PRAISE FOR

CW00818877

SILVER BLOOD is a carefull
mystery, squeal-inducing romance, and everyone's favorite...
vampires! If you're looking for something to fill the *Castlevania*-sized hole in your life, then look no further. —**RITA A. RUBIN**, AUTHOR OF *OF KNIGHTS AND BOOKS AND FALLING IN LOVE*

A tantalizingly slow burn vampire romance! Lots of action, lots of intrigue, and just a little bit of spice combine to make SILVER BLOOD a page turner. —**JOSIE JAFFREY**, AUTHOR OF THE SEEKERS SERIES

A queer starcrossed lovers tale between a vampire and vampire hunter filled with unique lore, a fascinating mystery, vampiric politics, amusing banter, and very unabashed—and very gay—flirting. —**CARA NOX**, AUTHOR OF *A HUNT OF BLOOD AND IRON*

In what is likely Morgan's most expansive work yet, SILVER BLOOD encapsulates much of what is loved about gothic stories, skillfully captivating elements of the tragic and the sublime. Combining mystery and romance, this epic tale is both intriguing and touching. A must-read for all vampire fans. —**JUNIPER LAKE FITZGERALD,** AUTHOR OF *THE MODERN MYTHOS ANOMALY*

A vampire romance that goes above and beyond, SILVER BLOOD wastes not even a moment captivating you to Cyrus's tale as he faces the trials and tribulations of seeking belonging outside the cruel world that fate bore him into. Truly a marvelous experience both gorgeous and gruesome that will enamor you to the very last page. —**SENNA BYRD,** AUTHOR OF *LORD OF THE NIGHT REALM*

A lovely romance with a heartfelt underlying message. Morgan weaves together intrigue and romance to show that the power to escape your nature comes through finding someone that believes you are more than what you were born to be. — **CAROLINA CRUZ**, AUTHOR OF *BLOOD IN THE WATER*

SILVER BLOOD

BOOKS BY T.L. MORGAN

Silver Blood

Sweet Sorrow

Faded Moon

PUBLISHED AS TALLI L. MORGAN

The Windermere Tales Series

Meliora

Transcendence: An Anthology of Change

SHORT FICTION

"The Wisdom of Stars" in *Indie Bites* vol. 11

"Mightier Than the Sword" in *A Chronicle of Monsters*, edited by Rita A. Rubin

"The Gluttonous Ghosts of Cobblebridge" in *Indie Bites* vol. 16

SILVER BLOOD

T. L. MORGAN

Print ISBN: 9798990782921

Ebook ISBN: 9798990782938

Cover illustration by Jan Falk (@thistlearts)

Interior design and typography by Talli L. Morgan. Scene break graphics and decorative page borders by GDJ (Pixabay, via Canva). Chapter heading graphics by Tuleedin Digital Art (via Canva).

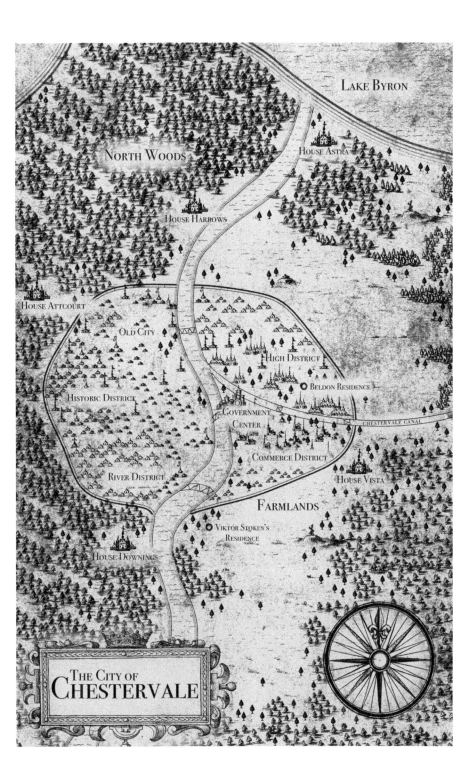

LAKE BYRON

NORTH WOODS

HOUSE ASTRA

HOUSE HARROWS

HOUSE ATTCOURT

OLD CITY

HIGH DISTRICT

BELDON RESIDENCE

HISTORIC DISTRICE

GOVERNMENT CENTER

CHESTERVALE CANAL

COMMERCE DISTRICT

RIVER DISTRICT

HOUSE VISTA

FARMLANDS

VIKTOR STOKES'S RESIDENCE

HOUSE DOWNINGS

THE CITY OF
CHESTERVALE

For the ones who fight for the world we dream about.

AUTHOR'S NOTE

November 6, 2024

This is a love story.

I wrote *Silver Blood* during a time of fear and uncertainty in the United States and the wider world. My research and writing process for this book provided a welcome escape from the turbulence, but the thing about Gothic literature is that it wants you to feel your fear. It wants you to find that monster in the shadows, unveil it, and then it wants you to embrace it. In Gothic literature, we open the wounds that no one wants to talk about and we let them bleed, and then we find catharsis—not only in the release of that fear, but also in the reassurance that we are not alone in our fears.

I wouldn't have this book in my hands—nor in yours—if I had not sat with my fears. I thought of everything that scared me about the future of this country and the people trying to dismantle its democracy, and I channeled every ounce of my rage at the rampant injustice and hatred into this story—this story that follows two men stuck in their own hopeless situations, wondering if anything will ever change.

This is a love story, but it's also a story about two people digging in their heels and adamantly refusing to continue the cycle of violence. It's about fighting the status quo and resisting the careless decisions made by the insatiably power-hungry people in charge. It's a story that asks "Is it worth it to try if the problem is too big for us to fix?" And it's a story that juggles hopelessness and despair with optimism and ever-burning hope.

This is a love story, but it's a love story with teeth. May your love, your rage, and your hope be your resistance.

T.L. Morgan

PART ONE

We are all, in the end, slaves to our families' wishes.

— ALUCARD TEPES, *CASTLEVANIA*

Chapter ONE

CYRUS BELDON WAS BORN TO KILL VAMPIRES.

Just like his siblings, his father and uncle, his grandfather, and gods-know-how-many generations of Beldons before them. They were a family as ancient and secretive as the Honorable Families of vampires themselves, and in the city of Chestervale, they had exactly one noble duty.

A duty at which Cyrus was currently failing.

He had the vampire cornered and weakened, bleeding its unnatural silver blood from the wound Cyrus had sliced across its throat—a wound that would've been instantly fatal for a human, but only a silver blade through the heart would kill this monster for good, and here, even with that lethal blade gripped tightly in his hand, was where Cyrus froze.

If Cyrus was like Arthur, his eldest brother, he would tear the vampire's heart out of its body while the thing still lived and *then* run it through with a blade, leaving the vampire to convulse while it watched its own miserable life spill out. If he was like Poppy, his sister, or Joel, her twin, he would've had the vampire staked, beheaded, and reduced to ashes within minutes. And if he was like his father—if he was *anything* like his father—he would've relished the creature's fear before inflicting a slow, merciless death, letting his reputation speak for itself.

But Cyrus had none of his siblings' efficiency nor his father's brutality. He'd already slit the vampire's throat; it *would* die, albeit slowly, and Cyrus *could* just walk away now and leave it to bleed out.

Or he could stop being such a goddamned coward and finish the job.

Cyrus gripped the knife until his hand ached. Enough stalling. The vampire in front of him had lost the last of its strength and collapsed to the muddy cobblestones. Its chest heaved beneath its blood-soaked shirt, each breath a wet rattle that spilled more of its life from its lips. Long strands of reddish-brown hair stuck to its sweat- and blood-stained face, and its eyes—deep, complete black —glared up at Cyrus with weakening hatred. The thing had put up a decent fight, but if Cyrus hadn't clocked it as a recent turn by its failure to hear him tracking it and its inability to heal the smaller cuts Cyrus had inflicted before he'd sliced its throat, its immediate depletion of strength after the silver blade parted its flesh was evidence enough.

Stop stalling, he begged himself. A bleeding vampire was not a dead vampire. *Do it right*, commanded Marcus Beldon's voice in his head. *Do it well. Come home with your blade and your trophy, or don't come home at all.*

Are you a Beldon or not?

He was. Even if he wasn't like the others, he was still a Beldon, and after tonight he'd officially be a hunter. *Then* he could do things his own way.

Tonight, it had to be Marcus's way.

The vampire heaved a rattling breath. "What'll it be, little Beldon?" It bared its fangs, stained silver. That it could still speak around a cut throat was enough of a surprise to stay Cyrus's hand. "The others make it quick. Are you begging penance first? As if your gods would forgive wretches like your bloody family." It spat a glob of blood onto the cobblestones and sank further to the ground. "If we're a plague," it wheezed, "the Beldons are a *curse*. On us, on the city, and especially on yourse—"

Cyrus didn't give it a chance to finish. He drove the dagger straight into the vampire's chest and twisted. Cold silver blood spilled over his hand and soaked the cuff of his sleeve; its metallic stench overtook his senses. He watched the life fade from the vampire's eyes, and only when it slumped dead against the stone wall did Cyrus wrench the knife out of its chest. Its body collapsed to the cobblestones, then lay still.

Cyrus's fingers twitched on the hilt of the knife. His job wasn't properly done until the thing was beheaded, but he suddenly couldn't move. Blood dripped from the end of the silver blade, hitting the stones with loud splats that rivaled the pounding of his heart. He watched the vampire's body turn white, then ashy gray, and then start to rot. The flesh withered and flaked and disintegrated to dust, and in a matter of minutes, only bones remained beneath a heap of tattered clothes. Cyrus reached down and fetched the skull—his trophy.

He should have been proud. His siblings had described their first hunts as thrilling rushes of adrenaline that left them floating on a high that lasted all night. This was the turning point of a Beldon's life, the moment they went from a child who happened to bear the name to a true hunter deserving of their place in the family. Each of his siblings had the skull of the first vampire they killed proudly on display in their rooms; Cyrus had had a spot reserved for his own as long as he could remember.

But now that the object was in his hands, bearing its macabre grin, the thought of taking it home and placing it on a shelf next to his books made him want to vomit.

Break off the fangs, and this was a human skull. A recently-turned vampire had been human itself not so long ago. Where was the line, he wondered, between *hunter* and *murderer*?

But he knew this was the danger of vampires—they walked among mortals, they masqueraded as human, and most of the time, no one looked twice. Everyone knew there were vampires in Chestervale; the Honorable Families practically had their own little kingdoms that intertwined with the city and its workings. Vampires and humans had shared blood in this city and the province, but that only made them more powerful and more dangerous. They walked in plain sight among their prey. They were sneaky, silent hunters, experts at hiding their true nature until it was too late.

Even monstrous people had human faces; a mortal appearance didn't take the monstrosity out of the vampire. Cyrus knew that whoever that man had been before was dead now; once a person was bitten and turned, a different, worse life began. The hunter families called it *deathlife*; an aimless, ghostly, lonely existence. It was Cyrus's job, as a hunter, to put the poor souls out of their misery in hope that, if there was still somehow a human soul in there, the Night God might find them and lead them to a peaceful rest.

This was the duty of the Beldons, the Sheridans, and the Barlows. The hunter families went back nearly as far as the Honorable Families; the world could not have one without the other. For every vampire, there was a hunter to keep it in check.

The vampire Cyrus had killed tonight had apparently attacked a judge's daughter and drank her blood, leaving her at the brink of death. Gods knew how long the teenager had suffered before her life had finally left her; she was found yesterday with the telling punctures in her neck and hardly a drop of blood left in her stiff, pale body. The distraught judge had called on the Beldons at once, and Marcus had flung the assignment at Cyrus. His first hunt was to be an act of justice.

Okay, well, justice was served, then. The thing was dead. Why did Cyrus feel like shit?

"I'm *tellin'* you, this was no wolf. You think I don't know what a wolf looks like?"

Cyrus startled out of his thoughts at the nearby voice. Dawn was creeping into the sky, and in this part of the city, that was most pub-goers' signal to head home. Cyrus took it as the same sign; he'd been gone too long already, and he wasn't particularly interested in being caught behind a restaurant with a dagger in one hand and a skull in the other. He swiped the flat side of the blade across his thigh to wipe the blood off, then returned it to its well-worn sheath and tucked the vampire's skull under his coat. As he crept toward the road, he waited in silence for the shuffling footsteps and slurred conversation to pass.

"Maybe it was diseased, I don't know. But what you said—"

"Yeah, yeah. *Impossible.* Easy for you to say. You didn't see the size of the thing's teeth."

The voices faded into the distance and Cyrus darted off in the opposite direction. He needed to get home; despite the successful kill, he'd get an earful from his father.

Your sister could've done that in an hour.

Arthur would've been home before midnight.

Did you even kill the thing at all?

Cyrus could practically recite the conversation in his head before it even happened. Same old bullshit. At least he was used to it.

THE BELDON ESTATE was still slumbering when Cyrus returned to the city's crisp upper streets. Fog clung to the grassy grounds and haunted the trees that stood guard along the path that led from the gates to the mansion's front doors. Cyrus waved at a trio of groundskeepers getting an early start on their work; they didn't wave back. They never did. It didn't stop Cyrus from extending the courtesy anyway.

The mansion slept with one eye open, and Cyrus felt it watching him as he approached the front steps. A single window in the east wing was alight, beckoning him in. Everyone else would be waking soon enough, when the birds began their songs, but only Marcus kept these inky hours. On a normal morning, he'd have been awake for an hour already. Today, however, he would've been up all night holding vigil while Cyrus was on his hunt. It was a ritual he kept for each of his children on their first hunt, and though Cyrus was far from his father's favorite, Marcus was nothing without his traditions.

All the more reason he'd be pissed that Cyrus took all night to kill one vampire.

The sun was just beginning to peek over the horizon at Cyrus's back when he reached the massive hawthorn doors of his home. He paused on the marble steps, consciously procrastinating this conversation with his father, and looked over his shoulder at the city sprawled below. The upper streets, home to the city's wealthiest and oldest families, zig-zagged their way around flowering trees and glowing streetlamps until the Commerce District abruptly cut off the greenery in favor of its own forest of marble and limestone. Chestervale's steep, narrow streets spread every which way, corralling lower-class houses and businesses toward the banks of the river that slithered down the center of the city. Far beyond the patchwork of rooftops, roads, and fields, dense forest swallowed the land as far as Cyrus could see.

Somewhere out there, within or past those woods, were other cities. Other lifestyles, other worlds. He'd never had the privilege of venturing beyond the walls of Chestervale, but on maps, the cities that sprawled on the shores of the northern lakes and the towns that huddled in the bends of the rivers looked close enough that if he threw a stone he'd hear it plunk into the water. Yet it seemed that every time he took in this view—whether from these steps or from his own third-floor bedroom window—those other worlds moved a little farther out of his reach.

Were there vampires in those towns, too? Did they have their own family trees of hunters engaged in a forever game of cat-and-mouse with blood-sucking predators, or were those places left to fend for themselves while Chestervale and its bigger neighbors to the east enjoyed the luxury of a willing minority with the skills to hunt the predators?

Why couldn't Cyrus be sent on a hunt somewhere out there, in those little towns, where he might conveniently get lost and never return to this mansion again?

The daydream was sweet, but foolish. There wasn't a place for him on earth other than here. Cyrus needed to get his head out of the damned clouds.

He took another second to relish the sun's early warmth on his skin, then fished his key out of his pocket and pushed through the front door. The foyer held stubbornly to its chill; the servants hadn't gotten to the fireplaces yet. Cyrus suppressed a shiver and crossed the foyer to the eastern corridor, holding tight to the skull concealed beneath his coat.

As he passed by closed doors and faded tapestries, he debated breaking the skull. It would disintegrate to dust just like the rest of the vampire if he so much as cracked it. He could tell his father he failed—*You were right, I'm useless at this vampire hunting thing. Guess I'm not worthy to be a Beldon, so I'll be on my way!*—but that daydream was as foolish as the rest that tested Cyrus's loyalty. Even failure to kill a vampire wouldn't get him exiled from this family, because Marcus probably knew that that was precisely what Cyrus wanted. And even if Marcus had no use for a cowardly Beldon, that was still not reason enough to give Cyrus what he wanted.

So he steeled himself for his father's gruff voice and harsh words, and approached the ajar door to Master Beldon's study. Golden light spilled across the polished floor, suggesting a warmth Cyrus knew better than to expect within. He knocked once, softly, then moved a single step into the room.

Marcus Beldon sat in his high-backed chair by the fireplace, which currently housed the dying remains of a fire. His usual items were close at hand on the table to his right: a weathered, pocket-sized leather notebook, a ceramic mug that had likely cradled numerous servings of black coffee throughout the night, and his round glasses, folded atop the notebook. His pipe lazily balanced at the corner of his mouth, emitting fragrant smoke that hovered in a cloud over his head and contributed to the permanent aroma of this darkwood-paneled room.

"You've returned." Marcus spoke quietly, but his gravelly voice at once sent all other sounds cowering. He lowered his pipe from his lips and inspected it instead of looking up at Cyrus. "Successfully, I trust?"

"Yes, sir." Cyrus moved further into the room and approached the other chair by the fireplace, but didn't dare sit without an invitation. He opened his coat to reveal the skull and presented it to his father. Its cold, dry texture made his skin crawl.

Marcus regarded him coolly. His stony expression betrayed nothing. While he studied the skull as if searching for a tell that it was somehow fake, Cyrus studied him right back. There were times, like now, when Cyrus looked at his father and tried to see him like the rest of the city did. The indomitable Marcus Beldon. There was no doubt he carried his legacy proudly—Cyrus saw that much—but where was the charming, honorable man that so many people worshiped? Where was the jovial father figure that so many fools envied? Cyrus had once been told he was lucky to have Marcus as a father, and when he'd burst out laughing at the comment, he was met with a scowl.

Cyrus tried to see those traits in his father now, but his blue eyes were cold and his lined face was harder than stone.

Apparently satisfied with his inspection, Marcus leaned back in his chair and finally looked at Cyrus. "An easy kill?"

"Easy enough, sir." It had taken Cyrus longer to find the vampire than to actually kill it.

Marcus narrowed his eyes. "Then why, for hell's sake, did it take you all damned night to come back?"

Ah, there it was. Cyrus caught himself wincing. "It...was a simple kill. Not so much a simple hunt."

"I gave you a precise location, right down to the three pubs where the bastard was most frequently seen. How hard could it have been?"

Sure, that *would* have been easy, if the vampire had actually been in one of those three pubs. But Cyrus had had to weave his way through three *others* before he'd spotted his target, and then waiting for the vampire to leave alone had eaten up an additional several hours, during which Cyrus had had to linger without looking suspicious and he couldn't even have a drink to pass the time.

"Well?" Marcus's voice broke into his thoughts.

What was he supposed to say? It wasn't *his* fault the vampire hadn't followed the guesswork pattern Marcus had come up with. "It didn't go as planned. Perhaps I could have been more efficient, but I found the thing in the end. It's dead. The judge's daughter is avenged. You'll get your coin. Are we done?"

"Mind your tone, boy," Marcus muttered. He scowled, but it seemed more directed at the skull than at Cyrus. "Very well. You completed the job. You have your trophy. Go, now that you've wasted the whole night. Arthur and Poppy won't delay morning drills just because you lost yourself hours of sleep."

The dismissal was clear, but Cyrus hesitated, waiting for his father to continue. To say something like, *Congratulations, son* in a surprisingly earnest tone. Or maybe even, *Now you're truly a Beldon hunter.* He didn't think his father would go so far as to say he was proud of Cyrus—if he did, Cyrus was sure he'd drop dead —but he expected something. An acknowledgment that he had completed the rite of passage, that he was no less of a hunter than his siblings. They had years of experience on him, yes, but hadn't they all started just like this?

Marcus eyed him as he would an ornery dog. "Did you leave your brain behind in those pubs? Why are you still here?"

Cyrus drew himself up taller. He remembered what Poppy had told him a few years ago, when Cyrus had complained that Marcus seemed to respect all of his children except for Cyrus: *He knows that you're afraid of him. Be a little bolder, and you'll start to gain his respect.*

He met Marcus's eyes. "Is that all you have to say to me, Father, when I am now, by your terms, a true Beldon?"

Marcus stared at him for several heartbeats that Cyrus felt in his skull with increasing volume. The corner of his father's mouth turned up just slightly, then a low laugh shook his shoulders. His gaze turned contemptuous, and Cyrus knew he should have left when he'd been dismissed.

The cold laughter tapered off and Marcus shook his head with what Cyrus could only describe as disgust. "Get out of my sight, boy."

Cyrus didn't wait to be told twice. He fled, still clutching the vampire skull, burning with shame that painted his face and crawled down the back of his neck. He kept his eyes fixed on the floor as he followed the brightening halls up to the third floor, but he stopped when his feet reached his bedchamber door.

His gaze wandered up the ornate chestnut wood, then down again to the skull in his hands. Its empty eye sockets stared back at him; its crooked teeth curved in a mocking grin. As if the remains of a twice-dead man had somehow won tonight, rather than the man who had wielded the silver dagger.

Cyrus whirled around and slammed the skull onto the marble floor. It shattered with a satisfying crack that echoed down the corridor, and in seconds the bone shards crumbled to dust.

Cyrus turned his back on the remains, and stormed into his room.

Chapter  TWO

"YOU'RE GOING TO GET YOURSELF KILLED!" ARTHUR stabbed the tip of his sword into the sand and threw up his hands in an exasperated *What the hell are you doing?* gesture that didn't need words.

Cyrus dropped his own weapon and doubled over with his hands on his knees. His chest hurt with every breath he struggled to gasp in, and his muscles were jelly after a morning of strength training and swordfighting that followed about forty minutes of sleep. Arthur could easily run two miles around the estate, dead lift over four hundred pounds, and then dance his blade around Cyrus without breaking a sweat, but Cyrus felt like he was going to die.

"Do you think the fucking vampires are going to give you a chance to catch your breath?" Arthur scoffed. His black boots moved into Cyrus's unsteady field of vision. "Pick up your weapon. Let's finish this."

Cyrus had thought that dropping his sword was signal enough that he was done, but apparently Arthur wouldn't be satisfied until Cyrus wound up sprawled in the sand like he normally did at the end of their spars. He flicked a glare up at his brother. "I *am* finished. Go stab something else."

Arthur scowled and roughly shoved Cyrus's shoulder, tipping his balance. He stumbled, but Arthur closed the distance and hauled him upright by a fistful of his sweat-dampened shirt. His

scowl was threaded with the same contempt that Cyrus knew well in his father.

Cyrus struggled to wrench himself free of his brother's grasp, but Arthur held fast. Six inches taller than Cyrus and built of solid muscle, Arthur Beldon was an imposing sight. The ragged scar that slashed from his left cheekbone to his chin only roughened his appearance and, ironically, made him a younger mirror of Marcus. Five years, two years, even one year ago, Cyrus would've cowered before his brother like this. No more. He wasn't afraid of Arthur Beldon.

And maybe that made him stupid.

"You're pathetic," Arthur spat, finally shoving Cyrus away from him. He had his sword back in hand before Cyrus had caught his balance. "I can't believe that vampire didn't rip your throat out last night. How'd you really do it, Cyrus?" He sneered. "Did you sweet talk and puppy-eyes your way into its good graces so you could take two hours to convince yourself to kill it before it killed y—"

Cyrus didn't give him a chance to finish the sentence. He elbowed Arthur hard in the sternum, and though it did little more than knock the wind out of him, it gave Cyrus a chance to retrieve his own weapon from the ground. He had the mere skin of a second to spare before Arthur came at him, swinging.

Cyrus stumbled back, reflexively blocking Arthur's blow, but Arthur was inside his guard and Cyrus didn't know how to maneuver himself away. He wanted his daggers, not this ridiculous rapier. This blade required far more grace than Cyrus had; he felt like he was fighting with straw.

"You make this so *easy*," Arthur snarled. He danced and turned around Cyrus, sword singing through the air. Cyrus blocked each strike with a clash of steel, but Arthur didn't give him a chance to strike back—or grab the dagger he had sheathed on the back of his belt.

He knew his brother wouldn't give him such an opportunity. Arthur had never made his fights fair and he wasn't about to start now. This wasn't a lesson so much as it was a power move: a reminder to Cyrus that Arthur was superior, *Arthur* was the strong one, *Arthur* was the favorite, the heir, the Beldon prince.

As if Cyrus wasn't already well aware of that.

Cyrus gritted his teeth and when Arthur pivoted for another strike, Cyrus drove his elbow hard against Arthur's forearm. It threw him off, just a little, and Cyrus seized the chance to dart out of Arthur's reach and grab his dagger.

He didn't wait for Arthur to attack first. He rushed at his brother, dagger tight and sure in his hand, and he felt the world narrow to himself, his weapon, and his opponent. He felt that slow elongation of time, stretching heartbeats into hours, and there was a moment where Cyrus almost forgot to flip his dagger around to spare Arthur the blade. Time rushed back like a tide filling a cave, and the steel hilt of Cyrus's dagger slammed into Arthur's ribs.

Arthur stumbled backward with an audible wheeze, but didn't falter. He tightened his grip on his rapier and let out a growl, then charged at Cyrus again.

But Cyrus had an advantage now, with his preferred weapon. *I do know how to fight.* Beldons weren't raised without knowing how to fight, how to survive, how to kill when it was necessary and how to injure when it wasn't. Cyrus sidestepped his brother's strikes and raised his dagger to block and redirect each swipe from the sword. The smaller blade set Arthur off balance; Cyrus knew it was difficult to strike a small blade with a larger one, and he used that— and his smaller stature—to his advantage.

"You little rat," Arthur hissed, trying and failing to fight his way closer to Cyrus. His movements were getting sloppy; he was over-exerting himself, meanwhile despite Cyrus's exhaustion and aching muscles, his carefully-timed strikes and dodges kept him moving but not working too hard. It was a cowardly way to fight, but it worked.

"I'm sorry, I thought you said to reserve my strength?" Cyrus's pulse thrummed in his ears. He'd never felt this exhilarated in a fight, especially not with Arthur. Then again, he'd never had the upper hand. "Am I not"—metal clanged as he blocked a strike—"doing precisely what you taught me?"

Arthur bared his teeth and growled, falling back a few steps only to come back at Cyrus with renewed fury. Cyrus flinched as Arthur's blade slammed against his own, surprised at the force behind the blow. His heels sank into the sand as he pushed back with his entire weight, but Arthur was stronger, and that one misstep was all he needed to regain his control.

Cyrus hissed a curse and gave a final shove, only for Arthur to shove back harder and send him sprawling. Cyrus barely managed to scramble back to his feet as Arthur advanced on him again, blade raised.

"Wait!" Cyrus flinched as Arthur swung, instinctively throwing up his arm to block the strike. But either Arthur didn't realize or didn't care that Cyrus had dropped his dagger; the rapier's blade gouged across his forearm.

Cyrus screamed as hot pain spiked up his arm. He staggered back from Arthur, gripping his bleeding arm with a shaking hand, and glared up at him. "You son of a *bitch*! What the fuck!"

Arthur sneered. "Move faster next time."

Cyrus grasped his arm harder and clenched his teeth. Hot, sticky blood dripped over his hand and skimmed down to his elbow; bright spots of crimson stained the sand. His vision tilted. Distantly, he knew he was rapidly losing blood; Arthur's blade had cut deep. He needed to find the physician. But he was stunned in place as his brain caught up with the fact that Arthur had actually hurt him. Despite all the threats and the rough shoves, part of Cyrus had not believed his brother would spill blood.

"*Cyrus.*" Arthur's voice was a stab into his hazy thoughts. "Come on, you're fine. Wrap it up and let's continue."

"I—I can't." He felt every throb of his pulse in his arm, and the blood wasn't slowing. The coppery smell of it stuck like bile at the back of Cyrus's throat. He feared he'd either vomit or pass out before he even made it to Adriyen's office in the infirmary.

"For gods' sakes." Arthur roughly grabbed Cyrus's uninjured

arm and hauled him across the training field. "Then stop sniveling and go to Adriyen. Be a fucking man, Cyrus."

Cyrus shrugged off Arthur's hand and started to snap back at him, only to stop short when he realized they had company: Two tall figures dressed in black finery approached them from the path leading up to the house.

Arthur halted and squared his shoulders as the man and woman drew closer. "What are you doing here? I told you I'd come to you."

Cyrus squinted, trying to make out their faces. It wasn't until they came within a few feet of the field that he realized with horror that they were Honorable Ones.

"Arthur," Cyrus muttered, "come on. Whatever they're doing here—"

"Doesn't concern you." Arthur glanced back at him. "Go, Cyrus."

Cyrus hesitated, glancing between his brother and the Honorable Ones. They wouldn't hurt Arthur—wouldn't dare lay a finger on any Beldon—and while it wasn't entirely unusual for members of the Honorable Families to visit Marcus, Cyrus and his siblings had always been advised to stay out of their way. Yet it sounded like Arthur *knew* them, and Cyrus had a bad feeling about it.

His chance to flee evaporated when the vampires came to a stop before Arthur. The woman—Cyrus couldn't think of her name—chuckled softly and exchanged a glance with the man beside her. "An entitled little princeling, isn't he, brother? He thinks himself so important that everything we do *must* be his bidding." Another icy laugh. "I've always said that pride will be the death of the Beldons."

"Leigh." The dark-haired man spoke in a low voice. "We still need him."

Leigh: The name rang a bell, yet Cyrus still couldn't place her family name. He ran through the names of the Honorable Families in his mind, but the worsening pain in his arm made his thoughts stumble.

The woman named Leigh whirled on her companion with a snarl. "If there is one thing in this world we don't need, Philip, it's *Beldons*. This one can be of use in other ways."

She turned on Arthur, then, and time slowed. Cyrus understood too late; before he managed to move a step, the vampire attacked Arthur with a vicious swipe of claws across his chest. Arthur stumbled backwards, pale with shock. He scrambled to grab a weapon, but barely managed a swing of his rapier before the vampire pounced again and went straight for his throat.

Arthur flailed, blood gushing down his neck and painting his bare chest crimson. His sword dropped from his hands and he collapsed to his knees. The vampire wrenched back, tearing out a dripping mouthful of sinewy flesh. The chunk of gore fell from her teeth with a wet *splat*, and she turned to Cyrus with a fang-bearing grin.

He heard himself scream. Suddenly he was moving, suddenly he had Arthur's sword in his hand. Cyrus heard it sing through the air as he swung. He felt it sink into flesh. Then something struck him across the face and he fell, the world upending around him. Agony throbbed through his head and radiated viciously from his bleeding arm. He felt sand under his hands and dug his fingers in for purchase, struggling to drag himself upright. He had to help. He had to save—

Arthur. He was there, right in front of Cyrus. His eyes were wide and panicked, his mouth twisted in terror. Cyrus reached out to him, but froze when his unfocused eyes fixed on the blood coating his own skin.

And then Arthur's face came into sharp relief. His blood: splattered on his face, still gushing from his throat. His flesh: wet and pink and torn to shreds. His eyes: blank, unseeing, and dead.

Cyrus tried to scream, but it got stuck in his throat. The sickly-sweet stench of blood clogged his senses. He scrambled away from his brother, but got no farther than a few inches before he was slammed back to the ground.

He fought and kicked blindly, shoving his pain to the back of his mind in favor of survival. His weapons were gone, his brother was gone, and he stood little chance against two supernaturally strong vampires. If Arthur couldn't beat them, Cyrus was as good as dead. But he wasn't a Beldon if he didn't fight to his last breath.

Still, the vampires were stronger. The vampires were always stronger. A hand closed around Cyrus's throat, sharp nails digging in hard, and he froze. His instincts abandoned him. He couldn't kick, couldn't move, couldn't think. A pale face appeared, lips stretched around a deadly grin. Cyrus's heart pounded one, two, three seconds; the vampire opened its mouth.

A rain of cold blood splattered Cyrus's face. The vampire's head tipped sideways with a squelch and then dropped, landing with a wet thud inches from Cyrus's own head. The body collapsed on top of him, and only then did his senses come rushing back.

With a strangled cry, he flung the vampire's bleeding body off of him and scrambled across the grass. He shook uncontrollably; his breaths came too fast, his heart was beating too hard. He couldn't tear his gaze away from the dead vampire; he stared until it turned to dust and blended with the training field's blood-soaked sand.

Then it occurred to him to wonder who had killed it.

"Cyrus."

He turned his head, still dazed. His surroundings were a blur of green and brown, but a familiar face loomed over him. "Poppy?" His voice came out rasped and wobbly.

His sister stood a sword's length from where the vampire had fallen, twin weapons still drawn at her sides. Silver blood dripped off the blades.

"Are you hurt?" Poppy asked.

It was the last thing Cyrus heard before he passed out.

CYRUS CRAWLED BACK to consciousness in short, reluctant seconds that teetered him between asleep and awake until he could finally open his eyes. His bedroom came into hazy focus, dim but for a faint glow from the fireplace on the other side of the room. The soft light melded with the faint, foggy brightness that peeked around the heavy curtains drawn over the windows. He blinked slowly, staring with unfocused eyes at the rows of bookshelves opposite his bed as he pieced his memory together.

His head throbbed. His throat felt raw. His left arm pulsed with a burning ache that brought back the clearest memory: his spar with Arthur, and its bloody end.

That bastard, he thought. He winced as he turned onto his back. When he didn't feel like a sack of shit, he'd go find Arthur and give him a rematch he wouldn't soon forget. *Then* Arthur would respect him.

The slippery end of a memory nudged doubt against that thought. *No, that's impossible*, and not just because Cyrus had little chance of actually besting his brother in a fight. There was something else wrong; Cyrus felt it like an itch at the back of his throat, but he couldn't grasp why.

His memory offered hazy flashes of the training field, the pines surrounding it, the blood spattered on the grass...

And Arthur's dead eyes, inches away from his face.

Everything viciously came back to him, then. He saw it all in vivid clarity as if the scene was still playing out before him: Arthur's blood pouring from his body, his blank eyes, the sound his flesh made when the vampire had torn out his throat. Cyrus could still smell it.

He forced back the bile that rose in his throat and dragged himself up to a sitting position, leaning back against the headboard with his face in his hands. The cold, hard wood against his bare skin chased off the last of the haze in his brain, but he couldn't puzzle out how many hours had passed between that spar and this moment. If Arthur was dead, the house must be in an uproar; no wonder the bandages on his arm looked like they hadn't been changed in a while.

Cyrus glanced at his bedside table, where a full glass of water awaited his attention. He could practically sense Dr. Adriyen's glare as she directed him to drink it. It was only because she wasn't in the room that he reached for it.

As if his compliance with her passive plea for him to drink water summoned her, Cyrus heard footsteps approaching his room, accompanied by voices.

"What?" That was Dr. Adriyen's sharp tone, unmistakable even through the walls. "You know that's—Please, Poppy. Don't be absurd. I beg your pardon, but I've neglected your brother long enough."

"Doctor, please, I swear—"

"Not now." The doctor's voice could've cut diamond. "Your suspicions are ungrounded and fueled by shock and grief. I advise you to see Leif about that. And for gods' sakes, don't speak a word of what you just said to me to your father."

There was a pause, and then angry footsteps stormed off.

The door to Cyrus's bedroom opened before he had a chance to ponder what he'd just heard. Dr. Adriyen entered and immediately scowled at the room's darkness; she strode across the sitting area and flung open the curtains over one of the windows before finally turning to Cyrus's bed.

"Oh! Cyrus, forgive me, I didn't expect to see you awake so soon." She approached his bed and gently touched the back of her hand to his forehead, then made a satisfied hum. "How are you feeling? I'm relieved to see you upright." She flicked a glance at the now half-empty glass on the table. The faintest hint of a smirk touched the corner of her lips. "*And* staying hydrated."

Cyrus grumbled and replied to her question with a shrug. The late afternoon light streaming through the window across the room was steadily draining his desire to have his eyes open.

"How's your head?" Adriyen asked.

He frowned. "How'd you know my head hurts?"

"You're squinting at me even though it's like a cave in here. Besides, now that I'm seeing you upright and all those curls are somewhat where they should be, I can see the goose egg on your skull." Adriyen stepped closer to the bed and lifted a hand. "May I?"

Cyrus nodded and inclined his head toward her, but she tipped it back up and parted his hair to poke at his scalp. He winced when she found the spot that hurt.

"Right there, hm? Yeah, that's quite the bump." She drew back and studied him; Cyrus couldn't read her expression. He never could. She was perhaps the only person in this house whose moods were an utter mystery to him; he suspected that she knew he was good at reading people, and schooled her expressions accordingly. Cyrus would've been impressed if it wasn't inconvenient.

"Do you remember what happened?" the doctor asked softly.

"Mostly." He rubbed the sore spot on his head, and startled when he felt the bump. Shit, it felt like *two* goose eggs. He gaped at Adriyen. "Am I going to *die*? How is it okay and normal to have a bump that big on my head?"

"I promise, you are not going to die." Adriyen laughed softly. "Trust me, I wouldn't be this calm if you were. That swelling will go down soon. I'll get you some ice. Do you feel dizzy or nauseous? Any spots in your vision?"

Cyrus shook his head, wincing as a muscle pulled painfully in his neck. He lifted his hand to massage the bump only to recoil when the touch made it worse. He blinked a few times at Adriyen, struggling to chase a memory. Hands around his throat, claws tearing his skin. So much blood.

He swallowed thickly. "They almost killed me, too, didn't they?"

Adriyen placed a warm hand on his shoulder. "What matters is that you're alive, and you're going to be okay. Try not to get yourself worked up over the gaps in your memory; it'll come back once the shock eases. Right now, you should rest. I'll be back later with ice for your head and something to eat."

"But—"

She silenced him with a hard look. For a woman of thirty-something, she had an uncanny talent for resembling a disgruntled grandmother. Cyrus had learned long ago that arguing with her was useless.

Her harsh expression didn't stay long. "If you want, I can ask Leif to concoct something that might help jog your memory. They'll probably suggest hypnotism, but let's not go that far quite yet. The brain has a tendency to surprise us. Let's let yours rest before we send you digging into its recesses."

Cyrus breathed a nervous chuckle. "I must be in truly dire straits if you're willingly bringing Leif into this. Haven't you always said they're a quack?"

Adriyen pursed her lips and shrugged. "Our understandings of medicine are very different, and they experiment with the absurd more than I would like, but when they're right, they're brilliant." A fond smile softened her face. "Let's just say we've settled *some* of our differences." She winked and then abruptly made for the door.

Cyrus's mouth fell open. "What? Wait— Are you—?"

"Ring for me if you need anything or start to feel dizzy!" Adriyen called, and then was gone.

Cyrus blinked at the door. Unbelievable. Adriyen and Leif— the physician and the mystic—had been vicious rivals as long as Cyrus could remember, probably as long as the two of them had been employed by House Beldon. Cyrus had heard numerous rants and complaints from both of them about the other, but he'd once had the misfortune to witness one of their verbal battles and it had compelled him to avoid seeking either of them for months, even when he'd come down with an illness that had him emptying his guts for a week.

Adriyen was a control freak, and her word was law when it

came to medicine. Leif's unconventional methods, alternative treatments, and general spaciness mercilessly stomped on Adriyen's toes and she hated it. Cyrus had always assumed she hated Leif themself, too.

But apparently not, if that cheeky wink was any indication of what was really going on.

If this was a normal day, if Cyrus wasn't in all kinds of pain, and if there wasn't something strange going on, he'd make it his mission to dig up every last piece of gossip about the physician and the mystic.

But unfortunately for him—and lucky for Adriyen—this was very much not a normal day, and he had more pressing concerns. Resting be damned; what had happened to him out there? Who were those vampires? He needed to find Poppy. She'd been there; she would tell him.

He took a deep breath and threw off his blankets, then stiffly turned to get his feet on the floor. The cold wood seeped the warmth from his bare skin; he focused on that discomfort while the aches in the rest of his body settled. When he didn't feel like he'd shatter if he moved, he gritted his teeth and pushed to his feet.

The room tilted; he grabbed the bed's headboard so he didn't tip with it. Once the dizzy spell passed, he shuffled a step forward, then another, gradually regaining his balance. He'd almost made it to his bedroom door when it creaked open.

He froze. But it wasn't Adriyen who poked her head into the room; it was his sister.

Cyrus let out a breath. "Poppy."

"Why the hell are you out of bed?" She shut the door in her wake and approached him, giving him a quick once-over. Her gaze lingered on his bandaged arm for a second before she met his eyes. "You look awful."

"Thanks, so do you." He scowled and shuffled back to his bed, then sat down. Poppy lingered where she'd paused, and Cyrus realized that she truly *did* look awful. Her black hair was tangled and unwashed, wild around her face. Her eyes looked sunken and red around the edges, and she was wearing the same clothes from the training field—tight-fit trousers, knee-high boots, and a snug vest over a white blouse, cravat firmly in place. When she moved, Cyrus caught a glint of silver staining her shirt.

She tucked a strand of hair behind her ear and then rubbed her forehead with a sigh. "Can I sit?"

Cyrus nodded and gestured at the empty space beside him. Poppy plopped down heavily and put her face in her hands.

Cyrus didn't know what to say. He'd never seen his sister like this. She was the cornerstone of the family, the one who always had a solution to any problem. Back her into a corner, and she'd climb up the walls to get herself out. She wasn't afraid to tell Arthur off for being a brute, didn't hesitate to scold Joel for acting too impulsively, and she feared no wrath from Marcus. To Cyrus, she was the closest thing he'd ever had to a friend.

He dragged shaking hands through his hair. "Is it true? Arthur... Arthur's dead?"

Poppy turned her head. "You don't remember?"

"I— I do now, I think." He didn't realize he was shaking until Poppy gripped his shoulder.

"I killed the vampire that nearly got you, but the other one got away." She scowled. "No one else believes me, Cyrus, but they were Honorable Ones. House Harrows. I'm a Beldon, for gods' sakes, I know the fucking Honorable Families. And I know you do too." Poppy met his eyes.

Cyrus shook his head. "I don't—"

"You have to back me up on this, Cyrus." Poppy turned to face him. "Father won't do anything against the Families without solid proof."

"Because that would be suicidal," Cyrus said flatly. "Poppy...if you really killed an Honorable One..."

"I was *defending* my *family*," she growled. Then she sighed. "You really don't remember who they were? You didn't recognize them?"

He searched the piecemeal of information in his mind, but it was all still scrambled. Only flashes, nothing coherent. It had all happened so fast. "Poppy, I've been awake for like twenty minutes. It's still coming back to me. But if an Honorable One did kill Arthur...shit."

"Yeah. Shit."

Cyrus couldn't wrap his head around this. The Honorable Families had a truce with the hunter families—a truce of their own making. They agreed to spare any relative or ward of the hunter families while the hunter families were absolutely forbidden from killing an Honorable One or anyone protected by them. The truce was the only thing keeping an utter bloodbath at bay; that an Honorable Family would break it by killing the heir to the Beldon family was so improbable that two days ago, Cyrus would've laughed at the suggestion.

Now the possibility filled him with dread. If this was all true, Marcus Beldon was going to rain hell upon the Honorable Families, and likely get his entire family killed in the process. It would be war, and Cyrus had no interest in being a martyr for his father's bloodlust.

"There's something else." Poppy straightened and then leaned back on her hands. "Arthur's body is gone."

Cyrus stared at her. "What?"

"I..." She clawed her fingers through her hair. "After I killed that vampire, you passed out. You were bleeding a lot, and I— Arthur was..." She winced, swallowed, tried again. "I couldn't do anything for Arthur, so I...left him. Brought you to Adriyen, told everyone I saw what had happened. We went back outside to collect Arthur's remains, and...he was gone."

Cyrus blinked a few times. "Dead bodies don't just get up and walk away, Poppy. What, did someone *steal* it?"

"No." She crossed her arms over her chest. "Doubtful. No one else wants to say it, but...I think he was turned."

Cyrus barked a short laugh. "No. That's—That's impossible. Why would they—"

"Do you have a better explanation?" Poppy snapped.

"They *ripped out his throat*," Cyrus snarled back. "You didn't see it, Poppy. You didn't see how they killed him." Cyrus's heart was beating too fast again. "They didn't just bite him; they *mauled* him. Like a fucking animal. There is no way he could have survived even if he had been turned." Cyrus studied her for a second. "And you know that, which is why you left his body out there. You knew he was too far gone for it to be possible."

"I assumed so," Poppy muttered. "But now I think I was wrong." She got up and paced toward the windows. "There could be another explanation, but right now, the most logical one is that he was somehow turned—even if it wasn't done correctly or perfectly. Gods know what happened to him if that's the case, but we have to find him, Cyrus. Vampires have control over people they've turned; if Arthur is still alive as a vampire, the Honorable Families could use him in any way they please. He'd be their perfect spy."

Cyrus frowned. "Right, because we wouldn't think it suspicious if our dead brother walked through the front door like nothing happened? You're not making sense, Poppy."

"*Nothing* makes sense anymore, Cyrus!" She turned to him and flung out her hands. "Our brother is dead, Father won't speak a word of it, you almost died, and House Harrows just broke the fucking truce!"

Cyrus watched her steadily. Another memory flickered in his mind; he closed his eyes to chase it. The vampires—a man and a woman, similar in appearance. Siblings. Black hair, angular faces. He knew their names now that he wasn't panicking: Leigh Harrows, the family's heir, and her brother Philip.

Poppy was right.

Cyrus carefully stood up. "We're working with your brief glimpse and my hazy memory. None of this is certain."

"But it's enough to convince Father to listen to us."

"I will be doing no such thing," Cyrus said.

"Do you want to find out why our brother was killed?" Poppy snarled. "This wasn't an accident, Cyrus. The Harrows vampires were here for a reason, and they killed Arthur for a reason. They would've killed you, too, if I hadn't been heading out to the field at just the right time. They're targeting us, and I can't be the only one who wants to know why."

With that, he could agree. But he was too exhausted to even start to spin theories. He went to Poppy and touched her shoulder, then to his surprise she gathered him in a crushing hug. He froze, stunned. Try as he did, he could not remember the last time his sister had hugged him. He wondered if she ever actually had.

When she let go of him, her eyes were watery. Her jaw was clenched tight; Cyrus knew she was struggling to hold back tears. That was another thing he'd never seen from her, but if there was ever a time for her to drop her stoic Beldon strength, it was now. She should be allowed to cry over her brother's gruesome death.

Cyrus gave her shoulders a light squeeze. "I won't try to tell you it's okay, because you won't believe me. Nor should you. But I am sorry, Poppy."

She turned her head and inhaled slowly through her nose. "He was your brother, too."

Cyrus winced. Hardly. Arthur had never shown him any affection, and vice-versa. Still, the loss did sting in some odd, unfair way. By all logic, he should not care that his cruel brother was gone. Yet he did.

"We'll figure out why this happened," Cyrus said to Poppy. "Even if Father won't."

A tear escaped down Poppy's cheek and she quickly swept it away. "Right. Well." She drew back from Cyrus and tucked her hair behind her ears. "We've got work to do, then, don't we?"

Chapter  THREE

CYRUS PUSHED THROUGH THE HEAVY DOORS INTO THE library and guided them silently shut behind him, then shuffled across the polished wood floor. The cavernous space was well-kept, but no amount of upkeep and dusting could fully banish the smell of old paper and mold. This library didn't want to be alive. Despite the massive windows high on the walls, there never seemed to be enough light in this room.

Honestly, Cyrus hated this place. In any other circumstance he would die before he said he disliked a library, but the Beldon library was less of a haven for readers and more of a grotesque museum. The collection of books tucked neatly on their shelves in each ten-foot bookcase was secondary to the main attraction: display cases housing relics—trophies—of generations of vampire hunting. Weapons that had belonged to Cyrus's grandfather, great-grandfather, and so on, lay on velvet beds with little cards beside them noting the weapon's owner and how many monsters it had slain. Everything from daggers and swords to things as large and impractical as scythes and axes slumbered in their glass houses, following the main aisle all the way to the collection of skulls that stretched the length of the back wall.

Cyrus spared them only a glance as he walked by. The skulls—many of which were yellowed and cracked, but all still intact—grinned back at him with their bared fangs and empty eye sockets.

Sometimes he swore he heard them snapping their teeth and hissing.

Which was preposterous, of course. But a room housing so much death was bound to attract ghosts, and Cyrus wasn't keen to meet any vengeful vampire spirits. He kept his distance.

He finally left the macabre display behind and found his way to the farthest corner of the library. Here, the stacks were nestled closer together and the walls closed in, creating a cozy nook that was the only spot Cyrus could tolerate. It seemed his sister was of a similar mind.

"Poppy." He tried to announce his presence gently, but she still jumped.

"Gods, Cyrus." She huffed. "Wear bells next time."

"Ah, but then I'd never be able to sneak away from Adriyen." Cyrus approached the round table where Poppy was seated. Several books were stacked by her elbow, but only one was open—a huge leather-bound tome with yellowed pages and faded, nearly illegible print. "What have you got?"

"Refreshing my memory." Poppy patted the stack of books beside her; Cyrus recognized the one on the top as the book of vampire physiology from which every Beldon learned their trade. "It's been a while since I've gone after a fresh turn; I spent some time reading up on their weaknesses."

Cyrus pulled out the chair opposite her and sat down, folding his knee up to his chest. "Fresh turns are easy, though. They're unstable. Push them into a sunbeam and"—he snapped his fingers—"whoosh. Gone."

Poppy looked up at him. "This is our brother we're talking about."

Cyrus winced. He shouldn't have forgotten that so easily.

"You're right, though, that freshly turned vampires are unstable. They don't know their limits; they're still getting used to deathlife, and think they're invincible." Poppy leaned back in her chair and tapped the giant book open in front of her. "But Arthur isn't a typical case. He was turned in an act of violence. And according to this old thing," Poppy smoothed her hand down one of the crinkled pages, "that could make him a Wild vampire."

Cyrus stared at her. "A what?"

Poppy rolled her eyes. "Did you retain *anything* from Uncle Emerson's lessons?"

"Just the trauma from a childhood of verbal abuse."

"You're so fucking dramatic. Emerson's just blunt; don't take it personally." Poppy turned the book around to face Cyrus and flipped back a page. An illustration of a hunched figure with leathery skin, black eyes, overlong fangs, and clawed hands snarled up at him. Its long limbs were jointed in a way that suggested it could run on all fours, and a pair of giant batlike wings extended from its back.

Cyrus glanced up at Poppy. "Okay, I'm not *that* stupid. You expect me to believe this is real? Come on, Poppy, we both know vampires don't look like that."

"Wild ones do."

"Bullshit. This is an absurd exaggeration, just like the drawings from all the folklore we had to study. For gods' sakes, I didn't go through two decades of Beldon education to not know what a vampire is." He pushed the book back toward her. "Cut the shit. What really is a Wild vampire?"

"Do you really think I'd pull your leg with something like this when it's our *family* we're talking about?" Poppy snapped. "This isn't representative of all Wild vampires, but this is what they become if they're not killed quickly enough after they turn. It's already been almost two full days since Arthur was turned, meaning we have *maybe* another day before he reaches this point. Monsters like this don't get better, Cyrus, they only get more monstrous."

He stared at the crude illustration as Poppy's words sank in. The thing was grotesque, each joint and vertebra pushing through the veiny skin. Its eyes were depthless, soulless.

Cyrus had never been close with his brother, but to imagine him like this—a thoughtless abomination, likely in unfathomable pain—was enough to steel Cyrus's resolve. Poppy was right. If they, as Beldons, had one duty, it was to put monsters like this in their graves. Even if, this time, that monster was one of their own.

He looked up at his sister. "What's our move, then? How do we kill this thing?"

"Well, first we have to find him. *It.*" She grimaced and flipped the book shut. "Are you up for some investigative work?"

"If Arthur's running around looking like that," Cyrus nodded toward the book, "it's going to be the talk of the town. I don't think we'll have to *investigate* so much as eavesdrop."

"Exactly." Poppy stood up. "Let's get going, then."

Cyrus didn't move from his seat. "Where, exactly, are we going?"

"Where else do you go for gossip?" Poppy shrugged. "The pubs, obviously."

Cyrus looked at her wearily. A pub and all its noise and ruckus was the last place he wanted to be.

"Unless you're not up for it?" Poppy put her hands on her hips and pursed her lips. "Oh! Idea: Let's go see Leif. I'll bet they can give you something to boost your energy, even if it's just for a few hours."

"Oh, yes, they'll boost my energy, for sure, with some kind of questionable drug that'll make me hear colors." Cyrus rubbed his temples. He did want to help Poppy, but he knew he wouldn't make it all the way into the city and back in his current state. If he went to Adriyen, she'd tell him he absolutely could not leave the house. Leif, at least, could be persuaded, if only by the prospect of annoying Adriyen.

"Fine." Cyrus dragged himself to his feet. "But if I start muttering prophecies or seeing ghosts, Adriyen is going to kill you. And me. And *definitely* Leif."

Poppy snickered and started across the library. "Then this had better be worth the risk. Come on, we don't have all night."

Leif Trysz lived in the attic of House Beldon, which was odd considering that, upon beginning their service to the family, they would've had their choice of comfortable, furnished rooms like the rest of the high-ranking staff. The attic would not have been one of those choices, but given Leif's personality, Cyrus wasn't surprised that they had asked for it specifically. It suited them, in a way, and Cyrus sympathized with the introverted desire to have a haven away from judgmental eyes.

The attic was only accessible via a tightly spiraled staircase hidden in the walls of the fourth floor. Poppy dragged the plain white door open—to which the door protested loudly—and at once the two of them encountered a sickly-sweet cloud of incense.

"Ugh." Poppy waved her hand through the air. "It's a good thing they're in the attic. If the whole house smelled like this, I'd burn it down." She jogged up the first few steps, then looked down at Cyrus. "Are you going to be able to make it up here?"

He'd been wondering the same thing himself, sore and winded as he was from climbing all the way up to the fourth floor. But since Poppy had asked, he was determined to do it. "Of course I am. Go ahead. I'll catch up."

"Try to be quick about it, yeah?"

"I can't be quick if you're in my way." Cyrus grabbed the metal railing and dragged himself up a couple of steps, stopping just behind Poppy.

"Just making sure you're not going to topple backwards and break your neck."

"Then don't tell me to hurry."

Poppy huffed and continued up the stairs. "I take it back. I hope you do break your neck."

Cyrus snickered to himself and followed her as quickly as his tired muscles would allow. The circular ascent didn't do him any favors, but he managed to make it up to the landing without tripping or toppling or any such misfortune. Poppy graciously waited for him to catch his breath, then did the honors of knocking on Leif's door.

This cramped space had seemed almost magical to Cyrus the first time he'd come up here as a child. It had been just after his mother had died, and wanting nothing to do with any of his siblings and especially not his father, he'd run to the farthest part of the house he could think of, where no one else went. He'd never tried to open the attic door, believing it to be forbidden to him like so many things were, but that day he hadn't cared. He'd clambered his way up here, feeling like he'd entered another world, and burst right through Leif's door. And Leif, though likely startled at the sudden and unexpected appearance of a distraught Beldon child, had calmed him down and introduced him to what was still his choice tea when he needed to settle his anxiety.

Leif *was* weird and spacey, but they were kind. Even if that didn't matter to anyone else under this roof, it mattered to Cyrus more than anything.

"Why are they taking so long?" Poppy shifted impatiently on her feet. She lifted her hand as if to knock again, but decided against it. "They *must* be here if they have incense burning. It's too strong to be a remnant from earlier."

Cyrus shrugged. It *was* late. Leif could be asleep, or it could be that the reason Cyrus hadn't seen Adriyen in a while and the reason Leif wasn't answering the door were one and the same.

Poppy knocked again before Cyrus could tell her to forget it. Moments later, the door swung open and Leif appeared, looking flustered and mildly irked. Their expression softened only a little when they saw Cyrus.

"Er, good evening." Leif pulled their long, oversized cardigan tighter around their shoulders. "Are you both well? What brings you all the way up here at such an hour?"

"Sorry, Leif, we hate to interrupt your night," Poppy said, earning herself a subtle yet distinctly annoyed look from the mystic in question. "But we have some important work to do, and after the whole ordeal Cyrus went through—"

"I just need something to give me some energy," Cyrus interrupted. He cringed at Leif's unimpressed look. "Please?"

"You dragged me out of bed in the middle of the night...to give you an apothecary's equivalent of a cup of coffee."

Cyrus exchanged a glance with Poppy, then plastered on a grin. "Yes?"

"A cup of coffee wouldn't strengthen him the way your medicines could, Leif," Poppy added.

They pursed their lips, then sighed and pinched the bridge of their nose. "All right. Thankfully that's easy, and lucky for you, you caught me in a good mood. Wait here. I'll be right back." They retreated back into their flat and closed the door.

"Whatever they give me had better work, for their sake." Cyrus rubbed his eyes, trying to soothe the instant headache the potent incense had stabbed into his skull.

"I do feel bad for waking them up." Poppy pushed her hair behind her ears. "But I don't see what other choice we had."

"I don't think we woke them up," Cyrus muttered.

"...Oh."

Leif returned then, bringing a fresh plume of incense with them. Cyrus sneezed, and Leif's eyes widened. "Oh, *shit*."

"What?" Cyrus rasped.

"What's wrong?" Poppy said.

"Go downstairs," Leif ordered, waving them away from the door. "Go! I didn't realize— Seriously, *go*."

Poppy hurried down the steps, Cyrus scrambling after her with Leif on his tail. They all clambered out of the attic stairwell and spilled into the hallway. Leif shut the door and turned to Cyrus and Poppy, looking frazzled.

"Sorry. I didn't realize you could smell the incense from out there." Leif fiddled with the stoppered vial in their hands. "Not ideal for you."

"But it's fine for you?" Poppy frowned.

Leif sighed. "It's an aphrodisiac, if you must know. Can't have you two inhaling that, can I? Of course, if you *asked*, I wouldn't judge, but this is neither the time nor the place. Anyway." They turned to Cyrus and presented the vial. It was filled with a clear, pinkish liquid. "Drink all of it, but not too fast. Don't down the whole thing at once. Give it twenty minutes or so, and it'll perk you right up. Just don't do anything extremely strenuous. No running, no fighting, no slaying vampires. Deal?"

Cyrus gave the vial a little shake. "What exactly is this?"

"Not important. Do you trust me?"

"Yes, but—"

"Then just follow my instructions and you'll be fine." Leif smiled.

"No, what is it going to do to me?"

"Keep you awake, and restore your strength," Leif said. "Is that not what you asked for?"

"Yes, it's perfect, thank you," Poppy interrupted. She grabbed Cyrus's arm and dragged him away. "Sorry for, uh, interrupting, Leif! Good night!"

"Wait, Poppy—" Cyrus pried her hand off his arm and halted. He did trust Leif, but he'd learned the hard way to always ask for side effects of their remedies.

"It's not going to kill you, Cyrus!" Poppy continued down the hall toward the stairs. "Drink the stuff and let's *go*. And let Leif return to whoever's warming their bed."

Cyrus glanced back, and sure enough, Leif had already disappeared through the attic door. He closed his hand around the vial and followed his sister. "Aphrodisiacs, huh. I guess I shouldn't be surprised."

"That mystic's probably into some weird shit." Poppy was already at the third floor landing. "What are you waiting for? Drink it! We've already wasted a lot of time. At this rate we'll be out all night, and I promised Joel I would go for a run with him in the morning, which I'm already regretting."

Cyrus caught up to her and popped the cork out of the vial. He brought it hesitantly to his nose and sniffed. A faint floral scent did little to mask the onslaught of something sharply alcoholic. Cyrus cringed and glanced up at Poppy. "If this kills me, you're the only one allowed at my funeral."

He tipped the vial to his lips and swallowed half its contents. The stuff was smooth but had a sharp aftertaste that stung the back of his throat and made him gag. He forced himself to drink the rest of it even as it left an unpleasant tang on his tongue.

Poppy snorted. "I wish you could see your face right now. At least we know we won't find *you* at the pubs."

"*Thith ith dithguthting.*" Cyrus barely wanted to touch his tongue to the inside of his mouth.

Poppy rolled her eyes and continued down the stairs. "Deal with it, Cyrus. You'll be thankful for it by the time we get downtown. Hope you're ready for a long night."

Chapter FOUR

CYRUS AND POPPY STEPPED OUT OF THE COACH INTO A startlingly loud corner of the city. Chestervale was always noisy, always humming and grumbling, but tonight the lower Commerce District was a cacophony. Crowds of people hustled by, and *everyone* was talking.

It was rapidly worsening Cyrus's headache.

The coach they'd hailed back in the High District only brought them as far as the last Commerce District stop, from which point they continued on foot along the river and toward the bridge into the River District. Cyrus kept pace with Poppy as they trotted down narrow stone steps and wound around sharp corners, and the streets grew noticeably danker as they ventured out of the nicer parts of the city, but not any less noisy. Doves cooed from their nests on windowsills, the wind rustled through dying flowers bedded in window boxes, and teapots sang from within darkened houses. Wheels clattered over cobblestones. Horses snorted, reins snapped. People coughed and grunted and called to each other. The street that Cyrus and Poppy turned down next was deserted, yet the noise carried. Cyrus had half a mind to jump into the river if only to muffle it all.

Even the rowdy River District was *never* this loud. What were so many people doing out this late at night?

Harsh laughter erupted somewhere behind them, and Cyrus jumped. A quick glance showed him an empty street—must be a group of particularly rowdy pub-goers from the next street over—but they sounded like they were right behind him. Cyrus quickened his pace to keep up with Poppy.

"Why is it so loud?" he wondered aloud, risking another glance back. He'd been taught from childhood that if he ever found himself in the River District, the last thing he wanted was to look lost or paranoid. Predators lurked in these run-down, drunken streets, and they had an eye for fresh meat.

Poppy had been keeping a brutal stride since they'd left the upper streets, but now she slowed and turned to him, frowning. "What?"

Cyrus stared at her. "You haven't noticed how many people we've passed? Like, entire groups of them. It's as if it's noon on a festival day. And they're *all* talking. Even inside the houses we've passed. Everyone's talking."

"Cyrus...We haven't seen a single person since we left home."

He waited for her to crack a smile, to snort, to smack his arm and say she was messing with him, but her concerned expression remained.

Cyrus pressed his fingertips to his temples. "What the *fuck* did Leif give me?"

"It's probably best that we don't know." Poppy still eyed him like he'd sprouted a second head. "But hey, maybe we can put your hallucinations to use." She glanced up and down the street again, then tugged his arm to bring him to the edge of the road, in the shadow of the stone building that loomed over them. "What do you hear? How much can you see?"

Cyrus rubbed his eyes. "I thought it was just because it's dark, but the people I've seen have all been sort of...half there. I can hear them clearly, though. But Poppy, I don't think they're hallucinations. I think they're... echoes. O-Or memories? The *city's* memories of everyone and everything that has passed through these streets."

Poppy's eyes widened. "Fascinating. That sounds like hell,

actually. But close your eyes. See if you can focus on individual sounds."

Cyrus obeyed. Somehow that made everything louder. City noise, amplified a hundred times, blended and tangled in his mind.

"Look for a scream," Poppy said. "Er, there's probably a lot of those, so try a growl, or a roar, or something inhuman. See if you can find Arthur."

Cyrus opened his eyes. "You can't be serious. You think I can *control* this?"

"I don't know! Try it!"

He rolled his eyes and then closed them. He was not at all confident that he'd be able to accomplish what Poppy was asking, but if it worked, it'd be faster than asking around the pubs. Safer, too; Cyrus and Poppy were not low-profile in this city. If they went asking around about Wild vampires mere hours after news of the Beldon heir's death...even the drunks would put the pieces together.

He squeezed his eyes shut tighter and concentrated on the phantom noises around him. Poppy had suggested searching for a growl or a roar, and it was only because of that illustration in the book she'd shown him that led him to believe a Wild vampire would sound more animal than human. The thrum of city noise was difficult to tune out, but beneath the rowdy voices, rumbling carriages, and clattering horseshoes, Cyrus heard *something*.

It was faint, but it undoubtedly did not fit.

Where are you? What surrounded that odd growl? Footsteps, voices... But no carriages, he realized. The steps were softer, muffled. The voices echoed far and wide. There was a whisper of wind through trees, and something else, some other quiet murmur, some kind of...animal sounds?

Cyrus opened his eyes, pulse spiking with excitement. "He's near the farms."

"There's a dozen farms outside the city," Poppy pointed out. "Which one?"

Cyrus scowled. "I managed to figure all that out with the whole damned city ringing in my head, and you're not even a *little* impressed?"

"I'll be impressed when we actually find him," Poppy hissed. "We can't search every farm. See if you can tell which direction it's coming from. Hell, he might've even moved on by now, and might still by the time we get there." She kicked a loose stone, sending it skittering across the road.

Cyrus considered that, then shook his head. "No, Poppy, think about it. Why would he seek out a farm, of all places? He wouldn't have just wandered there; he went on purpose."

Poppy's eyes lit up. "To feed."

"Exactly. The sounds were very faint from here, with everything else going on. But once we get closer, I can probably figure out which way to go."

Now Poppy looked impressed. She clapped him on the shoulder, then strode ahead toward the end of the street. "I take it back. Genius."

Cyrus didn't try to hide his smile.

They hurried their way back across the bridge, but it was still the better part of an hour before they even reached the outer city walls. By then, Cyrus could feel his energy waning. He was still in better shape than he would've been without the medicine from Leif, but his feet hurt and his legs ached and his headache was threatening to split his skull in half. Even if they took another coach back to the High District, the thought of trudging up all those damned hills to get home made him want to lie down and die on the spot.

He *would* be skipping training in the morning, no matter what anyone said.

"Can you hear anything here?" Poppy finally slowed and paused as they reached the road that would take them out of the city.

Cyrus rubbed his temples in an effort to ease the throbbing behind his eyes and tried to focus on the sounds again. He was relieved to find a less overwhelming cacophony, but rumbling wagons and shouting guards drowned out the gentler noises. He shook his head and looked up at Poppy. "We have to get closer. I can't hear anything under the noise from the gates."

He expected her to surge ahead, but she just stared at him. "This is so weird."

"You think?" Cyrus deadpanned.

"I kind of want to be there when you tell Leif about this."

"I truly don't think Leif needs to be encouraged." Cyrus started up the road. "It's handy, though, I'll admit. Too bad it's not permanent, then maybe I could actually do something useful with my life instead of getting kicked around by Father for the next few decades until he dies."

Poppy's footsteps caught up with him and she scoffed. "Come on. You don't mean that."

He just looked at her.

"Cyrus." She nudged his arm. There was still humor in her eyes and the slight curl of a smirk at the corner of her mouth; she thought he was joking. "You *are* useful to this family, and now that you've killed a vampire on your own, you'll find your place like the rest of us have. This is who we are. This is what we were *born* for. Don't tell me you didn't feel even a *little* thrill when you hunted that vampire the other night."

Cyrus couldn't mask his horror. Was that what hunting was to her—to all of them? A game, an adrenaline rush, a high? Where had Cyrus missed the memo that he was supposed to feel that way while cold blood gushed over his hand and the light died from a human face?

"What?" Poppy gave him an odd look. "Oh, come on. Really, Cyrus, it's not like you killed a *person*."

But I did. He turned his head down and stared at his feet. Lanterns fixed on metal poles along the sides of the road lit their way in pools of golden light; they passed through three bright puddles before Poppy spoke again.

"Cyrus, you are a Beldon. We all had the same training: vampires are not human, and they are not people." Now she was starting to sound like Marcus. Her voice deepened, her tone turning serious. She wielded that voice like one of her shortswords when she had to; it was a weapon all on its own. But it didn't weaken Cyrus; it only grated on him. "Like it or not, you are one of us and you share our duty. The Honorable Families, the other hunter families, and the city itself trust us to make quick work of vampires who step out of line. If not for us, innocent people would be falling victim to those monsters left and right. Is that the world you want to live in?"

Cyrus clenched his teeth. This spiel wasn't new to him, but he hated it nonetheless. It was such a foolish, narrow-minded way to look at the world. Vampires had likely existed as long as—if not longer than—humans. Of *course* there were other ways to peacefully coexist with them. Everything that made this city tick—the truce included—had been built by people and therefore could be *changed* by people. Cyrus did not believe for a second that this was the natural order of things.

"I don't care if the vampires I kill are ruthless criminals," Cyrus muttered, "I am still never going to enjoy taking a life. Human or not."

Poppy gave him a pitying look that nearly ignited his temper. "You'll get over that."

And that *did* spark his temper. Poppy strode ahead, but Cyrus halted. Adrenaline and anger burned through him. "And how old were you, when you *got over it*?"

She lifted her hands in a shrug without turning or stopping. "I dunno, thirteen?"

"Bullshit!" Cyrus shouted. "We're *human*, Poppy! We have fucking hearts! You can't make me believe you're not affected by killing them when they *look like us*."

"Cyrus, stop shouting." Now Poppy paused and turned to him. "If you hadn't waited so long to decide to actually do your job, you wouldn't still be this sensitive to it at age twenty-fucking-one. I wasn't being callous when I said you'd get over it. You *will*.

But in order for that to happen, you have to keep doing it. I promise, it gets easier every time."

Cyrus was close to fully panicking; he hadn't realized how hard his heart was racing until he tried to take a breath and couldn't. He'd been so caught up in his shock the past few days, between his first kill and Arthur's death and his own injuries—it was all hitting him now, all at once.

He didn't want to fucking do this. This couldn't be his life. It *couldn't* be. Why did he have to be born into this family? Why couldn't he be a normal person in this city? Why did he have to be a killer?

He didn't ask for any of this. And he'd never been given an option to choose.

If Poppy noticed his distress, she did not appear to care. She turned on her heel and continued through the gates, and Cyrus had no choice but to follow. He focused on calming his breathing as he dragged his feet, pressing a hand to his pounding heart. Cold wind whipped over the farmlands ahead, snapping the ends of his coat and chafing his ears. It was unpleasant, but it grounded him. A low murmur of voices and wagon noises followed him, and he concentrated on them in an effort to banish the lingering threads of panic that had his heart and lungs in a vise. The sounds tugged his attention every which way, all overlapping with each other as if he was caught in the middle of a giant, echoing room packed with people. It gave him nervous flashbacks to the parties his father used to host.

"...save him, can't you?"

Cyrus surfaced from his reeling mind and looked up at Poppy, who was a smudge of shadow on the road ahead. "What?"

She turned her head over her shoulder. "What is it? Keep up."

"Did you just say something?"

"I said, keep up. You're lagging."

"No, before that."

"No? It was probably echoes again." She upped her pace. "Come on, we still have a couple miles to go."

She was probably right, but that voice had been louder and crisper than the rest, as if spoken in real time directly next to Cyrus. He suppressed a shiver and walked a little faster.

"...too far gone. I can—"

"That's impossible. You can't *undo* it."

Cyrus startled and looked around, but of course, there was no one there. There were two voices now, sharply distinct from one another. The first was deep but soft, the second gruff and snappish. Both were loud and clear amid the other echoes. This conversation must have happened recently, perhaps hours ago, on this very road.

"I have done it before," the first voice said. "I hesitate to try again, but for him..."

"You're a madman, Stokes," scoffed the second voice.

"Please, Viktor." A third voice spoke up, strained and desperate. "I don't know what else to do. I can't let him suffer like that. I can't let him become a monster."

There was a pause, and Cyrus feared the conversation had ended or the people had walked off in a different direction. He slowed his pace, desperate to hear more. What sort of monster were they referring to, and what did they mean about *undoing* it?

At last, the softer deep voice responded. "Bring him to me. I will do all I can to reverse the turn, if it is still possible. We must act quickly. Do not delay."

The voices quieted after that, distant and buried beneath the murmur of countryside noises, but those last words were enough to halt Cyrus in his tracks.

Vampires. They were talking about vampires, and the possibility of *healing* one—reversing the turn. Making it human again.

If it was true, if it was possible, and that man—*Viktor Stokes*—could achieve it...

Cyrus's mind was running too fast. He didn't know what to do with this revelation, but he desperately needed more information. He had to find those people, or at least that Stokes fellow, and beg him to tell Cyrus what he knew. Because if vampires could be reversed—if humans could be healed from the curse of deathlife—then there was no need for families like the Beldons to kill them. Cyrus could rewrite his family's legacy and shape it into something new—something he could wear with pride.

"Cyrus." Poppy was suddenly in front of him, snapping her fingers in front of his eyes. "Are you okay? You can't space out on me now. We're almost there."

He blinked and shook his head. "N-No, I'm good. It's, uh, hard to focus with all this noise. Um..." He debated telling Poppy what he'd heard, but shut the thought down after a second. She'd probably laugh in his face if he presented a mostly-guesswork theory about saving vampires, especially since she'd just assured him he'd get over his dislike of killing.

"Can you still hear Ar— Er, the Wild vampire?" Poppy asked.

He closed his eyes and focused. Out here, farther from the city noise, it was easier to single out the sounds that didn't fit. He searched beneath the faint tones of rumbling wagons, barking dogs, rustling and bleating farm animals, and easily pinpointed an unnatural growl.

"He's close," Cyrus confirmed. He continued forward until the road branched in a fork; the growling grew louder as he did. "Wait, he's *really* close. Probably right up there." He pointed at the farmhouse just ahead, off the road to the right. "Can you hear it? I don't think I'm hearing echoes anymore."

Poppy joined him and went still as she listened, blue eyes fixed on the house. After a second, her gaze snapped to Cyrus and she nodded once. Her right hand found the sword belted to her hip and she mouthed, *Let's go.*

Cyrus reluctantly went after her, keeping his steps as light and soundless as possible. They followed the road and then turned up the gravel path leading up to the dark farmhouse; only one light was lit inside, high up in a third-story window. Whoever lived here was likely oblivious to the monster lurking about.

As they neared the front porch, Poppy reached out and touched Cyrus's arm, pausing him. Metal scraped against leather as she drew one of her swords, then she motioned for Cyrus to go around the far side of the house, implying that she'd circle around the other way.

He started to argue, but she stopped him with a hard squeeze of his shoulder. Her eyes looked stormy gray in the night's gloom. "You can do this," she whispered, and then left him there and darted across the front yard on silent feet.

Cyrus cursed under his breath. He unsheathed the dagger from the back of his belt and took a steadying breath before venturing around the side of the house.

He didn't need any drug-induced heightened senses to hear the monster now. If Cyrus didn't know what he was hunting, he would've thought a wolf was on the prowl rather than a vampire; he'd never known them to make sounds like this—grunting, moaning, growling. It set his teeth on edge. Whatever Arthur had become, it was so very far from human.

Cyrus reached the back corner of the house and pressed himself against the whitewashed stone, then poked his head around to survey the yard. It was too dark to see Poppy on the other side, and a small porch blocked his view. He could hear something snuffling and breathing heavily, close enough to raise the hair on his arms, but the trees surrounding the farmhouse blocked the moonlight and Cyrus could see only shadows. He could make out a few shapes: a woodpile, an ax stuck in a tree stump, a chicken coop, a pen with a little shelter for goats and sheep.

Everything was eerily still and silent. Even the monster's breathing quieted.

Heart in his throat, Cyrus slid around the back wall of the house. His boots moved silently in the grass, but every swish of weeds across leather was like the crack of a whip in this absolute silence. He reached the back porch, and—

Oh, gods. Oh, he smelled it now: blood. A lot of it. The tangy, metallic stench choked his senses along with the added delights of guts and gore and shit. He had to press a hand to his nose to keep himself from gagging.

Nearby, a low growl rumbled across the yard. The monster took a deep, rattling breath, and then stepped out of the trees' shadows, and Cyrus beheld the thing that used to be his brother.

It was not a vampire. It was so much worse than an immortal humanoid with sharp teeth. Its hulking body melded with the dark, but the pale moonlight revealed precisely the image Cyrus had scoffed at mere hours ago.

The thing that had once been Arthur Beldon was easily three times the size of a human, with grotesquely elongated arms and legs that bent at disturbingly-angled joints and ended in curved claws rather than fingers and toes. Its back was hunched, each vertebra bulging through leathery skin. Cyrus could hear its bones cracking as it pushed itself onto its back legs. Its jaws parted, and something heavy and wet hit the grass with a loud *WHAP*. Cyrus dared a glance down and confirmed his suspicion of where the farm animals had gone.

Bile burned the back of Cyrus's throat, but he swallowed it back and inched a few steps forward. His little dagger wouldn't do a thing against this beast, but he tightened his grip on it anyway.

The monster allowed Cyrus only three more steps before it snapped at him. He froze, and it dropped to all fours, lowering its head and hunching its shoulders. Eyes black as pitch pinned Cyrus in place; bloody drool dripped from a mouthful of teeth the length of Cyrus's fingers. Yet, ironically, the thing's face bore the most human resemblance compared to the rest of it; the skull structure was vaguely similar, albeit much larger and with a wide, curving jaw to accommodate all those teeth.

Cyrus didn't know what to do. There was no way in hell he could fight this thing, even with Poppy's help. He hated to admit it, but they needed *everyone* for this, Marcus included.

He moved a step along the back porch to find Poppy and tell

her just that, but the monster had other plans. It growled and lunged forward with a swipe of its claws that missed Cyrus by a breath. He leapt out of its reach with a yelp, clambering over the porch railing.

"Cyrus!" Poppy's voice echoed across the yard. The monster turned its head.

Damn it. "Poppy! Where are—"

The monster gave a bone-grating roar and launched itself to the other side of the yard. Cyrus heard a cry that sounded too human to have come from the beast, and then the thud of a body hitting the ground.

"No!" Cyrus ran across the porch and vaulted over the railing on the other side. His boots slipped on blood-slicked grass as he hit the ground and sprinted toward the monster, praying he wasn't too late.

Gods forgive him, he didn't like his siblings all that much, but if there was one of them he couldn't bear to lose it was Poppy.

Please, not Poppy.

He charged at the monster, dagger gripped tight in his hand. For just a few seconds, he had the advantage of surprise; he leapt and aimed for the thing's neck, but no sooner had his feet left the ground when something heavy slammed into him and sent him sprawling. He rolled across the wet grass and pushed himself up with a groan. Pain throbbed in his ribs, and when he looked up, he thought for a moment that the drug from Leif was playing tricks on him.

"Uh...Uncle Emerson?" Cyrus blinked hard and dragged himself to his feet, but before he could move to retrieve his weapon, his uncle stopped him with a strong hand on his shoulder.

"Stay back, and stay silent." He pushed Cyrus toward the porch and drew the longsword at his hip.

Cyrus hadn't even caught up with his uncle's presence, let alone his instructions. "Wh—What are you—"

"Saving your ass." Emerson fixed his grip on his sword and charged the monster with all the bravado of a soldier leaping into battle. In swift, graceful movements, Emerson spun and stabbed and swiped at the Wild vampire until it was thoroughly pissed and focused solely on Emerson. It finally left Poppy behind and engaged Emerson in a fight that would've had Cyrus smeared across the grass in a matter of seconds.

The mutated vampire fought mercilessly, stomping and swiping, but Emerson was quick and lithe and avoided the strikes with apparent ease. In a matter of minutes he managed to dart close enough to drive his sword between the monster's exposed ribs, burying the weapon to its hilt and through the beast's heart.

I've really got to get better with swords, Cyrus thought faintly. And then his mind turned again to his sister. He started in her direction, but a blood-curdling screech from the monster tore his attention back to the fight. The thing reared back and writhed, flinging Emerson off his feet. Cyrus rushed forward and dragged his uncle out of the way just in time for the monster to crash back down and collapse.

"Damn it, Cyrus—"

"You're welcome," he snapped, releasing Emerson's cloak. "Is it—"

A piercing howl answered Cyrus's question before it fully left his mouth. The monster rolled in the gory mess it had made as it tried to dislodge the sword still stuck in its body. Cyrus watched with morbid satisfaction that the silver blade not only punctured its flesh and organs, but burned all the way down. Thick, black blood gushed from the stab wound and spilled out of its mouth, yet still its limbs flailed, tearing up chunks of earth and flinging blood and animal carcasses across the yard. Cyrus feared that once it got its bearings, it would resume its attack despite the injury.

"I have to behead it," Emerson said, confirming Cyrus's fear. "A simple stab isn't going to kill something like this." He swept his black hair back from his forehead, then looked at Cyrus. "Go to your sister. Keep her alive. I'll make this quick."

Cyrus nodded mutely.

Emerson strode toward the monster, empty-handed. While he

distracted the beast, Cyrus jogged toward the side of the house where he'd last seen Poppy.

He heard her before he saw her; her heavy, labored breaths led him around the side of the house, where he finally found her slumped against the building with her head bowed and arms wrapped around her torso. If Cyrus couldn't hear her fighting for breath, he would've thought she was already dead.

"Shit, Poppy." He dropped to his knees in front of her and gripped her shoulders. "Hey. Poppy, look at me." He gave her a light shake and she groaned, then weakly shrugged off his hands. She tried to speak, but coughed up blood instead.

"No, no, stay with me." Cyrus tipped her head up, but her eyes wouldn't focus on him. His insides seized with fear. "Please, *please* stay with me. Gods, what the fuck were we thinking, Poppy?" He glanced back at the monster, which continued to put up a fight despite the blood visibly pouring from multiple wounds. Emerson had his sword back, at least.

"F-Family...duty," Poppy rasped. One of her hands gripped Cyrus's wrist; her skin was slick and warm with blood. "I-I'm proud...of you."

"Hey." He snapped his attention back to her. Panic threatened to overtake him. "Stop that. You're not going to die." He flinched as the beast howled, but a glance back confirmed it was still alive and on its feet. *Come on, Uncle, kill the thing already.* Poppy didn't have much time.

"You're going to be okay," Cyrus told her. "Uncle Emerson is here, and he'll kill the vampire, and then we'll go home and Arthur won't be suffering and you'll get some help. And everything will be fine."

He said it to reassure himself as much as her. He knew the words sounded empty, like the reassurances you'd offer a child who woke up from a nightmare. But if he didn't fill the silence, if he didn't grasp at some semblance of optimism, he'd lose his last grip on his emotions.

Poppy's head rolled to the side, supported only by the wall

behind her. Cyrus lightly tapped her cheek to keep her awake, and though her eyes fluttered, she was quickly losing consciousness. Cyrus glanced over her body, trying to find the source of all the blood soaked into her clothes, but it was impossible in the dark. *Keep her alive*, Emerson had said, but Cyrus didn't know what to do other than plead with the gods or whatever divine forces out there that Emerson quickly wrapped up this fight.

He looked again over his shoulder at the persisting battle. The Wild vampire had grown sluggish, its movements labored. It dragged half its body on the ground as it tried to swipe Emerson off his feet, but Emerson danced around it easily now. Cyrus couldn't fathom how he hadn't tired himself out yet, but for once he was grateful for his uncle's seemingly endless well of stamina.

"C-Cyrus." Poppy squeezed his wrist.

"I'm here. You're okay." He didn't take his eyes off the fight. Part of him—the part that still, stubbornly, wanted to impress his father—was fascinated by the way Emerson fought. If Cyrus didn't already resent his uncle, he'd ask him to train him with the sword, but he knew that was really asking for a verbal lashing as well as a physical one.

"We were right," Poppy rasped. Cyrus finally tore his eyes away from the monster and looked at his sister. Her eyes were barely open, and a steady trickle of blood ran down her chin. "That thing...It's Arthur. I saw...I saw him..." She inhaled a deep, rattling wheeze. Fresh tears cut clean lines through the dirt and blood on her cheeks.

Cyrus shook his head. "That monster is not our brother, Poppy. Arthur died out on the training field yesterday."

As if to punctuate Cyrus's words, the monster howled again, but its cry cut off abruptly with a sickening crack. Cyrus flinched and turned to look even though he already knew what had silenced it.

Emerson stood over the beast's head, shoulders heaving, his cloak in tatters. Steam billowed from the monster's decapitated body. A tremor quaked through the ground as its legs collapsed and its body fell, gushing black blood into the grass. A sickly smell of rot filled the air.

Cyrus squeezed Poppy's hand. "It's over. We're safe."

But Poppy didn't reply, and when Cyrus turned to her again, she had bowed her head and gone still.

Chapter FIVE

CYRUS HATED THE FAMILY INFIRMARY. SEQUESTERED IN the farthest wing of the first floor, it was a cold and harsh series of stiff, sterile rooms that smelled sharply of herbs and alcohol. The white tile floors leeched all warmth out of the space, and the white curtains over the narrow windows gave the receiving room an artificial brightness in a vain attempt to offset the otherwise dreary atmosphere.

It did not help that Adriyen brought a hurricane of stress with her every time she blew through the doors.

Cyrus sat in an uncomfortable wooden chair with his elbows on his knees. Through a set of double doors to his right was the examination room where Adriyen had brought Poppy. He didn't know how many hours had passed since Emerson had rushed Cyrus and Poppy here, but it seemed like an eternity. Adriyen had called in other physicians and surgeons from the city, and Cyrus had watched them all rush around like frenzied bees while he and the rest of his family waited anxiously in this little room. Adriyen had come out periodically, blood smeared on her apron and gloves, to speak quietly with Marcus, and though Cyrus strained his ears he couldn't make out any words. The pit of dread in his stomach deepened each time Adriyen returned to her work, making the sign of the Night God over her heart and leaving Marcus looking grave.

Eventually, Marcus left. Joel lingered longer, but in time he departed as well. Dawn snuck in, lightening the sky behind the white curtains. Cyrus remained. The doctors worked. Time passed. Adriyen did not come out with news.

Cyrus stared blankly at the wood-hewn four-point star mounted on the wall between the two windows. No one in his family had ever been religious, but he knew Adriyen was; she wore a pendant depicting the symbol of the Earth God, and now here was the symbol of the Night God watching over the infirmary. Cyrus had never been one for praying, but if those gods really were listening and if they really gave a damn about little mortals, he begged them to do something for his sister.

He didn't know what he would do if she died. She was the only Beldon he could tolerate, the only one who had ever been his friend. Arthur had treated him like a nuisance; Joel considered him an acquaintance, and Marcus's disdain and blatant dislike of Cyrus was not a secret. If *anyone* in this family loved him at all, it was Poppy.

What was left for him here, if she was gone? A broken family led by an angry, broken man who had been chasing vengeance for fifteen years. And now that lust for vengeance would double in the wake of two dead children. Cyrus would be expected to fill the void left by Poppy, held to a standard he couldn't possibly reach. Joel would become the golden child, the new heir, and he, in time, would harden to stone the same way Arthur had.

Cyrus would become a ghost. Figuratively, at first, but if things got bad enough, well...

It wasn't as if anyone would miss him.

The soft click of a door shutting drew Cyrus out of his hazy thoughts. Footsteps shuffled across the tiles, approaching Cyrus with a familiar heavy gait that he normally dreaded, but right now he was too tired to care.

He turned his head and looked up at his father.

Marcus Beldon looked tired. Cyrus wondered if he'd endured a sleepless night as well, even if he wasn't here in this room. He hid his exhaustion well, though; it only showed beneath his eyes, where the deep lines were sharper than usual. The rest of him, from his neatly groomed hair and beard to his ever-present formal attire, betrayed no hint of a long and stressful night.

"Cyrus, go to bed." Marcus sighed and sank onto a chair beside him, but didn't look at him. He clasped his calloused hands together between his knees. "You know Dr. Adriyen won't leave her side, even after the work is done. There's nothing you can do for her."

Cyrus knew that, but he still felt obligated to stay. Part of him thought, irrationally, that he was the last thread tethering his sister to her life, and if he left, she would slip away.

When Cyrus didn't respond, Marcus turned his head. "I'll stay for a bit. Get some rest, boy."

They were the softest words Marcus had ever spoken to him, and for a second Cyrus didn't know what to do. Getting up meant severing this calm moment, this unspoken and fragile camaraderie that was the closest thing to a father-son understanding he'd ever had with Marcus. It was a minuscule gesture, but *get some rest* was a monumental expression of care compared to the things Marcus normally said to him.

"I'm serious, Cyrus." Now Marcus's voice gained back its usual hardness. "After tomorrow, your training doubles. Not only to make up for Arthur and Poppy's absence, but to make sure this does not happen again." His blue eyes were frigid. "Because if Poppy doesn't pull through, you'll have killed two of your siblings in as many days, and that, boy, is the last you will ever fail me."

Cyrus stared at him, horror freezing his bones. He couldn't even conjure a defense—*But I*—or a refute—*No, I didn't*—because Marcus was right. It was his weakness, his inability to help his siblings, that had cost one and almost two their lives.

"Leave, boy," Marcus growled. "I won't tell you again."

Cyrus bolted to his feet, trembling with fury. "Call for me if anything changes."

And he stormed out of the infirmary.

He was hardly aware of his movement through the house. His body ached with exhaustion, but his heart pounded with rage-fueled adrenaline. He took the stairs two and three at a time until he felt a burn in his legs, and didn't slow down until he reached his bedroom doors. He shoved through and slammed them, savoring the loud shudder that ran through the walls.

Fuck this family, honestly. Why should he stay and wait for an excuse to leave, one way or another, only when things got worse? He could leave now. No one would care—in fact, they'd be better off without him. His father would grumble about his goddamned disappointment of a son—which wasn't new—and then write Cyrus out of existence. Joel and Poppy, if she survived, would forget him. Emerson would pretend he'd never existed at all. And right now, in the wake of the past days' chaos, no one would notice if Cyrus disappeared, and by the time they did, he would be long gone. On to the next city or province, all notions of Chestervale and vampire hunting far behind him.

Okay, but you still have to eat, murmured a crumb of rationality in his mind. *You still need a roof over your head, and that does, in fact, require money.*

Cyrus had no qualms about stealing from his father—he'd always thought it was unfair, anyway, that Marcus kept all but a small fraction of the gold the Beldons were paid for their hunting jobs, regardless of who had actually wielded the blade—but realistically he knew he could only take so much, and it wouldn't last. Besides, wasn't the point of leaving to detach himself from the Beldon family? That included their money.

His eyes fell on his bookshelves. His beloved collection, packed neatly and orderly on ceiling-height shelves, was the one thing he had that he was proud of. He'd started purposely collecting and keeping these books when he was eleven; ten years later, he had an impressive variety of gold-foiled, leather-bound volumes that had come from all over. Some were rare in this province, others unavailable anywhere in the country. They'd been expensive, even by his family's standards, which meant they'd fetch a hefty price if Cyrus found the right buyers.

It would hurt to part with his treasures, but in the end, they were just objects. Staying here would be worse than any regret he might feel at passing a book into another set of loving hands. He could always find more wherever he ended up; he gravitated to them, and he liked to think the books themselves found him when he needed them most.

Right, so that settled it. First chance he got, Cyrus was going to leave.

But for now, all he craved was rest.

CYRUS WOKE to a bright room after what felt like ten minutes and pulled his blankets over his head with a groan, determined to sink back into sleep. But almost at once, his brain took off at a sprint, reminding him of everything that had happened last night and the day before and all the things he still didn't know. Like why Arthur had been killed by Honorable Ones. And if Poppy had made it. And that echo of a conversation suggesting vampires could be reversed. *That* itched his curiosity more than anything, so with a resigned grumble, Cyrus sat up in bed and rubbed the sleep out of his eyes.

He blinked at the grandfather clock across from the end of his bed; just after eight, meaning he'd only slept for about three hours. Wonderful.

He slid out of bed and rolled the stiffness out of his shoulders, then dragged his hands down his face. He felt grimy, more so after collapsing into bed in yesterday's clothes, still caked with dried blood. Though he was anxious to check on Poppy, he reasoned that someone would've told him if she'd died while he was asleep—if not Marcus, then probably Joel or Adriyen—so he shuffled into his bathroom and filled the tub.

He stripped off his ruined clothes and dropped them in a heap on the floor, making a mental note to advise the staff to literally burn them instead of trying to wash them. He gathered the soaps and shampoos he wanted from the shelf next to the sink, and when the tub was full and the water steaming, he sank in to his chin and closed his eyes.

Yes, this was precisely what he needed.

As he scrubbed the dirt and grime from his skin, he let his fear and stress from the past few days dissolve into the water with it. He let go of his worry about Poppy; either she would pull through and recover, or she would be gone, and either way, Cyrus did not have to stay here to endure the aftermath. He washed away his anxious fears of what might come next, of what would now be expected of him now with two Beldons out of commission. He let himself believe, at least for this moment, that he was in control of his life and he was not trapped.

In the safety of his own room, in the bath's serene embrace, it was easy to believe that. The pessimistic voice in his head scolded him for thinking he'd ever be in control of his life, but he silenced it with a dunk underwater. He massaged a fragrant soap into his hair, rinsed it, then for once actually worked it through with the oil that was supposed to make his curls more manageable. He rarely spent this much time pampering himself, but this morning, it was warranted. Despite his fitful sleep, he felt refreshed.

When the water was thoroughly clouded from all the dirt and blood, Cyrus reluctantly climbed out of the tub and reached for his towel, only to realize he'd left it hanging behind the door across the room. He grumbled at his own forgetfulness and crossed the room in an undignified, tip-toed prance in an effort to touch his feet to the cold tiles as little as possible. Towel claimed, he padded into his bedroom as he dried off, and found that someone had come in and opened the curtains and lit a fire while he was bathing. He lingered within the reach of its warmth for a few minutes while drops of water dripped from his hair and slid down his back.

Relaxed and warm, he had half a mind to go back to bed for a few hours. Venturing out of his room and chasing his unanswered questions would resurrect all the stress he'd just left behind in the bath water, and he was in no hurry to pick up that whirlwind of trouble when he'd finally managed to set it down for a few minutes. Right now, all of those things seemed small. Even Arthur's death. Even Poppy's close call. And even the sharp accusation Marcus had thrown at Cyrus this morning.

Prickles of anxiety started to return the longer Cyrus stood idly by the fire. All the things that had woken him from his restless sleep crept back into his mind. His moments of peace never did last long; of course he couldn't stay here all day and pretend nothing was wrong. These problems were too big to ignore; if he tried, he'd only end up caught in a spiral of his own anxiety, likely pacing a rut into the floor.

Despite his growing urgency, he took his time getting dressed, selecting a simple outfit from his wardrobe and adding a splash of color with his favored green waistcoat. He paused at his vanity and ran his fingers through his damp hair in an effort to guide it somewhat in the correct direction, but as usual his hair did what it wanted. He left it alone, tied a cravat around his neck, and then shoved on a pair of loafers on his way to the door.

A few housekeepers buzzed around in the hallway, darting in and out of the rooms as they went about their daily cleaning and tidying. Cyrus nodded in greeting to one woman as he passed her, and she gave a shy nod in return.

Aside from a few servants here and there, the halls were deserted as Cyrus made his way down to the first floor and across the mansion to the infirmary. When he reached the white doors, he could hear soft voices within, but the receiving room was empty. The sliding doors that led into the recovery room were, however, slightly ajar.

Cyrus nudged the doors open wider and slid through. His eyes went first to Poppy, who lay in one of the beds with white blankets pulled up to her shoulders and a stack of pillows propped up behind her. Her head was tilted away from him, but he could tell she was alive.

He let out a breath he felt like he'd been holding all night. She'd pulled through, but were Adriyen's treatments enough to keep her alive?

Cyrus turned to Joel, who sat by Poppy's bedside. He'd pushed his glasses up onto his head where they tangled with his disheveled hair, and he'd loosened his tie and undone the buttons on his shirt collar. Stubble shadowed his jaw and purplish smudges darkened the skin beneath his eyes. He'd probably been here since Cyrus had left hours ago.

"How is she doing?" Cyrus asked.

Joel gave a light shrug. "She's alive. Dunno how. Adriyen and the others were working on her almost all night. Thought for sure..." He pressed his lips into a thin line.

If Cyrus was more like a brother and less like an acquaintance to Joel, he would've set a hand on his shoulder or offered some other small comfort, but as it was, he instead opted to stand uncomfortably a few feet away from Joel's chair. His gaze wandered back to Poppy.

She was alive, for now, but how much time did she have? Had Adriyen saved her, or merely curbed her suffering so her life could slip away peacefully?

And why the hell did some sick part of Cyrus feel disappointed that she was still alive?

Across the room, a door softly opened and shut, and Cyrus recognized Adriyen's light but hurried footsteps. He glanced up as she approached; for having been awake and frantically working all night, she hardly showed it. Her hair was neatly swept back with a white bandanna and she'd changed into a clean set of clothes, free of blood. Her eyes looked tired, but her exhaustion did not slow her down.

"Cyrus. Good morning." She came up to Poppy's bedside and touched her forehead, then her cheek, then drew back the covers to Poppy's waist. Thick bandages wrapped snugly around Poppy's torso, crossing over her collarbones and around her shoulders. Adriyen nodded in satisfaction that no blood had leaked through the dressings, then replaced the covers and sighed.

Cyrus toyed with one of the buttons on his vest. "How...is she?"

"Doing better, all things considered." Adriyen looked up at him. "Did anyone tell you about the procedure we did last night?"

"Uh, no." Funny that Adriyen thought anyone told Cyrus anything around here.

She nodded as if she'd expected that answer. "She suffered extensive damage to her torso, internally and externally. I don't use this term lightly, but it is a *miracle* that her heart and lungs were not damaged. Still, I had to call in surgeons from the city to help, and we ended up having to remove a significant fraction of her breast tissue. We did some skin grafts, closed up her wounds, and fixed what internal damage we could. The rest will have to heal on its own, gods willing." She gripped the symbol of the Earth God that rested on her chest. "She has a very long recovery ahead of her, but...she'll make it."

"And thank the gods that she has the best physician in Chestervale taking care of her." Joel flickered a tired smile.

Adriyen smirked. "I shall do my best. But there's one more thing. I already spoke to Master Beldon about this, and he was... understandably unhappy. But I want to be transparent with both of you, as well. Even when Poppy recovers, I strongly advise against her returning to hunting."

And just like that, Cyrus heard the door lock on his cage.

"*What?*" Joel sat up straighter. "But Doctor—"

"I'm aware of the strong sense of duty you all have," Adriyen said, "even if I can't claim to understand it. But you both need to understand that Poppy wasn't just *on* death's door, she was halfway through it. It will be months before she can function normally, perhaps up to a year before she can so much as pick up a weapon. Her body has endured significant trauma, and to put it through more stress after she's healed is unwise. Even with training, I doubt she would regain the full strength and abilities she had before."

"*Bull...shit.*"

Cyrus, Joel, and Adriyen turned in simultaneous alarm toward

Poppy. Moments ago she'd been soundly unconscious, but now her eyes were cracked open.

"Poppy," Adriyen gasped, "you shouldn't be awake. Hold on." She darted off, and Cyrus expected his sister to slip back under, but instead she turned her head to him.

"I am...not as weak...as you think I am." Her chest rose and fell with heavy, labored breaths. "I *will*...return to my duty. Or I will die."

You've lost your mind, Cyrus thought with disgust. No sane person would go back to such a dangerous lifestyle after this close a call. Marcus had brainwashed all of them.

He hated that, in his father's eyes, Poppy's words made her a better Beldon than Cyrus would ever be.

"For gods' sakes, Poppy," Joel muttered. "Don't think of that now. Just rest, sister. Just rest."

And though she fought it, blinking hard, sleep took her once again.

Cyrus lingered a few minutes longer, then quietly slipped out of the room.

So Poppy would be okay. That was objectively a good thing. But even if she did decide to return to hunting, it would be months —if not more than a year—before she was physically able to. Cyrus could already feel the weight of doubled expectations settling on his shoulders. He'd be expected to take her place, and he already knew he would fail.

But with everyone's guard up in the wake of this disastrous week, would he even be able to disappear? He couldn't see way out that wouldn't have the Beldons breathing down his neck for the rest of his life; he knew that if he just left, they would find him before he could take more than two steps out of the city.

And then he'd really be a prisoner.

Well, there was always one way he could get out. There was no shortage of sharp objects in this house, and he could easily steal away somewhere where he wouldn't be found until it was too late. Cyrus hated that he'd thought of it enough times to have something like a plan—one to only be used as an absolute last resort—but if things got bad enough, death would be kinder than continuing to live under this roof.

Yet, the foolish and stubbornly optimistic part of him wasn't ready to quit yet.

Cyrus surfaced from his thoughts and found that his feet had brought him up to the third floor. He paused at the head of the hallway that housed his and his siblings' rooms, and for the first time in years, he looked up at the portrait of Julius Beldon, the founder of the family. One entire year of Cyrus's education had been devoted to family history, and he knew so much about Julius that sometimes he forgot that the man had been dead for three centuries.

This portrait, imposing in size alone, had stood guard over this hallway for decades, and Marcus treated it like a shrine. Every year on the anniversary of Julius's birth, he placed white flowers in a vase below the portrait, and on the anniversary of his death, he offered black roses. Marcus didn't pray to any gods, but he worshiped Julius.

Cyrus studied his ancestor now and wondered what Julius would think if he could see what this family had become. Would he be proud? Or would he, too, wish to smother the Beldon name and everything it stood for?

The family portraits in this house all had an uncanny realism to them. Cyrus had always felt like they were watching him whenever he passed by them, this one especially. He consciously tried not to look at the harsh, cold glares of his ancestors, but he met Julius Beldon's ice-blue eyes now with a challenge.

Julius had carved his legacy with a silver blade, passing down a duty he thought was noble to countless descendants who now thought that nobility meant getting themselves killed in his name. Their legacy was bathed in blood—crimson *and* silver—but why should it have to stay that way? What gave one man who had lived hundreds of years ago the right to dictate the lives of descendants he would never meet?

"I don't care what you think," he muttered. "I don't care if I'm a disgrace to this family. If what we are now is all we are meant to be, then we don't deserve to go on. We can be different. We *will* be different."

He drifted a few steps back from the portrait, daring its lifeless gaze to judge him. "It started with you. It'll end with me."

He turned his back on Julius Beldon and went upstairs to find Leif.

Chapter SIX

Tense silence followed Cyrus up to the fourth floor. The halls were quiet, void of voices and even the servants' light footsteps. House Beldon held its breath, not yet daring to relax lest something else go wrong.

Cyrus didn't mind the quiet, even if it was unnerving to have everyone walking on eggshells. He consciously lightened his own steps on the stairs until he reached the top floor, which he found deserted as usual. Other than the door to the attic, the fourth floor boasted just one other room: Marcus's private study, to which he stole away when he didn't wish to be bothered with the business that often approached him in his usual downstairs office. Marcus expertly charmed and commanded his way through social obligations and negotiations as the head of the family, but Cyrus couldn't blame him for needing a space where he didn't need to don a mask and pretend he wasn't annoyed when his work was interrupted. That was the singular similarity Cyrus shared with his father.

Cyrus stopped at the attic door and dragged it open, then followed the spiral stairs up to the landing. It didn't occur to him until he knocked that Leif might not even be home, but after a moment he heard their steps approach and they appeared with an apprehensive frown. It cleared quickly, though, when they saw Cyrus. "Ah! Morning, Cyrus. How are you feeling?"

"Eh." He shrugged. "I've been better. I wanted to ask you something, if you've got a few minutes."

"Sure! Come on in." Leif pulled the door open wider. "I promise there's no aphrodisiacs in the air this time." They winked and turned on their heel, sending their long shawl flourishing around them.

Cyrus resisted commenting on the aphrodisiacs and followed Leif into their home. The flat was small, but cozy for one—or sometimes two. The living space was open, kitchen and living room blending into each other, with narrow steps up to a small loft that presumably housed Leif's bedroom.

Leif invited him to sit at the island counter in their tiny kitchen, then grabbed a pot off the woodstove. "I just brewed coffee. Care for a cup?"

"That sounds great, actually. Thank you." Cyrus slid onto one of the wood stools.

"Mhm!" Leif fetched a mug and poured it. "Milk in it?"

Cyrus cringed but nodded, resigning himself to an upset stomach later. But he'd rather endure that than drink black coffee.

Leif shot him a knowing look but didn't say anything as they added a generous pour of milk to his coffee. They slid the blue ceramic mug across the counter to him, then poured themself their own coffee and wrapped their hands around the cup. "So, little Beldon, what brings you up here two days in a row? I'm beginning to actually feel needed around here."

Cyrus took a sip of coffee to stop himself from snapping at the phrase *little Beldon*. "I wanted to thank you, firstly, for whatever it was you gave me the other night. It was weird, but it did help us find what we needed."

"Oh, good!" Leif smiled, fiddling with one of their dangly earrings. "Hallucinogens are dicey, you know, so I'm glad to hear you didn't have any adverse effects." They paused a second. "You... didn't have any adverse effects, right?"

"Um. Not exactly?" Cyrus frowned. "Why the hell did you give me *hallucinogens* when I asked for something to keep me awake?"

"The tincture I gave you is a stimulant," Leif explained. "In very small doses, taken with care, it does give you an energy boost and keeps your mind awake. But we have to be careful with these things, of course, otherwise you could end up seeing *too* much."

Cyrus didn't have a response to that.

Leif eyed him nervously. "What happened? Oh, gods, did you get night terrors? Sleep paralysis? I hope you didn't see the—"

"I'm gonna stop you right there." Cyrus held up a hand. "No, I didn't see anything *weird*, but I did see things. Heard things, too."

Not for the first time, Cyrus was immensely grateful for Leif's presence in this house, because if he had said this to anyone else, they would've thought he'd lost his mind.

Leif's eyes widened. "Did you hear dead people?"

"What? No!" Cyrus stared at them. "Is that—Is that *common*?"

"Sometimes."

Thank the gods Leif hadn't given him more of that stuff. "Well, that sounds horrifying, and what I heard were more like...echoes, I guess. As I walked through the city, I could hear remnants of voices and noises that had occurred that day. Wagons, carriages, animals, boats, shouting and talking...It was like the entire city was talking to me all at once." Cyrus wrapped his hands around the warm mug. "It was overwhelming."

"Huh." Leif leaned their elbows on the counter and tapped their nails—currently painted black, but chipping on their thumbs —on the granite surface. "That is fascinating. And it sounds overwhelming, yes, but as far as side effects go, you lucked out. Was it this ability that led you to find what...or *who* you were looking for?"

"You're really bad at pretending to be clueless," Cyrus said.

"I'm a mystic who communes with forces beyond most people's understanding," Leif said. "I know things."

"So you know what we found out there."

"Yes," Leif said quietly. "And I'm very sorry."

Cyrus waved their sympathy away. That wasn't what he'd come

here for. "It's fine. But as strange as all that was, there's something else I wanted to ask you."

"Hm? Oh, do you—Wait." Leif grimaced. "I shouldn't give you drugs."

Cyrus blinked. "What?"

"You're not—? Okay, never mind." They grinned. "What is it, then?"

Cyrus glanced away, then back at Leif. "Are you implying that my siblings have asked you for drugs?"

"Nope!" Leif's grin didn't falter.

They were full of shit, but Cyrus let it go. "...Okay. Anyway, I wanted to ask you if you've ever heard of vampires being cured."

At that, Leif's smile faded. Their expression turned gravely serious and they crossed their arms, pulling their knit shawl tighter over their chest. "When you say *cured*, do you mean...reversed?"

Cyrus nodded once. "One of the echoes I heard was of a conversation I think happened mere hours before we were there. There were three people, and one of them was desperate for one of the others to save someone who had recently been turned into a vampire. The man seemed to have done so before, and he agreed to try again. I—I know how crazy this sounds, but if anyone would have heard of this being possible, it would be you."

Leif nodded slowly, mulling over his words. "Did you hear a name?"

"Viktor Stokes."

Leif's eyes darted up, but just as quickly they blinked and feigned ignorance. Cyrus had seen it, though: a flicker of alarmed recognition. They knew that name.

"Leif," he prompted. "What do you know?"

"Truly, not much," Leif said. "I've heard that name before, but never in this context."

Cyrus's spirits lifted. "So you know who this Stokes fellow is? You—Are you saying that reversing a turn *is* possible?"

"I'm saying I've heard of it as a theory," Leif corrected, sipping their coffee. "And I have heard Mr. Stokes's name before in your family's circles, but not for a very long time. This is very interesting indeed."

"Leif," Cyrus lowered his voice, "it would be *revolutionary*. Imagine it: the Beldons becoming known for *healing* rather than killing. If I can figure this out, it...it would give me a reason to stay."

Leif tilted their head to the side. "To stay here? Or to stay alive?"

Cyrus sipped his coffee and glanced away, letting that be his answer.

"So go."

Cyrus blinked. "What?"

"You have a name and a lead to follow." Leif shrugged. "Follow it."

"But where? All I have is a name and three people's voices."

"Wrong." Leif pushed off the counter and spun around, shawl fanning in their wake. They grabbed the kettle from the stovetop, snatched a cylindrical green tin from a shelf on the adjacent wall, then turned back to Cyrus. "Where were you when you heard this conversation?"

"The south end of the city, just outside the gates," Cyrus said. "Near the farms."

"And I imagine the voices disappeared at some point, perhaps as you kept moving and they did not?" Leif stirred a pinch of leaves from the tin into a steaming teacup.

"Or they went in a different direction," Cyrus said. The voices had died away as Cyrus and Poppy had approached the farmhouse where they'd found Arthur, which could mean the trio had simply fallen into silence, or it could mean they had turned down the road along the river. But that way went into the forest, and no one traveled that road on foot; it was a long distance through those woods to the next town, and the wolves were not known for their hospitality. Cyrus hadn't heard any hoofbeats or carriage wheels, so the trio must have been on foot, which meant they were most likely heading for the farmhouses.

It was a place to start, but Cyrus didn't have the time to waste wandering around until he happened to hear Viktor Stokes's name again.

"Only so many ways they could go," Leif said, as if they'd heard Cyrus's thoughts. They gave the tea another stir, then set the spoon aside and drew up a tiny leather pouch on a cord around their neck, then sprinkled something powdery into the cup. Cyrus watched in wonder as the rosy-brown liquid turned bright red.

"I hope you don't expect me to drink that," he muttered.

"Not you, no." Leif watched the substances swirl together in the cup, then spread their hands in the air above it as if warming their palms on the steam. They closed their eyes.

Cyrus studied the tiny tattoos on Leif's fingers while they did whatever it was they were doing. Delicate line drawings of leaves, flowers, and celestial bodies decorated their pale skin, including several phases of the moon that traced the lines of tendons down the back of their right hand. Cyrus flexed his own fingers and inwardly cringed at the thought of how much that must've hurt on Leif's bony hands.

Leif wrapped their hands around the teacup, then slowly brought it to their lips and drank the contents in a quick gulp. Their eyes flashed open, but they seemed to look right through Cyrus rather than at him. "He lives outside the city, alone. Secret. The house is black. Spires, gargoyles...old-fashioned, and *old*. It sits in a valley in the south."

Cyrus's mouth fell open. "How do you—"

"The land around it is barren," Leif continued. "No trees, no bushes, just empty land. You'll find something, I'm sure of it." They blinked a few times and focused their gaze on Cyrus. "Is that enough to start?"

"Y-Yeah," Cyrus stammered. "How did you do that?"

"Good old-fashioned divination." Leif smiled. "If you lost track of the conversation near the farmhouse you and Poppy visited the other night, retracing your steps there would be a good start. This Viktor fellow's house is likely not far, especially if you have reason to believe the conversation occurred late in the day. He was probably heading home."

Cyrus nodded and finished his last sip of coffee. Possibilities swirled in his mind—of finding precisely what he wanted, and of hitting a brick wall. And what would come next, even if he did learn something revolutionary from this mysterious Mr. Stokes? How far would he be able to pursue such an idea before his family duties caught up with him? He already felt like he was out of time.

"Come back and see me after you've spoken to Mr. Stokes," Leif said, interrupting Cyrus's worries. "I think you're unwell."

"Huh?"

"Hmm, yes, something is definitely wrong with you." Leif widened their eyes pointedly, and when Cyrus merely stared back in confusion, they leaned over the counter and dropped their voice to a whisper. "Don't be dense, little Beldon. If I'm going to help you, you need a good reason to steal away up here so frequently, and the position of secret lover is already taken. How old are you, anyway? Seventeen?"

Cyrus scoffed. "Twenty-one."

"Still too young for me."

"Don't make it weird, Leif."

"Trying not to." They put their chin in their hand and studied him. "Oh, I've got it: Dairy intolerance."

"What? No!" Cyrus's stomach took that moment to make an unhappy noise.

Leif smirked. "It runs in your family. Yet you didn't refuse the milk in your coffee."

"I'm fine." Cyrus crossed his arms. "Can't I be seeing you for something less humiliating? Like...headaches?"

"Boring."

"Anxiety?" Gods knew Cyrus had plenty of that.

"Still not giving you drugs."

"I never asked you to?" This mystic was so weird. "Do you *want* me to ask you for drugs?"

"Go ahead."

Cyrus blinked. "C-Can I have some drugs?"

Leif snorted. "Oh, you really are the straightedge of the family. No, Cyrus, I will not give you drugs until you know what to ask for. In the meantime, sure, you can be seeing me for help managing anxiety. That's believable enough in the wake of everything that's happened. Go follow your lead, and when you come back, I'll hopefully have figured out why the name Viktor Stokes rings such a bell."

"Y-You're really going to help me with this?" Cyrus couldn't help feeling a little incredulous. What did Leif have to gain here?

They nodded once. Their gold rings clinked against the teacup as they rolled it between their palms. "I want to see you succeed here."

"Why?"

Leif met his eyes. "I'm not just the weird mystic who lives in the attic, you know. I've been caring for you and your siblings for almost fifteen years. I care about you. Master Beldon might be desensitized to seeing his children beaten and bloody, but it doesn't get easier for me or Adriyen each time one of you gets injured. Your older siblings claim it's your family's duty, but I can't see the honor in a line of work that puts children in such danger. If there's another way..." Leif sighed and ran their hand over their shorn hair. "I want you to find it, too."

Cyrus's resolve cemented, then. For the first time in his life, he had an ally, and knowing that he wasn't the only one who saw the problems in this house ignited a spark of hope that he'd done his best to smother a long time ago. But it came back to life now, and Cyrus was determined to keep it burning.

"You have strength in you, Cyrus." Leif pushed away from the counter as Cyrus slid off his stool, and walked him to the door. "Don't let anyone else in this house tell you otherwise. You are here for a reason. You are a Beldon for a reason. You may not see that reason yet, but the universe has a plan for you."

If that was true, Cyrus hoped that plan turned in his favor

sooner than later. He flickered a smile at Leif and opened the door to leave, but Leif lightly touched his arm.

"One more thing," they said softly. Their tone at once put Cyrus on edge. "If you ever want to talk about anything—your life, your family, what happened the other day, or if that's too much, then just what you've been reading—you can confide in me."

Something tightened in Cyrus's chest. His first reflex was to brush off Leif's words and insist he was fine—because he *was*, and he couldn't be anything other than fine—but that insistence sounded weak even in his head.

He glanced up at Leif, but couldn't hold their gaze for more than a second. "Thanks, Leif."

They gently squeezed his shoulder, then let him go.

CYRUS DIDN'T WASTE any time. While everyone else in the house was occupied with their daily tasks—with the exception of Joel, who hadn't left Poppy's side—Cyrus stole away without notice.

The day was chilly and overcast, threatening rain, but the High District was busy in spite of the gloomy weather. Cyrus kept his head down and his eyes on the bricks, hoping he blended in well enough that no one would recognize him. If anyone did, they did not call out to him.

Just as well. The aristocrats who surrounded the Beldons might be their neighbors, but they were not friends.

The city smelled of dampness and petrichor as Cyrus left the brick roads behind in favor of bumpy cobblestones. The usual noises greeted him: fog horns, rattling carriages, horse whinnies, hurried folks calling out to one another. It took Cyrus almost two hours to wind his way through the city, and by the time he made it into the

Commerce District, he was ready to smack the next person who bumped into him or tried to sell him something. Truly, this was why he never ventured down from the High District; he could not fathom how anyone put up with this chaos every day. He would be filled with insatiable violence if he had to regularly deal with lost visitors who didn't know better than to stop walking in the middle of the road.

The sky steadily darkened as he made his way out of the city and trekked up the muddy countryside roads. Chestervale's ever-present fog became a light drizzle that dampened Cyrus's hair and beaded on his coat; he turned up his collar and shoved his hands in his pockets, but it was little use against the chilled wind that swept across the hills.

He found the farmhouse that he and Poppy had visited the other night, and saw now that there was a third branch in the forked road that disappeared around a bend and down a hill. Anticipation thrummed through him; that must be the way Viktor and his companions had gone. Where Cyrus stood now was just about where their voices had disappeared.

He swept his damp curls back off his forehead and turned down the narrow path. For about a mile, it led him along fenced pastures and fields that shimmered in the wind. The earth sloped downward, and a lush valley spread out before him, dotted with the occasional farmhouse or barn. The trees painted a backdrop of hazy gold, green, and red behind the scarce buildings, and with the landscape in such vivid color, it was easy to spot the one structure that didn't fit.

The house was precisely what Leif had described: solid black, weirdly old-fashioned, and surrounded by absolutely no plant life save for the dead grass. Compared to the other quaint dwellings, this house looked ghastly.

Strange. But maybe someone who dabbled in experiments with human lives didn't wish to attract attention. Though in Cyrus's opinion, having a bizarrely conspicuous house was not doing this man any favors. He wouldn't have looked twice at the other farmhouses, but this one was a beacon from quite literally a mile away.

Although, if Mr. Stokes's goal was to ward off visitors, he was admittedly doing a marvelous job. Cyrus tried to tell himself that the chill down his spine was because of the rain as he drew closer.

The wind blew colder and the drizzle finally committed to a full rain by the time Cyrus reached the bottom of the long hill. Mud squelched around his shoes and soaked his socks, and no matter how quickly he walked, the rain worked faster. When he finally stepped onto the puddled path that led up to the strange, black stone house, he was drenched, freezing, and fucking miserable.

He hoped this Stokes fellow was hospitable. Cyrus would kill ten vampires on the spot if it meant he could get his hands on a hot cup of tea.

A single iron lamppost stood at the end of the path, casting a weak orange glow in the gloom. Cyrus gave the house a last once-over before approaching the door, and he'd scarcely raised his hand to the brass knocker when a roaring howl erupted from inside.

Cyrus jumped back, stumbling as his foot crashed into a puddle. Something slammed into the door on the other side, rattling it on its hinges. Vicious growling followed, accompanied by the sound of claws scraping and scrambling on the floor. Cyrus had almost decided to give it up and flee when the door creaked open.

He braced himself to be pounced upon by whatever monster had just announced its presence, but several seconds lapsed and he remained on his feet. Slowly, he lowered his hands from his face and peered up at the figure that had appeared in the doorway.

Two pairs of eyes peered back at him. The first belonged to a man, pale-skinned and high-cheekboned, with receding black hair and round spectacles perched on his straight nose. The other was a wolfish dog, baring its bright white teeth at him. It maintained a low growl, but gathered in the man's arms like a child, it didn't appear as threatening as it probably thought it was.

Cyrus collected himself and stood up straighter. "Good morning. I'm looking for Mr. Stokes. Might he be in?"

The man arched a thin eyebrow. "And who is looking for Mr. Stokes?"

"Uh—" It occurred to him that he shouldn't give his family name. Not right away, anyway. He wanted to do this alone, free of the influence that came with his surname. "My name is Cyrus." He glanced around and picked the first object his eyes landed on. "Cyrus Bush. I'm a student, and I heard Mr. Stokes is... Er, I've heard extraordinary things about the work Mr. Stokes does. I just have a few questions for him about his research."

Cyrus had no idea where he'd pulled this story from, but he prayed it was strong enough. As long as this man didn't ask for many details...

The man shifted the dog's weight in his arms and eyed Cyrus, understandably skeptical. "What did you say your family name is?"

Cyrus made himself meet the man's eyes and prayed to the gods he didn't believe in that he didn't come across as the terrible liar he knew he was. "Bush."

"Hm." The man patted the dog's side. "I was gonna say that you look an awful lot like ol' Master Beldon's late wife, but my eyes aren't as reliable as they used to be. I beg your pardon. What sorts of questions do you have for Mr. Stokes?"

Cyrus let the tension out of his shoulders. He was getting somewhere. "I would be happy to explain, but, er...perhaps inside?" He nodded toward the downpour behind him.

"Ah, of course." The man stepped aside to allow Cyrus to enter. The dog, however, growled louder and snapped at him when he stepped over the threshold. He just barely skirted out of reach of its teeth.

"Your dog doesn't seem thrilled about a visitor," Cyrus said with a nervous chuckle. He flicked a glance around the dim foyer; the place was dark and bleak, and somehow colder than the outdoors. The candelabras and chandelier were unlit and covered in cobwebs, and the scarce furniture appeared centuries old.

"Oh, Mina? She's harmless." The man set the wolfish dog down, and as if to demonstrate exactly how harmless it was, the canine immediately lunged at Cyrus with its jaws open wide.

Cyrus didn't realize he had screamed until he heard the echo of it ringing off the stone walls. Then it took him a moment longer to realize he *didn't* have a dog hanging off one of his limbs; when he opened his eyes he found the giant, previously-snarling animal crouched in a playful bow before him. Its whole body wiggled with the rapid wag of its fluffy tail.

Soft laughter drew Cyrus's attention up to the man. He stifled his chuckles behind his pale hand. "I am sorry. She's all bark and no bite, truly, but the roar-barking really gets you, don't it?" He clapped Cyrus on the shoulder. "Good judge of character, she is. Wouldn't have let you through the door if she sensed something fishy about you. A friend of Mina's is a friend of mine. Welcome, Mr. Bush." He offered his hand. "My name is Viktor Stokes."

Oh. Oh *he* was Viktor. Cyrus was so used to being greeted by butlers that he forgot some people simply answered their own doors. He shook Viktor's hand. "A pleasure, Mr. Stokes. Thank you for having me."

He bowed his head, smiling, and all notes of suspicion were left outside when he shut the door. His demeanor was warm as he showed Cyrus across the foyer. "Let's talk in my study. I've got a fire blazing already."

Thank the gods, Cyrus thought. He rubbed warmth into his hands as he followed Viktor—and Mina the dog—across the room. Shadows slunk behind him, and he swore he saw a mouse scurry by. The walls were dull and spiderwebbed with cracks in the paint, and the last time the floors had seen a broom was probably before Cyrus was born. He wrinkled his nose at the musty smell that wafted out of Viktor's study when he opened the door, but quickly wiped the distaste off his face when Viktor turned and invited him into the room.

Cyrus stepped into the space and was immediately blasted with a sweltering gust of heat. The fire indeed blazed, threatening to breach its hearth. The tiny room wilted under the oppressive heat; Cyrus felt his own energy seeping out by the second. Viktor shut the door after letting Mina into the room, and Cyrus shed his coat under the guise of draping it over a chair by the fire to dry. He selected the farthest seat from the blaze, but already his high-collared, long-sleeved shirt threatened to suffocate him.

Meanwhile, Viktor planted himself in a plush chair that would've gone up in flames if it was any closer to the fireplace. He patted his knees, and Mina jumped up and settled in his lap despite being rather too large for lap sitting. Viktor placed his hands on her back and idly stroked her gray fur as he turned his attention to Cyrus.

"So, you're a student, are you?" He adjusted his glasses. "Whereabouts are you studying?"

"Oh, uh..." Cyrus's brain went blank for a panicked moment. "It's, er, more of an independent project."

"Oho, got a private tutor, do you?"

He nodded and hoped it looked convincing. "Yeah, you could say that. It's unusual research, so I'm mostly doing this on my own. There's... a bit of a story behind it."

Damn it, why did I say that?

"That so?" Viktor scratched Mina behind her ears. "Well, my time is yours, Mr. Bush. I'm interested."

Cyrus hesitated. This was going better than he'd anticipated. He'd found Viktor Stokes, and Viktor Stokes hadn't kicked him off his doorstep. Yet the ease with which Viktor had welcomed Cyrus needled a worry at the back of his mind. It was almost *too* easy, wasn't it?

Or maybe Cyrus was being paranoid. Maybe this man, who could allegedly reverse vampiric turns, simply wanted to help.

Cyrus caught himself fiddling with his family ring and stopped, smoothing his hands down his thighs. "A few days ago, I was attacked by a vampire."

Viktor sank back in his chair. "Oh, dear."

"It's fine." Cyrus glanced at him, then flicked his gaze to the fire. "It—I mean, *he*, didn't really hurt me. I was able to defend myself. But what stuck with me, Mr. Stokes, what I can't get out of my head, is his eyes. There was intelligence there, and fear. Even animals have desperation behind their eyes when they attack. This vampire had far more than that. He wasn't a monster. Wasn't a *creature*. He was a man, and I...I killed him."

Viktor was quiet for a long second. "He attacked you first, did he not?"

No. In the true version of the story, he had not. The vampire that Cyrus had killed had been doing nothing but minding his own business, strolling between the pubs on a crisp night, and Cyrus had ripped his life away from him. All for some hateful, vengeance-fueled family duty.

Cyrus looked up at Viktor. "Still. I watched the life fade from his eyes, knowing that I took it from him. My point, Mr. Stokes, is that there was still *humanity* in that vampire. And now I can't help but wonder if—if there's a way to help them. To...save them."

"Ah." Viktor let out a heavy sigh and shifted in his seat, careful not to disturb the snoozing dog sprawled upon his legs. "So you've heard of my experiment."

"Yes." Cyrus decided to stop dancing around his reason for being here. "I heard that you successfully restored humanity to someone who had been turned into a vampire. And I want to know how."

Viktor rubbed his chin. "Right. See, Mr. Bush, the thing is that I don't know."

Cyrus blinked. "I'm sorry?"

"The experiment was a success," Viktor said, "but it was also an accident. I tried countless combinations of formulas, catalysts, components, what have you. So many methods, trials, last-minute adjustments...I lost track of what I was doing. Some things didn't get written down. I couldn't replicate my success if I tried, and trust me, I tried."

Cyrus couldn't believe this. What sort of scientist worked like that? Gods damn it, he knew he shouldn't have gotten his hopes up. This *was* too good to be true.

"Oh, I regret it, too." Viktor patted Mina's rump, and with a disgruntled groan she hopped down from the chair. Viktor dragged himself to his feet, wincing as his knees cracked, and went to the cluttered desk that faced the windows. Cyrus noted it was the only fixture in this space that wasn't dusty.

Viktor rummaged through papers and books strewn across the desk. "Could've changed the world with that damned experiment. Despite my efforts, word still got out, and now I've got people like you asking all kinds of questions, and people like poor Mr. Harper begging me to help their loved ones." He paused and shook his head. "I fear that the conditions are just too delicate to reliably replicate. It took me years of work to do it once, and even then it was risky. The man I saved is lucky to be alive. Alas, I can't picture an outcome where this becomes a common practice, sadly. But..." He glanced up at Cyrus. "I see in you what drove me to my very first wonderings. You're not like the rest of 'em."

Like the rest of whom? Cyrus wondered.

"So I'll give you this. Ah." Viktor unearthed a small leather-bound book from the jungle of miscellany on his desk. "Within this book, my boy, are the bones. These notes guided my experiments and led me to my success. I will not cease trying, because if it could be done once I believe it could be done again. Perhaps you, also, might stumble upon the answer."

"Me?" Cyrus swallowed a scoff. "I apologize if I've led you to believe otherwise, Mr. Stokes, but I'm no scientist. I wouldn't know where to start with an alchemist's notes." He eyed Viktor suspiciously. "Why would you give this to me?"

Viktor gripped the book in both hands. "Because I want a reason to hope for the things I've deemed impossible."

Cyrus let his gaze fall to the book. One small volume, less than two hundred pages, was all that stood between him and a different, better life. No, he had no idea how to interpret whatever complicated science was in that book, but he'd be a fool to turn away.

He stood and went to the desk. When Viktor offered the book, he took it. The leather cover was smooth, if a bit dusty, and the book was worn but well cared for. Cyrus tucked it against his chest. "I don't know if I have the resources to do what you did," he said, "but if this can help even one person and save them from that miserable deathlife, it's worth a try." He met Viktor's eyes. "Right?"

Viktor smiled; his eyes were warm behind his glasses. "Precisely."

By the fireplace, Mina snorted as if in agreement.

Cyrus found himself smiling, too.

Viktor showed him to the door with Mina trailing behind. Cyrus was relieved to see it had stopped raining. "Thank you for visiting," Viktor said as Cyrus stepped outside. "Good luck, Mr. Beldon."

It wasn't until Cyrus turned onto the road up the hill that he wondered whether he'd misheard Viktor, or if the man really had called him Beldon.

But no, he couldn't have. Must've been a trick of Cyrus's ears.

Chapter SEVEN

"HE JUST *GAVE* THIS TO YOU?" LEIF MARVELED AT THE
book as if it was made of solid gold, inspecting it carefully as they
turned it over in their hands. "All his work, right here? Handed
over like it was nothing?"

Cyrus shrugged and sipped the tea Leif had instantly placed in
his hands when he'd returned to their loft. "He seemed like he
didn't really need what's in there. Maybe he has the most
important notes written down somewhere else, or maybe he
doesn't actually plan to try his experiment again. For some
godforsaken reason, he thinks *I* could do it."

"Well, maybe you could." Leif set the book on the table
between their two chairs.

Cyrus threw them a doubtful look. "Leif, I'm the farthest thing
from a scientist you could get. I won't understand a single thing in
there."

"Did you look at it?" Leif turned sideways in their chair and
swung their legs over the arm, dropping their slippers off their feet.

"Well, no, but—"

"Then how do you know?" They leveled their gaze on him.
"You're operating on assumptions of your own incompetence."

Cyrus frowned. "Ouch, Leif."

"And by that response, I know I'm not wrong." A tiny smirk
curled the corner of their lips, but not unkindly. "If it's any
consolation, that's not unusual for the baby of a family. Certainly

this family's renowned name and high expectations are a contributing factor as well. You're under a lot of pressure, Cyrus. Give yourself some grace for that. But don't assume you'll fail at something before you've even tried it. If your calling is not vampire hunting, perhaps it's science or medicine or even alchemy." They reached over and pushed the book across the table toward Cyrus.

Thoroughly chastised, he set his tea aside and flipped the book open. The marbled endpapers were faded at the edges and peeling in one corner, but the binding was strong and intact. A white square of parchment had been pasted in the center of the first page, bearing a wax seal that depicted a circle of thorny rose branches with an elegant letter *V* in the center. Aside from the letter, it was shockingly similar to the Beldons' family crest.

Leif abruptly stilled his hand when he went to turn the page. Cyrus glanced up at them and found them gaping, wide-eyed, at the seal. "Holy shit."

"What?" Cyrus studied the image again, but it carried no further clues. It must have been a family symbol, but it wasn't one Cyrus could immediately name. Logically it would belong to Viktor Stokes, wouldn't it?

"T-Turn the page," Leif stammered. "Go to the title page, see if there's anything else there. I think…" They bit their lip and leaned farther over the table, visibly impatient as Cyrus struggled to part the old, brittle pages. When he reached the title page, he found a faded ink stamp in the bottom right corner.

His heart missed a beat. The stamp was almost identical to the wax seal, except this image had curving, elegant script nestled within the ring of thorns: *From the Library of House Vista.*

Cyrus was holding a book that had come from an Honorable Family.

"*Why* did that man have this book?" Leif whispered. Their face had noticeably paled; they stared at the book as if it was posed to bite them.

"I mean, this is definitely shocking," Cyrus said, "but isn't it also convenient? This might be exactly what I need. Who would know the ins and outs of vampire physiology better than vampires themselves? If they know how to turn a human into a vampire, I'm sure they know how to reverse the process as well."

Cyrus ran his thumb over the stamp and felt that thrill of excitement again. This was far more than he'd expected to get out of following one lead. Part of him had suspected that Viktor Stokes was full of shit, but with this book in his possession, maybe the man really had reached a revolutionary breakthrough. Maybe Cyrus wouldn't have to keep silencing his hope.

But when he looked up at Leif again, they were shaking their head. "Cyrus, this is more dangerous than we anticipated. You're not just dabbling in experimental science now. Getting the Honorable Families involved..." They grimaced. "I can't let you do this."

"I don't need your permission, thanks very much." Cyrus scowled. "Seriously, Leif, look at me. Look at my life. Hell, think of what happened to Poppy and Arthur. Our entire existence demands that we play with danger. Delving into a book from House Vista is probably the *least* dangerous vampire-related thing I could possibly do."

Leif still looked reluctant, perhaps even a little scared.

Cyrus set his hand on the book so they couldn't snatch it away from him. "No one else has to know. Right?"

They glanced away from him and ran their palm over their hair. "Cyrus..."

"What are you afraid of?"

They straightened and met his eyes. "I'm not *afraid* of anything. I'm concerned about where this might lead you."

"A few hours ago, you were *excited* about where this might lead me."

"That was before this." They tapped the stamp on the title page.

Cyrus narrowed his eyes. "You're having a...a sense, aren't you? You can feel something."

Leif kept their gaze fixed on the book. "I can't tell you that."

"Why?"

"Because it would influence your actions and your future." Leif settled back into their chair, folding their legs up beneath them. They grabbed their teacup and entwined their hands around it. "The future is not mine to reroute."

"Isn't the whole point of being a mystic to guide people in the direction they want to go?" Cyrus tapped his fingers on the book. "If you already know what I'm going to do, aren't you influencing the future by trying to stop me?"

"No. Nothing is set in stone." Leif spoke to their tea rather than to Cyrus. "Your life is knit together with millions upon millions of choices and possibilities. Of course I can't see all of them. But I have a sense about this moment—this is a precipice. You will, in the very near future, choose a path that will significantly change the course of your life. I don't know what it is, and I don't know what will change or what the consequences will be. But it starts here, with this book."

No, Cyrus thought, *it's not the book. It's that name. Vista.* That was what had halted Leif in their tracks.

What was it, then, that House Vista had in store for him?

Cyrus's pulse picked up. He felt the precipice too. Here was an opportunity before him, the threshold of possibility. This was a point of no return; his life *was* about to change, by his own terms, and wherever that path led him, it would be different and it would be *better* than what he had now.

It had to be. He vowed that it would be.

"I can't give up, Leif," he said quietly. The stamp seemed to glow on the page, beckoning him further into this book. "I've barely started. I have to do this. I know that interacting with the Honorable Families is a risk no matter the business, but they're not the ones turning into Wild vampires. Maybe they'd even be willing to help me, if it means fewer vampires that the Beldons need to kill. I don't know, but I can't abandon the possibility of helping people just because it's risky."

Leif was quiet for a moment, then sighed and took off their

glasses to rub their eyes. "Do not make any choices lightly. That's the most I can say."

"Will you still help me?" Cyrus asked.

After a second of hesitation, they nodded. "We haven't tackled all that anxiety, have we?" A faint smile touched the corner of their mouth, but didn't reach anywhere near their eyes.

Cyrus wanted to press. What was so unnerving about the path ahead of him that had Leif so uncharacteristically shaken? What could they see? His success—or his failure? Which was worse?

Yet he couldn't let Leif's nerves soften his resolve. He did not know what they saw and they wouldn't tell him, so all he had to follow was his own instinct, and right now he knew it in his bones that this was the right path.

And that path started, as so many good things did, with a book.

CYRUS APPRECIATED Leif's confidence in him, but this book made no goddamned sense. And that wasn't to say Cyrus didn't believe in his own intelligence; he probably knew more about vampires than a lot of people in this city, but his knowledge was of killing them—or recognizing an Honorable One and *not* killing them. This book was all about how vampires *lived*, a subject equal parts unfamiliar and incomprehensible to Cyrus. The text and its accompanying diagrams and illustrations really wanted to teach him about circulatory systems and blood cells and the logistics of deathlife and immortality, but Cyrus had lost it after the third six-syllable word referring to an organ or bone or muscle that definitely had a more colloquial name.

He rubbed his eyes until colors danced in his vision. The candles he'd lit hours ago were melted down to waxy stumps, and the sky outside the window above his desk was starting to lighten. An uneasy sense of urgency crawled over him; dawn already, and he'd gotten barely twenty pages into this book. At this rate, he wouldn't get anywhere before he'd be expected to pick up Poppy's slack.

The clock was ticking. Soon, everyone's shock would wear off, and Cyrus would be expected to take up his role in the family. He *had* to make a breakthrough before his time and his freedom were snatched away.

So if this book couldn't explain all of this in a way he understood, maybe its owner could.

Whether they *would*, especially to him, was a different question entirely. But Cyrus had to try.

He flipped the pages back to the title page and skimmed his fingertips over the stamp again. *From the Library of House Vista.*

It was an insane idea, but it was the only way he could see forward. However, if he was going to pay House Vista a visit, he needed a good excuse. This wasn't a place to which he could sneak away unnoticed; word would travel back to his father if he went knocking at the Vistas' door asking questions about an old book, and then Cyrus's whole project would crumble to sand in his hands. Marcus could not find out what he was doing, but if he played his cards carefully, maybe he could frame this visit in a way Marcus would approve.

There was still a murder to investigate, after all.

Cyrus shut the book and put the candles out of their misery. He'd done enough for one long night; after a few hours of sleep, he would find a way to convince Marcus to let him visit the Vistas.

And hopefully walk out with his life.

CYRUS HAD SPENT SO MUCH of his life avoiding his father that to seek him out on purpose felt odd. He'd go if Marcus summoned him, of course, but as he made his way downstairs, he couldn't think of the last time he'd intentionally sought a conversation with his father. His siblings, on the other hand, had frequent casual chats with Marcus, because of course they did, but Cyrus had never been encouraged nor did he wish to speak to his father about his personal life.

Not that he'd have much to talk about if Marcus *did* ask.

The door to Marcus's study was ajar when Cyrus turned down the front hallway. Golden lamplight spilled through the crack and mixed with the daylight that streamed in through the windows. But the sunshine knew better than to invade the cavelike darkness in Marcus's study; Cyrus had once joked to Poppy that Marcus was the vampire of the Beldon family, with his reclusive habits and preference for the dark.

Poppy had not found that funny. Cyrus still thought it was.

He raised his hand to knock, only to freeze when he heard voices from within. At once he recognized his uncle's low tone.

"...said, this is too delicate to be swept under the rug, Marcus. Natasha's death was one thing. This is entirely different. You can't—"

"Watch yourself, Emerson," Marcus growled. "Do you really want to toe that line?"

"You're not seeing my point." Emerson audibly sighed—a tell that he was getting frustrated. When he spoke again, his voice was strained with forced calm. "We both know that Arthur's death was an intentional hit. How could it not be? I know you don't want to believe it, because the implications are...frankly, fucking horrifying. But we cannot let this slide. We must make a move against the Honorable Families."

Cyrus's eyes widened.

Several heartbeats ticked by before Marcus spoke. "What you are suggesting, Emerson, will shatter the fragile balance we have with the Families."

"It's *already* been shattered," Emerson hissed. "They shattered it themselves when they murdered your son! How can you not see that they're up to something? You of all people should see it clear as day, close as you are with Master Harrows."

"So why would House Harrows, of all the Honorable Ones, murder my son, given our closeness? Your theory is ridiculous and unfounded."

"Both Poppy and Cyrus confirmed that it was Leigh Harrows and her brother that attacked Arthur that day," Emerson said. "If you won't believe your own children, I don't know what else will make you see it. They are up to something, Marcus. And if we don't retaliate, they will strike again."

"So let them!" *Slam.* Cyrus flinched. "Let them pick off their targets one by one. It won't break me. If they want a war, let them bring it. Let them think they can crumble us. They will never succeed. They think they're gods, and on my life, I will remind them who really rules this city."

Emerson chuckled darkly. "You'd let your children die for the sake of spite?" His voice dripped with disgust. "I think I'm beginning to understand why Natasha—"

A sharp clap—unmistakably the sound of a slap to the face— cut off Emerson's words. Cyrus heard him stumble and then move several steps closer to the door. Heavy silence filled the room and crept into the hall; Cyrus held his breath for fear that his father and uncle could hear his pounding heart.

Then Emerson spoke, his voice low and even. "You're a fucking bastard, Marcus Beldon. The next time someone in this house goes and kills themselves—"

"Get out."

"—because they can't stand living under the same roof as you—"

"*Get out!*"

"—you will have no one to blame but yourself."

Cyrus scrambled away from the door and flattened himself against the wall. He stared up at the crown molding and tried to calm his racing pulse, but he still flinched when Emerson slammed the door on his way out of the study.

Cringing, Cyrus turned his head. His uncle regarded him coolly; Cyrus couldn't read beyond his stoic mask.

"Um." Cyrus cleared his throat. "I..."

Emerson held up a hand. "Not here. Come." He inclined his head toward the hallway before them, and Cyrus followed him without hesitation.

"Son of a bitch," Emerson muttered, rubbing his cheek. His skin was slightly red where Marcus had struck him. "Of all the brothers in the world..." He scowled and glanced at Cyrus. "Whatever you intended to speak to your father about, I assure you it can wait."

Cyrus nodded. "Clearly he's not in the mood."

"How much of that did you hear?"

"Only him shouting at you to get out of his office." Obviously Cyrus was not about to give his uncle the truth. He needed time to unravel what he'd heard before anyone tried to cover it up with lies.

"I only wish I'd shouted back," Emerson grumbled. "Never have been good at standing up to him. I suppose you and I understand each other in that regard, being the youngest brothers in our families."

Cyrus had never once felt an ounce of camaraderie with his uncle and he wasn't about to start now. Sure, Emerson had never laid a hand on him the way Marcus had, but his words struck deeper than any smack across the face could; Cyrus was not keen to sympathize with him now when he'd guilted and berated Cyrus to tears for most of his childhood.

He made a non-committal noise that was neither an agreement nor a refute, and said nothing.

Emerson let the tense silence persist until they reached the end of the front hall and stepped into the atrium. Pale, late morning light spilled from the glass dome overhead; the potted plants that Leif insisted be kept around the edges of the room seemed to lean forward to reach the sun. Emerson, rather, stopped just outside the bright patch of floor.

He turned to Cyrus but said nothing. Cyrus studied his

angular face and tired eyes, searching for a hint of what to expect next. If Emerson was angry—at Marcus or just in general—he hid it very well. If he had some kind of critique for Cyrus for being elusive and lazy these past few days, Cyrus was surprised he hadn't said it already. Anticipation crawled up his spine as he waited for the shoe to drop; he shifted restlessly on his feet.

Finally Emerson straightened and looked down at Cyrus. "I want to show you something. Come with me."

Cyrus hesitated; he didn't have time for a detour. But Emerson started across the atrium without waiting for Cyrus's agreement, so Cyrus had no choice but to follow. He did still require someone's permission to go to House Vista, and Emerson's blessing was as good as Marcus's. Especially when Marcus was in a foul mood.

Emerson led Cyrus down one of the corridors branching off the atrium and then opened a door near the middle of the hall. A gust of cool air carried up a strange smell.

"Is this a trick?" For all of Cyrus's life, his uncle's alchemy laboratory had been strictly off limits—even more so than the old tower behind the mansion. Cyrus didn't even want to know what sort of punishment Emerson would have dealt if Cyrus or his siblings had tried to sneak down there. He wasn't sure if even Marcus had ever stepped foot down these stairs.

Emerson sneered. "No. Though, it is good to see that the lessons you learned in youth are still strong. Some of them, anyway." He flicked his hand, beckoning Cyrus to follow, and descended the steps.

Cyrus glanced back once, then stepped into the dark.

Dim light flickered from candelabras along the wall at the bottom of the stairs, but that glow hardly lightened Cyrus's path. He kept one hand on the wall to steady himself as he carefully felt his way down each stone step; meanwhile, Emerson descended with phantasmic ease.

Cyrus expected a dark, dank dungeon, like the lair of an evil wizard from a fairy tale. Instead, he faced a clean, open space illuminated brightly by a massive chandelier overhead and numerous candelabras and oil lamps throughout the room. A large oak desk hugged the far wall, and a wide work table stood opposite. Shelves along the stone walls carried books, jars, and bottles of all shapes and sizes. Instruments Cyrus couldn't name were tucked alongside other supplies on the tables and shelves, and some bright red concoction bubbled in a glass container on the work table. A sharp scent of herbs and something chemical permeated the air.

Not that Cyrus had any basis for comparison, but the room was rather *normal*. No big secrets or taboo experiments. None that were obvious, anyway.

He turned to Emerson, who was scanning a bookcase along the wall. "So... what did you want to show me?"

"Have somewhere to be, do you?"

Yes, actually, I do. He scowled at the back of Emerson's head. "Just curious. Am I so bad at hunting vampires that my father told you to teach me alchemy instead?"

Emerson chuckled and pulled a book from the shelf, then strode toward his work table. "No. And even if he did, I doubt you'd do any better. Alchemy requires a sharp mind for puzzles, for numbers and formulas and equations. Not only is it mathematical, it's transcendent. Only the best minds, the ones willing to think outside the known constraints of human understanding, can tackle alchemy. You hardly retained simple history. Keep to what you know."

Cyrus clenched his jaw and stared hard at the bottom shelf of the bookcase to his left. His ears turned hot. He had half a mind to leave, but he resisted the impulse. He still needed Emerson's permission.

A dull thump drew his attention up as Emerson set another book on the table and opened it. "I've been thinking, in light of recent events, of the unfairness of mortality."

Cyrus raised an eyebrow. "So you're having an existential crisis?"

He savored the twitch of annoyance that passed over Emerson's face, knowing that it was only because there was half a room between them that Cyrus hadn't just gotten a smack to the head.

"Marcus, perhaps, but not I." Emerson smoothed his hand down his cravat. His silver family ring glinted in the candlelight. "No, Cyrus, if there is a crisis in this house, it is because of Marcus's denial of the dire situation at hand. But that is not what I wished to show you today. Come here."

Reluctantly, Cyrus did. He stood opposite Emerson, keeping the wide table between them, and slid his hands into his pockets so he'd be less tempted to fiddle with the objects in front of him. "What is all this?" He watched the crimson substance bubble in its vase.

"Another unsuccessful formula." Emerson sighed and switched off the flame beneath the glass container; gradually, the liquid ceased its bubbling and turned a deeper, darker red. "I fear it will be quite a while before I make any progress on this one. I thought I was close to a breakthrough, but...such is the way with science." He shrugged and nudged his glasses up his nose. "But wouldn't you agree, Cyrus, that it is unfair that we—the protectors of this city and humanity itself—are restricted by the inconvenience of mortality?"

"I...can't say I've ever thought about it." Why would he? Death was an unavoidable fact, especially for his family. He'd made his peace with that a long time ago.

"No?" Emerson looked surprised. "You haven't ever wished that, say, your mother had another chance?"

Cyrus frowned.

"You never thought once this week, with your sister being on death's door, that it wasn't fair that she might die so soon, so young? And what about yourself? Do you not wish for more time?"

Cyrus folded his arms across your chest. "What are you getting at, Uncle?"

"Mortality is too trivial a constraint for people like us. We deserve better." Emerson leveled his cool gaze on Cyrus and lowered his voice. "If the monsters are awarded immortality, why not the monster hunters? Why should we die while they live?"

Cyrus could only stare at him. He still didn't know why Emerson was telling him this or what Emerson might want from him, but what he was suggesting was not only dangerous, but absurd. Cyrus smothered a scoff. "You want us to be immortal. Like vampires."

"It would level the playing field, would it not?"

Cyrus held his gaze. "Why are you telling me this?"

"Because I know that you have never been satisfied with this life," Emerson said earnestly. "And though I think it's an immature and ungrateful dissatisfaction, I do understand the desire for something more. Think of it, Cyrus: an immortal life, with all the time in the world to be everything you want to be. You could live multiple lives without ever running out of years."

Cyrus couldn't deny a flutter of interest. But it was impossible, so it wasn't worth wanting. Well, unless he became a vampire, but he'd rather die. "Plenty of people manage to pull that off without immortality. I could do it right now."

"But realistically, you can't."

"Right. So there's no use wishing for it."

Emerson studied him. "And does knowing that stop you from wishing for it?"

Cyrus scowled and said nothing.

"Instead of wishing," Emerson said with smug satisfaction, "don't you want to do something about it?"

"Yes, actually," Cyrus said. "But not by becoming immortal. Sorry, Uncle, but you've chosen the wrong guinea pig. Try Marcus. I'm sure he'd love to live forever."

Emerson's face twisted in a way that made clear his desire for the opposite. With that, Cyrus agreed.

"I do have a question for you, though," he said.

"Oh?" Emerson folded his hands together on the table.

Cyrus took a second to gather his logic. "I've been thinking about what happened to Arthur. I know it seems like a straightforward case, and I know it's undeniable that Leigh and Philip Harrows are at fault for Arthur's death."

"Try telling that to your father," Emerson muttered.

"But there's clearly a deeper motive," Cyrus went on. "Why would they do that? Who *ordered* them to do that? Why Arthur and not Marcus himself? And why did they turn him Wild instead of just killing him?"

"Poppy seems to think the Wild turn was an accident," Emerson said, rubbing his beard. "She also blames herself for it, since she failed to ensure Arthur would not turn. But your other questions are valid. You are not alone in asking them. But what is it you need from me?"

"Even if we know that House Harrows is responsible for Arthur's death, I think it's worth investigating the next closest Honorable Family." Cyrus took a deep breath. "I think we should speak to House Vista."

Emerson narrowed his eyes. "Why?"

"They might know something we don't," Cyrus said. "House Harrows attacked us, yes, but what if that was one piece of a bigger plot that all of the Families are involved with?"

"And if that's true, do you really think the Vistas will tell you that?"

"No, but some sneaking around might get us a few clues." Cyrus wrung his hands. "And even if that's not the case, if House Harrows has gone rogue, don't you think House Vista would have something to say about it?"

Emerson was quiet for a minute, absently stroking his thumb down his chin as he considered Cyrus's logic. "Why you?"

"Because I feel useless," Cyrus said with all the honesty he could muster. "I want to know why this happened to my brother, and this is the way I can be most helpful."

Cyrus held his breath until Emerson gave a small shrug. "All right. Go visit House Vista." His gaze turned sharp. "Choose your words and your actions carefully. Do not break etiquette. Hear me, Cyrus, if you embarrass us in front of an Honorable Family, I will see to it that you find yourself a long and miserable way from Chestervale."

"I understand." Although, if Cyrus fucked up, he'd likely be smeared across the floors of the Vista manor before Emerson even got a chance to get his hands on him.

I can do this. He might not have Poppy's sharp perception, Arthur's strength, or Joel's charisma, but Cyrus was stubborn. Maybe the vampires would respect that.

Or maybe they'd rip his throat out as soon as he stepped through the door.

He'd find out soon enough.

Chapter EIGHT

CYRUS WAS SICK OF WALKING ACROSS CHESTERVALE, SO he stole a horse. Well, it wasn't really *stealing* since the horse did belong to his family, but it wasn't his horse—he was the only one in the house without his own horse, but that was okay since he didn't really like horses, so he wasn't bitter about it at all—it was Poppy's horse. Cyrus didn't trust Arthur's stallion, but surely Poppy wouldn't mind if he brought her mare out for some exercise. She wouldn't be needing the animal anytime soon, anyway.

He made his way across the city at an easy pace with the reins wrapped tight around his hands. He sat perfectly straight, not because he knew what he was doing, but because he fucking hated riding horses. His knees already ached from how tightly he had them pressed against the animal's sides, and he'd have imprints of the leather reins on his hands once he let go, yet he still feared with every lurch that he'd slide right off the saddle. Every time he directed Demeter around a corner or down a hill, his stomach dropped through his ass.

It had been at least ten years since he'd been on horseback. He had no idea what to do if Demeter got spooked or bolted or even decided to stop and smell the roses. He had exactly no control over this animal, and part of him suspected that she knew it and would buck him off her back at her first convenience.

Thankfully, so far, she seemed content with their little adventure.

Once he was out of the busy parts of the city and well into the countryside, he gently nudged his heel against Demeter's side and she picked up her pace. The ride was smooth now that there weren't dozens of people and carriages around them, and Cyrus let himself relax a little, loosening his grip on the reins and the tension from his muscles.

This side of the city walls was like a different world. The noise faded to a distant hum, muffled by the cover of trees and chatter of birdsong. Cyrus rode beneath a rare patch of clear sky, and for a few wonderful moments, felt the autumn sun on his face. A vague sense of peace settled over him for the first time since this hellish week had started.

He wondered when it was all going to hit him. Everything still felt numb. Or, worse, maybe he'd emotionally distanced himself from his family so much that he simply didn't care.

But no, he must care, otherwise he wouldn't be out here on his way to visit House Vista. He cared about this research he was trying to do, so that he could...

What? Be special and different from the other Beldons? So that he didn't have to live like they did? Was it really the family legacy that he cared about, or just himself?

Gods, he really didn't care about the rest of them, did he?

An abrupt disappearance of sunlight brought Cyrus out of his thoughts. He blinked his surroundings back into focus and found that he'd entered the woods; densely packed trees knit their branches together in a canopy overhead that blocked nearly all daylight but for a few dappled patches on the dirt road. The air temperature noticeably dipped.

Well, he must be getting close.

"Dramatic lot, aren't they, Demeter?" he muttered, shifting in his seat. He glanced around at the gnarled, moss-covered trees. Many of them had already dropped their leaves, but those that hadn't were painted red, gold, and everything in between. It made for a beautiful landscape, but Cyrus couldn't help thinking the lack of sunlight did it a disservice.

"All this shade and darkness for a family that doesn't need it." Vampires as old as the Vistas didn't need to avoid sunlight. They could enjoy the days as humans did, hiding in plain sight, without so much as a sunburn. But no, even still, they embraced the night and reveled in their darkness.

Cyrus nudged Demeter again. "Come on, let's find this place."

IT WASN'T MUCH LONGER before he stumbled upon the main gates of the Vista manor. Tucked away among the trees, the black stone mansion loomed over Cyrus, its towers blending in with the treetops. Ivy crawled up the walls, and the wrought-iron gate before Cyrus was rusted to hell and back. A path laid with mossy stones led from the gate up to the front steps, where two lanterns on either side of the tall doors steadily flickered.

All was quiet, as if it was midnight rather than midday. Light glowed from several windows on the front side of the house, but if anyone spied Cyrus from behind the latticed glass panes, they did not come out to confront him. Still, House Vista watched him, waiting.

Cyrus clambered down from Demeter's back and winced at the stiffness in his thighs; it took him a few steps to get his legs to work properly.

Demeter bumped him with her head and snorted, and Cyrus gave her a small pat on the nose. "It's all right," he assured her even as it was the last thing he was sure of. He brought her to one of the brick columns that marked the end of the path leading to the Vista gates, and looped Demeter's reins around the stem of the lantern atop the column. It wasn't the most secure spot for a horse, but he didn't see another option, and at least it would be easy for Demeter to get away if she needed to.

He might not be so lucky.

They're just people, he reminded himself. Honorable Ones were not like the vampires the Beldons hunted, and they were nothing close to the Wild vampire Cyrus had faced with Poppy. They followed a strict etiquette code, just like the hunter families and other members of high society did. Cyrus might get hit with scathing glares and underhanded insults coated in pretty words, but he would not be harmed here.

He approached the gate, shaking out his hands to quell his nerves. He ran a hand through his hair, straightened his cravat, and took a deep breath. He could do this. He was a Beldon. This was his chance to prove he wasn't useless.

Today was the day everything would change.

Cyrus pushed the gate. The hinges screamed and Cyrus flinched at the noise, but he made it up the path to the front doors without incident. Part of him expected the doors to swing open immediately, but even after a minute, they remained still.

Gathering every ounce of courage in his body, Cyrus struck the brass knocker against the door.

The sound echoed loudly within the mansion. Cyrus stepped back, putting some space between himself and the doors, and held his breath as he waited to hear footsteps. It was several minutes before he finally did, and as one of the doors groaned open, Cyrus wasn't sure if his lightheadedness was because he'd deprived himself of oxygen or because he was so anxious that his brain was giving up.

He didn't have time to pull himself together before someone stepped out of the house.

A child stared up at him. *Victoria,* his memory supplied; a girl of maybe nine, with shiny black curls and round crimson eyes. Her face was pale, as many vampires were, devoid of the rosy blush of life. She eyed Cyrus with trepidation at first, and then beamed a bright, toothy smile.

"Well, hello!" She gave a polite curtsey, delicately raising the edges of her black gown. "Who are you? Is Papa expecting you?

He's meeting with the staff right now, which is why Oscar didn't get the door. Sorry for the wait."

Good, because Alastair Vista was the last person Cyrus wished to speak to. He'd take the family's heir, or even a cousin, before he'd approach the master of House Vista.

He offered a small smile and inclined his head. "Good afternoon. I admit I'm not an expected guest, but I do wish to talk to someone here." He pulled the book out of his satchel and opened it so the girl could see the family seal on the title page. "I believe this belongs to someone here. I'd like to speak to whoever that is."

She peered closer, and her eyes widened. "Oh! That's gotta be Lucien's. Books are his whole personality. Come inside, I'll go get him!"

Cyrus hesitated. "Are you sure? Shouldn't you let someone else know I'm here?"

The girl had already disappeared back inside, and now dragged the door open wider. "Nope, don't need to! If you try to hurt me, I'll kill you. Easy-peasy. Are you coming or not?"

All right, well, that was fair. Into the lion's den he went, ushered by a small child with ringlets, a lacy black dress, and supernatural talents for killing.

House Vista was cavernous and miserable. Cyrus's home was a cheery coastal palace compared to this; everything was dark—the walls, the floors, the rugs, and even the lights didn't seem to burn as brightly in this space. A high ceiling vaulted overhead, all dark wood beams and cobwebs so dense Cyrus could see them from all the way down here. The center of the foyer rose upward in a dome that bore an intricate mural, the details of which Cyrus couldn't make out. He tore his eyes away and hurried to follow the girl before she left him on his own in this labyrinthine mansion.

She led him up a wide staircase carpeted in blood-red, then turned into a corridor brightened with numerous sparkling chandeliers. The girl brought him to a large set of white doors, knocked, and then turned to him. "If he's not here, he's probably in the library, and if that's the case we could spend all day looking for him. But around this time of day, he's *usually* here in the study hall. What was your name, again?"

Here goes nothing. "Cyrus," he said. "Cyrus Beldon."

The girl's eyes widened and she jerked back, and in the same second the doors flew open and someone leapt in front of the child. Cyrus found himself facing another vampire, this one tall and lithe with a cascade of silver hair and vivid crimson eyes. He bared his fangs and forced Cyrus back a few steps.

He quickly lifted his hands. "Wait, I—"

"What the *hell* are you doing here?" the vampire snarled.

Slowly, with a shaking hand, he reached for the book tucked under his arm and offered it to the vampire. "Please. I did not come here to harm anyone. I have this, and I—I'm hoping you can help me...so I can help you."

For several long heartbeats, the vampire continued to glare at Cyrus with his teeth bared. But gradually his hostile expression eased and he straightened, regarding Cyrus with cold suspicion. He did not take the book.

"Help us? *You?*" He crossed his arms over his finely tailored vest. The ruby pinned to his cravat glinted. "And what makes you think we need it, especially from a *Beldon?*"

The way he spat Cyrus's family name, with so much venomous hatred, settled a sick feeling in his stomach. Not that it wasn't justified, but a lifetime of hearing only respect for his family made the vampire's tone jarring. Cyrus had only heard the Honorable Families' names spoken with reverence: in public, to their faces, and even in private. But if this was how an Honorable One spoke the name Beldon *to* a Beldon, then all their respect for Cyrus's family must be a façade. Sure, he knew that the Honorable Families disliked the Beldons—they had every reason to. But hearing it straight from one of them—all that ire, mixed in with a little disgust—made something flip in Cyrus's mind.

All his life, he'd been told that the Beldons were heroes. Saviors. Protectors.

But to this vampire and his family, the Beldons were murderers.

Cyrus exhaled slowly and stood up straighter, meeting the man's gaze. "I don't claim to be any kind of savior. My family has committed too many crimes to ever make that a possibility. But this book, which I believe belongs to you, contains information that could help a lot of people, human and vampire alike. If... If these are your notes, Honored Vista, my simple ask is that you help me understand."

His expression shifted from suspicion to contempt. He tilted his head to the side, long hair falling in a shimmering wave over his shoulder. "Oh, *so* noble. Why would I spare a second of my time helping you when the most your family has done for mine is begrudgingly agree not to slaughter us in our beds?"

Cyrus winced. He didn't have a good answer to that. Nor could he plead innocent of his family's crimes when he himself had silver blood on his hands.

But he had to try something. He had to make this vampire see where he was coming from. He was *not* like the others. "Because the rest of my family doesn't care whether you live or die or turn Wild. I do."

That got the vampire's attention. He raised a sharp eyebrow. "What did you say your name was?"

Cyrus told him his name and dared to feel a flicker of hope.

"Cyrus." The vampire's smooth voice softened the syllables. "I am Lucien Vista. Yes, those are my notes. And I will entertain you, Cyrus Beldon, not because I believe what you've said, but because I'm *very* curious to know where you found that book."

It took a second for the Vista heir's words to sink in. He was... saying yes? Sort of? He wasn't refusing to hear Cyrus out, and that was a start. Oh, gods, that was *such* a start.

Cyrus was determined not to screw this up.

"Join me downstairs in the parlor," Lucien said. He exchanged a glance with his sister, who had moved to his side. "I'll call for tea."

Cyrus nodded. "Of course, Honored Vista. I'd be happy to."

He smiled, and Cyrus suddenly couldn't picture the violent

hostility that had twisted his face moments ago. "Wonderful. I'll show you the way."

IF SOMEONE HAD TOLD Cyrus even three hours ago that he would soon be sitting in a luxurious parlor having tea with the heir to House Vista, he would've laughed in their face. He had had passing interactions with Honorable Ones before, mostly as they came and went from meetings with Marcus, but Cyrus realized as he sat across a small table from Lucien Vista that he'd never had a full conversation with an Honorable One. Or any vampire, for that matter. They were always either at the end of his blade or a careful distance away.

If Lucien sensed Cyrus's bafflement with this situation, his posture didn't show it. He lounged in his seat with one knee crossed over the other as if this was completely normal; as if he and Cyrus had already been acquainted. He cradled a black teacup decorated with gold floral details, slender fingers threaded together around the delicate object. Cyrus studied the rings on his fingers; sure enough, one on the middle finger of his right hand bore an engraving of the seal he'd seen stamped in the book.

"Is the tea to your liking?" Lucien spoke softly, conversationally, with absolutely none of the venom he'd spat earlier. Cyrus couldn't blame him for that initial reaction to finding a Beldon in his house, but he did prefer Lucien's current demeanor. It settled *some* of his nerves.

"Yes, thank you." Cyrus caught himself bouncing his foot and set his free hand on his knee so he'd stop. He took another sip of tea, then lightly cleared his throat. "So...you asked about the book."

"Indeed." Lucien reached up and tucked a loose strand of hair behind his ear. "It's been missing from my collection for quite some time. I loaned it to a colleague, who promised to return it promptly, and then never saw it again. Where might you have come across it?"

"It was given to me by a man named Viktor Stokes." Cyrus watched for a reaction to the name, but all he caught was a slight twitch of the eyebrow. Lucien hid his surprise well. "He's a scientist," Cyrus went on. "Sort of an alchemist, but it sounds like he delves into medicine too. He claimed that, using the contents of this book, he reversed a freshly turned vampire. Healed them. Made them human again."

Lucien's manicured eyebrows slowly crawled up to his hairline. "Successfully?"

"Apparently. I didn't see any proof of it, but..." He explained how he'd heard Viktor's name in conversation—leaving out the unusual circumstances of that eavesdropping, of course—and how the man had been so fickle with the experiment that he couldn't manage to replicate it.

Lucien flicked his eyes to the side in what was perhaps the most polite way one could roll their eyes. "He is exceedingly lucky he didn't do something irreversibly catastrophic."

"I would agree." Cyrus set down his tea on the table and picked up the book instead. "But is that really what's in here? The science behind undoing a vampire? I tried to read it, but I didn't understand it."

Lucien brought his teacup to his lips and took a slow, contemplative sip. "It isn't precisely that, but I can see how someone with that ridiculous goal in mind might use it to that effect. I have doubts about Mr. Stokes's success. Not that I don't believe your tale, but I don't believe his claims. Turn reversal is impossible. That's a simple fact."

Cyrus tapped the cover of the book. "Then what is this for?"

Lucien studied him closely. Those vivid crimson eyes fixed on Cyrus unflinchingly; they were almost unsettling in their intensity, and Cyrus got a prickling sense that Lucien could read his thoughts as easily as he read his facial expressions. "Are you familiar with Wild vampires?"

Cyrus clenched his teeth. "Quite."

Amusement alighted in Lucien's eyes. "Ah, did we have a run-in with one?"

Was he joking? The Vistas *must* know about Arthur's death; all of the Honorable Families likely did by now. Leigh Harrows had probably gloated to them all the minute she left the Beldon estate. Cyrus scowled. "Don't bullshit me, Vista."

He quirked an eyebrow. "I was wondering how long it would take for the polite façade to drop."

"Was it ever there? You threatened me immediately upon seeing me."

"Because you're a fucking Beldon and you're in my house."

Cyrus feigned a scandalized gasp. "Honored Vista, I don't believe such language is proper in polite society." He smirked, but returned to his earlier scowl when Lucien's expression didn't change. "You know very well that my family is *more* than familiar with Wild vampires. And for once, to no fault of ours."

To Cyrus's confusion, Lucien looked genuinely lost. "I'm afraid I don't actually know what you're talking about, Mr. Beldon."

"Ugh. Call me Cyrus." The words were out before Cyrus could stop them. He cringed at Lucien's surprised expression. "I...don't like being called that."

"Oh? Which is it you don't identify with? *Mister*, or *Beldon*?"

The question threw him, but he did appreciate the subtle courtesy. "Beldon. It feels like a weight I can't carry."

Why am I admitting this to a fucking Vista?

Lucien sipped his tea and relaxed back in his chair. "What happened?"

"My twenty-one-year saga of family trauma is a bit of a long story for our meeting today, don't you think?"

For gods' sakes, Cyrus, shut up shut up shut up.

Lucien rolled his eyes, but this time a hint of amusement hid at the corner of his mouth. "Indeed it is. What I meant to ask is, what happened with the Wild vampire?"

Cyrus still didn't understand why Lucien didn't already know. Unless he did, and he hoped to get additional information? If Cyrus was half as intelligent as anyone else in his family, he wouldn't say another word to this vampire.

But he still needed answers. He still needed help. If Lucien could trust him enough to have tea and a conversation, then Cyrus could offer some trust in return. He saw no way forward otherwise.

So he told Lucien Vista about his brother's death—leaving out the names of the culprits, of course—and about the Wild vampire he and Poppy had followed. He told him of the bloody fight that had ensued, and the utter monstrosity of the thing that had once been Arthur Beldon.

Chills scattered over his arms and he folded them across his chest. "I can't even call that thing a vampire, Honored Vista. It was like nothing I had ever seen. If...If whoever killed Arthur is going around intentionally making more of those monsters, they have to be stopped. And if the victims can be helped in any way..." Cyrus shrugged. "I have to try."

Lucien had watched Cyrus intently through his tale, and now he leaned against the arm of his chair and propped his chin in his hand. "And what makes you the savior, Beldon? Why have you decided that you should be some kind of peacemaker? You're nothing. Your family's legacy speaks for you, as does mine for me. We cannot change our blood."

This vampire was missing the point. "I'm not trying to be anyone's savior," Cyrus said. "We want the same thing. If a bunch of Wild vampires start springing up, it won't be any better for your kin than it will for mine."

"Why do you want to help us?" Lucien narrowed his eyes. "Why do you care?"

Cyrus swallowed. "Because I want to make a difference in this goddamned city without innocent blood on my hands. You say my family name is my legacy, and you're right. But I don't want the legacy that my father has made. I don't wish to be synonymous with slaughter."

"You think you can rewrite your family name?" Lucien's doubt dripped from his words.

"Yes." Cyrus held his gaze; he couldn't tell whether the vampire was on the same page, or if he thought Cyrus was insane. Lucien's steady expression revealed nothing.

After a few moments, he broke Cyrus's gaze and shifted in his seat, running his fingers through his hair. His eyes found their way back to Cyrus as he settled, and he absently tapped the pointed tips of his nails against his lips. "You wish to be different." It wasn't so much a question as a curious observation, and Cyrus held his breath as Lucien pondered and deliberated what Cyrus had said.

There were so many ways this could go wrong—Lucien might not believe him, or might flat-out reject him, or he'd take everything he'd heard today to the rest of his family and then word would get back to Marcus Beldon who would proceed to flay Cyrus alive—endless, endless possibilities of failure. Cyrus felt the doubts hovering around his head like a swarm of bees.

Because what reason, really, did the heir to House Vista have to believe a word out of Cyrus Beldon's mouth? He was more likely to be a spy than an ally. Lucien had come at him with fangs bared for simply being under this roof; was Cyrus really so naïve as to hope for a second that this vampire would help him?

But that was just it. Yes, he was. Naïve, sure, but also hopeful. He was so tired of looking for the worst in people before he even considered the best.

"Are you alone in this fight?" Lucien's tone was still cool, revealing nothing beyond a mere hint of curiosity.

"If you're asking whether anyone else in my family knows what I'm doing, the answer is no." He twisted his silver signet ring around his finger.

"No secret allies? No fellow rogue Beldons?"

Cyrus shook his head.

"Good." Lucien sat up straight and leveled Cyrus with that intense gaze again. "Because you may not speak a word of this to *anyone.*"

Cyrus stared at him. Wait, was he agreeing?

"I don't care what lies you must conjure," Lucien went on. "I don't care if they try to torture it out of you. If you reveal a single word from this book to your family, I'll make your life a living hell, Cyrus Beldon."

Cyrus nodded along with Lucien's words, accepting the terms and vague threat without really letting it sink in. Oath of secrecy under consequence of torment at House Vista's hands—great, acceptable, completely reasonable. All that mattered was that Lucien was saying *yes*, and Cyrus had a path forward.

His heart threatened to burst out of his chest. He really might get a chance to change everything.

Lucien rose gracefully from his chair and extended his hand. Cyrus did the same and clasped Lucien's hand—but failed to muffle a gasp at the coldness of his flesh. He should've expected it, but feeling that lack of warm blood was jarring.

A soft smile played across Lucien's lips. "We have an agreement, then?"

Cyrus met his eyes. "We do, Honored Vista."

"Hmm." Lucien let go of Cyrus's hand. "If you insist on leaving your family name at the door, surely I can as well. Call me Lucien, and let us perhaps be associates rather than...generational enemies."

Cyrus found himself smiling. "Thank you, Lucien. Truly. I can't express how grateful I am that you're willing to help. Though I have to wonder...why agree to my odd request? And from *me*, of all people?"

Lucien slid his hands into the pockets of his trousers. "Because I'm tired of it, too."

The answer surprised Cyrus to silence.

"I exist to be a threat," Lucien went on. "I'm the heir to House Vista, to this centuries-old family and all its so-called honor, but at the end of the day, everything I am is tied to my usefulness in my kin's cat-and-mouse chase with yours. Why do the Honorable Families still stand, if not to hold the sword over the hunters' necks? I'm not a person. I'm a weapon in a war that might never start, and might never end. And I never asked for that." He shook his head. Strands of silver hair fell to frame his face. "I love my family, but...where does it end? Where does the cycle end?"

Cyrus couldn't conjure a response for a long minute. He studied Lucien Vista, and for the first time, he saw not a vampire but a person as unmoored and lonely as Cyrus himself was. He saw more of himself in this man he'd known for half an hour than he ever had in his own family.

He glanced down at the book on the table, then reached for it and offered it to Lucien. "Here. It could end here."

Lucien hesitated, then accepted the book and tucked it under his arm. His fingers reverently stroked the leather spine. "It's...a start."

"And isn't that more than anyone in either of our families has ever done?" Cyrus met Lucien's eyes and realized he was searching for a reflection of the hope that had awoken within him. There was still some reluctance there in Lucien's gaze, some hesitation, some doubt. But Cyrus saw his determination, too, the same sort of stubbornness that drove Cyrus forward. "This work you've done is brilliant. It works in ways you never anticipated. It doesn't need to be reinvented. Just perfected."

Lucien nodded slowly. "Come back tomorrow. Meet me in the carriage house, no later than noon." A small smile warmed his face. "I'll be waiting."

Chapter NINE

LOUD KNOCKING ROUSED CYRUS FROM THE BEST SLEEP he'd gotten all week. With a groan, he turned his head toward his bedroom door and blearily opened his eyes, but in the half-light he couldn't see anyone there. "What," he called, voice cracking.

"Mr. Beldon?" A servant's voice responded from the other side of the door. "I've been instructed to check on you, sir. Master Beldon and the others are already ready."

What? Cyrus rolled onto his back and rubbed his eyes, but even having them closed for a second threatened to drag him back under. "Ready for what?"

"Er...your brother's funeral, sir."

My brother's...? "Oh, *shit*." Cyrus bolted upright. That was *today*? Since when? Was anyone going to tell him that sooner than five minutes before he had to be ready?

Cyrus grumbled a string of curses and stumbled out of bed and into the washroom. A splash of cold water to his face chased away that last of his sleepiness, and he moved through the rest of his routine in a hurried blur. When he got to his wardrobe he grabbed the first three pieces of black clothing he saw, and in less than five minutes he was dressed and out of his room. He tied his cravat as he ran down to the first floor, where he found the rest of his family —minus Poppy—in the foyer.

"So glad you could join us," Joel muttered dryly.

Cyrus shot him a sneer and straightened the hastily-tied cravat.

It probably looked sloppy, but he didn't care. He ran his hands through his hair and reluctantly turned to his father. "I apologize. Overslept."

Marcus pursed his lips and said nothing, then strode toward the doors. Emerson followed him, trailed by Joel, and lastly Cyrus. Arthur and Poppy's absence hit him then; their order was thrown off—it was always Arthur behind Marcus, and Poppy and Joel following Emerson. Cyrus was always at the end, but he was used to having more people ahead of him.

Only one of them was truly gone, but Arthur's absence alone was a gaping hole in the family.

They walked in a somber cluster along the gravel path that wrapped all the way around the mansion. Cyrus hadn't thought to grab a jacket and now regretted it; the air carried a cool reminder that the warm part of autumn was done. Dew clung to the grass and dampened Cyrus's shoes, and an insistent breeze chilled the back of his neck. He couldn't fathom why they all had to walk around the house instead of through it and out the back door, especially since this funeral was clearly not a public affair. A procession would make sense if they had half the city following, but across the grounds, at the end of the main path, the gates were shut. The street was quiet. Either Arthur wasn't important enough for a public funeral, or Marcus wanted everything under wraps.

Cyrus assumed the latter. Besides, it wasn't as if they had a body to bury.

Silence cloaked the family for the duration of the hike across the back gardens and up the hill to the graveyard. Cyrus had been up here only once before, for his mother's funeral fifteen years ago, and never since. The space was tranquil; long grass, garlic stalks, and wildflowers swished in the light wind, but to Cyrus it was unsettlingly still. The world seemed to hold its breath here, as if the slightest sound or movement would wake something up.

It was a stupid superstition, he knew, but he still kept his steps light.

Corralled by a rusted iron fence consumed by overgrown

brambles, the rectangular patch of land was dotted with the moss-coated, eroded, often slouching grave markers of generations of Beldons. A granite obelisk in the center with the family name engraved boldly at its base marked the resting place of founder Julius Beldon, who was clearly compensating for something with the size of that sculpture. Older graves—Julius's wife and children, their children's children, and so on—surrounded the obelisk, their engravings mostly illegible at this point. Closer to the graveyard entrance, the stones were newer, from great-grandparents to grandparents to mother, and now brother.

The four of them gathered around their slice of the graveyard, where a crisp new stone marked an empty swath of earth. BELDON proudly crowned the upper part of the rounded slab, with ARTHUR LAURENCE and his birth and death dates in smaller text below it. Beldon first, person second. As always. A wreath of thorns with two swords crossed through it was engraved beneath the words; the same symbol adorned every stone in this graveyard—except for Cyrus's mother's.

He glanced up at his mother's grave, slightly behind Arthur's. He felt a stab of guilt that he had never come up here to visit his mother's resting place since she was buried, but something about that spot unsettled him more than the entirety of the graveyard. There was a coldness to it, a sadness that felt infectious.

Beside Natasha's marker was a nearly identical slab of granite with Marcus's name and date of birth, but a blank spot awaiting the details of his death. Cyrus wondered if there would be a body to bury in front of that stone, or if they would all gather around another empty grave when Marcus's time was up.

Cyrus returned his attention to his father when Marcus cleared his throat. He stood beside Arthur's grave marker, one hand reverently rested on the granite. "It pains me to have to do this. One never expects to bury one's child. And to do so in this way, without a body to purify and lay to rest, disturbs me all the more." Marcus clenched his jaw and tore his gaze from the tombstone to look up at the others. "This family has been dealt too many tragedies. Too many injustices. Enough is enough. I will not stand here again until it is my body beneath the earth. If the Honorable Ones will not show us the same respect that they demand from us, then they are not deserving of such respect. They seem to have forgotten our strength. I intend to remind them."

Cyrus stared at the wet grass and wildflowers at his feet and prayed that his face didn't give away the horror he felt at Marcus's words. The man was insane if he thought he could successfully retaliate against the Honorable Families. Even if he rallied the other hunter families, they were all merely human. Against centuries-old vampires? None of them stood a chance, even Marcus Beldon and his delusions of invincibility.

Cyrus didn't ask for this, and he didn't want any damn part of it.

"But," Marcus went on, in a softer tone, "today is not for vengeance. Today, I want us to think of Arthur and his bravery. His unflinching loyalty to this family and our purpose. Arthur honors us even in death, despite what those monsters did to him. My son will be remembered not by his death, but by his honorable life."

Cyrus doubted that.

Marcus lowered himself to one knee and struck a match to light the incense in the basin that sat before Arthur's grave. The leaves ignited at once and filled the air with a sharp fragrance. White puffs of smoke drifted skyward and unfurled in the breeze.

"May I say something, Father?" Joel asked.

Marcus nodded and gestured for Joel to move forward.

Cyrus slid his hands into his pockets and glanced around for something interesting to capture his attention while Joel rambled an anecdote about Arthur's strength and bravery and brotherly loyalty. Cyrus struggled not to roll his eyes.

What would he say, he wondered, if he was encouraged to talk about Arthur? No one would ask him—he was sure of that—but where to start? Maybe that time when Cyrus was eight and Arthur had decided Cyrus was too old to still have the blanket his mother had knitted when he was born, so he'd stolen it and flung it into the pond so Marcus would throw it out. Or, even better, when Cyrus had started his hunter training and Arthur had decided that meant he could hit Cyrus all he wanted because now Cyrus "knew how to fight back." Maybe Cyrus would share each occasion—of which there were many—that Arthur intentionally hurt him during a spar, but not badly enough to get him scolded, only enough to leave Cyrus in significant enough pain that he had to miss lessons and fall behind, so Arthur would always be better and always be stronger and Cyrus would never be enough.

He curled his hands into fists in his pockets. *Honorable life.* Right. Was endlessly tormenting and seriously injuring one's brother *honorable*? Was acting like you were king of the world and everyone else was beneath you *honorable*? Were cruelty and arrogance and a thirst for violence this family's ideas of honor?

Of course they were. And how, Cyrus wondered, did that make them any different from the Honorable Families?

Arthur would have been a perfect successor to Marcus. Cyrus was glad he was gone.

When Joel finished his tearful stories, Emerson shared a few commendations of Arthur's intelligence and skill, and lamented the loss of such a strong asset to the family. *Beldon first, person second.* Rustling trees filled the silence that yawned over the graveyard when Emerson finished speaking, and after several minutes, Marcus was the first to break away. He lifted a small pouch out of his pocket and scattered its contents—wildflower and garlic seeds mixed with rice—on the threshold of the graveyard. He said nothing as he left, and no one else moved until Marcus had reached the bottom of the hill.

Emerson departed next, long cloak sweeping behind him as he descended the slope.

Cyrus didn't know why he was still here. The incense was starting to give him a headache, worsened by his empty stomach. He should go, have something to eat, and then flee to the Vista manor while everyone was still distracted by the funeral. This day and this service felt like the end of a chapter—the beginning of the end of Cyrus's freedom. The shock had worn off, and Marcus's anger had rekindled. Cyrus was closer than ever to being out of time.

"Do you think he knew it?" Joel asked, cutting into Cyrus's thoughts.

Cyrus glanced at him; his shoulders were slumped, his eyes tired. "Knew what?"

"What he was, at the end." Joel swallowed. "Do you think he knew he was a monster?"

"No." Cyrus was positive of it. "There was not a trace of Arthur left in that thing."

Joel nodded slowly. "Good."

Cyrus waited for him to say more, and when he didn't, Cyrus quietly drifted away. He cast a final glance at his mother's grave, then descended the hill.

CYRUS COULDN'T SEE the sun when he reached the gates of the Vista manor, but it was most definitely past noon. He'd stupidly decided to take a nap after he'd eaten breakfast, and by the time he woke up, the day was already creeping toward its midpoint. He'd ridden as fast as he dared across the city, but it wasn't fast enough. Sweat stuck his shirt to his back and frizzed the curls framing his forehead, and he nearly ate dirt in his haste to get off Demeter's back. He flung her reins over the lamp at the end of the path, then shouldered through the iron gates and ran toward the carriage house behind the mansion.

He didn't slow when he reached the doors, slamming through them with a grunt. "I'm—I'm here," he wheezed. Each breath burned his lungs. "I'm here, I'm sorry, I—"

He heaved a relieved sigh when he saw that Lucien was still here. He was perched on a wooden crate in the front corner of the room, a book open on his lap. And he was smiling, for some reason. "You're here."

"Yeah." Cyrus struggled to catch his breath. A painful stitch stabbed his side. "S-Sorry I'm late. I don't even know what time it is, but I had—Arthur's funeral, and then I—fucking fell asleep, I'm sorry, and it takes f-fucking forever to get through the city, a-and—"

"Beldon." Lucien's voice was warm with amusement. "Don't worry. You're only an hour late."

His mouth fell open. "An *hour*? But you said—"

"I gave you a specific time to be here so I would know if you were as serious about all this as you claimed to be." Lucien closed the book and slid down from the crate, brushing dust off his long, black coat. "If you had arrived early, I would have admired your enthusiasm."

"I—"

Lucien held up a hand. "If you had sulked in here precisely at noon, I would have concluded that you came only because I instructed you to do so." He took a step closer to Cyrus, heeled boots crunching dirt underfoot. "But you were late. And instead of dragging your feet without a care for the time, I believe you broke one of the latches on the door in your haste to get in." A smile eased across his face. "And that, Cyrus Beldon, allows me to respect not only your enthusiasm, but your commitment."

Cyrus exhaled and slumped back against the doors. He hadn't expected Lucien to be so understanding, but part of him suspected it was a one-time mercy. He couldn't be too trusting of the honesty in Lucien's eyes; he had to remember who he was dealing with.

"Well...Thanks, I guess," he said. "For giving me the benefit of the doubt."

"It doesn't help either of us for me to be unforgiving," Lucien said. Some of the warmth faded from his eyes then. "No one knows or suspects that you are here, correct?"

"Even if anyone saw me leave, this is the last place any Beldon would look for me." Cyrus moved out of the way as Lucien reached for the door handles.

"Hm. That's ironic, isn't it?" Lucien dragged one of the oak doors open, ushering in a gust of cool air.

Cyrus followed him outside and fell into step beside him. "How so?" He wondered where Lucien might be taking him as they passed through a gate into a garden that crept up to the back of the house. Its prime had passed with the summer months, but it was still exquisitely maintained. Bare, thorny vines crawled up a weathered pergola that arched over the path Cyrus and Lucien followed; in season, the whole space likely flourished with flowers.

Lucien turned his head to glance down at him. His long, silver hair shimmered as it shifted on his shoulders. "I do recall a piece of advice regarding keeping your friends close, but your enemies closer. I'm just surprised that Master Beldon isn't personally interrogating every member of every Honorable Family in response to your brother's death." He lifted an eyebrow. "Unless that is why you're truly here?"

Cyrus snorted. "If Marcus wanted to spy on the Families, he wouldn't send *me*. No, I don't know what my father will do now." Cyrus hoped he sounded earnest, because that was the truth. Marcus spoke of vengeance and putting the Honorable Families back in their place, but did he have the balls to actually make a move against them? Cyrus genuinely didn't know.

"Then it seems we must all tread carefully," Lucien said. "Which is why I'm bringing you in through the garden door. You took a risk yesterday, showing up on our doorstep unannounced. You're lucky it was Victoria who answered and not Oscar, our butler, who would have brought you straight to my father. I don't want him finding you here any more than you do."

Lucien stopped at a small ivy-covered door with a circular stained-glass window in its center. He turned to Cyrus. "I was not exaggerating the secrecy of our agreement, Beldon. Your presence here is a powder keg. If we are to work together, I dearly hope you understand that." He drew a key from his pocket and turned it in the lock, but only opened the door a crack.

"Of course I do," Cyrus said. "My father would skin me alive if he knew what I'm doing here." He didn't even want to imagine how that would go down. Thankfully, only Emerson knew of Cyrus's investigation of House Vista, so as long as Cyrus continued to tell Emerson what he wanted to hear, he was safe. And so, by extension, was Lucien and his family.

He didn't know how long he would be able to keep control over the situation, but for now, a few lies and some sneaky excursions would have to be good enough.

Lucien held his gaze a moment longer, then nodded and led the way through the door. Cyrus followed him into a dark, cramped entranceway and tripped his way up a steep set of stairs. Lucien opened another door that violently spilled light into the stairwell, and Cyrus blinked spots out of his eyes as he stepped into a warmly lit corridor. Arched doorways opened into a larger, darker room beyond, into which Lucien led Cyrus.

"Wait here," Lucien instructed after a mere handful of steps into the cavernous space. Cyrus lingered beside a niche in the wall housing a flickering candelabra, trying to make out the shadowy shapes surrounding him. Where had Lucien brought him?

A sudden swathe of bright light momentarily forced him to shield his eyes. When the burn faded, he looked up, blinking, and the air rushed from his lungs.

Cyrus gazed around at the grandest library he had ever seen. His home had its own library, sure, but this...this was *majestic*. Three stories packed with rows upon rows of bookcases hoarded thousands of volumes and likely centuries of knowledge. Towering windows, some of colorful stained glass, poured sunlight into the room and chased the shadows to the corners. Oak tables stood every few feet across the marble floor, matching chairs neatly tucked in against them. Cyrus took a deep breath through his nose and let the scent of leather and paper and ink fill his senses. His heart gave a little flutter of joy.

Lucien could lock him in this room for the rest of his life, and Cyrus wouldn't even be upset.

"Welcome to my slice of Vista pride," Lucien said. Cyrus turned to find him leaning against one of the tables, hands in the pockets of his well-fitted trousers. He'd shed his coat and draped it over the back of the chair beside him. "Ten generations of Vistas contributed to this library. I've spent countless hours of my life in this room, and I've barely scratched the surface of the knowledge and history stored in here. What we seek is experimental, risky, and frankly, unheard of. But if there is anything to be found, it will be here."

Cyrus had to consciously close his mouth to quit gaping at the rows of books. "Where do we even start?"

"Great question. I hope that nap prepared you for a long day." Lucien winked at him and pushed off the table, languidly making his way toward the nearest bookcase. He moved as if his feet didn't quite touch the ground, like gravity didn't have as tight a hold on him as it did everyone else. "Everything we have acquired in the past century is meticulously labeled and organized—thanks to yours truly—but the older collections have not been caught up. There's a directory of the entire collection at the far end of the room, by the main entrance. The end of each shelf has a plaque telling you what is contained in that row, and you'll find the corresponding numbers on—"

"I know how to use a library, Vista," Cyrus scoffed.

Lucien shot him a smug look. "Oh, all right, then. I'll leave it all to the expert. Good luck." He tossed the length of his hair over his shoulders and strode past Cyrus, heading toward that main entrance he mentioned.

"Hold on, you're leaving?" Cyrus jogged to catch up with him. "I thought we were working *together*."

Lucien's soft chuckle echoed off the marble floor. "Do you expect me to hold your hand? I can't raise suspicion by disappearing for hours on end. I sat waiting for you in the carriage house for an hour, remember. I have things to do. I'll come back later to make sure you haven't gotten lost in here."

Cyrus halted and watched him strut the rest of the distance to the doors, through which he disappeared with a flippant wave.

All right, fine. So Cyrus was on his own. He didn't need that vampire's help, anyway. He knew libraries. He could do this.

He found the directory Lucien had pointed out and flipped through the pages to get a general idea of the collection's layout. Three floors with dozens of shelves was a lot of ground to cover, but if he could figure out where the oldest parts of the collection were, that was a more promising start than the newer items Lucien had categorized. What he and Lucien sought was indeed obscure; such information wouldn't be a recent acquisition. Cyrus needed something old, something buried.

There was no efficient way to do this, but any start was better than none.

By the time Cyrus lost the sunlight, he had made it through nine bookcases and had a teetering stack of promising volumes heaped in his arms. He examined each row of books until it was too dark to see the titles, and then carried his haul to the nearest table and pored over them one by one with the scarce pool of light from the oil lamp on the table. He wagered it had about two hours of fuel in it; when it ran out, he would call it a night.

Lucien, despite his word, had not come back yet. But just as well. Cyrus preferred the solitary focus.

A LONG, curving stairwell stretched ahead of Cyrus. Ancient stone walls surrounded him, and mossy steps ascended forward. Behind him, encroaching darkness obscured his starting point. Ahead, a faint flicker of candlelight beckoned him onward. A damp, coppery scent blended with the smell of decay, but Cyrus felt no dread or unease. He continued his ascent, following the light.

Around and around a stone center, Cyrus climbed seemingly endless steps. The flickering light remained out of sight. He didn't know where he was going or what lay ahead, but an instinct within him pulled him forward. He needed to see what was up there. Everything would make sense once he reached the top.

Amid the sounds of dripping moisture and his own breaths, Cyrus heard a voice. Low, soft, soothing. It sang, calling to him with a lullaby that prodded a memory. He couldn't make out the words, but his heart knew the tune.

He climbed faster and faster, now taking the steps two at a time. His feet were steady on the stone; the steps did not trip him. Why hadn't he moved faster before, if there was no danger of slipping? Heart pounding, pulse racing, he hurried up and up and up. Finally, the light grew brighter. It was closer now, bathing the walls around him in a warm yellow glow. *Almost there. Just a little farther.* Then he would know; then he would see; then he would understand.

A cold gust of wind hit him with the force of a stone wall. He flew backwards, flailing, falling, falling, falling—

He jolted awake with a gasp.

It took him a minute to gather his bearings. Where was—Oh, the library. The *Vista* library. He'd been reading, paging through all those books. The room was dark, and he was cold.

It was then that Cyrus realized he was on the floor.

Still disoriented, he dragged himself off the cold marble and grabbed onto the table to pull himself to his feet. His body ached, a steady throb pinched behind his eyes, and on top of it all he was starving. How long had he been here? How long had he been *asleep*?

And what the hell was that dream?

It was already fading from his mind, but he swore he could still feel the dampness of the tower and that gust of wind. His pulse had yet to settle after the vivid sensation of falling. And though it was just a dream, he couldn't shake the feeling that he had seen that place before. If not in person, then in a previous dream that retreated to the depths of his memory. What was it? Why had his mind taken him there? And what was at the top of those stairs that he was so desperate to reach?

Miraculously, the oil lamp on the table still had some life left in it. Cyrus grabbed the wrinkled sheet of parchment he'd been using to take notes and scribbled down what he could remember of the dream. It would likely be nonsensical when he looked at it later, but he wanted to preserve the feelings in case it happened again and became worth a visit to Leif.

As Cyrus folded the parchment and went to turn off the lamp, he abruptly sensed another presence in the room. A shiver ran over his skin, raising the hair on his arms and the back of his neck. Slowly, he lifted the lamp as steadily as possible with a trembling hand, and turned in a circle.

Several feet away, concealed in the shadow of a bookcase, a human shape leaned against the shelf. The light caught and reflected off their eyes, and Cyrus's heart pitched with fear. He jerked a step backwards, but then the shape moved and Lucien stepped into the light's reach.

Cyrus let out a breath, scolding himself. He should've known it was just Lucien. "How long have you been there?"

"Long enough to be surprised that it took you so long to notice me." Lucien drifted closer to him in that fluid way that he moved. He glanced over the scatter of books on the table; Cyrus searched his expression for some sort of interest, but the vampire's pale face remained stoic. "I hope you noted the shelf from which you took each of these books so you can put them back where they belong."

Cyrus pursed his lips. He had not.

Lucien's crimson eyes flicked up to his face. "It's late, Beldon. You should go before your father sends an army here to rescue you."

"You overestimate how much my father cares what happens to me." Cyrus set the lamp on the table and stacked the books he'd collected into a neat pile. None of them had offered anything noteworthy, and not a single one had mentioned Wild vampires at all. "What about your book?" he asked. "The one I returned to you. Wouldn't that be a better place to start than whatever *might* be in this library?"

"No." Lucien shrugged. "Besides, did you expect to find everything we need immediately? You've been at this for half a day. Have patience."

"I don't have *time* to have patience," Cyrus argued. "While you can lounge around here as often and for as long as you'd like, I have duties and expectations on my shoulders that are only going to get bigger. I have to find something now and do something soon, before—"

He stopped himself. *Remember who you're talking to.*

Lucien tilted his head to the side. "Before what, Beldon?"

Before my father declares war, was what he'd almost said. But Cyrus couldn't betray that possibility, even if the Families already feared it. He couldn't risk someone taking another strike against the Beldons and worsening Marcus's rage.

Cyrus didn't even know if finding a way to reverse a turn would do any good against his father's hatred. He could make a world-altering breakthrough that ensured the Beldons never had to kill another vampire, and it might not matter at all. Marcus Beldon would likely keep killing them anyway simply because that was what he thought he was meant to do. But Marcus Beldon wouldn't live forever, and having some alternative to bloodshed meant that his successors had *options*. A silver sword was not the only answer. Cyrus was still determined to make a difference, even if he wouldn't see it for another decade or two.

All of this—snarky, unhelpful Vista heir included—would be worth it.

"Look." Lucien quieted his voice. "If you want to haunt this library until you drop dead from exhaustion, be my guest. I'm not your nanny, you can do whatever you want. But no matter how much you read or how many sleepless hours you stay here, this project cannot be rushed. I've spent years on this research already, and I've barely anything to show for it. You need to be prepared for a long road, Beldon, not a sprint to a deadline. If you can't commit to that, then we're done here."

Cyrus's stomach twisted with the realization that he didn't really know what he'd gotten into. Lucien was suggesting that he'd be buried in these books for months before he even had enough context for the notes in Lucien's journal, and after that, what? More months of study, trials, and experiments? *Years*? How much of his life had he thoughtlessly signed away? And what if it was too late by the time he got anywhere?

A vampire had all the time in the world to meander through research. Cyrus didn't have that luxury.

He met Lucien's eyes. "I don't intend to sprint. I intend to *work*. And I won't be dragging my feet. Or yours, for that matter. If you are willing to help me, then I expect you to work with me, Vista. Have you forgotten that our project is more beneficial to you than it is to me?"

Lucien turned his head away, which told Cyrus he'd struck a truth that Lucien couldn't deny. He shifted his weight to one leg and placed a hand on his hip. It was another second before he looked at Cyrus again. "You admittedly make a valid point, Beldon."

"Just say I'm right and let's move on."

Lucien's upper lip twitched, but he expertly schooled his expression to a calm, unaffected mask. Cyrus found it mildly entertaining that this vampire was so easily and obviously peeved by Cyrus's snark.

"You're right."

Cyrus stared at him. He had not actually expected Lucien to say it. And there was not a hint of condescension on his face, only sincerity. Maybe even a touch of...guilt?

It scattered an odd feeling through Cyrus that started in his stomach and fluttered its way upward. He realized that he'd been expecting a battle from Lucien, a resistance to their cooperation that would have them circling each other with knives behind their backs and never moving forward. To hear Lucien agree with him and admit his own fault finally released the nervous tension Cyrus had been gripping since he walked through the doors.

"You're right," Lucien said again, and Cyrus almost pushed him to say it once more but refrained. "I was being needlessly negligent. I do care about what we're doing—obviously—and I care about the future it could bring for both of us, and for everyone who comes after us. I know this is merely an excuse, but... part of me was still convinced you would not actually see this through."

"You have my word—whatever it may be worth to you—that I will," Cyrus said earnestly.

Lucien met his eyes. "And you have my word that I will give everything I have so that we can move forward. I can't expect you to do this alone, nor should you."

"Thank you," Cyrus murmured. Relief swept through him, and only then did he feel his exhaustion catch up with him. He stifled a yawn, but Lucien saw it.

A gentle smirk worked its way across the vampire's mouth. "Get some rest, Beldon. The books aren't going anywhere. In the meantime, I'll see what I can find on my own. We'll search with fresh eyes in the morning."

Cyrus nodded and stretched his arms. "First thing tomorrow?"

"If you insist."

"No time to waste, right?" Cyrus drifted toward the stairs.

"On the contrary, I have all the time to waste." Lucien flashed a grin. "But yes, first thing come morning. You know where to find me."

Cyrus didn't, really. Carriage house again? Here? He'd figure it out tomorrow. He left Lucien with a parting wave, and took his leave.

Chapter TEN

CYRUS FOUND LUCIEN IN THE CARRIAGE HOUSE AGAIN, seated on the same crate with a different book balanced on his knees. Cyrus tried to get a peek at the cover or the spine as Lucien flipped it closed and slid off his perch, but the vampire tucked the book under his arm too quickly, concealing any identifying text on the leather binding. The subtle secrecy piqued Cyrus's interest even more. He spent the walk from the carriage house to the garden door smothering the temptation to ask after Lucien's reading preferences. He didn't need to know what Lucien liked to read, nor should he care. They weren't friends.

Lucien brought him up to the second floor of the library and led him to a table already spread out with books and papers. Cyrus recognized one of the books he'd chosen last night and felt a flicker of pride in himself. If Lucien had agreed that text was useful, maybe Cyrus *wasn't* so terrible at this research thing.

Lucien leaned over the table and studied the array of items. He reached for a small stack of books and lifted two off the top to reveal the volume Cyrus had returned to him. "After we parted ways last night, I spent some time thinking about what you said about me being *uselessly unhelpful* to you."

"I didn't say you were useless," Cyrus muttered, even though it was true.

"Even so, you're not wrong." Lucien shrugged, unaffected, and caressed his long fingers over the book's smooth leather cover. "I left you to your own devices and assumed that you would figure it out, but what I didn't consider is your lack of knowledge." He held up a hand when Cyrus went to protest. "You admitted to me yourself that you didn't understand a word of this book, so before we can move forward, we need to be on the same page. It's hardly a hypothesis to say that your knowledge of vampires is vastly different than my own."

Cyrus shut his mouth. That much was true.

"There's nothing shameful in admitting a gap in understanding," Lucien said. "It's hardly your fault that you've only been taught what the Beldons want you to know. What matters is that you're here and eager to learn. So." He raised his eyebrows. "Are you ready to shatter some myths?"

He was, and it surprised him how earnest that feeling was. He wanted to understand how vampires lived, not just how they died, and he didn't want to be afraid anymore. "Yes," he said to Lucien.

"Excellent." A bare hint of a smile touched Lucien's lips. It showed more in his eyes; they squinted slightly at the corners, even when the rest of his face hid the expression. It vanished quickly, though. "And forgive me for repeating it yet again, but I can't emphasize it enough: you may not—"

"Speak a word. I know." Cyrus nodded. "You don't have to worry."

"Do you understand the magnitude of what I'm about to share with you?" Lucien lowered his voice to a hush. His crimson eyes darted nervously between Cyrus and the books; the emotion was foreign on the suave vampire's face, and it hit Cyrus then that for all their might and all their teeth and claws, the Vistas were just as wary of the Beldons as the Beldons were of them.

Two snarling wolves, circling each other with teeth bared and hackles raised, yet never attacking for fear of the other being much, much stronger.

Cyrus prayed for the day that all of this nonsense would end.

"I do understand," he told Lucien. "I know very well that if the rest of my family got ahold of the information you're about to share with me, it would be devastating. Catastrophic." Cyrus leaned over the table and met Lucien's eyes. "But I am not the rest of my family. Your hesitance to trust me is valid, but I hope...I hope that, in time, you'll see that I'm really not like the rest of them."

The words nearly choked him on their way out, but though the sincerity made him want to vomit, it was effective. Lucien's expression shifted, and Cyrus watched the last of his hesitation fade. He gestured to the chair to his right, and Cyrus went around the table and took a seat.

"Your honesty is admirable," Lucien said softly, and that was the last he spoke of trust.

"So." Cyrus drummed his fingers on the table as Lucien gathered a few pages of notes. He wished he'd thought to bring a notebook; he didn't trust his slippery brain to retain everything Lucien intended to tell him today, but he'd have to make do. "What do I need to know?"

"First," Lucien said, sinking into his own chair, "I need you to forget everything you've been taught about vampires."

Cyrus raised his eyebrows. "Everything?"

"Like every Beldon before you, you have been taught a litany of ways to kill a vampire," Lucien went on. He folded his hands neatly on the table. "I suspect that these lessons and methods have no finesse, only brutality. You've only been told what our weaknesses are—silver, sunlight, wooden stakes, rice, *garlic*..." He rolled his eyes.

Cyrus stared at him. "Is...Is garlic...not...?"

Lucien returned his blank stare, then pinched the bridge of his nose. "Spirits help me."

Cyrus waited for him to answer his question, but he moved on. "Anyway, these weaknesses have been passed down through generations of folklore, with no thought given to the origin of such stories or the truth of them. No one ever stopped to consider why people thought this or that of vampires; it's all taken at face value."

"Okay, but I do know that sunlight won't kill *all* vampires," Cyrus muttered bitterly. He didn't doubt that much of his knowledge was inaccurate and biased, but at least the hunter families knew more than the average citizen. "I also know that silver is always more effective than a wooden stake, and rice and garlic are *protections*, not weapons."

"My point is that there are nuances to all of these supposed weaknesses, just as there are with humans," Lucien said. "To say sunlight will kill a vampire is like saying...a piercing is a stab wound."

Fair enough.

"And I hate to break it to you, Beldon, but if you toss a sack of rice at me, I will not be overcome by an irresistible compulsion to count every grain." Lucien shook his head with an exasperated chuckle. "Honestly, I don't know where you people come up with these things."

Admittedly, that piece of superstition had never made much sense to Cyrus, either.

"Anyhow, vampires are weakest when they're young," Lucien continued. "Freshly turned vampires are far more vulnerable than those that are born, but both will be highly sensitive to sunlight and silver for up to their first two decades of life. Even then, it's not until we reach our first century that we grow into many of our strengths."

He started to go on, but Cyrus raised his hand. "Hold on. What do you mean by...those that are born?"

Lucien blinked in a way that Cyrus was beginning to recognize as a response to a stupid question. "Exactly what I said. Vampires that are born, as opposed to turned."

"What? But—"

"Do I have to spell it out for you? You see, Beldon, when two vampires love each other very much—"

Cyrus rolled his eyes. "Okay, I get *that*, but—"

"Do you?"

Cyrus scowled, unamused at Lucien's stupid smirk. "I didn't know that vampires could be born. Why would you ever turn a human, then, if you can just make vampire babies the way everyone else does?"

"Turning is easier," Lucien said with a shrug. "Our biology isn't really suited to, ah, reproduction."

It was Cyrus's turn to smirk. "Is that so? Right, I suppose a lack of warm blood would make some things *difficult.*"

"Shut it," Lucien snapped, which only made Cyrus laugh. Lucien huffed. "I answered your question, so we're moving on. The things you believe to be vampire weaknesses aren't entirely incorrect, but they are mostly harmful to young vampires, and usually a mere inconvenience to those of us who are far more mature."

"I'm supposed to think you and your sex jokes are mature?"

Lucien ignored him. "Let's take silver as an example. Hunters such as yourself are never without it on your person, correct? You think yourselves invincible as long as you wield that precious metal. I hate to be the bearer of bad news, but to a mature vampire, silver hurts no more than a minor burn."

"Silver *kills* you," Cyrus argued. "I've seen that firsthand."

"Not necessarily," Lucien said. "It is far more likely to be fatal to a young vampire than it is to me. The thing about silver is that we cannot heal wounds inflicted by it as long as it is touching our body. If you really want to kill a vampire and make sure they stay dead, then yes, run me through with a silver blade—but *leave* it. Do you know why it's in your repertoire to decapitate a vampire after you've already stabbed them?"

Cyrus frowned, thoughts racing. "Because you might heal yourself otherwise."

"Precisely. I can heal many wounds, but not a severed head. The moment your weapon is removed from my flesh, my body begins to heal. It takes longer, and it leaves a scar, whereas an injury caused by a weapon made of, say, steel, would heal without a trace. But silver halts the healing process. Young vampires can't heal as well as mature ones, and therefore silver often spells instant death.

That's why it's an effective weapon, not because the metal burns us."

"Fascinating," Cyrus murmured. "Okay, so what about sunlight? You obviously won't burst into flames, but does it have *any* effect?"

"It hurts my eyes, mostly," Lucien said. "Vampires see very well in the dark, which in turn makes us extremely sensitive to bright environments. It's no coincidence that this house is in a particularly dense part of the forest. Daylight gives me migraines if I'm out in the sun for too long. Besides, if any of my relatives decided to turn someone or have a child, we'd need to keep them out of the sun. Like I said, young vampires are most susceptible."

"Makes sense," Cyrus muttered. Then he frowned. "Garlic."

"What about it?"

"It really doesn't do anything?"

"No." Lucien paused. "Most of the time."

"Oh?" Cyrus grinned. "Come now, Vista, this is a safe space for honesty. What does it do to you?"

Lucien pretended to be very interested in one of the pages in front of him. "Some of us have a...minor yet inconvenient allergy to it."

Cyrus smothered his grin. "Noted."

"There's a thousand other details we could get into—weaknesses and strengths—but I won't bore you," Lucien said, looking up at Cyrus again. "Besides, it's mostly irrelevant. We want to focus on turning, as that's the root of our project, and spirits know there's a plethora of myths to debunk in that territory. I'll start with the most obvious." His eyes trailed down Cyrus's face before settling on his throat. "We are not filled with insatiable bloodlust at a mere glimpse of a human neck."

Cyrus blinked, confused, then glanced down at the cravat tied snugly around his throat. Reflexively, he reached up and straightened it. High-collared shirts, buttoned just below the chin and further secured with a tie or cravat had been the fashion standard in his family's circles for his entire life. He felt naked without something around his neck. But he'd never considered that this style had anything to do with vampires.

How many other social norms had been woven out of superstitions against vampires? Cyrus suspected he'd notice them everywhere now.

"Honestly, the idea that a vampire would recklessly attack anyone who dares to show their neck outside is preposterous," Lucien continued. "We're not animals. Turning is a delicate process, and most vampires wouldn't even try it if they're not of perfectly sound mind. It requires mutual trust as much as it requires consent, so it's not as though we're prancing about biting people at random."

Of all the things Lucien had told Cyrus so far, that was the most surprising. It wasn't that he thought vampires were akin to animals who couldn't think beyond their instincts, but the idea of a turn being mutually consensual was impossible for him to wrap his head around. Who the hell would ever agree to that? And why?

Another old myth claimed that vampires had hypnotic abilities, and therefore you shouldn't be alone with one for too long lest you fall under its spell. It sounded absurd, but Cyrus couldn't fathom another circumstance leading to a human agreeing to be turned.

"You're talking about Honorable Ones, though, right?" Cyrus asked. "Those of you bound by the truce?"

Lucien frowned. "No, I'm talking broadly about vampires. There's nothing special about Honorable Ones except for our social status."

"So just a normal, common vampire wouldn't be any more dangerous than an Honorable One?"

"Is a common thief more dangerous than a hired sword?" Lucien gave him that *stupid question* look again. "No, Beldon, Honorable or not, most vampires aren't monsters. You have only been led to believe we are." He sat back in his chair and regarded Cyrus coolly. "Your entire world and the lifestyle you know were built to cushion you and exclude me. Vampires live among humans and freely mingle with them, but only because we look very similar to you. Most people don't look closely enough to find the tells—not anymore, anyway. At least your kin have dropped some of their paranoia. But while we can glide through your society without much notice, we're far from safe among humans even if you aren't burning and staking people every other day. Everything we need to live, we can only find among other vampires. We take care of our own, because no one else will."

"Sure, but that goes both ways," Cyrus said. "Humans stick to fellow humans for all our needs, too."

"Yes, because spirits forbid a vampire comes anywhere near your sick or injured child."

"Oh, and bringing someone who's injured and *bleeding* to a *vampire* is *such* a good idea."

Lucien bristled, and Cyrus regretted the words. "Have you heard a *word* I've said? If you're not going to listen—"

"I am, I am, I'm sorry." Cyrus held up his hands. "I didn't—That was a stupid thing to say. I'm sorry."

Lucien continued to glare at him.

"I apologize, Lucien." His name sounded strange on Cyrus's tongue after three days of slinging his family name at him. "Look, I'm here with an open mind, but you have to understand that the things you're debunking are things I've been conditioned to blindly believe for my whole life. I want to unlearn the myths, but you can't expect me to be an expert overnight."

For a moment, Lucien's expression didn't change. Then with a blink, his anger vanished, and he closed his eyes. "You make a fair point. In that case, I shall lower my expectations." He glanced up at Cyrus, eyes scathing. "I did not realize you had a *toddler's* understanding of vampires."

Cyrus bolted to his feet, shoving his chair back. "Do you want my help or not? You're the one who told me to forget everything I know. If you're just going to infantilize me—"

"I did not ask for your help, Cyrus Beldon." Lucien rose to his feet, and their few inches' height difference seemed to expand exponentially. "*You* scurried in here yourself and begged me to collaborate on this suicidal crusade that could earn *both* of us a stake through the heart. *I'm* in over my head, you even more so, and no, you *don't* seem to understand that." Lucien pursed his lips. "I am *so* sorry that the wee vampire hunter got his feelings hurt, but I'm not infantilizing you. You *do* have an elementary understanding of vampires, and yes, I see that you want to change that, but I need you to understand that *everything* you know is going to be challenged. Everything Marcus Beldon and his brother have taught you will be turned over and shaken and torn apart by the things you will learn if you continue to work with me. Are you truly prepared, Beldon, for your reality to break? Because if there is one thing I can promise, it is that."

He paused, breathing audibly through his nose. Cyrus sat back down. Lucien held his gaze. "This is your last chance to change your mind and walk out, Beldon. I won't ask any questions. I won't stop you. You will never see me again. Make your choice."

Cyrus stubbornly glared back at him. Lucien didn't actually want him to go, because if Cyrus did—if he fled this place and its secrets—everything would slide back to normal. More humans would be killed and turned Wild. The Beldons would hunt them, and eventually the Beldons would fail. The Honorable Families would break the truce and betray the hunter families, and all hell would break loose. And the cycle would go on and on and on and peace would be impossible, all because Cyrus had too reactive of a temper to listen to the one singular vampire on earth who had chosen to hear him out and strike a deal.

Cyrus refused to throw that away. His ego and his pride could sit down and shut up. He would be stupid to let this go, and Lucien knew it too.

Thoroughly humbled, Cyrus let the tension bleed out of his shoulders. "No. I'm not going anywhere."

"No?" Lucien's voice dripped with doubt.

"No. I'm serious about all of this. But..." Cyrus sighed. "We won't get anywhere if we keep antagonizing each other."

"Who's being antagonistic? It's not my fault that you're prone to tantrums."

"Do you *have* to be such a supreme ass?"

"Yes, it's part of the family legacy." Lucien slid a book toward Cyrus. "Go home and read this. Or stay here and read it, I don't care. But read this, and then I want to hear how your encounter with a Wild vampire compares to the records in this book. Note anything you don't understand for lack of basic knowledge and I will fill in the blanks."

Cyrus didn't reach for the book. "Didn't you want me to learn the basics first?"

"No, that would be far too time consuming. But I hope that debunking the myths will spare me some of your inane questions." Lucien shot him a smirk and began gathering the other books. "You don't need to know everything; for now, focus your understanding on Wild vampires and the process of turning."

Cyrus was fairly certain he could handle that. He hesitantly brought the book closer to him.

"Which is it, then, stay or go?" Lucien moved away from the table.

"Wait, you're leaving again?"

Lucien batted his eyes. "Yes, daddy has to go do other things now, but he'll come back and check on you later, okay?"

"Fuck you, Vista."

Lucien snickered and stepped into the shadows between the bookcases. "Best of luck, Beldon."

FIVE HOURS LATER, Cyrus reached the conclusion that vampires didn't make any goddamned sense. The term *deathlife* was a bit of a misnomer, apparently; vampires weren't dead, but they also weren't really alive, but they also weren't reanimated corpses like so many people throughout history believed. They had beating hearts but cold blood; they aged but not indefinitely; they *could* reproduce but mostly chose not to. They were made of contradictions, and unfortunately, Lucien was right: Cyrus had, at best, a child's understanding of them. He got that some vampires were born and others were turned, but once the text got into the nuances of turned vampires versus born vampires versus born vampires who had one human parent, and so on, Cyrus's eyes slid out of focus.

He understood, at a basic level, that to become a vampire was to forsake humanity. Turned vampires weren't just immortal humans with pointy teeth and a taste for blood; they were something else entirely, arguably a different species. And then there were dhampirs, which were a whole *other* thing—neither human nor vampire, but a little of both. But what happened when someone was a quarter vampire? Or less? How strong were those traits through generations? Were vampire families related by blood at all, or did they flock together by choice and remain loyal?

The more Cyrus read, the more he wondered why he didn't already know some of this. Why hadn't he been taught about born vampires? Wouldn't this knowledge of the differing weaknesses between those born and those turned be beneficial to a hunter? Although, a stake through the heart was a stake through the heart, no matter how sensitive you were to silver or sunlight. What mattered to the Beldons was that their methods worked regardless of the vampire's age or how they were born.

Cyrus finally reached the end of a chapter and pushed the book across the table with a groan. He slumped forward with his forehead on the smooth wood and debated falling asleep here. Shadows had encroached around him while he'd been buried in those brittle pages; the sun had likely long since set. He should go home before anyone started to wonder where he was.

He didn't move from the table.

He was too mentally exhausted to read any more, but it irked him that the book had so far given him nothing useful. It had yet to mention Wild vampires at all—the topic seemed rather taboo; the only reference Cyrus had seen was a brief footnote acknowledging a Wild turn as a rare possibility, but it offered no details or further reading. Yet there must be more, or else Lucien wouldn't have assigned him this specific volume.

Cyrus lifted his head and rubbed his eyes. A glance at his watch informed him that it wasn't as late as he thought; he could stay a *little* longer without stirring too much suspicion. But he refused to stumble aimlessly through this book; he flipped to the back and scanned the latter half of the index, brightening when he found several entries under *Vampire, Wild*. He turned to the first page listed: a section of a later chapter titled *Maladies, Misfortunes, and Mutilations*. The first half of the chapter chronicled all the ways vampires could be hurt, killed, poisoned, or otherwise harmed, which Cyrus leafed by without interest until a full-page illustration halted his search.

Whoever had drawn this monster must have seen it firsthand; it was precisely what Cyrus and Poppy had found that night: a hulking, snarling, drooling monstrosity that had only rage in its black eyes. No longer human, no longer vampire—not even an animal. It had no sentience, only hunger. Only fury.

Cyrus suppressed a shudder and shifted his attention to the text on the page facing the illustration. He skimmed an introductory paragraph explaining that Wild vampires, while extremely rare, were a real and devastating danger. That, he knew very well. He was more interested in the following section, which promised the gritty details.

But he scarcely got to the end of the opening sentence when he heard the library doors crash open on the other end of the room.

He froze. Lucien didn't usually make that much noise; what could have him so angry that he'd slam the doors? Cyrus turned around in his chair, squinting in the darkness as he strained his ears for footsteps, but then his blood ran cold at the sound of multiple voices.

"...impossible," grumbled an unfamiliar baritone. Another Vista? "An *Honorable One*. There is no way. None of us are—"

"Or so we thought," replied a different voice. *That* was Lucien. His tone was even, but not without annoyance beneath the surface. He hid it well, but Cyrus had spent a lifetime learning to recognize the slightest hint of malcontent in otherwise calm voices; he knew frustration when he heard it. "You and I both see the implication here, Father, do we not?"

Father? Oh, fuck.

Cyrus stood from his chair as soundlessly as possible, taking care not to move it or bump the table or let the pen he'd been using roll a single inch. Lucien and Alastair Vista did not seem to be moving any closer, but Cyrus knew he'd be dead if he was caught. Lucien *knew* he was here; why would he lead his father anywhere near Cyrus?

Whatever the reason, Cyrus wasn't stupid enough to stick around. He snatched the books from the table but left the lamp burning, then darted down the nearest aisle of bookshelves. He let the shadows cloak him and tried not to breathe too hard as he clutched the books to his chest.

"Whatever implications you glean from this situation should be kept to yourself, boy." Alastair Vista's voice had the same sharp, cold edge that Cyrus knew all too well from his own father, though there was something noticeably softer about the vampire's voice; it was imposing but not rough. Like weathered parchment rather than grinding gravel. Cyrus could hear the centuries in Master Vista's voice, but that softness was surely not to be mistaken for lenience or kindness. Each word out of his mouth was a sharp warning to Lucien.

"There is danger in keeping this under wraps," Lucien argued. He still did not raise his voice or allow his obvious irritation to bleed through, but he also didn't quietly defer. Cyrus would have scurried away from Marcus by this point; there was the difference between Lucien's place in his family and Cyrus's place in his own

—Master Vista saw Lucien as a son, while Master Beldon treated them all—Arthur included—like pawns.

Footsteps scuffed the floor. "Father." Lucien dropped his voice lower. "I understand that we are all on a precipice. I know that recent events could tip the balance we've all been struggling to hold. But if we do nothing, if we don't bring our theories to the other Families, this will continue to happen. This time it was House Harrows, but what next? Attcourt? Downings? *Us*? Would you display the same nonchalance if it were me turned Wild, Father?"

"Of course not," Master Vista snapped. Cyrus winced at the sharp thunderclap of his voice. "Put such worries out of your mind, Lucien. It's not going to happen. I do not know what happened to Leigh Harrows, but the same cannot and will not happen to one of us. We are a strong, ancient bloodline. We can't be turned Wild."

Several heartbeats passed. Lucien's next words were so quiet that Cyrus hardly heard him over the pounding of his own heart. "That is what we thought of House Harrows."

"Now you're wearing my patience. Think outside of your stubborn hypotheses, Lucien. We all know the Families keep secrets. Leigh Harrows must have had some human blood in her if she turned Wild. That is the only explanation."

Leigh Harrows was turned Wild?

How?

And...did it have anything to do with her having turned *Arthur* Wild?

Cyrus didn't know where the connection was, but he did not think he would find it in these books.

"No," Lucien said in reply to his father, "that is the *convenient* explanation. The other—the one none of us wants to consider—is that even born vampires can turn Wild. But we're all too scared to think about that, aren't we?"

If Master Vista replied after several long beats of silence, his words were too quiet for Cyrus to hear. Cyrus's thoughts raced, weaving possibilities from fears and theories from possibilities. Who else could turn an Honorable One Wild but another Honorable One? But why would another Honorable Family attack House Harrows? And how could someone who had never been human be turned at all?

It didn't make sense. This puzzle was growing by the day and none of the pieces fit.

Cyrus surfaced from his thoughts just in time to hear two sets of footsteps drawing closer. He held his breath and sank further into the shadows, praying that Master Vista didn't glance this way. Vampires could see almost perfectly in the dark; if Cyrus so much as twitched, he'd be caught.

Lucien and his father paused by the table Cyrus had occupied mere minutes ago. The soft glow from the lamp illuminated Lucien, but threw shadows across his father. Cyrus didn't need him in direct light to recognize the similar traits; he and Lucien had the same long, straight nose and piercing eyes. But where Lucien was willowy, Alastair was stocky. Tall and imposing, his noticeably muscular build was obvious even beneath his exquisitely tailored clothes. He kept just out of reach of the light and placed one large hand on the back of the chair before him.

Cyrus's stomach dropped through his ass. His jacket was still draped over that chair.

Alastair Vista frowned slightly and looked down, running his fingers along the fine suede. "Has someone been here?"

To Lucien's credit, he did not betray a thing. "Only me. I was organizing some things earlier."

"This is yours? It must be old. Hardly your style." Master Vista removed his hand and flicked his fingers as if he'd touched something repulsive. "This library of yours is a lost cause, you know. Can't fathom why you waste your time trying to sort all of this when no one else will keep it in order."

"The organizing helps me think, Father." A slight strain in Lucien's voice betrayed his thinning patience.

Master Vista exhaled a *hmph*. "If you say so. I expect to be able to find what I'm looking for amid your rearranging."

"That's the goal, Father."

"Good. And Lucien, we shall not speak of the Harrows girl again. Tomorrow I will meet with the other heads of the Families and *then* we will have the truth. I don't want to hear another ridiculous speculation from you. Are we clear?"

A muscle twitched in Lucien's jaw as he slightly inclined his head. "Yes, Father."

Master Vista nodded once, then turned and went back the way the two of them had come in.

Cyrus waited until he couldn't hear his footsteps, and then waited for the sound of the doors shutting, and then counted another ninety seconds. Lucien also did not move from his spot by the table, and then after another minute, he finally turned his head precisely in Cyrus's direction.

"You are one damn lucky bastard."

Cyrus released the breath he'd been holding through that entire exchange. Still clutching the books, he moved toward the end of the aisle and cast a nervous glance in the direction of the doors. "Is he gone?"

"Yes, but I suspect he only left to fetch a cup of tea. He'll be back. Come with me." Lucien strode a few steps forward, then glanced back. "Don't forget your jacket."

Cyrus grabbed it and hurried after Lucien, who led him deeper into the library and along the back wall. Portraits of people Cyrus guessed to be past Vistas watched their trek across the massive room, until Lucien finally came to a stop at a shadowed corner.

"What's wrong?" Cyrus whispered, confused. He squinted through the dark, searching for a door, and saw none.

"Nothing." Lucien tipped the frame of one of the paintings on the wall. The nearest bookcase groaned, and Cyrus heard a lock unlatch. Lucien stepped closer to the bookcase and dragged it away from the wall, revealing a doorway behind.

Cyrus could not smother the delighted grin that lit up his face. "Oh, I *hoped* there were secret passageways in here."

"Is that what you were thinking about instead of our research?" Lucien smirked. "Come, we can speak freely in here. I'm the only one who knows how to open this door."

Cyrus stepped through the doorway and blinked to adjust his eyes to the sudden dark. Cool air surrounded him, carrying an earthy scent. He shuffled forward a step as Lucien followed him, swinging the bookcase back into place behind him and encasing them in absolute darkness.

"Um. Vista." No amount of blinking was going to help him in here. He inched another step in what he thought was the correct direction. "You know I can't—"

The ground dropped out from beneath his foot, and he tripped over what he realized too late was a step before tumbling painfully to the bottom of a set of stone stairs. He landed in a heap, ears ringing and head spinning.

From the top of the stairs, he heard the slightest muffled chuckle.

Cyrus groaned and felt around for the wall, then used it to drag himself to his feet. "Fuck you, Vista, you know I can't see in the dark."

"Oh, dear. That little fact slipped my mind." Lucien had soundlessly appeared beside him, and though Cyrus couldn't see his face, he knew he was smirking. Cyrus wanted to smack it off him.

Lucien moved a few steps past Cyrus, and then a flare of bright light burst to life. Cyrus flinched at the sudden onslaught, and when his eyes recovered he found Lucien holding a flickering torch. It cast him in harsh orange light, reflecting on his eyes in that strange, animalistic way.

Cyrus followed him in silence into a cavernous room with a dirt floor. The shadowy space threatened to gulp down the scarce light from the torch; Cyrus couldn't tell what he was looking at as he peered around the room. The air was damp, smelling of moss and something metallic.

"Where are we?" he asked, turning to Lucien.

"The cellar." Lucien placed the torch in a slot on the wall that was positioned between two massive racks stocked full of wine bottles. "No one will bother us here. We hardly ever venture into this dusty corner."

"These particular wines not good enough for you?"

Lucien let out a soft chuckle. "Oh, Beldon, you precious thing. It's not wine."

Oh.

Oh.

Right.

Cyrus swallowed and slipped his hands into his pockets, shifting a step away from the bottles.

"My father had a meeting with Chester Harrows today," Lucien said, tossing his hair over his shoulder. "When he returned, he informed me that Leigh Harrows, the family's heir, was somehow turned Wild by another vampire. Master Harrows called on your father to eliminate h—it."

Well, shit. And Cyrus hadn't been there for the job. Now Marcus would be suspicious, and sneaking away tomorrow to visit House Vista again would be doubly tricky.

"Master Beldon—or whomever he sent on the job—made quick work of the monster, I'm sure," Lucien continued. "But what concerns me, as you overheard earlier, is that Leigh Harrows was turned Wild at all. It's one thing for a human to be turned Wild, Beldon. It should not be able to happen to a vampire."

Lucien sighed and pushed his hair back from his forehead. "I'm not sure what to do. Someone is targeting the families that rule this city in a way that could put both humans and vampires in extraordinary danger if the culprit is not found. It must be someone in our circles if they managed to get close to Arthur Beldon and Leigh Harrows, but...I don't understand *why*. Why Wild turns? What's the message? And how do we stop it?"

Cyrus moved a step closer to him. "I think the research we've already been doing could answer all of that, too. If we can understand how Wild turns happen, we'll have a better idea of what sort of vampire would be powerful enough to do it, and if we can find a way to reverse those turns, we'll save people from the same fate as Arthur and Leigh. We'll find out who did this, Vista, and we'll stop them."

"You say that as if it won't be nigh impossible."

"If there's anything I've learned today, Vista, it's that *vampires* should be impossible. But that doesn't stop you from existing, does it? So why should impossible stop us from trying?"

Lucien considered him, his gaze contemplative. He gave a slight shake of his head. "You are infuriatingly optimistic."

That was far from how Cyrus would describe himself, but if that was what Lucien saw...There were worse ways to be perceived.

"It's refreshing," Lucien said softly.

Cyrus raised an eyebrow. "Not annoying?"

"Oh, I could list a hundred more things about you that *are* annoying. Your optimism is not one of them." A faint smile ticked the corner of Lucien's mouth. "Rather, it's a strength. I hope this mess we've uncovered doesn't kill it. Or you."

Yeah, Cyrus hoped that, too.

"But listen, Beldon, this changes things." Lucien paced toward Cyrus, circled around him, and then back toward the wall. "We may not have time to research as thoroughly as I hoped. You're right that our focus should remain on Wild vampires and their creation—their biology—but I fear that even my family's library does not contain the answers we need. I will pull everything I can from the shelves, but..." He paused beside Cyrus and met his eyes. "May I ask something risky of you?"

"This whole thing is risky," Cyrus said. "What's one more thing?"

Lucien nibbled his bottom lip. "It may do us well to consult *your* family's knowledge of Wild vampires."

Lucien looked as though he expected Cyrus to react harshly to the request, but Cyrus had already considered this. While the Vista family might have texts on the creation of Wild vampires, the Beldon family's collections would certainly have information on how to destroy them. No one—human or vampire—wanted Wild vampires running about, so for once the Beldon guides to killing monsters might come in handy.

And Cyrus had a perfectly good reason to be researching such a thing.

"Sure." He shrugged. "I can do that. I'll bring you everything I can find."

Lucien's relief was palpable. "Thank you. Oh— Here." He pulled something out of his pocket—an iron key dangling on a weathered leather cord—and offered it to Cyrus. "Take this. It unlocks the garden door that leads into the library, allowing you access when I cannot meet you. Just be careful."

Cyrus hesitantly took the key. The metal was coarse against his palm. "Is it really wise for me to poke around this place when you're not expecting me? What if someone else finds me?"

"That is why I will also give you this." He presented a small, shiny dagger with a polished wood hilt. He noticeably avoided touching the metal pommel—silver, undoubtedly. "Hopefully you do not have to use it."

Cyrus scowled at the weapon. He had an array of silver-bladed knives back home, but beyond that, this was a significant display of trust. A key to the house, and a means to harm anyone in it? The gesture made Cyrus uneasy.

He took a step back from Lucien, pocketing the key. "I think you forgot, Vista, that I don't suffer any shortage of silver weapons. Do you think I've been unarmed this whole time?"

Lucien hid his surprise well, but the subtle shift in his expression betrayed him. It pissed Cyrus off.

No, he didn't want the ruthless reputation that the rest of his family enjoyed. He didn't want to be seen only for the blades on his belt and the fury in his heart. He was more than that, but no one bothered to see it. Worse, people often wouldn't even consider him the bare minimum of a Beldon. *The youngest, smallest, weakest, kindest little Beldon can't even hold a knife.*

He was sick of being underestimated, and he hated that Lucien had thought of him the same way as everyone else. He snatched the knife from the back of his belt and lunged at the vampire, taking advantage of his lowered guard. Lucien reflexively dodged him, but Cyrus could tell he'd surprised him. Before Lucien could react, Cyrus threw himself at him again and slammed Lucien against the wall, knife across his throat.

To Cyrus's great satisfaction, Lucien stared back at him with unmasked shock. Cyrus knew he had very little leverage against this vampire, and if this was a real fight, Cyrus wouldn't stand a chance. But for this moment, he had the upper hand, and it felt goddamned *good*.

Lucien breathed a soft chuckle and slowly raised his hands at his sides. "Indeed, Beldon, I forgot who you were."

"This *isn't* who I am," Cyrus snarled back. He tightened his hand around the hilt of his dagger. "This is who the Beldons are. But you, like everyone else, assumed that since I don't act like the rest of them, I don't know what they know."

Lucien hummed. "I can safely say I won't make the same mistake again." His voice was a silvery murmur that only stoked Cyrus's anger. He wished Lucien would fight back. Struggle. Push him off. Anything. But he didn't so much as twitch when Cyrus slightly angled the blade against his throat. "Let me tell you a secret, Beldon."

Cyrus narrowed his eyes.

Abruptly, Lucien's hand closed around his throat. Cyrus gasped; his knife dropped involuntarily from his hand. Lucien grinned, fangs on full display, and squeezed just enough to make Cyrus wheeze. Bright, primal terror shot through him and rendered him frozen; his vision tunneled until all he saw were Lucien's fangs.

Lucien leaned in, lips nearly brushing his ear. "That little knife is nothing but a plaything. For each of your strengths, I have ten more. For each of my weaknesses, you have a hundred more. That's always been my favorite thing about humans, Beldon..." Lucien snaked his other arm around Cyrus's waist and slid his hand up his back, pulling him flush against his body. His voice dropped to a whisper, his breath a tickle below Cyrus's ear. "There are so many ways to take you apart."

Cyrus tried to jerk his head to loosen Lucien's grip, but Lucien didn't falter. Cyrus's breaths came short and quick, every second Lucien didn't let go edging him toward full panic. It occurred to him, faintly at the back of his reeling mind, that Lucien could very easily kill him and leave him here, and no one would know or care.

Just when Cyrus thought that was precisely the vampire's plan, Lucien huffed a mirthless chuckle and released him. Cyrus nearly collapsed onto him, but his last remaining thread of logic let him stumble back a few steps before he crumpled to his knees. He doubled over with his palms flat on the cold dirt floor, heaving in breath after shuddering breath. With shaking hands he reached up and clawed off his cravat, but even that didn't relieve the phantom pressure of Lucien's cold fingers.

In his periphery, Cyrus saw Lucien sink down to his level. He wordlessly offered Cyrus's dagger. "I respect you, Beldon, but we are not equals. Don't allow that ego of yours to let you forget that."

Cyrus gritted his teeth and glared at him. "You're a bastard, Lucien Vista."

He smirked. "You're too kind." He waved Cyrus's knife in the air. "Go on, take it, before I decide to keep it for my collection."

Cyrus snatched the knife and replaced it in its sheath on his belt as he shoved to his feet. He took another deep breath and straightened his shirt collar, but did not retie his cravat. He shoved the silk tie into his pocket instead and leveled Lucien with another glare. "Was that necessary?"

"You started it." Lucien arched an eyebrow. "I'm not entirely sure why, but if you find me that irresistible, there are nicer ways to get your hands on me."

Cyrus sputtered a scoff. Against his will, his face turned hot.

"Fuck off, Vista. I'm leaving. You may or may not see me tomorrow."

He stalked across the room toward the stairs, grateful there was at least some light now so he didn't trip his way up only to tumble back down. He made it up four stairs before Lucien called his surname.

Reluctantly, he turned his head. Lucien stood in front of the torch; its light illuminated his silhouette like some kind of divine apparition. His face was shadowed, but his eyes glowed.

"What?" Cyrus prompted.

"Don't forget the books," Lucien said, "when you come back tomorrow."

Cyrus scowled and stomped up the rest of the stairs. Hadn't he *just* said... Oh, but he knew, though he loathed to admit it, that he *would* trudge his way back here tomorrow regardless of Lucien's taunts and jabs and infuriating smugness. And Lucien knew it too, and Cyrus hated him for it.

Irresistible. As if.

At the top of the stairs, he slammed the secret door on his way out.

Chapter ELEVEN

MORNING CAME FAR TOO SOON GIVEN HOW LATE IT HAD been when Cyrus had returned home last night, but he woke up still pissed at Lucien and therefore did not mind throwing himself into a sparring match with Joel first thing after breakfast. For once in his life, Cyrus was ready for a fight; he wanted to hit something, and a burlap dummy wouldn't cut it.

Heavy rain soaked the city this morning, so Cyrus and Joel brought their spar to the indoor training room. "You're energetic today," Joel commented as he dodged a swipe from Cyrus's dagger. Unlike Arthur, Joel normally sparred fair, so he danced around Cyrus with a dagger of his own. Though while Cyrus was already winded and sweating, Joel hardly seemed affected.

Cyrus wasn't here to talk. He paused a second and swept his arm across his forehead and pushed back his hair before lunging at his brother again. Joel retaliated almost lazily, as if he was fighting a child. It reminded him of how easily Lucien had bested him yesterday.

A fresh churn of anger boiled within him at the thought of the vampire, and he struck at his brother with renewed fury. He caught a blink of surprise on Joel's face as his effort doubled, and *now* Joel seemed interested in their fight. He moved quicker, struck back stronger, and Cyrus matched it. Sand shifted beneath his feet with each step and pivot, and Cyrus lost awareness of everything outside of his tight focus. The dagger became an extension of his hand, striking hard and true against Joel's own blade.

"You're pretty good with that little knife," Joel said, spinning out of Cyrus's reach. "You'd be good with a sword, too, if you'd ever bother to pick one up."

Cyrus grunted in reply and made a stab at Joel's side; Joel only barely twisted his slender form out of the way. But as he turned to retaliate, Cyrus took advantage of his open guard and slammed the hilt of his dagger into Joel's ribs. Joel swore and stumbled backward, and Cyrus kicked his ankle and put him flat on the ground before he knew what'd hit him.

Then he backed off, letting both of them catch their breaths. Joel stared up at him with genuine shock. "Nicely done, Cyrus."

Cyrus grinned, running his hands through his hair. He pulled off his shirt and pressed his face into it to dry the sweat, but he found the fabric already damp. He tossed it to the ground and tipped his head back, closing his eyes to relish his victory. His body felt worn out, but in a satisfied way. This was far better than limping out of this room sore and bruised.

"I have to say, you've gotten stronger." Joel got up and brushed sand off his clothes. "Have you been practicing?"

Cyrus retrieved his dagger from the ground and sheathed it on his belt. No, he hadn't been practicing outside of regular training, but he never put this much real effort into a fight. He faked it until one of his siblings beat him, and then he quit.

"No," he told Joel. "But you don't normally catch me on a day when I *want* to spar."

"Are you...upset about something?" Joel eyed him curiously, without apparent judgment, but Cyrus didn't trust it.

"No. Why?"

"The way you fought just now—you were angry. I could tell by the way you moved and the strength of your strikes." Joel shrugged. "You don't have to tell me, but, you know...you *can*. Or if you need an outlet, we can always do this again."

He offered a smile and a nod, then strolled out of the sand pit and headed for the changing rooms.

Cyrus stared down at the sand and wondered when his siblings had actually started caring about him.

AFTER HE'D BATHED the sand and sweat from his body and eaten another meal, Cyrus went into the family library. He strode past all of the displayed weapons and vampire skulls, bypassed all the most commonly referenced sections, and found his way to the far reaches where even the light didn't venture. He returned to the cozy corner where he and Poppy had pored over that first unbelievable image of a Wild vampire and found that very book tucked on a nearby shelf. It was out of place, as if someone had shoved it there just to put it out of obvious sight, but it stood out at once to Cyrus. The numbers on the label pasted to the lower spine weren't even close to the rest of the books around it; Cyrus wondered if Poppy had done this on purpose, knowing Cyrus would wander back here to find it.

He carried the book to the other side of the sprawling library, where others of its subject were shelved. Amid centuries of vampire folklore, history, and even literature, the Beldons kept a robust collection on the monstrosity of vampires. Much of it was likely exaggerated, which dampened Cyrus's spirits a little, but with accurate information to back him up, even superstitions could lead him toward a truth.

He selected four more texts that seemed promising, then retreated back to the singular comfortable spot in the library and hunkered down.

Lucien was probably already expecting him at the Vista manor, but Cyrus didn't care. He'd set Cyrus in search of this information, anyway, so he could wait. Cyrus was in no hurry to see his smug face.

Taking his anger out on Joel had helped, but Cyrus was still pissed about yesterday. He couldn't articulate why, of all the ways Lucien got on his nerves, *this* had his feathers particularly ruffled, but their little wrestle had felt more personally insulting than every snarky comment Lucien had made. The obvious, unapologetic, arrogant display of the strength and power Lucien had over Cyrus cut deep into his bones. Maybe it was because it had been so easy to forget these past several days that Lucien was something dangerous, something Cyrus had been taught to fear and fight and kill. Cyrus had unconsciously separated Lucien in his mind from all other vampires, and that vivid reminder of *what* Lucien was had shattered Cyrus's comfortable perception of him.

He could not make that mistake again. He trusted Lucien more than he'd trust any other vampire on earth, but that didn't make Lucien human. And certainly not his equal.

Lucien was his better—socially and physically—and *that* angered him.

Cyrus shoved the vampire out of mind and spread the books out on the table before him. He started with the one Poppy had found after Arthur had been turned, and flipped until he found the illustration of the Wild vampire. Now, having seen the monster firsthand, Cyrus couldn't believe he'd scoffed at it. It was the stuff of nightmares, but it was an accurate representation. Even the one in the book from Lucien's collection had been a tame likeness compared to this.

Cyrus started reading. At once, this text took on a vastly different tone than the book from House Vista. This book didn't shy away from the discussion of Wild vampires; it was detailed, to-the-point, with a dead serious voice behind the words that all but threatened the reader. By the time Cyrus had finished a passage detailing all the horrid ways a Wild vampire could kill, maim, mutilate, and devour a human, he had curled himself into his chair with a nauseous pit in his stomach and a prickling feeling that he was being watched.

Between this text and the one from the Vista manor, Cyrus gleaned the basics: Wild vampires were created when a human was violently turned, against their will, and then left to suffer the transformation without care. Something went wrong during the process, and instead of a peaceful pass from one stage to the next, only the victim's fear and rage fueled the change.

(Cyrus couldn't imagine the process of becoming a vampire being peaceful at all, but clearly most people didn't or couldn't resist, otherwise the world would be overrun with Wild vampires.)

Vampires, like humans, were nuanced beings of myriad elements that made up their minds and bodies, but when only a select few primal instincts—such as fear and hate—existed at the time of transformation, the victim lost all other senses and feelings. Just like an abused dog knew only how to bite and knew nothing of a gentle touch, Wild vampires knew only violence and destruction. They craved blood to a maddening degree, and without the intelligence of a normal vampire, their hunger boiled down to an animalistic instinct to hunt and kill and eat anything that smelled like a meal.

So it was something to do with their brain functions, Cyrus concluded. The transformation failed. That made sense, but Cyrus needed something deeper. *How* did it go wrong? *What* went wrong, on a biological level? Even if Cyrus couldn't get his brain to bend around the science aspect, Lucien certainly could. If he'd filled a book with notes on how to reverse a vampiric transformation, clearly he was knowledgeable in this field. Cyrus was admittedly curious about that side of him; he wanted to hear what Lucien knew, even if he'd understand only a fraction of it.

Cyrus set the book aside and turned to the next one. This was an older edition of the text from which Cyrus and his siblings had learned nearly all of their vampire knowledge; it was anatomy, but from a killer's perspective rather than a healer's. Cyrus scanned the table of contents, faintly marveling at how much more information was in the updated text he'd yawned his way through as a teenager. He flipped forward until he found a chapter on vampiric anomalies, but it boasted only a small paragraph on Wild vampires and it didn't give him more than he already knew: stab it through the heart, sever the head with a silver blade, then burn the body so it could not rise again.

The book made it sound easy, no different than eliminating a normal vampire, which made Cyrus suspect that these authors had never actually faced a Wild vampire. He wondered if the updated version would be more helpful, assuming he could find it in his room.

He pinned the thought and delved into the third book he'd pulled, but found it written in a language he didn't know. Useless. He closed it and stacked it with the outdated text, then slid both of those back in their places on the shelf and took the one winning book with him out of the library.

The house was quiet as Cyrus made his way through the marble halls toward his room. Though all the curtains were open, the cloudy sky outside offered little light; rain pattered the windowpanes, and thunder rumbled distantly. The halls dragged the outside's gloom indoors; the flickering candelabras in their niches along the walls did little to warm the echoing spaces.

As Cyrus headed toward the stairs, it occurred to him that he should check on Poppy to see how she was doing, yet something held him back. Everyone in this house was highly perceptive, but Poppy was uniquely perceptive of Cyrus. He didn't know how she had such a keen sense of what was going on behind his eyes, but she could read him like a book and it made him nervous to talk to her when there was so much he had to hide. He couldn't risk having her dig all these secrets out of him. Not until he knew more, anyway.

He bypassed the way toward the infirmary and continued to his room. Poppy was at least out of the woods now, and if she took a sudden turn for the worse, someone would tell him.

He turned down the hall leading to his room only for a voice to stop him in his tracks. Soft, silvery, melodic, and almost familiar, it called his name in a gentle, beckoning way. Unlike how Cyrus usually heard his name in this house, it was not a warning or a reprimand; he turned around.

The sound had come from somewhere behind him and to his right, but all that was there was a wall and a window.

Maybe this was his brain telling him he needed to get more sleep.

He started to turn back around, but then he heard it again, louder: *Cyrus. I'm here.*

Okay, that was undeniable. Heart in his throat, he approached the window and slowly pulled the curtain aside.

A face in the glass stared back at him with wide green eyes.

He jumped back at the same moment he realized it was his own reflection. Annoyed at himself, he let the curtain fall back into place and turned on his heel.

A gust of frigid wind hit him in the back.

"What the fuck—" Cyrus spun around, gooseflesh prickling his arms. He was alone, yet he *knew*, despite his eyes, that he wasn't. Something else was here, but...But that was absurd. For all he spoke of ghosts in these halls, he didn't *actually* think the Beldon manor was haunted.

He tucked his arms across his chest and slowly approached the window again. *Cyrus.* The voice whispered in his ears. *Cyrus.* The hair on the back of his neck tingled, and when he pulled the curtain aside again he swore he glimpsed a humanoid shape behind him. But a blink dispelled the vision, and he instead looked out at the opposite wing of the house and the old tower behind it.

Cyrus. The soft syllables of his name were whispers on the wind, rustles through the trees. The yellow and orange leaves surrounding the ivy-choked tower swayed and waved, as if beckoning him there.

But...why there? A memory tickled the back of his mind—a flash of a place he knew he'd never seen. He ascended a spiraling stone staircase, chasing a light that never drew closer while a soft voice called him forward.

But he'd never been in that tower. No one was allowed up there except for Marcus, and Cyrus didn't even think there was a safe way to enter the crumbling structure. If there was anything at all in there other than rats and birds, what did it have to do with him?

Cyrus. And yet, it called him.

Movement behind him flicked his attention back to the present, and he stepped away from the window just in time to glimpse Emerson exiting a room at the far end of the connecting hall, Joel trailing after him. Neither glanced Cyrus's way, but the easy way Joel strolled beside their uncle, and the calm expression on Emerson's face, made Cyrus's stomach churn with envy.

He told himself every day that he didn't care what everyone else in this house thought of him, but he could say it a million times and that wouldn't make it true. He did care, and he didn't understand why nothing he did ever seemed to be enough. Marcus, Emerson, and Arthur all seemed to hate Cyrus on principle, for simply existing, as if that was Cyrus's fault. As if he'd begged and pleaded to be sheltered under this roof.

Why couldn't any of them just give him a chance?

He glanced back at the window and met his own eyes in his reflection, and then let his gaze fall to the book tucked under his arm. Clenching his jaw, he held the book tighter and strode toward his room. He didn't have time to wallow over his place in his family. Maybe, if he succeeded with this project, they'd see him.

Or maybe by the end of it, none of that would matter at all.

Cyrus closed himself into his room and dropped the book on the chair by the fireplace, then went to his bed. The small bookcase that served as his bedside table was packed beyond capacity with more volumes than it could hold, and Cyrus glanced over them even though he knew he wouldn't have shoved the textbook there. He spotted several journals he'd abandoned after only using a few pages, and novels he'd started but never finished. Many still had bookmarks tucked in the spot where he'd stopped, holding a place he'd likely never return to.

He kicked a blanket and an old pair of shoes out of the way, then dropped to his knees and pressed his face to the wood floor to peer beneath the bed. Decidedly not thinking about all the spiders that had probably taken up residence under there, he shoved his arm as far as it would go and felt around until he found something book-shaped. He dragged it out along with a truly impressive clump of dust and hair, and blew yet more dust off the leather cover. Sure enough, it was his old textbook.

That he was now going to use it to help vampires rather than kill them was a poetic sort of irony.

Cyrus grabbed a satchel, tucked both books into it, then thought again and grabbed the novel he was nearly finished with and brought that along too. He slung the bag over his shoulder and headed down the back stairs, out of the house and into the gardens.

He couldn't help but think, as he crossed the sprawling expanse of muddy green, that the Vista manor's gardens were far more impressive than these empty acres. The flora there grew wildly, mixing and mingling and climbing up the flowering trees that likely bloomed in the spring. The roses reigned over the gravel paths and marble statues, whereas here, the flowers cowered. They huddled close to the house, and every attempt they made to climb toward the windows was cut down. They were kept neat and orderly, not a leaf or weed out of place. Even at their peak bloom, it all looked so...artificial.

Cyrus followed the path back to the stables and led Demeter out once more, then rode across the city to the forest road. The day waned steadily toward evening, but Lucien *had* told Cyrus he could come and go as he pleased.

He hopped down from the saddle at the end of the cobblestone path, but decided to bring Demeter onto the grounds rather than leave her on the road. He approached the carriage house, then noticed a stable on the far side of the building and brought her there. The other horses—six shiny black stallions and a pure white one with unsettlingly blue eyes—perked their ears forward and eyed Demeter with suspicion. She snorted, resisting as Cyrus led her toward an empty stall, but he nabbed an apple from a basket by the door and Demeter made no further complaints. He left her with a pat on the side, then wove his way across the garden to find the back door.

The grounds of House Vista were their own forest. A long, sloping hill brought the land farther back into the dense trees; distantly, Cyrus could hear a trickling creek. Topiaries fashioned into various animals—a pegasus here, a lion there—watched over the garden alongside statues of people in graceful poses, sculpted robes falling artfully off of white shoulders. Slumbering rose bushes crowded the space, and Cyrus had to take care not to get his hair tangled in the thorny branches wound around the arbors that straddled the path. Old, gnarled trees shaded the space and whispered with the cool breeze that meandered through. Cyrus found himself longing to see this place in its blooming season.

Yet the sight of the Vista manor looming overhead still filled him with trepidation. The gardens might feel like a comfortable haven, but pretty flowers didn't make this place less dangerous. They all had thorns, after all.

He found the door Lucien had brought him through before and fished the key out from beneath his shirt. He fit it into the lock and wiggled it until the ancient mechanism clicked open, then glanced warily over his shoulder before sliding into the dark.

Clinging to the wall, he carefully felt his way up the steps and into the hallway, where there was at least a little more light. "Goddamned vampires," he muttered as he scurried into the library. Didn't they get sick of the dark? Didn't they get depressed when they didn't see the sun? Cyrus couldn't imagine living in shadows. He was certainly no creature of the night.

He slowed his pace as he ventured deeper into the library, now less worried that he'd be seen. With Lucien guiding him each previous time he'd been in here, he hadn't had a chance to truly take in the grandeur of this place. It welcomed him back as if he was a long lost friend, as if he was part of it, somehow. Strange. Frightening, even. But nonetheless the feeling was true.

Cyrus wandered his way to the far reaches of the library's first level, then found the stairs and went up a floor. There he spotted a cozy lounge surrounding a massive fireplace, the mantel of which displayed delicate glass figurines positioned around an antique clock. A bouquet of dried black roses centered the coffee table that stood angled between the chairs and the loveseat gathered around the fireplace; the flowers still retained their velvety scent.

He dropped his satchel on one of the chairs, intending to park himself there for the rest of the day and let Lucien find him, but a faint note of music made him look up. Far across the room, golden light spilled into the stacks through a half-open door, and from beyond, a gentle melody floated.

Curious, he approached the door. He nudged it open just enough to slip through, and stepped into a bright mezzanine with just two cushioned seats nestled together. Cyrus went to the balcony railing, and his breath caught.

Below, a shiny black piano stood proudly in the center of the cavernous room. Tall, uncovered windows poured sunlight across the gold-laced marble floor, and the high ceiling amplified each sweet note that rang from the piano. Seated at the keys was a familiar silver-haired vampire.

Cyrus barely dared breathe lest Lucien notice his presence. He edged away from the balcony just enough to be out of easy sight, but not so far that he couldn't see. Lucien had his back to the windows and was facing Cyrus, but the piano partially obscured him. At this distance, Cyrus couldn't see the minute details of his serene expression, but even still, there was no doubting his concentration. He played with his eyes closed, slender hands gliding expertly over the keys while his lips moved with an accompanying murmur. Bold, crisp notes rang from the lower end of the scale, and as Lucien moved gradually up the bars, his expression softened with the music. With a delicate chime, the notes slowed and tapered off, and a peaceful smile smoothed across Lucien's face.

Cyrus could have stayed there forever, hidden in the solitary embrace of that cozy mezzanine, but he took his cue to flee before Lucien opened his eyes.

When he stepped back into the comparatively dark library, he felt like part of him was still in that bright room. He couldn't put his finger on it, but he understood something more about Lucien now, even though the two of them hadn't exchanged so much as a glance.

He went back to the lounge in a daze, feeling like he'd just woken up from a dream.

He slumped into one of the chairs and pulled one of the books from his bag, but couldn't bring himself to open it. He stared at the clock on the mantel and watched the hands steadily tick.

Eight minutes went by, and then Lucien found him.

"Ah, hello." Lucien gracefully sank onto the chair beside Cyrus. He was dressed more casually than Cyrus had yet seen him; his silk shirt, tucked neatly into high-waisted trousers, wasn't restrained by the vest he typically wore, nor did he have a tie or cravat around his collar. His hair was pulled back in a long tail that rested loosely on his shoulder, though a few flyaway pieces still framed his face. "How long have you been here?"

Cyrus debated mentioning the piano, but decided against it. Let that remain a private moment—for both of them. "Not long," he said. "I had a lot to do at home this morning, but..." He tugged the textbook out of his bag and passed it to Lucien. "I brought this."

Lucien's brow twitched at the dusty, neglected state of the book, and then his eyes widened when he opened it and saw the title. His gaze flicked up to Cyrus. "This is..."

"The tool of the trade," Cyrus said, grimacing. He smothered a spike of anxiety that he'd made a terrible mistake by giving this book to an Honorable One. "Everything I know about hunting vampires started with this book. It goes into far more details about

Wild vampires than the texts I found here the other day, and I think I have a better understanding now, but I'm still getting stuck on the science." He tapped his fingernails on the cover of the book on his lap. "I'm hoping you can put the biological pieces together."

Lucien nodded and paged through the book in silence. Cyrus anxiously bounced his foot. As minutes dragged by, Lucien's expression grew darker and darker until finally he shut the book with a snap and spread his hand across his forehead.

For several heartbeats, he didn't move. Cyrus didn't dare speak. It would be stupid to ask what was wrong; Lucien held in his hands a step-by-step guide to killing others like him—a guide that had been passed down for generations in a family who made it their duty and their livelihood to follow these instructions to the letter.

This was information that, at an extreme scale, could wipe vampires out of existence. Cyrus suddenly felt ill that it had for so long been in Beldon hands.

Finally, he decided to voice the only appropriate thing to say. "I'm sorry."

It was several more minutes before Lucien responded, and even still, he did not look up or lower his hand. "We really are just brainless monsters to you, aren't we? Not even people. Just...*things*. Lesser than animals."

Cyrus didn't know what to say. To confirm Lucien's words felt too harsh, even if it was true. The Beldon family played nice with the Honorable Families in order to avoid mutual destruction; the peace was fragile at best, especially now, but that peace was never because of actual respect between humans and vampires. Rather, it stemmed from a deep-rooted fear of the worse alternative to being diplomatic with the most powerful vampires in the region.

Lucien went on before Cyrus could conjure any words. "I'm a *living person*. Do you—Do any of the hunters even understand that? Do you look at me and see another living being?" He shook his head. "I have been alive for over a century. I've seen this city at its worst and at its best. I've watched generations of people around me age and die. I feel love and hate and joy and sadness and fear and pain and anger and everything else. I'm not—I'm not some mindless beast that only exists to be hunted and killed. I want to *live*." His voice cracked and his throat worked as he swallowed. He spoke into his hand, still not turning his gaze toward Cyrus. "I want to be alive as much as you do. Why should only you deserve it?

"This can't be all there is." He lowered his voice to a murmur. "I've worked for so long to think of a way that we can both exist in this world without bloodshed, but will it ever be worth it? I could live forever, Beldon, and I'm not sure I'd see it come to fruition."

Cyrus resisted an impulse to reach over and touch Lucien's arm. He couldn't think of a single comforting word that would lighten Lucien's hopelessness; he felt it, too. He'd had the optimism beaten out of him long ago, and anytime it started to crawl back, this bleak reality screamed louder. This work he was beginning with Lucien was the first real sense of hope he'd felt in his whole life.

He remembered what Leif had told him, when Cyrus had wound up with a book from this house in his hands: *This is a precipice.*

"Vista," Cyrus said softly, "if there's ever a time to not give up, I think it's now."

Lucien glanced at him, and where Cyrus expected to see doubt, he found that same faint hope. That quivering, hesitant, fledgling hope—and the trust that came with it.

"I don't think we can fix everything," Cyrus went on. "But I think we can do *something*. I came to you saying that I wanted to be a different Beldon than all those before me, and I think I understand now why you listened to me."

"Oh?"

"I think it's because you want the same thing." Cyrus held his gaze. "I think you want to be a different Vista."

Lucien studied him inscrutably for a moment, then nodded once. His gaze fell to the book on his lap; he dropped it onto the table with a sigh. "Yes. And in my strongest moments, I do believe that we can do something. That we can be different, that we can change even one person's mind. But then I see this..." He eyed the book with disgust. "And it's like looking at my own death sentence, Cyrus."

Cyrus suppressed a shiver, caught off guard by Lucien's use of his first name. It was a sigh through his teeth, a whisper under his breath. Cyrus suddenly longed to hear it again.

He shoved that thought away. "I-I'm sorry," he stammered. "I didn't mean to upset you by bringing that. Maybe I shouldn't have—"

"No, I'm glad you did." Lucien sat back in his chair and turned sideways, draping his legs over the arm. "You're right that it could lend us some useful information, but in the interest of preserving my own sanity, I don't wish to read a single page of it. Tell me what you learned from it that will help us."

So Cyrus told him. He opened his notes alongside the book and went through everything he'd thought was relevant, while Lucien nodded along with interest. In the back of his mind, Cyrus marveled at the vampire's rapt attention; he didn't interrupt, and only asked a few clarifying questions that prompted Cyrus to elaborate. Gone was the mockery that had laced their previous interactions, and Cyrus realized that Lucien was now treating him more like an equal, worthy of his respect and attention.

If it had been that glimpse of the Beldons' knowledge of killing vampires that made Lucien finally look at him seriously, he had no choice but to be grateful for it, even if he regretted how it had to be done.

They talked, theorized, and read for the rest of the day. Cyrus's brain felt like a beehive—crowded and buzzing, humming with new information and ideas about vampires, Wild and otherwise. Lucien had done his best to explain the biology to Cyrus, but even he'd admitted the gaps in his knowledge. Little was known in general about how turns failed, which prompted the next step in their research.

Cyrus only became aware of how much time had passed when

his stomach twisted with an unhappy growl, and he realized he hadn't eaten since this morning.

Lucien glanced his way with a knowing smile. "Is it time to call it a night?"

Cyrus folded his arms across his middle. "I'm fine. Has that book offered anything helpful? I didn't look through much of it earlier."

"Don't change the subject." Lucien stuck his page of notes into the book and closed it. "I could eat, too. If you'll stick around a little while longer, I can prepare something."

Cyrus didn't know what sort of meal would be prepared in an Honorable Family's house, and he wasn't sure he wanted to find out. "Don't trouble yourself, Vista, really. Being a little hungry won't kill me. I don't want to inconvenience you more than I already have."

"Nonsense." Lucien unfolded himself from his chair and stood up, placing the book on the table with the others. "I insist. And before you fling another excuse at me, I promise, no one will suspect anything. I cook for guests often. Sit tight."

He slipped away before Cyrus could argue again.

Cyrus only *sat tight* for about a minute before his nerves got the better of him and he got up. He couldn't say why the idea of Lucien feeding him—*cooking* for him—had him more on edge than anything else about being here, but he suddenly felt like a caged animal. There was something different about this. Something gentle, hospitable, kind, even...*domestic*, and Cyrus didn't know what to do with it.

I cook for guests often. When had Cyrus become a guest rather than a stranger? No, he didn't want to stay on unsteady terms with Lucien, but now that they seemed to be leaving that vaguely antagonistic tension behind for something softer, Cyrus panicked.

He wasn't even supposed to be here. He was *absolutely* not supposed to be anything close to *friends* with an Honorable One.

He must have finally lost his mind for real.

Cyrus gripped the fireplace mantel and stared into the antique clock's face and told himself it wasn't that big of a deal. No one knew he was here, and no one was going to find out what he was doing here. As long as he avoided talking to his family—which he already did anyway—he was safe, and so was Lucien.

He didn't know when, exactly, he'd started caring about Lucien's safety, but that was beside the point.

"Beldon?"

He whipped around, startled by Lucien's soundless return. The vampire waited by the stairs with a sort of casual calmness that set Cyrus *more* on edge. How could he be so normal about this?

"Sorry," Cyrus breathed, and started to gather up the books, but Lucien waved a hand.

"You can leave them here. We'll come back for them after we eat."

Cyrus glanced at his family's textbook, lying plainly there for all to see, and shoved it into his satchel to at least get it out of sight. He met Lucien at the stairs, but instead of going back down, Lucien led him across the room, past the door to the mezzanine, and up a secluded staircase to the third floor. There, they followed the aisle of bookcases to the front end of the library and passed through a set of oak doors, leaving the library behind.

Where are you taking me? Cyrus wondered, but did not ask. He'd partially expected Lucien to bring their meal to the library, but no, knowing the care Lucien took to keep the place organized, he would never risk anything getting spilled on the books. Cyrus gained several levels of respect for him in that regard; reverence for books was a distinctly positive trait in his eyes.

So what would it be, then, a meal in the family's dining hall? How was that anything but a supremely stupid idea? Cyrus might be a guest to Lucien, but he was certainly no welcome visitor to the rest of the family.

He glanced around the vast, silent halls as they walked, distracting his worries by studying the faded tapestries. Despite all his reading, he didn't recognize any of the myths portrayed, and his mind wandered all too quickly. His anxiety rose higher with each step down the long corridor.

Finally, they reached the end of the hall and Lucien paused at a tall, white door with scarlet decorations. "Right, here we are." He glanced at Cyrus, then frowned. "What's wrong?"

Cyrus hadn't realized his uneasy mood was reflected so plainly on his face, but as long as Lucien was asking... "Well, to be frank, Vista, I don't trust a single person in this place other than you, and you just led me straight across your entire house as if begging the rest of your family to catch a glimpse."

"And we didn't encounter anyone, did we?" Lucien gave a placating smile. "I brought you down one hallway, Beldon, don't be dramatic. And I'll remind you that if anyone else discovered you here, it would surely be worse for me than for you. I don't wish to risk that for either of us. Come on and eat, before you entirely lose your wits."

Cyrus grumbled to himself and followed Lucien through the door. He faintly thought, as he shut it behind him, that this was an odd place for a dining room, and then his brain flung away any further thoughts when he turned around.

He froze, dead in his tracks, at the sight of what was very obviously Lucien's private chambers.

Three core Beldon rules drummed through his head:

Never meet them in their own territory.
Never let yourself be fooled by their charm.
Never let them lure you to a private space.

Cyrus's eyes darted wildly around the room, from the set tea table by the fireplace to the open bedchamber door to his left. Oh gods, *he* was the meal, wasn't he? Of course, *of course* the past days had only been a ruse to gain his trust and lower his guard, of course Lucien's friendliness today was only a game so he could lure Cyrus in, just like he'd always been warned, and—

Sharp, primal terror gripped him around the throat. He backed himself against the door and clasped his hand over his neck. When Lucien turned to him, Cyrus saw a flash of something predatory in his blood-red eyes, and a glimpse of those deadly fangs behind his lips. He saw those teeth gouging his throat, ripping the very life from him in the same way the Harrows vampire had done to Arthur.

His hand fell, shaking, to the door handle even as he knew beyond a doubt he would never be able to run fast enough.

"*Cyrus.*"

He gasped. The fog encroaching around the edges of his vision cleared. His pulse abruptly dropped its ringing adrenaline and instead beat a steady, slowing *thump, thump, thump.* He took in an unsteady breath and looked—*actually* looked—at Lucien.

He couldn't describe what he saw in the vampire's expression; it was there and gone in a heartbeat. Lucien quickly replaced it with a smile, but it was noticeably more forced now—far less genuine than the calm expression he'd worn just minutes ago in the library.

Cyrus had a sick feeling that he'd just shredded something between them that had only just begun to entwine.

Ducking his head, he joined Lucien in the sitting area before the fireplace. A crystal decanter filled with a rich, red liquid sat at the center of the table, one glass for each of them positioned beside places set with elegant dinnerware. Lucien invited Cyrus to sit, then he took the adjacent chair. He picked up and rang a little brass bell, and in moments a servant came in and set three covered platters on the table. Lucien thanked the man, and he scurried out.

Cyrus stared at the plates of food, stomach in knots. The savory smells made him nauseous.

Lucien did not make any move toward the feast. "Are we going to talk about what just happened?"

Cyrus didn't want to, but he couldn't stand the idea of eating in tense silence after the surprisingly pleasant afternoon the two of them had had.

Also, he owed Lucien a *strong* explanation.

"That..." He cleared his throat and made himself meet Lucien's eyes. "That was what two decades of Beldon training does to you.

I...I can't explain it any better than that. That was something deeper than fight-or-flight. That was a...a terrified certainty that I was about to die." Cyrus tore his gaze away from Lucien and set his head in his hands. "And it was entirely involuntary."

Lucien didn't say anything for a long minute, and when he did, his voice was a hush. "Are you afraid of me, Cyrus Beldon?"

"No." That was the rational truth. "But something deep inside me, the part that has been conditioned to fear and hate vampires, knows that you could end my life with very little effort. *That* part... fears you."

And that wasn't going to stop being true even as Cyrus gradually grew to trust Lucien. Even if Lucien wasn't a danger to him, that was not the same of all vampires. He *needed* to maintain a healthy fear of them, but at the moment he loathed himself for it.

He looked up again. "Lucien, I'm sorry. You have shown me nothing but respect and hospitality—I daresay even kindness—and I have no real reason to fear you. I...don't want to fear you."

"Likewise." Lucien nodded once. "I don't wish to give you any reason to fear me." A sly smile snaked across his lips. "Except for when you try to best me with a knife."

Cyrus chuckled, mostly out of relief at the break in tension. "Oh, no, I won't make that mistake again."

"On the contrary, I hope you do."

Why, Cyrus wondered, *so you can get your hands on me again? So you can nearly strangle me again?* He shot Lucien an incredulous look; Lucien flashed a smile in return, and then turned his attention to the feast.

He stood from his seat and lifted the lid off one of the platters, revealing a circular dish of roasted vegetables. The next plate bore an entire fowl, dusted with spices and drizzled with honey, and the next displayed a circle of tiny meat pies. Lucien plucked a white cloth off of a small basket nestled with a loaf of freshly sliced bread.

Cyrus's mouth watered. Nausea forgotten, his stomach made a loud groan.

Lucien flicked a smirk at him, then took his plate and selected a serving of everything from the table. Once heaped with food, he set it before Cyrus and prepared his own plate, then resumed his seat and at once grabbed his fork. When Cyrus didn't move to do the same, Lucien waved the utensil at him encouragingly.

"Go on, then. Or is something wrong?"

"Er—No! No, not at all." Warmth crept up the back of his neck. He spread the cloth napkin out on his lap and fiddled with the fork beside his plate. He was starving, and this food looked incredible, but he couldn't get over how odd all of this was. Maybe he was still in that dream that had begun in the mezzanine earlier.

He finally collected a coherent thought and looked up at Lucien. "You made all this?"

"Some of it." Lucien dug into a meat pie and ate a bite. "I prepared it earlier today and then told the cooks when I wanted it ready. Why?"

Cyrus glanced down at his plate. "This...was clearly planned for two."

"I anticipated your stay." Lucien shrugged as if that was normal. "I wouldn't be very hospitable if I didn't offer you dinner after we worked all day."

Cyrus chose not to reflect on that. "I thought you—I thought vampires didn't need to...eat...like this."

"Strictly speaking, we don't." He took another bite from his plate. "But I would argue that many things are often done for pleasure rather than purpose. It all still tastes good, even if I get no nutrition from it." He reached for the decanter and filled the glass in front of him, then turned to Cyrus expectantly. "A drink, Beldon?"

Now he was toying with him, Cyrus was sure of it. "I'm, uh... I'm good. Thank you." He finally dug into his food, and found the fowl—pheasant, he thought—to be tender and flavorful. Something spicy tickled his tastebuds, which he tried to alleviate by taking a bite of vegetables, but whatever seasoned the pheasant was also on those, and Cyrus soon found himself desperate for cold water. He set his silverware down and pressed the napkin to his mouth in a vain attempt to relieve the burning sensation on his lips.

"Is everything to your liking, Beldon?"

Cyrus sniffed and dropped the cloth back onto his lap. "It is. Everything's delicious. Er...I have to ask, what's on the pheasant?"

"The spices? A pinch of many things, but primarily paprika." Lucien chewed thoughtfully. "A favorite flavor of mine."

You can't have garlic but you can tolerate this? Vampires were a marvel.

Feigning fullness while his mouth was still cooling down, Cyrus leaned back in his chair and dredged up an earlier topic. "Not that this makes for pleasant dinner conversation, but I'm thinking about what you told me about the changes that make someone a vampire. If it's a full physical and biological transformation, done by replacing human blood with vampire blood, then how did that man I spoke to *reverse* the process? Wouldn't the victim need to regain all of their human blood for it to work? That doesn't even seem possible."

"It's not," Lucien said, slicing into the piece of pheasant on his plate. "Or rather, it *shouldn't* be. To try and reverse a turn should do you as much good as stuffing a butterfly back into the chrysalis and expecting it to revert to being a caterpillar. My theories and experiments were meant to save someone from turning Wild. *Not* from becoming a vampire at all. That someone claims to have fully reversed a turn...concerns me deeply. I fear for what he did to the poor soul who found themselves upon his operating table."

Cyrus grimaced. "I didn't think of it that way. So...vampirism isn't a curse, then, is it? It's just a different sort of life."

Lucien smiled. "Precisely."

He lifted his glass and drank deeply, and perhaps it was a trick of the scarce light, but Cyrus thought his lips looked darker—redder—when he lowered the cup. "If I can retrace my steps through those experiments and find the pieces I was missing before, we may have our solution to this Wild vampire problem. But I fear that in order to fill in the blanks, I'll have to seek help from someone...risky."

Cyrus frowned. "Your father?"

"Oh, no, I *wish* it was my father." Lucien took another sip of his drink. "No, this is someone notorious among the Honorable Families. She—"

A slammed door out in the hallway snapped off the end of Lucien's sentence. He jerked his head toward the door, and Cyrus tensed, ready to jump up and hide, but then Lucien's expression went blank with cold, vivid terror.

A heartbeat later, Cyrus heard screaming.

Chapter TWELVE

CYRUS EXCHANGED AN ALARMED GLANCE WITH LUCIEN, who immediately darted to his feet and went to the door before Cyrus could even think to stop him. He reached for the handle, but froze as another shriek pierced the air.

"Vista," Cyrus whispered; the syllables caught in his throat. He rose from his chair slowly, stiffly. His pulse thumped in his ears. From the hallway, he heard pounding footsteps, shouts, and agonized cries. Things crashed and shattered; muffled voices called to each other.

He didn't want to think it, and he certainly didn't want to be right. But there was only one thing that could be happening out there, and Cyrus didn't need to see any blood or swords to prove it.

Another door slammed, too close. Lucien jumped, then twisted the lock on the doorknob and strode toward Cyrus, grabbing his arm and dragging him across the room. Cyrus had no choice but to stumble after him; Lucien hauled him into his bedchamber, shut that door and locked it, and then pushed Cyrus toward the wardrobe opposite the bed. "Get in. Do not make a sound."

Cyrus couldn't think. He stared at Lucien and heard his words but none of them meant anything. He met Lucien's wide, terrified eyes, and found himself frozen. The shouting and crashing from the hallway continued, closer still, until a loud *crack* brought them through the door into Lucien's sitting room.

"Get in the fucking closet," Lucien hissed, and when Cyrus still didn't move, Lucien seized him by the front of his shirt and shoved him backwards into the wardrobe. Cyrus snapped out of his terror as Lucien let go, just long enough to grab him and pull him in.

Lucien tried to struggle, but Cyrus dragged him back further into the suffocating space and then wriggled around him so his own back was to the doors. He ignored Lucien's protests and pulled the doors shut as much as possible without something to grab on the inside, and then he clapped a hand over Lucien's mouth.

Please, Cyrus silently begged him. He didn't know for what, exactly. *Don't go,* maybe. *Don't go get yourself killed.*

Or, more likely, *Please forgive me.*

Because Cyrus already knew who would have so little logic and just enough rage to attack the Vista family in their own home. And the voices—crisp, cruel, familiar voices—that accompanied the bangs and thuds confirmed Cyrus's fears.

"He must be here somewhere," barked Marcus Beldon. "Search everywhere, and do not forget that they can shapeshift."

Lucien's breaths were quick and shallow against Cyrus's hand, still clamped over his mouth. Cyrus flicked a glance up at him; Lucien stared back with something deeper than fear in his eyes.

Something like horror. Like betrayal.

Cyrus shut his eyes and clenched his teeth until it hurt. Outside, the Beldons thrashed their way through Lucien's room and made their way ever closer to the bedchamber door. When it finally burst open, Lucien flinched, inhaling a gasp through his nose. Cyrus pressed closer to him, praying to gods he didn't believe in that the clothes hanging around them would be enough to conceal them if anyone opened the door.

Cyrus feared his and Lucien's heartbeats were audible as Marcus Beldon stomped around the room. Each time his steps neared the wardrobe, Cyrus swore this was the end. There was nowhere to run if Marcus found them.

"Joel!" Marcus snapped, *far* too close. "Anything?"

"No," came Joel's more distant reply. "He must have escaped another way, but I can't find any trace of a hidden door."

"Marcus," Emerson's low voice trickled into the room. "There was someone here who was not a vampire and yet shared this meal. Only one of these cups is filled with blood."

A beat of tense silence passed. Then Joel said, "Do you think—"

But his words cut off abruptly when another shrill cry split the room. Glass shattered and furniture crashed to the floor as another struggle ensued; Cyrus heard clashing metal, skidding footsteps, and—

And the unmistakable squelch of a blade piercing a body.

Marcus Beldon's voice cracked on a guttural roar that was followed by a thunderous *thud*.

"*NO!*"

"*Fuck—*"

More shouts exploded, voices overlapping. Footsteps retreated. Blades crashed. Another body fell.

Cyrus felt something wet touch his hand and snapped his attention back to Lucien. Silent, cold tears spilled from Lucien's horrified eyes. Cyrus could feel him trembling.

"Vista," Cyrus whispered, tightening his grip on Lucien's shirt. He hardly made a sound, but it was enough to break the trance, and Lucien finally shoved Cyrus away from him.

"Let me *go*," he whimpered, struggling to move around Cyrus in the tight space. "Let me go. *Let me go. Cyrus*, let me go. I can—I can h-help them, I can—"

"No! Lucien, *no*." Cyrus clung to him, nails biting, fingers bruising. He grabbed Lucien's chin with his free hand and forced him to look at him. "Lucien, they'll kill you."

Silence spread, hot and thick, over the room. Minutes dragged by. Beyond the stifling wardrobe, beyond their panicked gasps, pounding pulses, and silent tears, House Vista cowered, trembling.

Lucien jerked his head out of Cyrus's grip and then pushed Cyrus through the wardrobe doors. He streaked past before Cyrus had caught his balance, and Cyrus scrambled after him, but the bloodbath he found in the sitting room halted him and stole his strength. His knees hit the floor.

The room was splattered with crimson and silver. The coppery smell of it invaded Cyrus's senses, turning and twisting his stomach. But worse than the gore smeared across the room were the bodies that lay torn apart among it.

The first one Cyrus saw was Alastair Vista, whose body lay facedown but whose detached head stared blankly up at the ceiling.

The other was Marcus Beldon, whose throat was shredded to bloody threads. His clothes were stained black-red; if Cyrus didn't know better, he would've thought only a wild animal could maul someone so severely.

But if the stains around Alastair Vista's mouth and hands were any indication, it was neither an animal nor something Wild that had torn the life from Master Beldon.

Cyrus couldn't move. Couldn't tear his gaze away from his father's mutilated body. With every blink he expected the scene before him to vanish.

There was no conceivable way this was real.

Marcus Beldon couldn't be dead. He was too *much*. Too important. Too strong. Too cruel. Too powerful. Nothing could touch him. Nothing could break him. Certainly nothing could kill him. Cyrus had feared for most of his life that even time wouldn't dare touch Marcus Beldon. He was proudly, viciously human, but if there was anyone in the world whom Cyrus assumed had the immortality enjoyed by vampires, it was him.

A faint crackling sound finally made Cyrus avert his eyes from Marcus, and he watched the body of Alastair Vista start to rot. His skin turned ashy gray, shrinking around his bones until the flesh melted away and the body crumbled to ash. The horrid stench of decay clogged Cyrus's throat, and he doubled over, retching.

Shudders wracked his body. A sharp ringing filled his ears, and his lungs had forgotten how to take breaths. He stared with spinning vision at the fallen body of his father and wondered what the hell he was supposed to do now.

If things were out of sorts before, his life was about to be *chaos* now. His days of sneaking away unnoticed were over; there would be eyes on him every minute he was awake. The Beldon estate would become a true prison, now complete with iron bars in the form of hired guards.

It was all over. Everything with Lucien was over, and he had failed.

"You fucking idiot," Cyrus hissed at his father's body. "Why would you *do this*?" A sob shuddered through him, not out of grief for the man who had never loved him, but for the abrupt end of everything he and Lucien might have found. Even if they had gotten farther and succeeded, this incident—this slaughter—would ensure none of it mattered.

It would never end. Marcus had made sure of that. This was his war, and he'd left it for everyone else to endure.

"You've ruined everything." Tears spilled down Cyrus's cheeks. "As always."

Cyrus didn't know how long he sat there until he finally gathered the strength to stand. He held his breath as he picked his way across the wrecked room, following the smeared footprints Lucien had left behind.

Every door in the corridor was open, droplets of silver blood pooled at the entrance. Cyrus dared a glance into one room and found another heap of ashes and bones in a puddle of blood. He gritted his teeth and moved on, only to find the half-decayed bodies of two young men slumped against the wall at the end of the hall. Wooden stakes pierced their hearts, and one's head lolled to the side, attached by mere threads. The other's head had plopped into his lap, mouth open and fangs bared. They both crumbled to ash before Cyrus's eyes.

He stumbled away, pressing a hand over his mouth. *What have you done?* he mentally screamed at his family. *What the fuck have you done?*

He heard his father's response like a ghost at the back of his mind: *We are Beldons. This is our duty.*

"To *hell* with your fucking duty," Cyrus gasped. He couldn't look away, even when only ashes and bloodstained clothes remained of the two men. A faint memory supplied their names: Gregory and Roman, nephews of Alastair Vista. Lucien's cousins. Had he been close with them? Had they been like friends, like brothers?

An ear-splitting shriek from farther down the connecting corridor finally tore Cyrus away. He ran, shoes slipping in the puddles of blood, and rounded a corner so quickly that he would've run straight into Lucien if another heart-rending cry hadn't halted him in his tracks.

Sunken to his knees on the floor, Lucien clutched at a heap of ashes and bones. His hands clawed desperately across the tiles as his shoulders quaked with choked, breathless sobs.

Cyrus found himself on his knees, unaware of a conscious decision to join Lucien on the floor. He only noticed his own tears when they dripped off his chin and onto his lap. He hardly dared breathe, let alone speak. What was there to say? What could he *possibly* say?

How many of them, he wondered. How many of Lucien's family had the Beldons killed tonight?

Lucien's breaths grew heavier and deeper until he was outright sobbing, hands curled around fistfuls of ash. He clutched a crumpled garment that Cyrus recognized, with a pit in his stomach, as the dress that Victoria Vista had worn when she'd invited him into the house that first day.

Cyrus bit his lip to stifle his own cries.

He could not see Lucien's face behind the curtain of his hair. He didn't know if Lucien even knew he was there, and he couldn't conjure the courage to reach out to offer comfort. He mentally screamed at himself to do something other than sit here pathetically, but his body refused to move. Lucien's sobs pinned him, frozen, in place.

When Lucien finally swept his hair away from his face and straightened, Cyrus did not recognize the vampire he'd come to know. There was something wild in his eyes, a pain that cut so deep that it had shattered everything on its way down. And when he slowly turned that gaze toward Cyrus, noticing his presence for the first time, Cyrus suddenly understood that he had never before seen a true threat from Lucien Vista. His fear, until now, had been unfounded.

"*You.*" The word spilled out in a ragged breath. "Are you happy now? Did you get what you wanted?"

Tears ran down Cyrus's cheeks. "Lucien—"

He was on Cyrus in a blink; he seized Cyrus's collar and slammed him to the floor, teeth bared. "*You don't get to cry!*" he shrieked. "Save your fucking tears, Beldon—I'll bet they're out of relief that your family finally won."

Cyrus shook his head through all of Lucien's words. "No, no, no, Lucien, no, this wasn't—"

Lucien shook him violently, smacking his head against the floor. Cyrus tried to struggle free, but Lucien gripped his shoulders and dug in his nails. "This is what I get for trusting a Beldon, isn't it? Ohh, I am so stupid. None of you would ever be different, and I should've fucking known it." He shoved to his feet, standing over Cyrus. Cold fury twisted his features into something hideous, something unrecognizable. When he spoke again, his voice splintered. "You could have at least spared me the courtesy of killing me, too, when you had the opportunity."

Cyrus tried to get up but his strength failed him. He scrambled backwards across the floor until his back hit the wall. Tears poured uncontrollably down his cheeks. Nothing he said would convince Lucien, in his rage and grief, that he was not responsible for this. He was a Beldon and that was all he would ever be.

Lucien's glare turned dangerous. "Get out."

Cyrus kept shaking his head. No, because he didn't have anywhere else to go. If he went home he would never be able to come back.

"If you want to see the sun again, Beldon, go now." Lucien's shoulders shook with each heavy breath.

Cyrus's instincts screamed at him to run, but he was frozen. Lucien wouldn't—He wouldn't really hurt him...Would he?

"*GO!*" Lucien shrieked. He lunged at Cyrus and that finally unstuck Cyrus from the floor. He scrambled away from the vampire and ran.

"*Get out! Go! GO!*" Lucien's anguished screams followed Cyrus through the halls. He hardly registered the other smears of ashes or the blood slicking the soles of his shoes. As he put hallways and stairs between himself and Lucien, the vampire's shouts melted down to shrill, wordless cries.

Tears blurred Cyrus's vision as he stumbled his way out of House Vista. His shoes slipped on the floor, slowing his flight, and the doors—splintered and crooked on their hinges—refused to let him out. He fought his way through nonetheless and collapsed on the front steps.

Alastair. Gregory. Roman. Victoria. And four other remnants he'd seen on his way out: Loretta, Greta, Evelina, Roman Willem. If there were other members of the Vista family elsewhere, Cyrus did not know of them or their names. He knew only these nine, and with the exception of Lucien, only by name—this ancient, proud family that had survived centuries of hunters only to be snuffed by one angry, vengeful man and his thoughtless followers.

Cyrus had never hated his father as much as he did now.

And it wasn't just Marcus. Emerson had been here, and so had Joel. Poppy would have been if not for her injuries, and according to all of them, Cyrus should have been here on their side, flying through these halls with blades drawn and blood on his hands.

The thought churned his stomach. No. Never. He was not one of them. He never had been, and he never would be. He would sooner be slaughtered with the vampires.

This was not hunting for the sake of safety. This was murder, plain and simple: an unapologetic massacre and an undeniable declaration of war.

And damn him for it, but Cyrus hoped the other Honorable Families—and Lucien—sought their revenge. He hoped they all taught the Beldons a strong, bloody lesson.

THE BELDON ESTATE was frighteningly quiet when Cyrus finally slipped through the doors. In his haste to get away from House Vista, he'd left Demeter in the stables and made the journey across the city on foot. By the time he arrived home, his muscles ached, his head was throbbing, and dawn was breaking. He wanted nothing more than to bury himself in his bed and forget everything.

But first he had to reckon with his family.

Strained, anxious voices beckoned him toward Marcus's office on the first floor. Cyrus reluctantly went to the door, but didn't enter. Emerson stood in front of the fireplace, gripping the back of Marcus's favorite chair. Poppy and Joel, both looking stricken and exhausted, each slumped in a chair facing Emerson. Joel's clothes were rumpled and stained with blood—crimson and silver.

Cyrus braced himself and stepped into the room, scuffing his shoes on the floor to announce his presence.

Emerson's sharp gaze found him first, but before he'd opened his mouth, Joel darted to his feet. "Cyrus—! Oh, thank the gods." He rushed across the room and grabbed Cyrus by the shoulders; Cyrus jerked back, but Joel gathered him in a tight hug.

Cyrus went still. When Joel released him, Cyrus could only gape dumbly. His brother gazed at him with a haggard mix of shock and relief.

"I'm glad to see you're all right," Joel said softly.

"He thought you were dead," Poppy piped in.

Joel winced. "I didn't see another possibility. We couldn't find you, not here nor there." He swallowed hard. "I've gotten used to assuming the worst."

Yeah, Cyrus agreed, *I think we all have.*

Joel moved back to give him space, and Cyrus reluctantly approached the sitting area in front of the fireplace. There wasn't another chair for him, so he stood beside Poppy's and waited for the inevitable reprimand from Emerson.

It was a long minute before he spoke. "Did they turn you?"

It took Cyrus's weary brain a moment to understand Emerson's meaning. He swallowed a scoff; if he'd had more energy, he would've walked out at that. "No."

"How long were you their prisoner?"

Cyrus frowned. If he hadn't just walked across Chestervale in the middle of the night after witnessing several brutal murders, he might have snapped that he was nearer a prisoner *here* than he ever was at House Vista. And it was just as he expected: Emerson paid him so little attention that he was not aware of Cyrus's comings and goings from the house. He shook his head and said nothing.

"Uncle, he wasn't a prisoner," Joel cut in. His tone suggested they'd had this argument several times. "I saw Cyrus not a full day ago. He was here, uninjured and healthy. If the Vistas had been keeping him hostage, do you think they would have let him leave?"

Cyrus nodded once, agreeing with Joel's logic. If Alastair Vista had found Cyrus in that house and decided to keep him as a prisoner, he would not be alive by now. He would've been in that dank cellar, blood drained within an inch of his life.

Emerson leveled a hard glare at Cyrus. "Then *why*, boy, were you there?"

And there it was. Cyrus knew it was only a matter of time before he was faced with that question, and he still didn't have an answer that would satisfy his uncle while also keeping the necessary secrets. It was all too likely that his work with Lucien was done, but their agreement and Cyrus's promise of secrecy still held.

So instead of bullshitting a lie that Emerson would immediately see through, he leaned into the partial truth: "You're mistaken, Uncle. I've been to the Vista manor only once, about a week ago, after we first discussed speaking to them regarding Arthur's death. I haven't been near it since."

He held Emerson's gaze, praying that it was too dark in this room for anyone to see the bloodstains and ash on Cyrus's clothes.

Emerson slammed his hand on the side table next to the chair, making everyone jump. "Then where the *fuck* were you tonight when your family needed you?"

Play dumb. "W-What are you—"

"Gods, he doesn't even know," Poppy scoffed.

"Know *what*? What happened?" Cyrus glanced at his siblings but avoided Poppy's gaze. If anyone in this room could really see through him, it was her. "You all look like you've been to hell and back. I think I'm lucky that I wasn't here."

"Oh, yes, lucky for you, but unfortunate for us." Emerson scowled. "Had you been with us, as you were *meant* to be, you could've done us all a favor by dying."

"Uncle!" Joel snapped.

Cyrus glared back at him, unwavering. If Emerson wanted him dead, he dared him to do it himself.

"Emerson, *enough*." Poppy shoved to her feet, masking a wince. "We've had a taxing night. An impossible night. But that is not Cyrus's fault. Do you think the outcome would have changed if he'd been there?"

"No," Emerson said in a huff. "But it might've been his life instead of Marcus."

Cyrus didn't have to feign his shock. Though he'd literally stumbled over his father's dead body, hearing his death confirmed by Emerson was no less jarring. He glanced at his siblings again; Poppy glared hard at Emerson, while Joel had put his head in his hands.

"It's...true?" Cyrus murmured. "He's dead?"

Poppy turned to him and gave the slightest nod, pain written across her face.

Cyrus wished, for a heartbeat, that he had known the man Poppy had loved enough to mourn.

"Cyrus's presence on that stupid raid would not have saved our father," Poppy said to Emerson. "If he'd been there, we would be short *two* Beldons tonight. If *I'd* been there, we'd be short *none* and the Vista heir wouldn't have gotten away." She gritted her teeth with a growl. "Let's at least be glad there's four of us still standing, and get back to the real matter at hand: What do we do? Lucien Vista is a liability. The other Families won't let this go."

When no one replied, Cyrus ventured, "You all watched one of our family die tonight. Does the rest even matter right now?"

"When the king falls, the kingdom cannot move forward until an heir is crowned." Emerson crossed his arms over his chest. "In Arthur's unfortunate absence, we are at an impasse. Poppy and Joel are the same age, Cyrus is unfit, and the tradition states that a sibling shall only take over in the absence of offspring."

"And I will say it again: since I'm not yet recovered from my injuries, it would be unfair to the family for me to lead us when I'm not strong enough to defend us," Poppy said. "Therefore, I have no qualms with passing the role to Joel if he'll have it."

Joel was the only one who appeared unwilling to settle this issue tonight. He heaved a sigh and stood up. "If it's up to me, then we can all wait. I won't speak for all of you, but I'm in no mental state to make a decision like this when our father isn't even at rest yet. Cyrus is right: We've all endured the unimaginable, and we need to sleep."

Neither Emerson nor Poppy looked pleased, but neither argued either. Emerson waved his hand, dismissing everyone, and Cyrus would've been the first out the door if Joel hadn't beat him to it. Cyrus slid around him, but Joel grabbed his arm and dragged him into the next room, swiftly shutting the door and planting himself in front of it.

"Joel, come on." Cyrus fixed him with a weary glare. "Not in the mood."

"Where were you?"

Cyrus sighed. "Not here, which is apparently what everyone cares about."

"That might be good enough for Emerson, who doesn't actually give a shit about any of us, but it's not enough for me." Joel stepped closer to him, emphasizing the couple of inches of height he had over Cyrus. "Where. Were you."

Cyrus met his brother's eyes, and if not for the youthful face surrounding them he might've been facing his father. Arthur, Joel, Poppy—all of them had those ice-blue eyes. From that glare, teeming with disappointment, Cyrus would never escape.

"I was following a lead having to do with Arthur's death. Not that anyone else cares or noticed, but that's what I've been doing every day since he died. I want to know what the hell happened, Joel, and I think I'm close to the answer. But I have to do this alone."

Joel studied him closely, searching for a lie he wouldn't find. He'd inherited that from Marcus, too: an uncanny ability to tell when someone was lying to him. He narrowed his eyes and leaned back against the door. "What have you found, then, if you've been at this for so many days?"

Cyrus felt the thin ice crack under his feet. He chose his words carefully. "Potentially...a way to save someone from turning into a Wild vampire."

"Save them? As in, reverse the process?" Joel raised his eyebrows. Curiosity chased off his suspicion, and Cyrus relaxed a little.

"Ideally."

Joel's eyes darted back and forth behind his glasses as his thoughts raced. "That—That would be extraordinary, Cyrus, just imagine it! We'd be safe from *all* of them—Wild *or* Honorable. No more vampires...Gods, we'd finally be at peace."

Cyrus had to bite his tongue so he didn't betray more than he already had. He nodded stiffly. "Sure. But I'm not trying to save all of humanity as much as I'm trying to keep *us* safe. That's our duty, first and foremost, isn't it?"

The words tasted sour on Cyrus's tongue, but the pandering worked, because Joel smiled.

See? I can be a good little Beldon.

"Right. Still...it's an inspiring possibility." Joel finally stepped away from the door. "I'm sorry for cornering you as if you're the guilty one. I'm— We're all..." He trailed off, ducking his head.

"You're in shock," Cyrus supplied, then quickly amended, "We all are. I...can't believe he's gone."

Joel shook his head. "This house was his reign. Hell, this *city* was his reign, and this was his palace. It'll take more than death to banish him from this place. I think I'm going to be hearing echoes of his footsteps in these halls for the rest of my life."

Cyrus shivered. "Yeah," he murmured. "I think I will, too."

PART TWO

What man...would not gladly give a little, nay, much of his blood to rescue his beloved from the claws of death?

— GUSTAVE RUDLER, *THE BEAUTIFUL VAMPIRE*

Chapter THIRTEEN

THE DAYS DRAGGED AGONIZINGLY IN THE WAKE OF Marcus Beldon's death, and Cyrus couldn't stop thinking about Lucien. The rest of the house was caught in a cyclone of worries over the fate of the Beldon family and all of Marcus's unfinished affairs, but Cyrus skirted the edges of the chaos and stopped trying to pretend he was interested in participating. No one wanted his opinions, and certainly no one wanted his lack of expertise in official matters that he neither cared about nor knew anything about.

Just as well; he moved as if through quicksand. Each daily task tripled in difficulty, from eating to dressing to washing to simply getting out of bed. Each time he completed one step of one chore to take care of himself, a hundred more dragged him down, deeper and deeper into a pit. He spent his days in his room, reluctant to be seen, lest his uselessness be noticed and terminated.

At some point, he vaguely noticed that Emerson had begun sharing daily meals with Joel and Poppy, something that had never been done before, but now acted as an extension of their work as they organized everything Marcus had left behind. Cyrus was not invited to the family table, and did not wish to be. If he ate at all, he did it alone in his room and often left his plates half-full.

By the third day, easily a century after the slaughter at House Vista, Cyrus saw no point in getting out of bed. He lost track of time after that.

From his bed, bundled beneath a heavy quilt, Cyrus watched cold, white daylight poke through the gap in the curtains, bringing another sleepless night to an end. He turned over with a groan, tugging the blankets up around his neck, and his eyes fell upon his cluttered desk. A few of the books he'd pulled for his research with Lucien still lay there, but those were the unhelpful ones. The relevant ones were, as far as he knew, still on that table in the Vista library, open and untouched.

Even if Cyrus had the motivation to continue the project, he was back to square one here. He had nothing unless he went back.

I have to go back. He hadn't realized how severely he'd lacked a purpose until he'd had something to work on, something to chase, something to win. He couldn't return to drifting aimlessly like a ghost through these halls. How had that been his life for over twenty years? How had he *lived* like that?

But if he went back to House Vista, would Lucien even open the door? Or would Cyrus be chased out again?

Unconsciously, his hand found the iron key on its leather thread around his neck. He hadn't taken it off since running away that night, and more than once, he'd woken up to find it clutched in his hand. He ran his thumb along the length of it now, dragging his nail across the familiar grooves.

He *could* go back. He could let himself into that dark, empty fortress and beg Lucien to listen to him, to believe him. And if that didn't work, if Lucien chased him out again, Cyrus could at least say he tried. Maybe he could go back to Viktor Stokes and seek his help, or spend the rest of his life digging through the Beldon library until he found a different way forward.

Or maybe, if this absurd project was destined to be buried just like every dead Beldon, maybe Cyrus should be buried with it.

He blinked and turned onto his back, emptying his mind of those thoughts. They'd been screaming louder than ever these past days, but Cyrus couldn't go down that road. Not yet—No, not ever. He had to cling to what few scraps of hope he had left; he still had a purpose, still had work to do. There *had* to be a way to move forward.

The depth of his fear that it was over shocked him. It wasn't just the project itself that had given Cyrus a sense of purpose; it was Lucien, too. He was one of very few people in Cyrus's life who actually listened to him and respected him, who met him as *Cyrus* rather than as *Beldon*.

That couldn't be lost. Cyrus couldn't let his father take that from him, too.

He had to go back. He had to set things right. But he couldn't go without first finding out why that massacre had happened at all.

And unfortunately that meant he had to get up.

Cyrus threw the covers back and dragged himself upright. His eyes ached from lack of sleep and his head felt fuzzy after several days without enough food, but he ignored the familiar fatigue for now and told himself he'd get something from a shop or a street vendor on his way across the city. He grabbed the same wrinkled shirt and pants he'd been shucking on and off for several days, then shuffled to his bedroom door. There he paused, pushing the door slowly, and listened.

Silent.

He peeked out into the hall.

Empty.

Good.

He left his room behind and made for the back stairs. Down two flights, through several hallways, out several doors, he ran into no one else. He made it out into the back garden without glimpsing a single sign of life in the house, but before he reached the path that led down to the street, someone pointedly cleared their throat behind him and he froze.

He turned, already gathering an excuse on his tongue, but to his overwhelming relief, it was Leif. "Ah. It's just you."

"Just me." Leif knelt on a cushion among the overgrown herb garden. With a basil-green shawl draped over their narrow shoulders, they might've been one of the plants. "And just you. Having a walk? You look like hell."

He most certainly did. "Thanks, Leif."

"Care for a cup of tea?" Leif rose to their feet and dusted soil off their hands. "The earth is getting colder every night. I can't feel my fingertips after a few hours out here." They flexed their bony, tattooed hands. "I could use something warm to drink. Join me?"

Cyrus shifted on his feet. "I can't right now. I have...uh..."

"Somewhere to be?" They raised an eyebrow. "Yes, you do: it's in my flat, with a hot beverage in your hands. It'll make you feel better, I promise."

"But—"

"Oops, I'm no longer asking." Leif flashed their sweetest smile and jerked their thumb toward the house. "Let's go."

"WHERE IS EVERYONE?" Cyrus asked when they reached the fourth floor after a quiet walk through the house. Still he had not seen or heard any sign of his uncle or siblings, nor any staff.

"That you don't know is why it's not advisable for you to leave the house just now." Leif busied themself in their kitchenette. They washed the soil off their hands and turned to Cyrus with a flourish as they flung a towel over their shoulder. "Coffee or tea?"

Cyrus shrugged and slid onto one of the stools at the island. "Coffee, I guess. I could use the boost."

"Not sleeping well?" Leif filled the kettle and placed it on the little wood stove in the corner.

"You said it yourself that I look like hell." Cyrus slouched forward and leaned his cheek on his hand, watching Leif poke through various ceramic jars. He appreciated that they weren't staring him down as they talked to him; it was easier to tell them things when they were occupied. Their sharp perception made him uneasy, and he didn't like the feeling of being turned inside-out. Leif was the only person under this roof that Cyrus trusted enough to speak to freely, but two decades of keeping his feelings to himself still made it difficult.

Several silent minutes lapsed, and then Cyrus said, "I'm guessing I don't have to tell you what happened."

The kettle let out a shrill cry, and Leif hurried to lift it off the heat. "No," they murmured, briefly meeting his eyes. "And I'm very sorry."

"I shouldn't need to tell you, of all people, that I will not miss him."

"Oh, I wasn't talking about your father." Leif made Cyrus's coffee and set the steaming mug before him, then slid him a dish of sugar cubes and a small pitcher of cream. They busied themself with their own tea, giving Cyrus space to speak.

He wrapped his hands around the warm mug and stared into its rich depths. The coffee's aroma, usually comforting, now turned his stomach. "I should have known. I should've paid more attention. Maybe I could've..."

"What, talked them out of it?" Leif threw him a dubious look. "Talked your *father* out of it? Cyrus, if I know one thing about Master Beldon, it is that a simple plea is worthless against his will. Even if you had heard his plan—"

"Then I could've warned him!" Cyrus's hands started to tremble and he tightened his fingers around the cup. "I could've warned him and he could've told his family, and then he would've known he could trust me and he wouldn't have blamed me and he wouldn't have ch-chased me out."

Cyrus sucked in a breath and held it as a knot of emotions rose up his throat. He pressed the back of his hand to his mouth and swallowed it, buried it deep. He dared not even acknowledge the true root of his devastation; it was not his father's death, and it wasn't even that he'd heard and seen eight people slaughtered.

He smothered the thought, lest Leif's uncanny intuition hear it.

He didn't notice, until they spoke, that they'd taken a seat beside him. "My understanding was that you had a mutually respectful academic partnership with Lucien Vista. But is there... more to the story?"

"No." Cyrus stared firmly into his coffee. He was not friends with Lucien, and he certainly wasn't—*No*. He should not care about Lucien *at all*.

"No?"

"*No*, Leif." Cyrus couldn't bring himself to look at them. "It's absurd that you would ask that. That you'd *think* that. He's a fucking vampire, Leif, and I'm—I'm a Beldon."

Leif stirred their tea; the spoon faintly clinked the ceramic on each sweep around the cup. "He survived, then."

Now Cyrus looked up, unable to rein in his horror. *Fuck.*

But Leif fixed him with an amused look. "And what do you expect me to do with that information? Do I look like a Beldon to you? Do I look like a *hunter*?"

"No, but you're—"

"Employed by the Beldon family to offer comfort, psychiatric help, and remedies for simple maladies," Leif said. "Your secrets, Cyrus, have always been safe with me. Marcus knew and respected that confidentiality. So must Master Emerson."

Cyrus's relief momentarily drowned out everything else, but then he realized what they'd said. "Wait. *Master* Emerson?"

Oh, shit. *Shit.*

Leif nodded. "Emerson Beldon has solemnly stepped into his place as patriarch of the family. He and your siblings went downtown to sort it out with the city early this morning. They'd be on their way back by now, hence my insistence that you not sneak out quite yet."

"Fuck," Cyrus muttered. He took a gulp of coffee despite it still being black. He scowled at the bitter taste but drank more.

It wasn't the end of the world that Emerson was now the head of the Beldons. He was every bit as ruthless as Marcus, and in Cyrus's opinion he was cleverer than his hot-headed older brother.

Emerson was cunning, never without a plan to handle any situation, and his interest in alchemy made him an insatiable problem-solver. He looked at the world around him and seemed to unravel it in his mind just as he endlessly deconstructed materials in his laboratory, searching for the core.

Emerson would never have launched the Beldons into House Vista like Marcus had. If it had been up to him, it wouldn't have been a massacre but a carefully-targeted assassination—like Arthur's death. But that made Emerson no less dangerous, no less hateful.

"I don't know what changes are coming for your family, Cyrus," Leif mused, "but I don't think the turbulent uncertainty should stop you from chasing what you seek."

Cyrus turned his head. "Do you know what I *seek*, Leif?"

"I have an idea." They sipped their tea. "But I'm not sure that *you* know yet. I *do* know, however, that you're not looking for a way to reverse a turn. Not to save a human from becoming a vampire, anyway."

Cyrus opened his mouth to deny it, but Leif twitched their eyebrow and made the lie dissolve on Cyrus's tongue. There was no use lying to them. "Yes. That's true."

Leif nodded thoughtfully and gazed into their tea. "Vampires are dangerous. You'd be a fool to claim they aren't. But do you know what else are dangerous?"

Cyrus eyed them curiously.

"Wolves." Leif took another sip of tea. "But did that stop us from inviting them into our homes? Did that discourage us from deciding to love them instead of hunting them? And now, what have we got: loyal, loving companions who comfort our pain and bring us joy."

"You're comparing vampires to *dogs*?" Cyrus snorted, but as the metaphor sank in, a sense of comfort came with it. That same hope he'd felt in the best moments with Lucien warmed him again now: a hope for the future, that someday people would look back on these years and think it absurd that humans and vampires were once at odds.

Cyrus didn't know if that future was possible, but he was certain it wouldn't be if he didn't try to make it so.

"I know that what you saw the other night was...unspeakable," Leif said softly. "I can see it in your eyes and on your face. You're not okay. But you will have to go back there. It's going to hurt, and I don't know if Lucien Vista will forgive you, but you must go. First, though...forgive me."

"Huh?" Cyrus had hardly turned his head when Leif suddenly grabbed him by the back of the neck and clapped a cloth over his nose and mouth. Cyrus jerked back, but his mind and body lost the fight.

The last thing he was aware of was falling sideways off his seat.

CYRUS WAS in the tower again. Damp stone steps spiraled upward before him, and darkness yawned behind him. Ahead, a faint, flickering golden light beckoned him onward. *Just a little farther.*

He'd climbed these steps before. Why couldn't he move any faster? How many steps were there, and what was stopping him from reaching the top?

Frustrated, Cyrus tried to push himself faster up the stairs, but his legs dragged as if he had bricks tied to his ankles. Still he fought, but no matter how many steps he climbed there was always a turn ahead, just out of his reach. The light remained distant. The voice called him onward.

Cyrus.

"I'm here!" He meant to shout, but his voice was muffled in his own ears. "*I'm here!* Who are you?" He tried to scream, but he might as well have been underwater. "*Please*, hear me, I'm here!"

Cyyyyyyruuuussss...

"Who are you?" His lungs burned and his muscles strained, yet he moved at a snail's pace up the steps. "Where are you? Why do you keep bringing me here? Why won't you let me see you?"

See you?

See?

See? See? See? See?

Whispers echoed off the walls, spiraling down and down and down into the maw at his back. A cold breeze kissed the back of his neck and instinctively he turned, facing the darkness behind him for the first time. Several pairs of eyes, vivid and flashing, stared back at him.

Run, screamed his brain, but he couldn't move his feet. He tried to speak but no sound came out. *What are you?* He said it again and again but all he heard were whispers.

You want—

You want to see?

You mustn't—

You mustn't go up.

You can't be—

—belong here.

Mustn't go on.

A violent gust of cold air rushed at him, but this time he kept his balance. Then one of the things in the dark leapt forward, claws scraping on the stone. Cyrus caught a glimpse of grasping, bony hands and dripping black teeth before he whipped around and sprinted up stairs. Now his body let him move fast, but it wasn't fast enough. Howls and snarls echoed off the stone walls as the creatures gave chase; Cyrus could feel their closeness behind him—their icy breaths, the swish of their claws missing his flesh by inches, the spatter of something wet soaking through his clothes. He couldn't run faster.

With a howl, one of the creatures leapt in front of him, blocking the light and halting Cyrus unsteadily in his tracks. Gasping for breath, he gaped up into the drooling maw of a Wild vampire. Its hunched body gushed silver blood from multiple wounds, and its head hung loosely off its neck, attached by mere threads. Cold, pungent blood poured from its severed arteries and slicked the stones underfoot.

Cyrus whirled around, but any more than a step would have him in the clutches of more Wild vampires. Eight of them, all mutilated and bleeding, dragged themselves up the steps and reached for him with broken and bloody hands. One carried its own head in its arms; another tugged at a blade stuck in its chest as it lumbered forward.

A piercing howl broke through the monsters' groans and growls, and then something far bigger flung the lot of them out of the way and sent them tumbling, screeching, into the dark. The monster that remained filled the entire space: huge, hulking, with grotesque limbs and a mouthful of deadly teeth.

Cyrus ran. He barreled past the other, smaller Wild vampire blocking his path only for the bigger one to fling it out of its way. Cyrus could feel its breath at his back as it chased him; he couldn't move fast enough.

I'm going to die. The realization stole what scarce breath remained in his lungs. He was going to die here and he was never going to reach that light and he would never find her and *see*—

The Wild vampire let out a roar and yanked Cyrus's feet out from under him. He slammed onto the stairs, dizzy, and had only a second's glimpse of the monster's crimson eyes before—

Cyrus felt a hard tug, and all at once he could breathe again. His vision cleared and he found himself not in a dark stairwell, but in a warmly lit room that smelled of herbs and incense.

Leif's flat.

He was home.

He was sitting up in a small bed, blankets tangled around his bare legs. The air chilled him, which made him realize his upper body was bare, too, and damp with sweat.

His heart hadn't stopped pounding.

Cyrus closed his eyes and tried to breathe normally. He could still see them, those horribly familiar crimson eyes in the face of a monster. A shudder ran through him and he pushed the lingering nightmare away, returning instead to the cozy space that surrounded him now. The low, simple bed was tucked into a corner beneath a slanted ceiling; a skylight higher up poured golden light onto the wood floor. A table beside the bed presented an extinguished oil lamp and a folded handkerchief, and a tapestry pinned to the opposite wall served as a divider between this room and the space beyond. Compared to the rest of Leif's busy and cluttered living space, this room was plain, almost neglected.

Pieces of the day came back to him gradually. He'd been on his way out, intending to return to the Vista manor, but then he'd run into Leif and then...

Then it got fuzzy. What the hell had Leif done to him? Why was he here, rather than in his own room?

And why was he undressed?

With a spike of panic, he grasped for the key around his neck, then slumped back in relief when he found it still there. He cringed at the thought of what Leif might have assumed or suspected when they'd seen it, but he was still grateful that they hadn't touched it.

When he'd finally shaken the last of the nightmare from his mind, he unfolded his limbs and got up from the bed. A clean set of clothes had been left for him on top of a trunk at the end of the bed; he recognized them as his own, though the shirt was old and the maroon vest didn't really fit him. He wouldn't have chosen them himself, but he was also not about to scamper back to his room in his underclothes for better options, so he put them on. He ran his hands through his hair to get it in some kind of order, and was surprised to find it soft and clean, very much unlike its greasy state in recent days.

Okay...add that to his questions for Leif.

Cyrus scratched at the scarce stubble on his cheek as he slid around the tapestry and found a bright loft space beyond. There was a closed door to his right, a set of stairs ahead, and a short railing to his left that ran along the edge of the loft and looked down on the rest of Leif's apartment. Cyrus spotted them curled up in a chair with a blanket over their lap and a steaming mug in their hand; their attention was intently fixed on the book balanced on their knee.

On the stove, the kettle whistled, and before Leif could tear themself away from their book, someone else approached the stove. It took a second for Cyrus to recognize Adriyen with her hair down and without her usual infirmary garb. He smiled to himself.

"Thanks, love," Leif said absently.

Adriyen glanced at them, smiling, but Leif didn't notice. She poured the hot water into a mug and gave it a stir, then left the tea to steep and crossed the room to where Leif sat. She perched on the arm of their chair, and when Leif still didn't look at her, she touched her fingers to their chin and turned their face up to kiss them.

The book slid off their lap and hit the floor with a *thump.*

Cyrus took that as his cue to make his presence known. He padded down the steps and emerged into the room, announcing his presence with a quiet, "Um."

Leif and Adriyen leapt apart, Adriyen nearly falling off the side of the chair. She scrambled to catch her balance and pushed her curls behind her ears, cheeks flaming cherry red. "Ah—Cyrus. Good morning. Er, I mean evening?"

Leif snickered softly. "Cyrus. Did you rest well?"

"Yes," he said slowly, "but I have some questions."

"*Please* don't tell anyone," Adriyen blurted. She exchanged a glance with Leif, but they didn't mirror her uncharacteristic anxiety. "It's just...I don't want..."

"I understand," Cyrus told her. "It's okay. Your secrets aren't mine to tell, Doctor. I keep everything else from my family, so what's one more thing?"

Adriyen sighed and clasped her hands together in thanks. She leaned against Leif's chair and stroked her hand down their arm; Leif smiled up at her, and something pulled in Cyrus's chest.

He'd assumed, from the way Adriyen had hinted at her affair

with Leif, that it was something casual, but the way they looked at each other suggested otherwise. There was genuine love between them, and it warmed Cyrus's heart just as much as it made it ache.

"Well, now that we've cleared that up," Leif shifted to sit cross-legged, "I imagine you're a touch confused to be waking up here at such an odd hour."

"That, and I'm also wondering why I was undressed, why my hair feels clean, who picked out my clothes, and how far they had to dig into my wardrobe to find things I never wear."

Leif smirked at Adriyen; she scoffed. "They're very nice clothes, and I thought the maroon suited you," she said. "What's wrong with them?"

"Nothing, technically." Cyrus tugged at the vest, which gaped about two inches away from his body. "Just doesn't fit me as nicely as my newer things."

"That's because you don't eat enough," Adriyen said flatly. "And on that note, who wants biscuits? The dough's just about ready for the oven. Cyrus, do you want tea? And before you ask, *no*, I will not give you coffee, because unlike Leif, *I* don't take upset stomachs lightly and I *know* coffee upsets your stomach. So, tea?"

"It's not the coffee," Leif muttered, "it's the milk. I know you know that, because all of them have the same problem."

Cyrus wasn't awake enough to keep up with two conversations. He plopped into the chair opposite Leif and put his chin in his hand. "I don't want anything."

Adriyen pursed her lips but didn't argue, which was unlike her, which suggested she was trying to be extra nice to him, which made him suspicious. He rubbed his eyes. "Leif, what did you do to me?"

"I..." They exhaled. "Now, don't overreact. I gave you something to help you sleep."

"So you drugged me." Cyrus stared at them. "Leif, what the fuck?"

"I didn't—" They flattened their lips. "Okay, yes, I suppose I did drug you. But you needed to rest, Cyrus, and—"

"You *drugged* him?" Adriyen shouted. The spoon she'd been holding clattered to the floor. "What the hell, Leif!"

"I obviously didn't give him anything that would harm him!" Leif waved a hand, then studied Cyrus. "How are you feeling? Any nausea? Headache? You're not vomiting uncontrollably, so that's a good sign."

"Is that a side effect I should have known about?" Cyrus snapped.

"It can be. Answer my questions."

Cyrus pinched the bridge of his nose. "I feel fine. I'm just tired. I didn't sleep well, despite the drug-induced slumber." He flicked a glare up at Leif.

They frowned. "I checked on you often and you didn't seem restless. Did you wake up frequently?"

"No." Cyrus hadn't planned to talk about the dream, but now that he'd had it more than once, he wanted to know what it meant. Especially if it was going to turn more horrifying with every iteration. "I've been having this dream."

Leif's eyes lit up. Behind them, in the kitchen, Cyrus saw Adriyen roll her eyes. "A recurring dream!" Leif grinned. "How exciting. Well, for me. It seems to be disturbing you, though."

"Normally, the only disturbing thing about it is that I can't seem to do anything in the dream." Cyrus told them about the spiral staircase in the dark tower, and the light ahead that was always out of his reach. "I just climb and climb without ever getting closer to the top. And...there's a voice calling to me. I don't know who it is, but in the dream it feels like I do. I—I know that doesn't make sense, but..."

"No, it does." Leif nodded. "Go on."

"Whoever is calling to me obviously knows who I am," Cyrus continued, "and she wants me to reach that light at the top of the stairs. But I can't, and now..."

Silver blood. Swiping claws. Bared teeth. Crimson eyes.

Cyrus folded his arms across his chest. "It's not usually a nightmare. Today it was. I was being chased."

"By?" Leif prompted.

He didn't want to say it. "Wild vampires." He swallowed. "I...I think it was the Vista family, all turned Wild. I woke up when one of them caught me."

"Which one caught you?"

Cyrus glanced at Leif and grimaced.

Leif nodded once. "I see. Well, then." They twisted one of their rings around their finger. "The usual dream seems like a pretty standard subconscious response to stress. There's something you really want, but it feels out of your reach. Close, but evasive. Not only do you feel like you're fighting an uphill battle, but you also feel like you're running in circles. Around and around with no end in sight, all the while someone's begging you to reach the top, building panic and urgency that makes you feel like this end—this light—will disappear if you don't reach it in time."

Cyrus mulled over Leif's explanation. That was all more or less how he felt about his project with Lucien; he wasn't surprised to find that stress mirrored in the dream.

"Leif, let me butt in for a second." Adriyen called from the kitchen. She slid a tray of doughy biscuits into the oven. "Cyrus, have you had any thoughts of death?"

He blinked. "What?"

Leif sighed. "Yen, please."

"No, listen to me. Leif, I love you, but you're *so* good at missing what's right in front of you." She leaned her hip on the island counter and crossed her arms. "You've been having a dream where someone is calling you toward a bright, enticing light. I've seen enough people on their journeys out of this world to recognize patterns when I see them. Almost every person I've spoken to who has had a near-death experience has described a pull toward an ethereal light. Some people even hear their departed loved ones' voices when they're close to death. Cyrus, you've had several close calls with death in the past month—which is neither healthy nor normal—so of *course* your brain is spinning it like a spool of thread in your subconscious."

Leif looked annoyed at Adriyen's explanation, but Cyrus didn't find it any less logical than theirs. He shrugged, and Adriyen came over and touched his shoulder.

When she spoke again, her voice was softer, her eyes gentle. "This is the point where any good doctor—medical *or* mystic— would ask you if you've been thinking about dying."

Her concern put him on edge. "Yeah, Adriyen, you could say that. My brother was killed and turned and then killed again, my sister almost died, I listened as the entire Vista family was slaughtered by my father and uncle, and then my father died. Who wouldn't be thinking about death when it's all around them?"

"Of course, Cyrus, but what—"

"She's asking if you've thought about taking your own life, Cyrus," Leif said, bluntly but not unkindly.

Oh. Cyrus swallowed and looked down at his hands. "No," he murmured, and that was *mostly* the truth. He'd wondered often in the past days what he would do with his life now that everything had been torn out from under his feet, but while languishing in bed and wallowing in his misery had been a tolerable option, ending his life had not crossed his mind in earnest. He'd wished he could stop existing, but never once had that wish turned into an impulse, and certainly not into a plan.

Adriyen squeezed his shoulder. "Good. You've got a lot on your plate, Cyrus, and when your mind is gnawing at you even in your sleep, it's easy to feel like everything—including your own brain—is out of your control. We're here to help you feel like you can keep that control."

"And I am also here to offer interpretations of your subconscious that others in the room may think are silly, but may nonetheless be comforting." Leif smiled when Adriyen threw them a look, then turned to Cyrus again. "What Adriyen described regarding your dream is not incorrect. It's very likely that this dream is an amalgamation of numerous pieces of your life all globbed together in one persistent, pesky vision. I'm not surprised that it turned nightmarish in the wake of what you witnessed the other night. Rather, I'm more surprised that it took several days for you to have the dream again. That alone tells me how poorly you've been sleeping."

"I'm still not thanking you for drugging me," Cyrus muttered. To their credit, Leif looked a little guilty. "So how do I make the dream go away?"

"Reach the light," Leif said.

"I thought we wanted me to *avoid* dying."

Leif *tsked.* "Not like that. The light *could* mean death, sure, but it could also represent a significant victory: an important goal, a major revelation that will change you. What is death if not a transition—a transformation from one existence to another? Yes, the other side of it is a mystery to us, but perhaps that's why the stairs are endless and the goal is out of sight. You can't see what you're reaching for, you just know that it feels right and it feels safe. And someone is calling you there."

By the time Leif finished talking, Cyrus's shoulders were touching his ears. His hands were clenched so tightly that his knuckles were white. Something that wasn't quite fear but wasn't far from it thumped through him with each heartbeat.

He hardly wanted to guess at what Leif was implying. A major change—yes, that was what his family and the whole damn city needed, and that was what Cyrus was working toward. But what Leif suggested was not just a change in Cyrus's life, but a change to *Cyrus.* And that scared him.

Did Leif mean he was going to die? Or...something worse?

A transformation from one existence to another. Cyrus didn't want to voice where his mind went with those words, lest Leif pick apart something that lurked deep, deep within him.

He suddenly needed to get far away from this room. He stood up. "I—have to go. Thank you both for the—uh, for taking care of me."

"Cyrus, wait." Leif got to their feet.

But they didn't try hard enough to stop him, and he fled. He scrambled down the steps out of the attic and didn't slow down until he was outside. He gulped the sun-baked evening air by the lungful until his frantic pulse had settled, then closed his eyes and banished all thoughts of death and deathlife and Wild vampires from his mind.

He weighed his options. The sun was sinking quickly, and it would take at least an hour on foot to reach House Vista. But everyone would be in for the night, probably poring over more things Marcus had left unfinished, and no eyes were on Cyrus. If he didn't go now, he didn't know if or when he would have another chance.

He glanced back once. Only a few windows were aglow, all on the far side. Even the house averted its gaze.

Cyrus touched the key beneath his shirt, and then strode across the garden and left House Beldon behind.

Chapter
FOURTEEN

By the time Cyrus reached House Vista, his heart was in his throat and his stomach was ready to heave itself out of his body. It took several tries to fit the skeleton key into its lock on the garden door; his hands trembled with a roiling mix of adrenaline and panic. When he finally got through the door, he dashed up the steps and beelined across the library, ignoring the fatigue that chewed his muscles after a hurried journey across the city.

A cold sense of dread crept over him as he moved deeper into the manor. Something wasn't right, aside from the stillness of night. The place had never been lively, but now it was as utterly silent as a crypt.

Cyrus found his way to the foyer and paused, panting as he listened. When a few minutes passed and he heard no sign of life, he called, "Vista?"

His voice was a clap of thunder in the hall, but all he heard in response was its echo.

He went up the main stairs and told himself, as he passed several dark and empty rooms, that the lack of light was normal. Someone who could see in the dark wouldn't take the time to light lamps and fires in unused rooms. Lucien was one person; what need did he have to illuminate every part of this mansion?

But the logic's comfort faded and ultimately perished with every step that Cyrus took without finding a sign of the surviving vampire. Cyrus could explain the darkness that huddled in these halls, but not the sense of *wrongness* that bore down heavier and heavier on his shoulders as he hastened his steps down each hall.

Several wrong turns inched his urgency toward panicked frustration. His pulse quickened alongside his steps until he finally found a familiar corridor and covered it in a sprint. He found Lucien's door and did not pause even to think before barging through.

Cyrus didn't know what he expected. The darkness, sure. The general disarray, certainly. But the disheveled room was in a worse state than when Cyrus had seen it last: Nearly every piece of furniture was overturned, books and broken glass were strewn across the rug, and the remains of the dinner Cyrus and Lucien had shared were still on the table—pungent and steadily rotting. One of the curtains and two of the chairs had four long slashes through the fabric.

It was only because Cyrus took a deep breath in an attempt to steady himself that he realized he could still smell blood.

"Vista?" His voice withered to a rasp. Hesitantly, he took a step further into the room. Clearing his throat, he tried again: "*Vista!*"

Beneath his thundering pulse, he heard a faint gasp from within the bedchamber.

Cyrus bolted across the room and slammed through the half-open door, only to trip over his own feet in his haste to stop short. The faint light from the outer room sliced into the bedchamber and fell upon an all-too-familiar figure slumped on the floor at the end of the bed.

"Vista—*Lucien.*" Cyrus went to him and dropped to his knees beside him, reaching for his shoulder. But Lucien didn't move, and then Cyrus saw all the blood.

He pressed his hand over his nose and mouth, staring in horror at the silvery sheen soaking Lucien's white shirt. It was everywhere: all over his body, his arms, his hands, his face. Rivulets of silver dribbled from his nose and the corner of his mouth, and his eyes were bloodshot and hazy, the lids purple. Cyrus couldn't stop himself from thinking of a corpse; if not for Lucien's audible, rattling breaths, Cyrus would have thought he was indeed dead.

"*Lucien.*" Cyrus shook his shoulder. Still, he didn't react. "Lucien, look at me. *Please.* Please look at me. What happened? Lucien, gods, what happened?" He grabbed him by both shoulders and shook him again, and this time Lucien groaned. His eyes fluttered as his head lolled toward Cyrus, and he took in a raspy breath.

Cyrus could barely look at him. He frantically sought the source of his injuries, fearing that it was something internal like poison until he moved out of the way of the light and found the hilt of a knife protruding from Lucien's chest—so close to his heart that a sharper-trained hand would've killed him instantly.

"Who did this?" Cyrus couldn't breathe. His voice trembled, no longer with panic, but with rage. "Who the *fuck* did this to—"

"I..." Lucien's weak, splintered voice cut him off. His mouth worked around words he couldn't get out. "I...missed."

"Wh-What..."

Blood leaked down Lucien's chin. "Missed..."

"No." Cyrus shook his head. "No, *no*, you stupid vampire, you're not going to die. Do you understand me?" He gripped Lucien by the shoulders again and glared straight into his crimson eyes. "You don't get to give up. Not unless I do, too."

Lucien wheezed a weak groan. Tears spilled down his cheeks.

Cyrus took a deep breath to steady himself. The knife was probably silver, preventing Lucien's body from healing as long as it was buried in his flesh. But if Cyrus removed it, would he have the strength to heal before he bled out? Could vampires even die by bleeding out, or would Lucien be left suffering, half-dead, forever?

Gods, all the years he'd spent learning how to kill vampires, and here he was, needing to save one instead. And he had no idea what to do.

Well. There was one thing. Lucien needed energy in order to heal; he needed a boost of life force.

He needed blood.

Cyrus looked into Lucien's eyes. "Bite me."

Lucien's eyes widened.

"It'll save you, right? It'll let you heal once this knife is out?" Cyrus swallowed hard against the tightness in his throat. *Will he turn me? Will he kill me?* How much control would he have, in this state? Did he care at all to keep Cyrus alive after what the Beldons had done?

None of it mattered. "If that's what it takes, Lucien, *bite me.* Use my blood—my life—to save yourself." A sob forced its way out of him. "*Please.*" He couldn't lose this vampire. Not when Lucien had ignited in him the only real sense of hope he'd ever felt. It wasn't just about their work; Cyrus felt valued by Lucien, as an ally and as a *person*, and he couldn't bear to lose that.

"C-Cyrus..." Lucien's voice was a weak rasp.

"*Do it!*" Cyrus tore the cravat off his neck and ripped open the buttons on his shirt, then grabbed Lucien by the shoulders again. "Please. Lucien, please, this can't be the end. Let me help you."

Lucien's head nodded back against the bed's footboard and he let out a low moan. His face screwed up with pain that made Cyrus's heart ache.

Cyrus moved to sit at his side and took much of Lucien's weight against his body. He gently turned Lucien's face toward him and blinked back tears of his own. "Please," he whispered. "I don't want you to die."

Dreadfully long seconds dragged by. Lucien found Cyrus's gaze and held it, all the while his life steadily leaked out.

"*Please,*" Cyrus begged. Prayed.

Then Lucien gave the slightest of nods, and Cyrus didn't wait for him to change his mind. He gripped the hilt of the knife and pulled; it came free with a sickening squelch, and Lucien cried out, slumping against Cyrus as his chest heaved. Fresh tears rolled down his bloodstained face, and when he looked up again, Cyrus saw the moment his instincts took over. Something deeply primal within him chased off the foggy hopelessness that had shrouded his eyes, in favor of grasping one last chance to survive.

Lucien abruptly wrapped his hand around Cyrus's neck—firmly enough to keep him still but not hard enough to cut off his air. Cyrus squeezed his eyes shut and braced himself as Lucien leaned closer and pressed his mouth to the side of his neck, right over his racing pulse.

Strangely cool breath kissed his skin. Cyrus suppressed a shudder and had but a second to inhale before Lucien sank in his fangs.

The immediate pain pierced deep, drawing a stuttered moan out of Cyrus, but then an odd sort of lightheadedness came over him and softened the sting to a dull ache. Warmth seeped through him, radiating from the sharp pricks of teeth and spreading like pins and needles to the farthest reaches of his body. He wanted to be disgusted; he *should* have been disgusted, but all he felt was invigorating warmth. His muscles loosened and bled out all of his fear; if not for Lucien's strong hold on him, he'd be a boneless heap. He felt his heartbeat slow, his lungs expand; gods, was he dying? He'd thought it would hurt more.

But no, it was a pleasant sort of pain, the kind that set every one of his nerves on edge in anticipation of what might come next. It was a pain that danced the line between agony and ecstasy—a sharp, aching torment that demanded to end in bliss.

Lucien groaned softly against Cyrus's neck and pulled him closer; warm and pliant, Cyrus couldn't have resisted even if he'd wanted to. He let Lucien drag him onto his lap, holding him as if cradling a child. His cool body was a welcome balm against Cyrus's own hot skin, and without thinking, he reached up and weakly grasped Lucien's shirt to draw him closer still. Lucien's nails dug into Cyrus's flesh, and the soft tingles under his skin sharpened to hot pinpricks that set his body alight. *More*, begged a delirious voice in the back of his mind. *More, more, more.*

Cyrus couldn't keep in a soft moan when Lucien bit harder. He moved his lips and tongue against Cyrus's skin as if kissing him hungrily, repeatedly, all the while those fangs cut deep. He could feel the warmth of his own blood on Lucien's lips, and heard each of the vampire's heavy breaths and ravenous gulps.

Cyrus realized only then how hard he was breathing, how hard his heart was pounding. But despite a lifetime of being told to fear this above all else, fear was the last thing on Cyrus's woozy mind. How could he be afraid, when Lucien held him as if he was something to be treasured—something to be *worshiped*? Cyrus barely felt the bite anymore; only warmth, and a deep ache for more. He wanted Lucien to *devour* him.

Was this the real danger of vampires? Not their strength, or even their bite, but their hypnotic *kiss*?

"*Lucien*," Cyrus breathed. His hands wandered, finding their way into Lucien's thick hair. "Lucien, I want..." He smothered his own words with another groan as Lucien slowly eased his bite. "*No*," Cyrus whined. "No, keep...keep *going*."

"Shhhhh." Lucien stroked his hand across Cyrus's cheek, then smoothed his hair back from his forehead. "I can't. You'll die if I take any more." His voice was heavy, ragged with what Cyrus could only describe as desire. "And you don't get to give up unless I do, remember?"

Cyrus fought to keep his eyes open. Lucien's face was a blur, hazy around the edges, but Cyrus fixated on those bright eyes—wondrously, blessedly alive.

Tears ran down Cyrus's face. "I'm sorry," he croaked.

"Sleep," Lucien said, and the last thing Cyrus felt was his lips—still warm with blood—touch his forehead.

To say Cyrus *woke up* was far too gentle a descriptor for how he'd clawed himself back to consciousness. His entire body felt hazy and drained, but worst was his pounding head. *What the hell did I drink*, he wondered faintly, *and why did I have so much?*

He lifted his hands to his forehead and felt an unfamiliar, bruised pain on his neck, and that made it all come rushing back to him.

Cyrus bolted upright with a gasp. "Lucien—*agh.*" His head swam as the fatigue abruptly caught up with him; he closed his eyes until it passed. "*Gods.*" He rubbed his temples. It wasn't as if he expected to be unscathed after letting a vampire drink his blood, but he had *not* expected it to feel like the worst hangover imaginable.

When he felt less like the room was spinning, he gingerly touched his fingers to the tender spot on his neck. To his surprise, the punctures had already scabbed over, and felt more like a bruise than a fresh wound. He wondered, as he idly traced the scabs, if they would scar. How long would the evidence of what he'd done —of what he'd let *Lucien* do—stay there, clear on his neck?

The full severity of it hit him then. He hadn't been thinking last night— not of this, not of the consequences. He'd been so desperate to keep Lucien safe and alive that he hadn't given a single consideration of everything that would follow the moment those fangs broke his skin.

What the fuck was I thinking? Lucien could've killed him. Or worse, turned him. Sure, he wasn't some slimy rogue vampire, but he very well could have lost control and drained Cyrus to death. And thank the gods that hadn't happened, but that didn't make this any less wrong.

Cyrus could never go home again. If he walked through the front door of House Beldon with the mark of a vampire's fangs on his neck, he'd be gutted immediately. They'd remove his name from history and pretend he'd never existed. And if by some miracle he escaped with his life, it would be ruined. *He* would be ruined. Never again would he know the comforts or privileges that came with his family name, and he'd be lucky if he could stay in Chestervale at all.

Isn't that what you wanted? murmured a voice at the back of his mind.

Well...yes. Cyrus *had* wanted to sever all ties to the Beldons and forge his own path. But not like this; he'd wanted it to be his choice, and he'd wanted it to be a *statement*. Something unforgettable, so that even when they erased his name from the family trees, his siblings would still whisper the story of the day Cyrus turned his back on the Beldons and everything they stood for.

Although, he guessed that letting an Honorable One bite him did make one hell of a statement.

Cyrus took a deep breath. It was done, and he couldn't take it back. And, anxieties aside, he didn't regret it.

He surfaced from his thoughts and eased his eyes open to get his bearings. He was still in Lucien's room—and in his bed, which...he chose not to dwell on—but the vampire was nowhere in sight. He'd clearly been here, though: there was a glass of water on the table next to the bed, as well as a dressing robe draped over the back of the chair beside the table. Cyrus spotted his bloodstained shirt and vest folded neatly on the chair with his cravat rolled up on top; the sight made him snort. He couldn't fathom why Lucien thought he'd want to keep clothes irreparably stained with blood, but the gesture was touching.

Cyrus scooted across the massive bed, took a gulp of water, then slowly eased to his feet. He had to wait for another wave of dizziness to pass, then he grabbed the dressing robe and wrapped it around his shoulders as he padded toward the door. He cracked it open and peeked out.

At first, he couldn't make sense of the view. The room had been a disaster the last he remembered, but now all signs of the incident the other night were gone—bloodstained rugs included. Each piece of furniture was back in its place, with the broken ones notably missing. The torn curtain was gone, too, and bright moonlight poured through the uncovered window, drawing Cyrus's attention to the vampire sprawled across the loveseat.

Lucien was about a foot too long for the tiny sofa, but nonetheless he slept soundly with one leg hooked over the arm, the other hanging off the side, and one arm over his eyes. He'd changed his clothes, and his hair spilled in a silver cascade over the pillows. Cyrus couldn't see most of his face, but his jaw was relaxed and his mouth was slightly open.

Even if only in sleep, even if only for this moment, he was calm. Relaxed. At peace.

Cyrus let out a breath he'd probably been holding all night.

He moved closer to the sofa and laid the dressing robe over Lucien. Cyrus let his hand linger on his shoulder for a moment, and when he started to draw away, Lucien made a soft noise and felt around until he found and grabbed Cyrus's hand.

"Don't go."

The words made him want to flee. He instinctively glanced around the room, as if the house itself was watching with judgmental eyes. But there was no one else here, no one to glare with scorn or warn him away from the bloodthirsty monster.

Cyrus buried those Beldon voices and settled on the floor next to the loveseat. He let his head fall back against the cushions and closed his eyes. Fatigue weighed heavy on his bones; his body hadn't yet recovered from the blood loss, and sleep was already pulling him back under.

"I'm here," he murmured, and let himself sink, still holding tight to Lucien's hand.

CYRUS STOOD before a door made of reflective glass. Golden light shone around the edges, illuminating his features in the mirror with an ethereal glow. The smell of damp rot was familiar to him now; he knew this place, but he had never made it this far.

He stepped closer to the mirror, slowly lifting his hand. What lay beyond this glass that so badly wanted to be known to him? He no longer heard its call or felt its urgency; rather, relief washed over him that he had finally made it here.

He reached farther until his fingers nearly touched the smooth surface, but then he felt a tap on his shoulder and froze. Glancing up, he found his sister standing behind him.

"Poppy?" Cyrus's voice was still, as always, a whisper.

"Don't," said Poppy. Her voice echoed down the spiraling stairwell behind her. "You don't want to know what's up here."

Cyrus was very positive that he did. Why else would this dream have visited him so often? Why would it be calling to him—not just in his sleep, but during the day? That voice that had pulled his attention toward the tower that day was the same one from this dream; he knew it in his bones. If Poppy knew what was up here, and Arthur likely did, and Marcus certainly did, why shouldn't Cyrus know? He was a Beldon, wasn't he?

"A Beldon?" Poppy snorted. "Have you seen yourself?" She suddenly grabbed him around the neck and wrenched his head to the side, tugging away his shirt collar to reveal the puncture wounds. "You really think a *Beldon* would let this happen? You think a Beldon would *beg* for it?"

Cyrus tried to shake his head. "I—"

"Oh, but it felt good, didn't it?" Now the voice that spoke was Lucien's, low and sultry. Cyrus glanced at the mirror and found the vampire where Poppy had been moments ago. His hand gently caressed Cyrus's neck while he snaked his other arm around his waist and held him close, tipping his head down to rest his chin on Cyrus's shoulder. His crimson eyes flicked up to meet Cyrus's in the glass. "It's exquisite, isn't it? Do you remember how you begged me for more? How you moaned for me to keep going until I'd drunk every drop?"

"No, I..." He closed his eyes, chasing the memory. Gods damn him, but it *had* felt good. A very small and forbidden part of him wanted it *again*.

"Why deprive yourself of it, Cyrus?" Lucien pressed a lingering kiss to his throat. "Open the door. See what you've been longing for."

But when Cyrus opened his eyes, the mirror and the tower had vanished and he was once again in Lucien's bed. And Lucien was there too—albeit more than an arm's length away and with his back to Cyrus.

Cyrus doubted for a second that he wasn't still in a dream. He didn't remember moving or being moved here from the sitting room, which meant that Lucien had brought Cyrus in here with him.

He tried not to overthink it.

While his pulse calmed in the wake of the dream, he watched Lucien's body slowly rise and fall with his steady breaths. A faint sense of unease crawled under his skin; he'd expected things to change between them in the wake of the murders, but this strange, new, fond closeness was not what he'd anticipated. Cyrus couldn't even name all the implications that floated around the simple fact that Lucien had pleaded with him not to leave him alone, not to mention that he'd brought him into his room and into his bed rather than leaving him out there on the loveseat.

Was it a side effect of drinking Cyrus's blood? Did Lucien feel some kind of impulse to keep Cyrus close, just in case he needed more? Did the blood intoxicate him in a way, making him feel closer to Cyrus than he actually was?

Or...was the care genuine?

Cyrus tore his eyes away from Lucien's sleeping form and stared up at the canopy over the bed. His hand wandered again to the wounds on his neck; the bruise was still tender, the memory vivid. If he pressed lightly, he could almost still feel Lucien's fangs...

Across the bed, Lucien stirred, and Cyrus flung the thoughts from his brain. That was quite enough thinking about that. He dragged himself up and rubbed his hands down his face. *Pull yourself together, Beldon.* He couldn't change his choice to let Lucien bite him, but it could *not* happen again, and he was delusional if he thought that vampire actually cared about him.

And that was that.

Cyrus slid off the bed as carefully as possible so as not to disturb Lucien's sleep, then slipped out of the room, leaving the door cracked on his way out.

He wandered across the sitting room to the uncovered window and looked out. It was just after dawn now; a pale sky peeked through the breaks in the treetops, but night still reigned in the shadows. Thick fog hugged the front gardens that sprawled out toward the road, throwing the bushes into obscurity. Only the lantern at the end of the path managed to break through the gloom, an eerie orange glow in the distance.

It seemed like ages ago that Cyrus had come through those gates and walked up that path, but impossibly it hadn't been two months. The version of himself that had quaked in his boots on the doorstep would never have fathomed standing here now, watching over a slumbering Honored One while dreams of his bite—and his kiss—prickled at the back of his mind.

Cyrus glanced back at the bedchamber door, torn. Part of him wanted to crawl back into that soft bed and not let Lucien out of his sight until he woke up. Another part of him couldn't stand to be near the vampire. And yet another, perhaps the loudest one, wanted Cyrus to run far away from all the feelings of fondness that stirred beneath his skin.

He opted for none of those choices and sought, instead, a scalding hot bath.

Chapter
FIFTEEN

HOUSE VISTA WAS GIANT, LABYRINTHINE, AND LONELY. Shadows crept after Cyrus as he wandered the halls, and shrank back only a little each time he lit a lamp. More than once, he poked his head into a room and startled at the glimpse of a person standing at a window or seated by a fireplace, only for the mirage to disappear in a blink.

More unsettling than the lingering spirits—which Cyrus had grown to accept after the third sighting—was the energy of the house itself. Perhaps it was because he was accustomed to the very different feelings within his own home, or perhaps it was entirely his imagination, but House Vista had an *aliveness* to it that Cyrus sensed like a physical presence. Its halls seemed to breathe as he passed through them, cracking the stiffness out of their bones and exhaling in relief whenever he stepped into a dusty, neglected room. Lamps and candles that he swore he didn't touch burst to life in the corner of his eye. The first day he'd set off on his meandering exploration of the house, he'd stumbled upon the kitchen precisely when he noticed he was hungry.

The house had positive energy, at least, but it was still strange. He wished he could ask Lucien about it, but the vampire had not stirred in two days.

Cyrus checked on him frequently. He didn't know if Lucien needed anything—food, water, more blood—but the glass of water Cyrus had left on the bedside table yesterday remained untouched, and Lucien's sleep was apparently unbroken. Maybe that was all he needed while his body healed. But Cyrus still expected him to be ravenous when he finally woke up, and if that was the case...

Obviously, Lucien had a supply of blood in the house. Cyrus had seen it himself, neatly bottled and stocked in the cellar. But he still wouldn't say no if *he* happened to be more easily accessible.

Try as he did to banish those thoughts from his mind, Cyrus could not stop thinking about Lucien drinking his blood. It haunted the back of his mind when he was awake and it painted his dreams when he slept. He'd found himself in the tower every night since, standing before the glowing mirror, wrapped in Lucien's arms with absolute bliss running through his veins while Lucien ravenously drank him.

Cyrus woke in the dizzying midst of it each time, hot and breathless. It made sleeping next to *actual* Lucien rather awkward.

But he still refused to leave Lucien entirely alone, so he endured the dream and the restless state it left him in, and it gradually became a routine to start his day with a cold bath to douse his fantasies before he set off wandering around the house.

On the third day, he got sick of the house's dreary darkness and made it his mission to light every candle and lamp he found. He started with Lucien's chambers and the hallway beyond, then made his way through each connecting corridor all the way down to the foyer. He burned through an entire matchbook before midday, but between the candlelight and the now-uncovered windows, the place gradually roused from its slumber and came back to life.

On the fourth day, Cyrus went back to the library. He found the books he and Lucien had been studying, still undisturbed in the lounge on the second floor. The scene was so strangely normal, oblivious of everything that had happened since these books had last been in Cyrus's hands. He'd set them down thinking he'd be back in an hour or so to continue his work; one of the books remained open, expecting the same. He reached down and closed it.

Their work was far from done, but for now, it would have to wait.

Cyrus left the books and wandered the second floor until he found the door that led into the mezzanine where he'd watched Lucien play the piano. The room was dark now; its many candles and lamps had been extinguished, and the wall of windows was smothered behind heavy black curtains. Shadows stretched and sprawled across the once-luminous room, and Cyrus couldn't stand it.

He backed out of the mezzanine and shut the door, then went back down to the main floor and opened every door he found in that corner of the house, determined to find the way into that room.

Ten doors later, he opened the last one that would reasonably lead to the piano room and found a closet-like space behind it. Frustrated, he went to shut it, but then felt a faint breeze from within the room. He stepped in and felt along the walls until his fingers met an unmistakable break in the paneling, then followed the edge down until his hand bumped a doorknob. He grinned and twisted it, pushing through the smaller door into, at last, the piano room.

Cavernous darkness yawned ahead of him, lightened only by the faint glow from the door behind him. Fractures of daylight poked through the cracks in the curtains, and Cyrus quickly crossed the echoing floor to drag them open. Warm, golden sunlight greeted him with each uncovered window and coaxed a smile out of him.

He turned his back to the windows and took in the room. The mezzanine was in the far upper corner to his left, supported by marble columns with bases sculpted to look like muscular men hefting the pillars on their shoulders. Similar columns lined the room's perimeter, and between them were yet more doors decorated with intricate filigreed swirls. Murals that occupied the entire width of the upper halves of the walls showed scenes of revelry and indulgence: dances in the woods, parties under moonlight, couples lounging in intimate embraces. Whoever had pored over these paintings had clearly harbored a deep appreciation for the human body—or, rather, vampire body, upon closer scrutiny—given the lack of clothing in each sensual scene.

Cyrus followed the paintings along the edges of the room until he circled around to the piano, and then approached the shining instrument. He looked around for a book or even a single page of scores, but found none; what Lucien had played the other day had been entirely from memory, a skill Cyrus himself had never mastered.

It had been years since he'd played at all, but his earliest memories of his mother were at her piano bench. He had sat on her lap and placed his small hands on top of hers while she'd played and recited the notes aloud so he'd learn which ones were where and made which chords. Cyrus faintly remembered getting the hang of it enough to play a little on his own, but when his mother had died, his motivation to learn music had died with her.

Now that he thought about it, there hadn't been music in the Beldon household since.

Cyrus sat down on the piano bench and uncovered the keys. Pristine ivory gleamed in the room's brightness, reflecting the windows' glare. Cyrus traced his fingertips over the keys and felt the weathered places where musicians' fingers had worn away the polish over time. How many years—how many *decades*—had Lucien been playing this very instrument? How many Vistas had sat in this spot and let the notes carry away their worries?

Cyrus closed his eyes and set his hands in the starting position on the keys. A tune surfaced in the back of his mind, a long-ago melody that he'd practiced over and over until he heard it in his dreams. It was the song his mother used to play, the one she hummed as she went about her day. Cyrus plucked the keys until he found the right notes, teasing out the melody over and over until his fingers didn't stumble. Up and down the scales, he increased the tempo until the gentle tune became the song he remembered.

*There was once a a dear young
Woman, fair and proud.
She met a vampire
And he taught her how to dance.
And she fell hard
For that creature o' the night
Ne'er to be seen again.*

Cyrus hadn't heard or thought of the song in years, but he still heard the words in his mother's voice. He'd never really paid attention to the little story within those lyrics before, but now it sank like a stone into his heart. Apparently the Beldons couldn't even have folk songs without mentioning the danger of vampires.

He slowed his hands and brought the song back to a gentler tune, letting out a slow breath as the music faded. Only then did he realize his cheeks were wet with tears that had welled and fallen without his notice. He quickly wiped them away.

And it wasn't until he went to place his hands on the piano keys again that he realized he was no longer alone.

Soundlessly, wordlessly, Lucien slid onto the bench beside him and placed his own slender hands on the lower half of the keys. He glanced once at Cyrus, then gently pressed a single note with the ring finger of his left hand.

Cyrus stared at him for a moment, and then played two soft notes.

Lucien played the next ones, and Cyrus soon recognized the tune he'd just been playing himself. He followed Lucien's lead, letting him choose the tempo. Lucien kept the pitch low, so Cyrus moved his hand closer to the middle, and though it was the same song, the tune they played together was far more subdued, the lingering notes almost ominous.

And to Cyrus's surprise, when the tempo reached its peak, Lucien began to sing.

There was once a foolish
Creature of the night.
He met a woman and she
Promised him her life
And he let that human
Shatter his pride.
Best ne'er to love again.

It was a clear parody of the song Cyrus knew, and he found himself chuckling. Of course, any cautionary tale humans wrote about vampires, vampires had one to counter it. Cyrus found the irony amusing, even if it was also disheartening. Even their songs were at odds.

Lucien kept the music going even after the lyrics ended, but Cyrus now struggled to keep up. His attention had abandoned the music in favor of Lucien himself; Cyrus couldn't stop looking at him, silently begging to hear that silvery voice again. He gazed in something like awe at this man who was so much more than what Cyrus had assumed. Exhausted, devastated, at the brink of utter ruin—yet still, miraculously, alive.

If Cyrus had done one good thing in his life it was this: sacrificing his blood, his very life, to keep Lucien in the world.

His hand clumsily hit a wrong note, jarring him out of his daze. Warmth flooded his cheeks and he refocused his attention to the music, but Lucien was already bringing the tempo back down, letting the notes fade out. The serenity that had softened his face in these past moments gradually faded too, and something darker crept back in.

He sighed and let his hands slip from the keys.

Cyrus folded his own hands between his knees. He stole a few glances at Lucien but didn't want to stare too harshly; Lucien would talk when he wished to, and Cyrus wanted to give him space.

But he also wanted to take him by the shoulders and shake the absolute hell out of him, all the while demanding to know what the fuck he'd been thinking when he'd tried to stab himself through the heart.

That night and that bloody scene had been surprisingly scarce in Cyrus's mind these past few days, but now, with Lucien beside him, Cyrus couldn't stop seeing him as he had been that night: Defeated, hopeless, and half dead.

Cyrus understood those feelings all too well. He felt them often. But either he was oblivious or Lucien hadn't betrayed a single sign that he'd go that far—that he was so desperate to be relieved of the burdens on his shoulders that he'd choose death, alone in the dark.

The days following his relatives' deaths must have been unimaginable. And Cyrus had left him here, in a bloodstained house of ghosts.

"Lucien." Cyrus's voice was thick. "I am so sorry."

He shook his head, dislodging a few strands of silver hair from behind his ears that fell to frame his face. "No. I am. I...chased you away. After all you've promised me and all you've done for this mad endeavor of ours...I chased you away."

"You were in shock," Cyrus said.

"That doesn't make it acceptable." Lucien turned to him. "I don't expect your forgiveness, but I do hope for it."

Cyrus rolled his lips between his teeth to smother the swell of emotions that jumped up his throat. "You stupid vampire," he croaked. "I forgave you before I was even out the door."

Lucien blinked a few times, then let out an unsteady breath and turned his head down so his hair obscured his face. Minutes slipped by, and when Lucien looked up again, his eyes traced down Cyrus's face before finally lingering on his neck.

Self-consciously, Cyrus touched the healing scabs.

"Are you okay?" Lucien asked softly. "I know it can be disorienting, and I regret that I wasn't able to take better care of you afterwards. I...I'm sorry that it was even necessary."

"You don't have to apologize," Cyrus said.

"Usually we try not to leave a mark." Lucien met his eyes. "I could heal it further, if you'd like."

Cyrus frowned. "How?"

"I'd have to kiss your neck."

Cyrus recoiled. "No." As if his dreams needed more fodder. "It'll heal on its own. I'm okay. But I can't believe you're worrying over *me* when you're the one who was at death's door. Are *you* okay, Lucien?"

His energy bled out of him; his shoulders sank and he bowed his head so Cyrus couldn't see his face. "No. I'm not."

Cyrus smothered an urge to touch his hand. "What can I do?"

Lucien was already shaking his head before the words were out of Cyrus's mouth. "Nothing. Nothing at all, Cyrus, you've done so much. You've done more than enough, more than I ever expected from someone I've known for mere weeks. My pain is mine. You are not responsible for it."

"But my family is," Cyrus said. "I had no part in what happened to your family, Lucien, nor did I have any idea what my father was planning. I swear to you that is the truth."

"I know."

"But I'm also not free of guilt. I've said from the beginning that *that* is not the kind of Beldon I want to be." Cyrus looked down at his hands and twisted his family's ring around his finger. Part of him wanted to rip it off and fling it into the canal, leaving it to tarnish and rot with all the other shit in there. Another part of him couldn't let it go, if only to remind him of what he was reaching for —and what he was leaving behind.

He could still be a Beldon without being *Marcus* Beldon.

"I know," Lucien murmured. He let out a heavy sigh and tipped his head back; his hair slipped like silk over his shoulders. When he opened his eyes he squinted at the windows, then his gaze wandered back to Cyrus. "Did you open those?"

"Yes. I...couldn't stand the darkness anymore."

"Ah. You lit all the lamps as well."

"Who else was going to do it?" Cyrus flickered a smile. "Need I remind you again that I can't see in the dark like you can?"

"Right. Well, assuming the staff haven't all fled, I thought perhaps they had lit the lamps." Lucien dragged a hand through his hair and shook it out as his fingers caught on numerous tangles. He made a face as his fingers skimmed over the silver locks. "Ugh. Before we do anything else or even talk about doing anything else, I'm taking a bath." He turned to Cyrus, frowning. "Have you eaten? Did you find the kitchens? I hope you helped yourself to anything—"

"Lucien." Cyrus smiled. "I'm fine. Yes, I found the kitchens, but I haven't had much of an appetite. It's been...a weird few days."

"Few *days*?" Lucien's mouth fell open.

"Lucien, you almost died," Cyrus said, more harshly than he intended. "I don't even know how you were still alive when I found you. Of course you were out for a few days—your body had a lot to heal. I'm surprised you're awake even now."

Lucien clenched his jaw and studied Cyrus in that close way that made Cyrus self-conscious about whatever his face was doing. He turned away and fixed his eyes on the piano keys, waiting for Lucien to snarl something about his capability to take care of himself, and Cyrus was stupid for worrying and foolish for getting so attached.

Instead, Lucien reached over and touched his arm. Cyrus startled, and the slight jump made Lucien pull back for a second, only to set his pale hand on Cyrus's forearm, gentler this time.

"In the interest of not being chastised, I won't apologize again," Lucien murmured. "But I hate that I caused you so much distress."

Cyrus couldn't believe Lucien felt even a *hint* of guilt for the past few days when *Cyrus* was the one with silver blood spattered all over his family name. "You're blaming yourself again," he muttered.

"Why shouldn't I?"

Cyrus met his eyes. "Because you're in unimaginable pain. You lost everything and everyone you care about in the span of an hour, and in the days following, you were alone. It is not your fault that you broke, Lucien. The blame is not yours to carry. Isn't the pain heavy enough?"

Cyrus saw it then, written across Lucien's features. It broke through the carefully schooled neutrality on his face and shattered it. He crumpled, pressing the heel of his hand to his eyes as tears welled and fell. A sob broke out of him and pierced straight through Cyrus's chest.

Tears burned at the corners of his eyes. He hadn't meant to push Lucien to break down, but he also saw that Lucien needed the release. If he was anything like Cyrus, he'd been drifting through numb fog these past days, bottling everything up to keep it at bay.

Cyrus held his breath and lightly touched Lucien's shoulder, spreading his hand across his soft shirt. He could feel Lucien trembling; part of him longed to pull Lucien into his arms and hold him the way the vampire had held him that night.

But that was too much, too raw, so Cyrus resisted, and wished with every beat of his heart that he could offer more. More comfort. More courage. More hope.

After some time, Lucien's breaths evened out and he dragged his hands across his face. When he straightened, his eyes were red and his cheeks were damp, but no fresh tears fell. He took a deep breath and let it out slowly.

Only then did Cyrus let his hand fall from Lucien's shoulder.

"I didn't know you could play." Lucien stroked his fingers across the piano keys. His voice was frail, on the verge of breaking.

Cyrus was thrown by the abrupt change in subject, but if Lucien didn't wish to speak more of the past days, Cyrus was content to lay the topic to rest for now. "I can't, really. My mother taught me when I was young, but I've forgotten nearly everything."

"You remembered enough to coax that tune to life earlier." Lucien softly pressed a low note, then let his hand slide off the keys. "Music has a magic to it, I think. It never truly lets you forget it.

I've always felt that magic in this room—a sense of connection to all the past versions of myself who sought solace in here. I come here when I need clarity, when there's so much on my mind that words aren't enough to let it out."

He reached up and pressed another key higher up on the scale. "The keys respond to emotions. Each strike carries nuance, never exactly the same as the last. There's so much you can say with music that can't be said in words."

Cyrus flickered a smile when Lucien glanced up at him. "Maybe someday I can relearn what I forgot."

"Maybe I could teach you." Lucien's smile was gentle, fragile as his voice and delicate as the tears that clung to his eyelashes. The rapid patter of Cyrus's heart begged him to look away, but he was caught. Pinned. And he had no desire to wriggle free.

It was a dangerous feeling, a treacherous and slippery slope toward something he hardly dared think about. So he let the feeling run its course, he felt its forbidden warmth, and he smothered any and all thoughts of what it meant. His emotions were going haywire; he couldn't trust any of them. He'd come to his senses once the shock of the past few days wore off.

Lucien finally looked away, and Cyrus remembered how to breathe. "What now, Cyrus?"

So, it seemed the first names were here to stay.

"You mentioned a bath," Cyrus said. Past that, he sure as hell had no idea what was to come next.

"Oh, did you want to join me?" Lucien flashed a grin, then laughed at the horror on Cyrus's face. Cyrus buried his mortification under sheer relief that Lucien had *laughed*. "I jest," Lucien assured him. "Unless...?" He quirked an eyebrow, and before Cyrus could figure out if he was *actually* joking or not, he chuckled again. "Truly, I jest. Yes, I wish to freshen up after several days of not leaving my bed, but what comes next? Where the hell do we go from here?"

Cyrus released a heavy sigh in an attempt to calm his pulse, forcing every thought of Lucien and baths from his mind. Really, after the plague of dreams about the vampire drinking his blood, this was the absolute last thing his imagination needed.

He dragged his mind back to reality. "You were going to tell me about someone who might be able to help us, weren't you? Someone sort of risky?"

Lucien grumbled something under his breath. "I didn't want it to come to that, but I don't think we have another choice at this point."

Cyrus nodded. "Lucien...I can't go back to the Beldon estate. Possibly ever. If I show my face there again, I'll likely never be able to come back here."

"Which begs the question," Lucien said softly, "do you trust me enough to stay?"

"Yes," Cyrus said, without hesitation.

Lucien nodded thoughtfully. "This contact I have...She doesn't live in the city. We'd have to travel—quite far, I'm afraid. It could take us up to a week to reach her. So I would understand if that's... too much to ask of you."

"Not at all. Wherever we have to go, whatever we have to do, I'm in. I'm with you."

He'd abandoned Lucien once. He did not intend to do it ever again.

Lucien studied him nervously for a moment, and then that gentle smile eased across his face again. This time, Cyrus made himself look away.

Yet the silence that stretched between them was comfortable as the new plan settled in their minds. How far was *quite far*, Cyrus wondered? How long would they be gone, and what sort of havoc might Emerson Beldon wreak in that time? Would he even care that Cyrus had disappeared, or had he already shrugged it off? And if he did care, would he come looking here?

Maybe it was for the best that Cyrus and Lucien would be getting away from Chestervale for a time.

Lucien rose from the piano bench, tossing his hair over his shoulder. "Right, I'm tired of feeling vile. Feel free to reacquaint yourself with the piano if you like, but you also may want to rest. If we're going north, we need to leave soon. At sundown, if we can manage it."

Cyrus raised his eyebrows. "Tonight?"

"We can't risk your family coming knocking again," Lucien said quietly. "If you've been here for several days, they've likely noticed your absence. I know you kept our work secret, but I fear this will be the first place they look."

So Cyrus hadn't been irrational in his fear of the same. Even if Emerson didn't care about Cyrus as a person, he still belonged to the Beldons, and Emerson did not like it when his belongings were missing.

"Okay," Cyrus agreed. "We leave tonight, then."

Chapter
SIXTEEN

THE FOREST GREETED CYRUS AND LUCIEN WITH A THICK
cloak of fog. They had left Lucien's home at twilight, each astride a
horse laden with leather bags that contained necessities intended to
last them until they were far enough from Chestervale that they
could safely stop. Until then, Lucien had warned, the canopy of
trees would be their shelter and the forest floor their beds.

Cyrus rode Demeter alongside Lucien's lithe stallion, which
snorted and tossed its head as it pranced along the worn dirt path.
The animal was clearly annoyed with the leisurely pace Lucien had
set; Demeter, on the other hand, seemed rather content with the
casual trot.

Though they had not yet crossed the official city limits, Cyrus
felt farther away from home than ever. Strange, that he'd looked
out over the city just a handful of weeks ago and thought of all the
places that lay outside of his world—and now here he was,
venturing toward them.

It felt wrong to be excited for the days ahead, given the reason
for their travels and the previous days, but Cyrus couldn't stifle his
anticipation. It wasn't just the promise of new sights, either; it was
the promise of freedom.

Finally, for the first time in his life, he was beyond the reach of
the Beldons' watchful eyes.

Lucien's horse gave another impatient snort, bobbing its head forward as if urging Lucien to let it run. Lucien glanced at Cyrus, winding his reins around his hands. "How do you feel about a quick sprint?"

"Sprint?" Cyrus considered Demeter. Compared to Lucien's mount, the tawny mare looked like a wobbly cow with a long face. "I don't even think Demeter *can* sprint. But clearly your horse has a spring in his step, so go ahead. I'll catch up."

Lucien pouted. "But that's no fun. Come on, Cyrus, race me."

"Does this look like a racehorse to you?"

"I'm sure she's still got it in her. Come on." Lucien grinned. "Winner gets to sleep on the one singular pillow I brought."

Cyrus pointed a finger at him. "You're on." He nudged Demeter with his heel; she surged ahead exactly one step with a halfhearted gallop, then snorted. Cyrus frowned.

Lucien snickered. "Maybe she needs some inspiration." He snapped his horse's reins and the stallion bolted, kicking up dirt and leaves in its wake. Demeter snorted again, tossing her head.

"You know what I think?" Cyrus muttered. "I think he just wanted to show off."

Lucien was a silver streak against the night, his hair the only bright feature betraying his presence. Soon the fog would swallow him entirely.

"Come on, girl." Cyrus nudged Demeter's flank again, and when she didn't react, he reached back and smacked her rump.

Which was the wrong thing to do, because Demeter reared back so abruptly that Cyrus only barely stayed in his saddle. He scrambled to keep ahold of the reins as Demeter leapt into a gallop.

Cyrus had never seen this horse move so fast in his life. And he sure as hell had no idea how to get her to stop.

But to his surprise, he was gaining on Lucien, who was close enough now that Cyrus could see the grin on his face. His hair flew in wild strands around him, framing his sharp cheekbones and that bright, unmasked smile. He rode gracefully, as if the horse was standing still; meanwhile, Cyrus was quickly losing feeling in his hands thanks to the grip he had on his own horse's reins.

"See?" Lucien called over the thunder of hoofbeats. "She figured it out!"

"Yeah, and nearly killed me," Cyrus retorted.

"Spirits, you're dramatic." Lucien swept his hair out of his face. "Race to the next crossroads?"

He didn't wait for Cyrus to reply before he snapped the reins and sent his stallion sprinting again. Cyrus rolled his eyes but found himself smiling; he urged Demeter faster until he was sure she couldn't possibly work her legs any harder, and though he didn't stand a chance at catching up with or surpassing Lucien, the mare kept a strong and steady pace until the crossroads came into view. Cyrus drew up the reins.

Only then, in the absence of hoofbeats, did Cyrus realize how quiet the surrounding forest was. A cold trickle of fear licked down his spine; Cyrus might not be *that* kind of hunter, but he knew how to tell when animals sensed a predator.

"Lucien," he whispered, and the name had scarcely left his lips when Lucien's horse reared back with a shriek as something tore out of the woods. It pounced on the stallion, and in moments more were upon them—huge, four-legged beasts that both outsized and outnumbered the horses.

Cyrus stumbled down from Demeter's back and let her go, then drew his knife and rounded on the animals. He counted four of them, at least, but he was blind in the dark. He heard Lucien's horse's pained screams, but saw no sign of the vampire until one of the beasts leapt, only to be thrown backwards into the trees. Cyrus glimpsed a streak of silver, but then one of the creatures snapped at him and he had to trust that Lucien could take care of himself.

Cyrus swiped frantically, trying to keep the beast away rather than trying to land a blow; if the thing got within stabbing range, he was dead. It was massive; its hulking form almost reminded him of—

Oh. Fuck. These weren't animals. They were Wild vampires.

Cyrus tightened his grip on his knife and wished, for once, that he had a larger blade. But silver was silver and a dagger could sever arteries just as well as a sword. The dark gave him a disadvantage, but if he could get past this one, he could find his way to Lucien and rely on the vampire's sight rather than his own.

One monster in his way. He could do this. It was in his blood.

Cyrus lunged before the creature had another chance. He went straight for its throat and jabbed the knife into its jugular. It roared and recoiled, swiping at Cyrus with deadly claws, but he ducked its clumsy blows and kept hold of his weapon. Cold blood poured over his hand and arm as he dragged the knife through the thing's thick flesh, and then finally the monster's wet breaths became ragged. It jerked and swayed, still trying to claw Cyrus away, but he was small and the beast couldn't reach him where he clung to its neck. Cyrus used the monster's erratic movements to rip the knife harder through its flesh with every jerk of its head.

When Cyrus at last freed his dagger, the Wild vampire reeled back with a howl, stumbling over its own legs. It thrashed madly, crashing into the other monsters before finally collapsing. Cyrus darted to its side and plunged his dagger into its throat. The blade was far too small to fully decapitate the beast, but he twisted it deeper until he was up to his wrists in the cold, torn flesh, and only when the monster stopped writhing did he draw back.

He had exactly a second to take a breath before another beast pounced.

Cyrus ducked and swiped at the creature's legs as he darted out of its reach. While it lumbered around, searching for its target, Cyrus followed the other growls and grunts in search of Lucien. He spotted a streak of silver—practically glowing in the dark—but when Cyrus neared he found not a vampire, but a white wolf.

He didn't have time to ask, and the canine's bright crimson eyes were answer enough. Another Wild vampire lunged at Cyrus with a roar; before Cyrus had raised his knife, Lucien flung himself at the beast and clamped his jaws around its throat. It howled and wrenched back, yanking Lucien off his feet, but Lucien held fast and thrashed until he fell from the monster's body with a dripping chunk of its flesh still in his teeth.

The creature collapsed to its knees; Cyrus jumped in and tore his dagger across its shredded throat. Its roars choked up with blood that spurted from its mouth, and the moment it crashed to the ground Cyrus gave it a final, lethal stab through the skull.

Breathing hard, he staggered back from the creature and sought Lucien—who had changed back to his usual appearance. His face, hair, and clothes were soaked with black blood, but not a trace of silver. He eyed Cyrus appraisingly and started to speak, but then his eyes flashed wide and he rushed toward Cyrus in the same moment something swept his legs out from under him.

He hit the ground hard and a scream tore out of him as white-hot pain shot up his leg. Blindly, he scrambled across the dirt, desperate to tear himself away from the source of the pain, but the movement only worsened it. Black spots crowded his vision and turned his surroundings into nonsense; he heard growls and roars and the squelch of bloody flesh, but as his mind fought for consciousness, he lost track of what was real.

Wild vampires. It took all of his focus to stitch even a single thought together. *Lucien. Help.* Cyrus gritted his teeth and shook his head, willing the dizziness away. He dragged himself upright and turned, searching for a glimpse of silver hair. Instead he saw the wolf again; his eyes focused just long enough to watch it bring down a Wild vampire, and then the last thing he saw was Lucien's panicked face before the darkness swallowed him.

CYRUS WAS RUNNING, and something at the back of his mind told him that should be impossible. Yet he sprinted through a dark, overgrown forest that clawed at him with thorny branches as he tore his way through it. Something was chasing him, and something ahead would save him. He just had to keep running.

The land sloped upward and his momentum slowed. The

forest floor gave way to loose rocks, and then stone steps. Darkness swallowed his surroundings, leaving only a faint glowing light ahead, just around a corner.

Cyrus knew this place. He ran faster. And this time, the light drew nearer.

Hope burned in his chest with each rapid step. Around and around he ascended until finally—*finally*—he reached the top of the steps and faced the mirror on the door. He glanced back once, but no one was there to stop him. He grabbed the brass knob and burst into the room beyond.

Warm, golden light welcomed him. The space smelled like cinnamon and cranberries, a scent he knew but couldn't place. In his baffled relief at finally opening the door, it took him a moment to realize there was someone else in the room.

Opposite the door, a woman sat at a piano with her back to Cyrus. Her wavy brown hair cascaded down her back, and she hummed a tune that instantly struck a memory in Cyrus's mind. Candles flickered on the windowsill above the piano; their glow highlighted the lighter strands of blond and gray in the woman's hair.

Cyrus took a step forward. The woman started to turn her head, but before he could get a glimpse of her face, something grabbed his ankle and tore him off his feet. He screamed and thrashed, kicking at the shadowy monster that had clamped its jaws around his leg, but it didn't relent. It dragged him out of the room and back into the dark, and the door swung shut on the woman at the piano.

"Cyrus. *Cyrus!*"

"No!" He grasped at the floor, nails scraping over the stone. "I'm here! Don't let me go! I'm *here!*"

"Cyrus! It's me." Someone grabbed his hands; their skin was smooth and cool, their touch gentle. "It's just me. You're okay."

He snapped open his eyes with a gasp and found himself in an unfamiliar space. The room was dim; a lantern burned low somewhere in a corner Cyrus couldn't see. He blinked, struggling to focus his vision, and finally his eyes found a familiar pale face.

"Lucien?" His voice scraped his throat. He tried to clear it, and then tried to move, but a shock of bone-deep pain canceled that idea at once. He groaned and slumped against the pillows beneath his head. "Where are we?"

"We're safe," Lucien murmured. He glanced over Cyrus's face with that slight crease between his brows that told Cyrus there was a lot more to the situation than them merely being safe. But they weren't in the woods anymore, so that was a start. "How are you feeling?"

"Fucking awful," Cyrus rasped. He searched his memory, but everything between racing Lucien through the woods and climbing that damned tower came up only in pieces. "How did we get here? The Wild vampires..."

"Are taken care of." Lucien folded his hands between his knees. He was perched on the edge of the bed where Cyrus lay, even though there was a chair only a few feet away against the wall. This close, Cyrus could see the deep lines of exhaustion beneath his eyes. Had he slept at all? Would it be strange to tell him he could lie here with Cyrus and rest as long as he needed to?

What? Of course it would. Cyrus shook the thought out of his head; he must still be half in his dreams. He rubbed his eyes and tried to sit up again, but this time Lucien stopped him with a hand on his chest.

It was only with the shock of that cold touch that Cyrus realized he was mostly unclothed. Again.

"Don't," Lucien said. He pulled back his hand, but his eyes lingered on the key that rested beneath Cyrus's collarbones. "You need to stay still. It'll be a few days before you can move."

"Where are my pants?" Somehow that question made it out before anything concerning the state of his injury. The pain chewing up his leg was answer enough to that.

"Probably ash by now." Lucien shrugged, but at least looked a little guilty. "We were both covered in blood. I was fairly confident that you wouldn't want your clothes back, so I burned them along with mine. I hope you brought extras."

"Well, yeah, but..." Cyrus took in the room for the first time. Small and sort of drafty, with graying white walls and peeling paint around the single window, it was a little worse for wear. A lantern sat, flickering, on top of a three-drawer chest across from the bed, and Cyrus spotted a heap of familiar bags slumped on the floor beside the chest.

Cyrus dragged his attention back to Lucien. "So our horses came back?"

"Demeter did." Lucien glanced away. "Spire...didn't make it."

"Oh." Cyrus grimaced. "I'm sorry, Lucien."

He shook his head. "Better him than you." A faint smile touched his lips as he met Cyrus's eyes again. "You fought well back there. I truly had no idea how we would fare against five Wild vampires, and I'm ashamed to admit that I did not expect you to take out two all on your own. It seems I've underestimated you, Cyrus Beldon."

"Well." Cyrus looked away, uncomfortable under the praise. "It was really just the one; you took care of the rest, and then I went and got hurt and left the others for you to finish off, so really I was quite useless." *Stop rambling.* He swallowed and grasped the first change in subject he thought of. "I guess I knew, in theory, that you could shapeshift, but I never expected to see it. That was...pretty incredible."

"I don't do it often," Lucien said. "It tires me out quite a lot, but in certain scenarios it's useful. Necessary, even. Especially when I have to rush to get help after a Wild vampire gnawed on your leg."

He said it lightly, but Cyrus still winced. "I guess we're lucky that this town was close. What is it?"

"A little village on the lake's edge." Lucien combed his fingers through his hair and gathered it all together over his left shoulder. He separated the length into three sections, and with deft fingers began weaving it in a braid. Cyrus watched the practiced movements and felt a tug of longing to run his own hands through those silver strands.

Gods, stop it, what is wrong with me?

"I planned for us to stop here eventually, so we're not off course," Lucien went on. "I've visited this little inn before; the couple who own it are kind acquaintances of mine. Thankfully when I showed up in the middle of the night desperately needing their help, they provided. Even went and fetched the village doctor, who got your injury cleaned and fixed. The couple was apologetic that they only had one room available, but I assured them it wouldn't be a problem." Lucien tied off his braid with a piece of ribbon he took from his wrist, then curled the strands at the end around his finger. "When you're feeling up to it, I can bring you something to eat. And let me know if the pain gets worse; the doctor left me something to help with that."

Cyrus found himself smiling. This side of Lucien was different; he hadn't expected him to be such an attentive caretaker. It was *almost* worth getting bitten by a Wild vampire.

And that thought sent a spike of panic through him. "Lucien?"

"Hm?"

"What's going to happen to me?"

Lucien frowned. "What do you mean?"

"That thing *bit* me. Am I—?"

"No." Lucien shook his head. "You'll heal from these wounds like you would from any animal's bite. Wild vampires can't turn people, and even if they could, it would've needed to take far more blood from you than it did. You're safe, I promise."

"Are you sure?" Cyrus couldn't get the fear out of his head. "There's so much we don't know about them. What if they *can* turn people—isn't that what we think happened to Leigh Harrows? What if they don't need as much blood as a regular vampire, or—"

"Cyrus." Lucien reached over and placed his hand on his arm. "You are safe. Nothing is going to happen to you. Trust me."

Cyrus met his eyes and realized he did. Really, truly,

wholeheartedly, he did trust Lucien. Because Lucien had spared his life twice now: he'd bitten him and drank from him without turning him, and he'd rushed to get help instead of leaving Cyrus to die in the woods. And yes, it would be foolish of Lucien to let Cyrus die when he needed him for their project, but studying the vampire now, Cyrus saw that it was more than that. Lucien cared about him, and Cyrus, admittedly, cared about Lucien, too.

"I do," Cyrus said softly. "I do trust you. Sorry, it's just...These things are terrifying."

Lucien nodded. "You're not wrong, there is a lot we don't know about Wild vampires. The mere fact that we ran into any at all is deeply concerning. Where did they come from? Who were they? And who turned them?"

Cyrus was too exhausted to even start to consider those questions, but they were worrying nonetheless. At the moment, though, he was more concerned about Lucien. "What about you?" he murmured. "Were you hurt?"

Lucien failed to hide a blink of surprise at the question. "Not really. Just a few scratches here and there. I'll live."

"You'd better." Sleep pulled at Cyrus's consciousness, but he didn't want to succumb. Not yet. He wanted this moment to continue.

"I'm doing my best," Lucien said. "*You* ought to try harder."

"It's not *my* fault we ran into a bunch of Wild vampires. *You* were the one who wanted to race blindly into the woods."

Lucien flinched a little. "Right. Perhaps that wasn't my greatest idea."

Cyrus reached up and poked his arm. "It's okay. We couldn't have known. And we handled it."

"Sure, but it certainly could have gone better." Lucien flicked a pointed glance toward Cyrus's feet.

"Could've gone a lot worse, too." Cyrus smirked. "Unfortunately for you, I lived, and you still have to put up with me."

Lucien snickered and stood up. "You say that like it's a bad thing." He lightly touched Cyrus's shoulder. "Get some rest. When you've recovered, there's a few things I want to show you."

Ominous. "Like what?"

He slipped out of the room with a sly smile, but no reply.

Chapter SEVENTEEN

A WEEK OF REST, MEDICINE, AND CAREFUL EXERCISES got Cyrus gradually back on his feet, only to find out that Lucien's secret plan was to kick his ass.

Following a note he'd found on the bed when he'd woken up, Cyrus had found Lucien out in a field on the edge of the little fishing town. Longsword in hand, he'd been practicing various movements while Demeter grazed nearby. Cyrus should've known he was doomed when Lucien had greeted him with a grin that fell somewhere between manic and evil.

"Let me know if you need to stop," Lucien had told him when they'd begun, and then hadn't been easy on him since.

Cyrus knew that a sword was far more effective against a vampire than his little daggers, but he still didn't like it. The weapon was too heavy; he felt clumsy. Every swing he attempted was painfully overcalculated; if Lucien was a real opponent, Cyrus would've been dead at least four times by now.

"Okay, pause," Lucien commanded, and Cyrus lowered his weapon. Lucien twirled his own in his hand as he approached. "Before you pull a muscle or break your wrists, let me show you how to hold it correctly. I just realized you haven't been doing it right at all."

"I did tell you *several times* that this isn't my preferred weapon." Cyrus flexed his hands on the hilt. His arms were already tired; he couldn't imagine what he'd feel like tomorrow. "I haven't picked up a sword in years."

"And it shows," Lucien said with exaggerated cheer. He moved to stand at Cyrus's side. "Firstly, your hands are too close together. You have no control over the weapon because you're not distributing its weight correctly. Hold it like this." He gripped the hilt just under the crossguards with his right hand, and placed his left hand closer to the pommel.

Cyrus copied the positions, but the weapon still strained his muscles. "This doesn't feel much different."

"It will. Your right hand—assuming you are right-handed, yes?"

"I'm ambidextrous." Cyrus swapped his hands and found that the sword felt more controlled with his left hand in the upper position. "Actually, this feels better."

"Interesting," Lucien mused. "That could be an advantage for you. But at any rate, your dominant hand should be in the upper position. This hand is directing your strike, while the other balances the weapon's weight. Your dominant hand leads, and the other hand follows. Does that make sense?"

"Sure." Cyrus moved a few paces away from Lucien and gave the sword an experimental swing, following the movements Lucien had shown him earlier. He could tell he had more control, but the sword still seemed awkward. He turned back to Lucien. "Even if I was holding it wrong, I think this sword is too big for me. Look." He stabbed the tip into the ground; the pommel was nearly level with his shoulder. "It's almost as tall as I am."

Lucien stared at him, then blinked a few times. "Oh. Well, that certainly is your problem, then. One moment." He placed his weapon on the ground and went over to Demeter, then returned with another, smaller sword. He offered it to Cyrus. "Try this one."

Cyrus took it and found he could swing it easily enough with one hand. He'd need practice, but at least this weapon didn't feel like it was going to snap his wrists or fly out of his grip.

"Much better," Lucien murmured. "But that didn't solve all of your problems, because you're still only using your shoulders and hands when you need to be using *all* of the muscles in your arms. Flex those biceps, Beldon, I know you're not all skin and bones." He poked Cyrus's arm, and Cyrus batted his hand away with a scowl.

But he did as Lucien said, and found it took a lot of strain off his wrists. He guided the sword through another slicing motion, and for the first time felt like he might actually be able to wield this in a real fight.

"Better?" Lucien asked.

"Definitely different."

"Great, now I can point out how sloppy your stance is."

Cyrus rolled his eyes. "I think I preferred this lesson when you were beating the shit out of me."

"Oh? You prefer a more hands-on approach?" Lucien stepped behind Cyrus and grabbed him by the hips, pulling him flush against his body. He leaned close to Cyrus's ear and purred, "Is this better?"

Cyrus tensed every muscle in his body, hardly daring to breathe. Half of his brain screamed at him to push Lucien away; the other half rendered him frozen. Lucien's presence was oddly cool, and Cyrus caught himself leaning into him more, seeking warmth he knew he wouldn't feel. A shiver ran down his spine as Lucien's breath feathered his neck; yet again, the memory of his bite returned unbidden.

"Oh, but now you're all tense again." Lucien slid his hands up Cyrus's sides, over his arms, and gripped his shoulders. "Relax. Release the breath I know you're holding. Your heart is *racing*, Mr. Beldon. I wonder why that could be."

Cyrus tightened his hands around the sword's hilt until it hurt. He tried to speak, but all that came out was a ragged breath. Lucien's touch froze him and burned him all at once; his closeness was electrifying, intoxicating, and dangerous.

Two things occurred to Cyrus in unison:

One, he most assuredly was attracted to this vampire.

And two, Lucien probably knew it.

Why would he be doing this otherwise? Unless it was all a game, which was most likely, but even still, if this was Lucien's game, Cyrus was more than willing to play it.

"You still haven't relaxed those shoulders," Lucien murmured. He squeezed harder until Cyrus finally managed to release the tension from them, letting out a slow exhale at the same time. "That's better. And look, you're finally using the proper muscles to hold that sword. I'm impressed that your hands aren't shaking yet. You're stronger than I thought, aren't you? I think you'll catch onto this quite quickly."

Cyrus tried to swallow, only to find that his mouth had gone dry as sand. He stared squarely at the blade in front of him and gripped it until his hands went numb.

Lucien breathed a soft chuckle that scattered gooseflesh up the back of Cyrus's neck. "It seems I should be conscious of how I direct my praise. Here I thought you could use some positive reinforcement, but I can be mean to you, if you'd prefer."

Only if it involves your fangs, Cyrus thought hazily. He didn't need more ridicule; he wanted the sort of *mean* that would bind his hands and deny him pleasure until he felt pain. And all the while, Lucien was *welcome* to sing his praises.

Cold bath, screamed his last shred of dignity. *Cold bath cold bath cold bath.*

Cyrus jolted himself back to reality just in time to catch the end of a sentence he'd entirely missed. It took him a minute to find his voice. "What did you say?"

"Something distracting you, Beldon?" Lucien slid his hands back down to Cyrus's waist. "I said, spread your legs."

Cyrus choked on his own breath. "*What?*"

Lucien snickered. "Not like *that*, you naughty thing. Shall I remind you that the whole point of this lesson is to correct your stance? Your feet are too close together. Spread them."

Cyrus shot a glare over his shoulder, but obeyed and shifted his feet to a sturdier position. To his great relief, Lucien then put some space between them, and the moment he was more than an arm's length away, Cyrus swung around and faced him with his blade raised. He smirked at Lucien's surprised expression.

"Diving into the deep end already? I've scarcely shown you the basics and you think you're ready for a fight?" He drifted toward his own weapon where it lay in the grass, but Cyrus got in his way.

"I'm a fast learner." He lunged at Lucien, absently marveling at how different the sword felt now that he had a weapon better suited for him—and knew how to hold it correctly. It was still heavier than he was used to and he had to concentrate on his balance, but he would learn in time.

Lucien easily skirted out of the weapon's path, but Cyrus could tell he was annoyed that he couldn't reach his blade. Each time Lucien tried to make a grab for it, Cyrus jumped in to block his path and Lucien had no choice but to backpedal or get sliced. Cyrus grinned; this wasn't much of a challenge, and it did nothing for his dueling skills, but he wanted to see how much it would take to truly anger Lucien. At what point would Cyrus feel the adrenaline rush he'd come to expect from a real fight?

It wasn't that he wanted to antagonize Lucien, and he wouldn't actually hurt him, but after the way he'd just made Cyrus feel, Cyrus had more than a little restless energy to get out. And fighting him was a *far* better idea than fucking him.

"Come on, now, do you want a fair fight or not?" Lucien let out a growl as Cyrus forced him back another few steps. His words were light, but the tension in his jaw betrayed his irritation.

"Would it be a fair fight if a vampire attacked me?" Cyrus shot back. "The ones I've fought have thus far been armed with nothing but their own brute strength. Surely you can manage."

Lucien bared his teeth and Cyrus's heart missed a beat, making him stumble as he swung the blade to keep Lucien away. Lucien saw his opening and zipped past Cyrus, claimed his weapon, and dashed out of striking distance in a blur of silver.

He didn't wait for Cyrus to catch his breath. He spun around and swung his blade, and Cyrus managed to parry the strike at the last second. *Now* Lucien wasn't holding back, and Cyrus would get not a fair fight, but a real one.

"Did you ever think, Beldon, that the vampires you fought were unarmed because they were *innocent*?" Lucien tore his blade away with a shriek of metal, then attacked again. Cyrus skipped backwards, clumsily blocking each blow.

Lucien's words broke his focus and sank deeper than any blade ever could. No, it had never occurred to him that the vampires he and his siblings were ordered to kill were innocent. How could they be? The Honorable Families passed the Beldons a list of names—rogue vampires who were a threat to the peace—and the Beldons took care of it. Those vampires *weren't* innocent.

Were they?

"W-Wait." Cyrus lowered his weapon, but Lucien didn't let up; he came at Cyrus with another swing and Cyrus had no choice but to parry. "Lucien, wait! Stop!"

He ducked just as he was sure that blade was going to sever his head from his body, but the sting of steel never came. He heard the weapon hit the ground with a dull clatter, and then before he had a chance to turn, Lucien seized him and twisted his arm behind his back. He dropped his sword. Lucien grabbed him around the neck with his other hand, and Cyrus stilled.

Each of his heavy breaths got caught on Lucien's tight hold. He was sure Lucien could feel his hammering pulse—he could probably smell the rush of his blood and sense every pitch of his heart.

"You lose, Beldon," Lucien hissed into his ear. Cyrus shivered. When Lucien spoke again, Cyrus could hear the smile on his lips. "But you don't seem too disappointed about it."

"Let go," Cyrus grunted. He tried to wriggle out of Lucien's grip, but the vampire held fast.

"You fight well," Lucien said. "You have the skills, but you're easily distracted, and that is your downfall. You can't let a few sharp words meant to disarm you do just that. And a flash of fangs shouldn't frighten you to the point of stumbling. Is that not an elementary Beldon lesson?"

"I wasn't frightened," Cyrus said, without thinking. And then promptly shut his mouth.

Lucien's laugh rumbled in his chest, flush against Cyrus's back. "I'll let that slide. But whatever the feeling, it broke your focus on the fight. If I didn't wish to keep you around, you'd be gutted like a fish right now."

"How kind of you to let me keep my guts inside me." Cyrus fought against Lucien's hold again, and when Lucien still didn't loosen his arms, Cyrus growled. "Let me *go*."

"But you're enjoying it so much. Or was that someone else's blood rushing about?"

This time when Cyrus struggled, Lucien released him. Cyrus put several feet of space between them, leaving the swords for Lucien to collect. He felt the vampire's eyes on him as he stalked across the field toward Demeter.

He paused beside her and stroked her soft nose; she made a happy noise and nudged his hand to encourage more pets, which he obliged, if only to let the gentle motion calm him and bring him back to earth.

"When did he become so...insufferable?" He dared a glance toward Lucien, who was still across the field where Cyrus had left him. He had his back to him now; the breeze lazily toyed with the long strands of his hair, plucking and twirling them as if with deft fingers. Cyrus buried the pit of longing that opened in his chest and looked away.

Demeter snorted. Cyrus smiled. "You're right. He's always been insufferable. I just don't know when I started to like it."

CYRUS SHOULD HAVE EXPECTED that Lucien wouldn't be satisfied with one swordfighting lesson. They stayed in the lakeside village for three more days, and each one dawned with Lucien dragging Cyrus out of bed and out to the field. Under pale skies and amid thick fog, they sparred until the sun was fully up. After breakfast, Lucien left Cyrus alone for a few hours, only to show up again before lunch and start their lessons anew. The pattern continued: practice, breakfast, practice, lunch, practice, dinner. Only in the evening hours between dinner and nightfall did Lucien let both of them rest.

Cyrus was more than ready to move on with their travels, if only to give the muscles in his arms a chance to recover. Between his injury from the Wild vampire and Lucien's ruthless lessons, Cyrus hadn't gone a day in this town without being sore.

Their last day in town, Cyrus shuffled back to their shared room after a particularly brutal afternoon lesson. He longed for a hot bath followed by an undisturbed nap before Lucien inevitably roused him to continue their journey north, but when he arrived at the room he found something occupying the bed: A long, narrow box took up the precise space where Cyrus wished to collapse. He approached it, intending to get it out of the way and investigate later, but he paused when he found a card with his name written on it tucked beneath the green silk ribbon tied around the parcel.

Cyrus glanced over his shoulder as if the answer to this mystery had snuck in without his notice, but he was alone. He plucked the card off the box and turned it over, hoping for an explanation, but found none. Just his name in a sweeping calligraphic script.

He dropped the card onto the bed, then pulled the ribbon off the box and lifted the lid only to find it packed with a thick cushion of tissue paper that obscured its contents. He tore several sheets of it out of the way until he unearthed what lay beneath, and at the first glimpse his heart fully stopped.

He pressed his hands to his mouth. Tucked in the bed of tissue, a gorgeous longsword gleamed in the room's warm light and reflected Cyrus's shocked expression in its polished blade. With trembling hands he cleared the rest of the tissue away until he found the hilt, wrapped in crisp leather dyed a deep forest green. Cyrus scarcely wanted to touch the weapon lest he ruin its pristine newness.

"Do you like it?"

He spun with a gasp and found Lucien leaning against the doorframe. His eyes were warm, his smile gentle.

It's stunning, was Cyrus's first response. Then, *How much did this cost you?*

Then, embarrassingly, *This is the most thoughtful thing anyone has ever done for me.* And, *I don't deserve this.*

But he couldn't say any of that; he hardly managed a nod. Louder than everything else, his thoughts screamed, *Why?*

The answer to that one scared him the most.

"It seemed right for you to have your own," Lucien said, as if the answer to *Why* was that simple. "Don't worry, I made sure it's the correct size and weight for you. Eventually, it'll feel like an extension of you in the way you've said your daggers already are. And, if you are to make a weapon yours, I wanted you to have a beautiful one."

Cyrus turned back to the sword in its box, too overwhelmed to even look at Lucien. Four days—no, probably more—of pent-up feelings and tension so thick it would split on the edge of a blade caught up with Cyrus and the weight of this gesture became too much.

Why had Lucien done this? What did it mean? After days of flirting and teasing and finding excuses to get close—*too* close— until Cyrus couldn't handle it, what the hell was he supposed to think of a gift like this? Was Lucien really just toying with Cyrus because Cyrus responded to it in a way that was entertaining, or...?

The answer was here, staring him in the face, but Cyrus turned his back on it and rounded on Lucien.

"Why would you do this?" The venom in his own words shocked him, and before Lucien had a chance to reply, Cyrus shoved past him and fled downstairs.

CYRUS FOUND himself no more relaxed after a bath. Though he'd spent nearly half an hour submerged in the steaming water, his thoughts refused to settle even as his muscles did. Physically, he felt refreshed by the time he climbed out and hurriedly dried off before the night's chill got to him, but a needling sense of unease lingered at the back of his mind. He didn't know what to call that feeling, but he feared that if he prodded it, it would unravel its many threads and tangle him in its clutches.

As he dressed and made his way from the bathhouse back to the inn, he tried to remind himself why he was here. He had not run all this way just because Lucien had a pretty face. Cyrus wasn't that shallow, and he still had something to prove to the Beldons. And if Lucien's friend up north really did know of a way to save vampires from turning Wild, maybe that knowledge could be passed to the Honorable Families in Chestervale and beyond.

Cyrus wasn't interested in any fame that might result in this discovery; he hadn't even considered that it would be a big deal for more than just their respective families if they succeeded. If Lucien wished to be known as the one who eradicated Wild vampires, he was welcome to the renown. Cyrus only wanted his name associated with the situation so history would remember him as the Beldon who chose to be different.

Yet at this point, even that seemed like wishful thinking. Who was he to assume history would remember him at all?

For now, he had to focus on the task at hand. He could deal with its rippling effects later. And these new, unsteady feelings toward Lucien needed to *go*.

He just had to endure a few more days with the vampire until they made it to his friend. And then a few more days after that while they traveled back to the city. And then...

Then what? It would all depend on what they found or didn't

find, but would they really just...part ways? Cyrus thought of Lucien returning to his dark and empty house and himself returning to the Beldon estate—where he'd likely be smited on the spot—and he felt an odd tug of sorrow in his chest.

He didn't want to go back to how it was before. This journey was supposed to change his life, not circle him back to where he'd been two months ago. If he went home, even with a way to save vampires from turning Wild, he'd still be expected to hunt them. He'd still be ordered to deal with vampires that stepped out of line. Wild or not. Honorable or not. He would still be a hunter, and he would still go home with silver blood on his hands.

Cyrus paused at the door to the inn and looked down at the Beldon family ring that, even still, remained on his left middle finger. One digit off from being a marriage band, binding him to that family forever.

He couldn't go back to that. But really, what other choice did he have? It wasn't as if he could expect to stay with Lucien.

Cyrus clenched his hand and then opened the door, only to be halted in his tracks by jarringly loud music. The tavern was dark, with low-burning candles on the corners of the bar but nowhere else. A quartet of musicians played as loud as humanly possible on stringed instruments while another pair each thumped a jaunty, reverberating beat on large drums. As Cyrus's eyes adjusted to the dark, he saw that the room was more crowded than he'd yet seen it; the space around the bar was packed with patrons nursing drinks or waiting for them. People lingered in pairs or groups on the room's edges, some merely chatting and laughing while others sloppily kissed while grinding together to the music's beat. A few bolder— and drunker—people gathered around the musicians and danced, some together and some alone. For all their flailing, they did look like they were having fun.

Cyrus kept his head down while he made his way around the lively tavern-goers, aiming for the back stairs that would take him up to his room. He hoped Lucien wasn't around; the thought of seeing him again—and that sword—brought a scowl to his face.

And his mood only soured further when someone crashed into him.

"Oops! Sorry, friend!" A very drunk woman stumbled out of Cyrus's way, one sloshing drink in each hand. "Dark in here, innit? *Heyyy*, you're *cute*. Wanna dance?"

"Uh." Cyrus glanced away. "Sorry, I'm not here for...this." He gestured at the ongoing party, then took a step toward the stairs. "Have fun, though?"

"Ohh, come on!" The woman thrust one of her cups toward him. "At least have a drink, friend! You look like you need it."

Cyrus accepted the drink if only to placate her enough that she'd leave him alone, and sure enough, she lifted her own glass in a woozy toast and then flounced away.

Cyrus studied the drink. He had no idea what it was; it was too dark in here to discern any colors, and when he sniffed it, he only came away with a strong tang of alcohol and a hint of citrus. Hesitantly, he took a tiny sip.

It only then occurred to him that it could be drugged, but it didn't taste weird. He swallowed more, finding that he actually rather liked it. The sharp bite of alcohol drowned out whatever it might have been mixed with; this could mess him up quickly if he wanted it to.

And he sort of did want it to.

He glanced back at the hall leading to the stairs. What was waiting for him up there? A flirty vampire with damnable doe eyes and heartfelt gifts? Fuck that. Cyrus swallowed another gulp of the drink, then downed the rest in one go and made a beeline for the bar.

He found a vacant stool and took a seat between a man with a long ponytail and a pair of women who shared hushed murmurs between kisses. Cyrus tried not to look at anyone around him lest they try to start a conversation; he fixed his eyes on the barkeep until he noticed him. It was only thanks to the slight buzz already numbing his brain that he remained here at all; truly, he was out of his element.

Some of his anxiety eased when the bartender at last turned to him with a smile. Cyrus noticed a little patch on their apron that had "*they, them, their*" stitched in bright thread. *Just like Leif,* Cyrus thought absently.

"Evening! What can I get for you?" The bartender was around Cyrus's age, with a voluminous heap of dark, wavy hair that fell over their forehead but curled out of their eyes just so. The sides of their head were shaved while the top remained long; Cyrus had never seen anyone with that sort of style, but he liked it.

He realized that while he'd been thinking about the bartender's hair, they had asked him a question. His face warmed. "Sorry, um... honestly, I don't know."

"No problem!" They flicked a small towel over their shoulder. "I'll give you a minute to think about it?"

Cyrus didn't want to think; that was the whole point of being here. "No, I mean...I'm not from around here, so I don't know this place. This isn't my usual scene, you know?" He tapped the side of the glass in his hand. "I've no idea what this was, but it was pretty good. What would you get?"

He had forgotten how much alcohol made him ramble.

Thankfully, if the bartender noticed, they didn't seem to mind. They pursed their lips and thought for a minute, then nodded and went about concocting something. "I have a suspicion it was Quinnie who put that cup in your hand, and if I'm right, it's probably that vaguely-citrus-but-mostly-alcohol drink she loves so much. So if you liked that—maybe for the zest?—I'll get you something better." They shook the ingredients together in a metal canister.

Cyrus found himself smiling. "What's your name?"

"Saffron." They retrieved a glass from beneath the counter and flipped it upright, then poured Cyrus's drink. They placed a sprig of some leafy herb in the glass, then slid it toward him. "Yours?"

"Cyrus." He took an experimental sip. The herb turned out to be mint, and it was an unexpected yet satisfactory complement to the sour drink. "Oh, this is really good. Thank you. Er, how much?"

Saffron smiled and shook their head. "On the house."

"A-Are you sure?" Cyrus started to reach for his pocket, but the bartender waved their hand.

"Positive. Enjoy."

"Oh. Well—Thank you." Cyrus took another sip of the drink. "I do find that I often need a boost of encouragement to linger at these sorts of gatherings."

Saffron tilted their head to the side. "Where are you from, if you don't mind my asking?"

"Uh...Chestervale."

"Ah, that makes sense."

Cyrus wasn't sure if that was a good thing. "How so? Do I have an accent?"

"No," Saffron chuckled. "You just talk a lot more formally than anyone I know around here. Not in a bad way, though—it's charming."

Charming, huh? Cyrus reckoned he sounded like a posh kiss-ass.

Before he could think of another route of conversation or ask Saffron about their life in a way that wouldn't sound invasive, another patron waved for their attention. They sent Cyrus an apologetic smile. "Duty calls. But please do let me know if you want anything else." Was that a wink? "Enjoy the party!"

Cyrus watched them as they made quick work of a few other people's drink orders, and maybe it was his imagination, but they didn't appear to be chatting with anyone else quite as much as they had with him. Maybe they already knew those people? It was a small town, and this was a central place. But wouldn't they chat *more* with friends and acquaintances?

He decided not to overthink it. This was not a night for thinking. He grabbed his drink and, taking generous sips every few seconds, wandered his way across the tavern.

Now he knew the alcohol was *really* getting to him, because he actually wanted to join the throes of people dancing and singing along with the musicians. The music swallowed him whole. The thump of drums, the strum of strings, and the clamor of voices drowned out everything else; if he closed his eyes, he could believe it was just him, alone, and the contagious energy of this room. He felt it all: the beat, the heat, the swirl of intoxication in his body. For this moment, he didn't have to care about home. He didn't even have to care about going upstairs and seeing Lucien and his stupid beautiful face and that stunning sword that he'd probably paid *hundreds* for. But Cyrus didn't care. He didn't care! Right now, nothing mattered, and at last, he started to relax.

He swayed with the music, no longer caring when people bumped him. If anyone tried to talk to him, he didn't know it. He was happily lost in his little bubble of fuzzy oblivion, and was quite content to let this delightful drink further cloud his mind.

He was only drawn out of his own head when someone lightly but intentionally touched his arm. Blinking as if waking from a dream, he found Saffron the bartender at his side with a drink in their hand. "Oh! It's you!"

"It's me." They grinned. "Having fun?"

"Actually, yeah!" Cyrus was sure he sounded precisely as drunk as he felt, but he didn't care. "What are you doing out here?"

"They *do* let me out from behind the bar every so often, you know." Saffron's smile laughed on its own. "I'm off for the night, so I get to actually enjoy the party without having to make sure everyone's happy. Now I can just make sure *you're* happy."

Ohh, they're flirting with me, Cyrus registered faintly. And he found that he did not mind. It sent a little thrill through him, to be approached so blatantly. It was a refreshing change of pace from that fucking vampire's puzzling glances and infuriating teases.

"But what about you?" Cyrus said. "I can't be happy if you're not. Let me buy you a drink!"

Saffron laughed. "I already have one!" They raised their cup and clinked it against Cyrus's. "I think we're both set, don't you?"

Had Cyrus noticed that they already had a drink? He couldn't recall. "For *now*, maybe. But the night is young, isn't it?" He met their eyes. "There's plenty more fun to be had."

A knowing smirk curled at the corner of Saffron's lips. They drifted closer to him. "Is that so? And what *would* make you happy, Cyrus of Chestervale?"

Hell if he knew. But for the moment? Fuck it. He closed the space between himself and Saffron and kissed them. They grabbed him by the collar of his shirt and kissed him back vigorously; Cyrus happily opened his mouth when they ran their tongue along his bottom lip. His thoughts melted away with the rest of his surroundings, and he didn't realize the two of them had moved at all until Saffron shoved him back against the wall and pinned him there with their hips. They'd abandoned their drink and now wandered their hands down his body, plucking at buttons and pulling fabric until they got their hands under his shirt. One skimmed upward, the other down, over his stomach and down the front of his pants.

"*Fuck*," Cyrus breathed. His head fell back against the wall; Saffron didn't waste a moment before their mouth was on his neck. But when they roughly kissed the spot where Lucien had bitten him, Cyrus suddenly snapped back to his senses and pushed Saffron off.

They backed up, confused. Cyrus saw their mouth form the words *Are you okay?* but he didn't hear the sound. His thundering pulse drowned out everything, even the music's deafening beat.

"It's not you," he mumbled, and then fled across the tavern. He downed the last of his drink, left the glass on a table, and then dashed up the stairs to his room.

He wasn't sure if he was relieved or disappointed to find that Lucien wasn't there, but whatever feeling piped up when he found the empty room quickly sloughed away. Cyrus took off his shirt, thanking Saffron for dealing with the buttons so he didn't have to, flung it onto the floor, and then flopped down on the bed. Lucien had moved the box containing the sword; Cyrus could see it in the corner of his eye, leaning against the wall near their other belongings.

He heaved a sigh and pressed the heels of his palms to his eyes. He was fairly sure his head would never stop spinning. It was starting to turn his stomach. He would kill for some water. It was too hot in here.

With some difficulty involving buttons and gravity, he kicked off his pants and sprawled across the entire width of the bed. If Lucien came back after Cyrus fell asleep, he could sleep on the floor, for all Cyrus cared. Why he continued to share a bed with that vampire *without* caving into the desires he'd rather not think about, he had no goddamn idea.

It was still too hot in here.

Cyrus cracked open his eyes and glanced at the window on the other side of the room. Too far away. If he got up—if he even could —he suddenly doubted he'd make it more than a few unsteady steps. Gods, those drinks had been strong. Cyrus was *not* getting up. Lucien could open the window whenever he returned from wherever it was he'd gone.

In the meantime, Cyrus was alone for the first time since they'd left the city; he reasoned he might as well take advantage of it and finish what that handsy bartender had started.

Chapter EIGHTEEN

CYRUS WOKE UP TO A HARD KICK TO HIS ANKLE. HE surfaced from a wonderfully dreamless sleep and grumbled at the disruption, turning onto his side. Just as his consciousness started to dip back out, the kick roused him again, and this time he sat up with a scowl.

"*What*," he hissed, twisting around to glare at the offending vampire. But Lucien wasn't awake. He thrashed erratically in his sleep, visibly trembling. His face was mostly buried in his pillow, but the half Cyrus could see was scrunched in distress. Each of his rapid breaths was nearly a whimper.

"Hey." Cyrus fully turned around and grasped Lucien's shoulder. When he didn't react, Cyrus gave him a gentle shake. "Lucien. Hey. Wake up."

He made a soft, muffled cry and turned his face further into the pillow. Cyrus shook him again, harder. "*Lucien*," he said, louder. "You're dreaming. Wake up."

"*No*," he mumbled, over and over. "*No, no, no no no no, not you —not you, please, not you—*"

Cyrus didn't know what else to do, so with a whispered apology, he roughly shoved Lucien onto his back and then smacked his cheek. Lucien's eyes snapped open, but his gaze was panicked and unfocused. He bolted up with a strained gasp and grabbed Cyrus by the shoulders.

Cyrus kept his own hands on him as he caught his breath and

regained his bearings. Something noticeably changed in his eyes when he took in Cyrus's presence; his face crumpled, and he dropped his head onto Cyrus's shoulder with a deep sob.

Cyrus dared not move a muscle. Part of him wondered if he was still asleep, if his mind had conjured this unexpected tenderness along with all of the other desires swimming around up there. The sound of Lucien's heavy breaths and the strange shivering coolness of them against Cyrus's bare skin was vivid enough to raise gooseflesh, yet Cyrus slid his hands gently down Lucien's shoulders, just to be sure this was all real.

"You're okay," he murmured. This softness felt so fragile. He didn't want to ruin it by speaking, but Lucien was still trembling, and stronger than his reluctance to break the silence was his need to soothe Lucien's fear. "It was just a dream. You're safe."

"Cyrus..." His name was a hush, a feather-soft breath on Lucien's lips. Lucien inhaled shakily, then slowly lifted his head and met Cyrus's eyes. For several long, lingering moments he simply gazed at him, brows pinched in that thoughtful crease. Cyrus wanted to smooth the worry lines from his face and dry the tears that clung to his eyelashes.

"I'm here." It was all he knew to say, even if it felt like far from enough. There was too much that was yet unspoken; if Cyrus said anything more, he feared it would all spill out.

"You're here," Lucien murmured, as if confirming the truth of it to himself. He brought a slender, shaking hand to Cyrus's cheek; Cyrus closed his eyes and held still, forcing himself not to lean into the touch. Too soon, Lucien lowered his hand, and then lay back on the bed with a sigh. His hair spilled in a pale puddle around his head.

Cyrus inched back over to his side of the bed and settled down. He lay on his side, facing Lucien, and propped his head on his hand. A fluttering sense of unease knotted in his chest. Until now, the two of them had never been awake at the same time in this creaky bed that was better suited for a pair far more comfortable with each other. So until now, Cyrus had not noticed just how little space there was between them.

It made him ache. He gazed at the man beside him—his elegant features, his depthless eyes, the gentle slope of his parted lips—and he wanted to smother the last remaining inches that kept them apart. If he was still drunk, he might have. Unspoken words be damned.

But he couldn't help but fear that if he crossed that line, those unspoken things would remain as such. He didn't want that.

And it didn't really matter what he wanted, did it, because of all the things he might desire, Lucien was one that he absolutely could not have. Cyrus had forgotten, too easily, that Lucien wasn't just any attractive man with whom Cyrus had undeniable chemistry. He was a fucking Honorable One, and Cyrus was still, always, forever a Beldon.

Lucien turned his head toward Cyrus and Cyrus avoided his gaze, fearing that Lucien had somehow read his thoughts. Dawn was breaking outside the window across the room, washing the space with pale light that softened Lucien's skin and hair to barely separable tones of gray and white. Even his eyes paled, their vivid crimson muted but no less striking.

Cyrus's chest tightened. A prickling feeling burned behind his eyes and he blinked frantically to make it stop.

He didn't know what exactly Lucien saw in his face, but it made him frown. "What's wrong?"

Oh, so much. He wouldn't know where to start even if he did want to answer. Where *had* it started? Out in that field, with swords in hand? At the piano? In the library? Cyrus couldn't pin it, and didn't even dare to name it. It was wrong. Here he was, a son of Beldon, in bed with a fucking vampire. And worse: attracted to, enchanted by, infatuated with an Honorable One.

He shook his head in reply to Lucien's question. "I should be asking that of you."

"Nightmares," Lucien said simply. "You?"

And Cyrus could have spilled it all, right here in the hand's breadth between them, but instead he shook his head again and rolled over, turning his back to Lucien so his face didn't answer for him.

Lucien's sharp sigh broke the floodgates. Cyrus squeezed his eyes shut as hot tears rolled down his cheeks. He wished he could scream. Instead he swallowed back the stupid sobs that lodged in his throat and let them out one soundless hiccup at a time while his tears salted his lips and dampened his pillow.

"Why do you keep doing this?" Lucien whispered.

And though it was a weak, useless farce, Cyrus pretended to be asleep.

DESPITE HAVING BEEN WOKEN in the middle of the night and then having all of his emotions crash down on him at once, Cyrus slept well for those last few hours before the sun fully rose. He woke slowly and reluctantly from his slumber, turning his back on the window to hold onto the darkness of sleep a little longer. Faintly, he was surprised it was the sun and not Lucien that had woken him.

At that curiosity, he cracked open one eye and found the vampire in question just a few feet away from the bed. He was bent over the heap of traveling bags, sorting through and packing his belongings. After a moment he straightened, gathered his hair forward, and then pulled off his shirt. Cyrus shamelessly let his gaze follow the lines of muscle down Lucien's back and wished it was his hands rather than his eyes tracing the slope of his spine.

His view was interrupted when Lucien tossed the length of his hair over his shoulder, curtaining most of his back with the thick fall of silver. But then he turned slightly as he shook out a fresh shirt, and Cyrus was treated to a glimpse of toned pectorals, a ripple of muscle down his stomach, and—to his surprise—a glint of metal pierced through his nipples.

Cyrus thanked the gods that Lucien thought he was still asleep, because he didn't even try to pretend not to stare. So much for feeling relaxed; a fresh prickle of desire tingled beneath his skin. He turned onto his stomach and shoved his face into his pillow before his body had a chance to betray him.

"I know you're awake."

Cyrus held absolutely still.

"You forget that I can sense your blood," Lucien said, a coy edge to his voice. "And right now it's racing quite unusually for someone who otherwise seems sound asleep."

Fuck. Cyrus indeed had forgotten that detail. He grumbled into his pillow. "I had a good dream."

Lucien laughed. "Apparently so. Consider me jealous. My imagination chose to torment me last night."

Well, that was one way to kill the mood. Cyrus rolled over and then finally sat up. Lucien had since put on a shirt, though it remained mostly unbuttoned, and now that Cyrus knew the piercings were there he couldn't stop noticing the slight tease of them beneath the fabric. He forced himself to drag his eyes up to Lucien's face. "I know. I'm sorry."

Lucien looked at him with an expression that Cyrus couldn't quite translate, and Cyrus quickly glanced away as he remembered the rest of their conversation last night. Guilt twisted in his stomach and he changed the subject before Lucien could say more.

"I'm surprised you didn't haul me outside to train before we leave." He slid off the bed and stretched his arms over his head; his muscles were still sore from the sword lessons, so he wasn't exactly disappointed to not have one today, but the thought of getting back on that horse wasn't so thrilling either. When Lucien didn't say anything, Cyrus turned to him.

He could only describe what he saw in Lucien's eyes as *hunger*, sharp and raw. And he could only assume that that was precisely how he'd been eyeing Lucien just a few moments ago. It made his knees weak; unconsciously, he plopped back down on the bed. Part of him expected Lucien to take that as an invitation and pounce on him.

No such luck. Lucien suddenly shook his head and turned away, busying himself with the buttons on his shirt. Cyrus ran his hands through his hair and wished someone would smack some sense into him. He longed for another bath—a cold one this time —but Lucien had resumed his efforts to pack up their stuff and now sat to put on his boots, and Cyrus didn't think he'd be willing to wait.

"So we're going?" he asked.

"Yes, and unless you wish to treat everyone we pass on the road with your rather impressive array of scars and abdominal muscles, you might want to get dressed."

Self-consciously, Cyrus crossed his arms over his bare chest. He got up and successfully stayed on his feet this time, then retrieved last night's clothes from the floor and dropped them with the pile of stuff that had accumulated on top of his bag. He grabbed the shirt he'd worn least, shrugged it on, and set to work on the buttons. When he reached the top ones he remembered that the only cravat he'd brought had been burned with the rest of his bloodied clothes.

Out here, away from high society, no one would care that his neck wasn't properly covered, but it still felt weird. He couldn't remember a time when he hadn't worn something around his neck; even as a child, he'd worn first a loose ribbon and then, as he aged, a proper cravat. He felt oddly exposed without it now.

Well, he'd have to get used to it. A piece of fabric wasn't going to protect him against any leering vampires, and if *this* vampire wished to gaze longingly at his neck and the scars he'd left there, he was more than welcome to.

Cyrus finished dressing, then unceremoniously shoved the rest of his clothes back into the bag and flung it onto the bed. He went to retrieve his shoes when his eyes fell on the gift box once again.

He sighed and turned to Lucien, who had drifted over to the

window. "Vis—" Cyrus started, but no, they were past that. "Lucien."

He turned his head.

"Thank you for the sword," he said, as earnestly as he could manage. When Lucien didn't say anything, he continued: "It's beautiful. And it was...startlingly thoughtful of you to give it to me. I'm sorry for how I reacted yesterday."

Lucien studied him for a long minute before a smile worked its way across his face. "You're very welcome."

Cyrus didn't quite know what had changed, but he could accept the gift now. Maybe not everything it implied, but the object itself. He lifted it out of its tissue bed and held it up, turning it so the blade caught the morning sunlight. Again it stole his breath; it truly was a marvel, perfectly polished and pristine, flawless in its craftsmanship. As he admired it, he noticed a detail he hadn't yesterday: at the base of the hilt, just above the gleaming pommel, two letters were stamped into the leather.

C. B.

The sword was well and truly made for him.

"There's a scabbard for it underneath the rest of the paper in the box," Lucien said. He slung his bag onto his shoulder and made for the door. "Are you ready?"

Cyrus swallowed the swell of emotions that threatened to choke him and unearthed the sword's sheath from the box. "Yeah, just about." His voice caught in his throat; he hoped Lucien didn't notice. He grabbed the rest of his things and followed Lucien out of the room.

Downstairs, the tavern smelled wondrously of food. Cyrus's stomach growled, reminding him that he'd consumed nothing but alcoholic drinks since yesterday afternoon. As they passed through the dining area, he debated requesting a quick stop to eat, but then Lucien himself paused at the counter. Cyrus didn't hear what Lucien said to the woman there, but he came back with a small basket and wordlessly passed it to Cyrus before continuing outside.

Cyrus peeked beneath the white cloth covering the basket's

contents and found it packed snugly with a variety of fresh rolls and biscuits, dried fruit, a few apples, a bundle of grapes, and two small wedges of cheese.

He looked up at Lucien, blinking in surprise, but the vampire neither turned nor offered a word. Cyrus continued staring at the back of his head as they went around the back of the tavern to the stable. It wasn't even that grand of a gesture, having some food set aside for him to enjoy on the road, but it was that Lucien had thought of it at all. The food, the sword, the attentive care while he recovered from his injury—this vampire seemed determined to take care of Cyrus, and Cyrus couldn't decide if he liked it or not. On one hand, he wasn't a child and he could take care of himself. On the other, he desperately wanted Lucien to care.

Yet it frightened him that Lucien actually *did*.

He broke out of his thoughts when the stablehand presented him with his horse. Demeter gave a happy snort when Cyrus approached her with his hand outstretched, though Cyrus suspected she was more excited at the potential for a treat than she was to see him. Cyrus patted her nose, then went around to her side and secured the bags and his sword to the saddle. Then he turned to Lucien.

"So where's your horse?"

He strapped his own bag to the saddle and frowned. "I told you: he didn't make it."

"Right, but...I guess I figured you'd go out and get a new one?"

Lucien looked offended. "Getting acquainted with a new horse isn't like—like replacing a broken carriage with an identical new one. It takes time and contemplation to even choose one, let alone get to know it. I lost an animal, Cyrus, not an object."

Cyrus winced. "Right. Sorry. So..."

"So this is what we've got." Lucien patted Demeter's side. "She's a sturdy beast, she can handle it. I did not anticipate this being an issue."

Objectively, it wasn't. Cyrus had just spent over a week sharing a room and a bed with Lucien; really, this should not have him so off-kilter. "No, it's—It's fine. Um, who's driving, then?"

Lucien waved a hand toward Demeter. "She's your horse."

Indeed she was. But Cyrus didn't move.

Lucien flourished his hand. "After you, sir."

"Don't call me sir," Cyrus grumbled, and finally unstuck his feet from the ground. He climbed onto Demeter's back and told himself that at least he didn't have to look at Lucien if the vampire was behind him. But then Lucien got up and settled behind him, and all at once his nerves were on edge again. Lucien's thighs straddled Cyrus's hips, his knees bumping the backs of Cyrus's legs. If Lucien's body were warm, Cyrus would've been drunk on his heat. As it was, Lucien's presence was a shiver down his spine.

Cyrus wrapped the reins around his hands until it hurt. Wherever they were going, he hoped they got there quickly. He dared a glance over his shoulder. "Which way?"

"North out of the village, then stay on the main road and I'll direct you as needed." A smirk eased across Lucien's lips. "You don't have to be so tense, Beldon. Although I will warn you..."

He leaned forward, and any closer, he would've kissed Cyrus. His smirk stretched to a wicked, fanged smile. "I bite."

Chapter NINETEEN

THE AUTUMN SUN CHASED THE NIGHT'S LINGERING clouds from the sky and bathed the landscape in gold. Trees of orange, red, brown, and everything in between framed the packed dirt road that stretched endlessly into the woods, while the lake sparkled bluish-gray between the tree trunks. The sun managed to break through the dense treetops in dappled golden patches, offering brief respites of warmth as Demeter carried Cyrus and Lucien through the shadows.

Aside from occasional brief chats, they remained comfortably quiet. Crows cawed, critters scurried, and the rare traveler waved when they passed. As the day wore on, Cyrus grew bored of the silence and found himself desperate for Lucien to start a conversation. He didn't trust himself to initiate it; the pressing topic on his mind was also the one he didn't want to touch.

He supposed he could ask Lucien about the person they were going to see, and why Lucien seemed to treat her like a last resort, and why she was allegedly risky, and what on earth she could possibly know that would lead Cyrus and Lucien to what they wanted to know. But though Cyrus was curious about all of that, he also reasoned that silence was easy. He didn't have to endure any teasing or flirting or sly smiles or innuendos if they didn't talk.

And yet, curiosity itched in his mind. As close as the two of them had gotten in the past weeks, there was still so much Cyrus didn't know about him. What was it like to live for over a century?

How long had he been studying the sciences, and when did the Wild vampire research start? What got him interested in all that? Did he have friends? Did Honorable Ones even have time to have friends?

Cyrus was so busy in his own thoughts that Lucien startled him by speaking. "May I ask about your brother?"

"My brother?" Cyrus glanced back at him. "Which one?"

"Arthur," Lucien replied softly.

Cyrus had figured as much, but it was still unexpected. "What do you want to know?"

"What was he like? Firstborn of Marcus Beldon...those are quite the shoes to fill."

"I guess." Cyrus shrugged. It didn't matter how large those shoes were, given that both Marcus and Arthur were dead, and no one would be filling Emerson's shoes anytime soon. "If he felt pressured as the Beldon heir, he never showed it. Being the eldest Beldon came with its big responsibilities and high expectations and all that, but Arthur loved it."

Lucien hummed thoughtfully. "Lucky him."

Cyrus chanced another glance back at him. "I...imagine that you have similar feelings, as the Vista heir?"

A shadow of grief clouded Lucien's eyes as he gazed out at the trees. "Well...I was far more confident in my position before..." He swallowed. "When I was simply the heir and not...Master Vista."

Cyrus winced. "I'm sorry."

Lucien shook his head. "He sounds quite similar to your father. Arthur, I mean."

"Frighteningly similar," Cyrus agreed. "Arthur was basically Marcus's shadow, and Marcus loved it. He raised a copy of himself, which was precisely what he wanted. I'm surprised he bothered with more children at all."

Lucien didn't reply for a minute, and Cyrus thought he was done talking. But when he glanced back again, he found Lucien's soft eyes on him. "I am glad he did," he murmured.

Cyrus turned away.

"Marcus Beldon was prouder of his family's legacy than most Honorable Families are," Lucien went on. "It was annoying, to be honest. My father respected him because he had to, but I also often heard his petty rants about Marcus Beldon and his insatiable ego." He sniffed a bare hint of a chuckle. "If there was ever a Beldon to find my research, I am exceedingly relieved it was you, Cyrus. That book in your father's hands...The thought of it haunted me after you went home that day we met."

"What, you think Marcus would have used it against you? Against the Families?" Cyrus frowned incredulously.

"No," Lucien said, "I think he would've tried to use my research to make himself immortal."

Cyrus twisted around. A laugh bubbled out of him. "But that's...impossible."

"Most likely," Lucien agreed, "but the Beldons—especially Marcus, but his ancestors too—have always been obsessed with their legacy. They want to live forever, mortality be damned. Marcus might not have had the mind for alchemy, but his closest confidant certainly does, and I know for a fact that Emerson paid numerous visits to my father under the guise of diplomacy so he could snoop around. Eventually my father kicked him out because he got too nosy."

Cyrus's thoughts took off at a sprint. "Wait, wait, *Emerson* visited you? When? What was he looking for?"

"What else would an alchemist be looking for in a house full of immortals?" Lucien flicked his hair out of his face. "The secret to eternal life, of course."

Of course. And who deserved to live forever more than the Beldons? Certainly not vampires, not in Emerson's eyes. And now he was Master Beldon, with all the privileges and resources that came with that title.

But if Emerson had approached Alastair Vista for information that he thought the family had, why had he turned around and murdered them?

Oh. Because Alastair had cut him off, and Emerson hadn't

gotten what he wanted. So he charged in there, swords swinging, and eliminated everyone who would've stood between him and the knowledge he desired.

Yet *still*, that was so *rash* for someone as cunning and contemplative as Emerson Beldon. It was a Marcus move, but what motive would Marcus have had to go after the Vistas? Why not the Harrows family, if vengeance was his goal? And if Emerson had convinced Marcus to attack the Vistas, why take such a drastic step before being absolutely sure that the information he sought was even written down? Alastair Vista was a centuries-old vampire—a living, breathing treasury of knowledge—and it was very unlike Emerson to stab first and ask questions later.

Although, if he had been to the house numerous times and had seen and explored that library, maybe he'd seen enough to assure him that he would find what he sought within those books. If that was the case, all he needed was free reign of the place, with no one there to kick him out.

Shit. Was he really so petty that he'd slaughter an entire family just to get a look at their books?

Cyrus's skin crawled at the thought of Emerson tearing apart that house and that library in search of alchemical secrets he wasn't likely to find. At least Lucien's research journal was—

Wait.

"Lucien..." Cyrus turned around and met his eyes. "You have that journal, right? The one with your notes?"

Lucien's eyebrows slowly made their way up his forehead. "I thought *you* had that book."

They stared at each other. Cyrus felt all the blood drain from his face. "It was on the table in the library, the night that..."

"And we left everything where it was." Lucien's voice was dangerously low, calm but edged with an unmistakable whisper of horror. "Fuck."

"*Fuck*," Cyrus agreed. They had left the Vista manor empty and unattended, and this far from the city, there was absolutely nothing they could do. "Wait, but, you mentioned staff...?"

Lucien shook his head. "They'll be long gone by now. We have a protocol: in the event of an emergency, they escape through the cellar and get to safety. Which means that nearly all of the house's defenses are useless without people to man them." He dragged his hands down his face. "Why the *fuck* didn't you bring that journal?"

"Don't pin this on me! You forgot, too!"

"You spent a week wandering around my house waiting for me to wake up," Lucien snapped. "Were you too busy lighting all the candles that you didn't have time to put the books away or stop to think that maybe you should hang onto the one source of solid information we have?"

"You could've done that just as easily," Cyrus snarled. "Or—imagine this—you could've *asked*. You could've used your goddamn words for once instead of expecting me to read your mind."

"I'm *sorry*, it wasn't a priority of mine to nanny you mere hours after waking up from a near-death experience."

"A near-death experience that was your own fucking fault!"

Lucien shut his mouth. Cyrus immediately wished he could snatch the words back. Gods damn his temper.

"Lucien—"

"Stop the horse."

"Lucien..."

"Stop. The horse."

"I'm—"

"Stop the fucking horse, Beldon!"

Cyrus pulled up on the reins and Demeter halted with a snort. Lucien swung down from the saddle and stormed off the road into the foliage. Cyrus clambered down and followed him.

"Lucien, I'm sorry!" He tugged Demeter along behind him as he stepped over bushes and saplings that came up to his knees. "That was a stupid thing to say."

"Yes, it was," Lucien called back. He was nearly out of sight; only his pale hair gave him away amid the golden trees.

"It was stupid and thoughtless and just cruel," Cyrus went on.

"Especially since I witnessed everything you went through. I'm sorry." He looked up and stopped when he realized he could no longer see or hear Lucien. He flailed his hands. "Come on, really? Where the hell did you go?"

A silent minute slipped by; jays and songbirds laughed at Cyrus from the treetops. Then with a rustle of foliage, Lucien reappeared. "You're like a fucking duckling," he grumbled. "Do I follow *you* every time you piss? You have a short temper and you say hurtful things when you're angry, but I still don't plan to leave you behind." He bumped Cyrus's shoulder as he trudged past him.

Cyrus turned and trailed after him sheepishly. "You're still angry."

"Excellent observation. I'm sure I'll get over it, though, like you seem to have gotten over hearing my entire family dying in front of us."

Cyrus wished he hadn't opened his stupid mouth. "Lucien, I'm sorry."

"I know you are. That doesn't mean I get to stop being angry." He turned to Cyrus when the two of them stepped onto the road, and the intensity of his glare halted Cyrus in his tracks. "You drive me mad, Beldon."

That feeling, at least, was undeniably mutual.

Lucien climbed back onto the horse, but Cyrus stalled, fiddling with the straps securing their bags to the saddle. Lucien let him get away with it for half a minute before he huffed, "What is it?"

"I'm sorry I forgot the book. I was preoccupied, and I didn't think of it. I was..." Cyrus's hands trembled as he fed the end of the leather strap through the buckle and pulled it tight. He made himself look up at Lucien and meet his eyes. "I was thinking only of you."

He climbed onto the saddle and settled with his back to Lucien without waiting for a reaction. His heart thundered and he hated that Lucien could sense it; already he was kicking himself for saying that. It was too sincere, the closest he had come to revealing any of his feelings, and he desperately wished he could take the words back lest Lucien read into it too much.

Cyrus urged Demeter onward and their journey continued, silence resumed.

THE HORSE'S BUMPY, jostling gait was the only thing keeping Cyrus awake. Well, that and the sharp ache in his back and thighs that assured him he would not be able to walk correctly when he finally got down from this fucking saddle. The sun had set hours ago, at which point Cyrus had asked Lucien when they should stop, but Lucien had said to just keep going. So they had. And now it had to be close to midnight, and Cyrus wanted to die.

Or at least sleep for ten days. After a long, hot bath.

His stomach growled.

And a meal.

He tipped his head back and let out a quiet groan, yearning for those fluffy biscuits they'd gotten from the inn back in that lakeside town. The stale bread and hard cheese that remained in his bag were about as appetizing as dirt; he wanted *real* food, like a hearty stew with colorful flavors and bits of tender meat. Or one of those potato pies from that one shop in the city. And maybe a sweet pie, too. Cranberry. Or pumpkin, with a big dollop of whipped cream on top.

Cyrus's stomach growled again, and cramped itself in a knot for good measure. He heaved a sigh. "Lucien." He tried not to whine, but it was a vain effort. "Are you hungry?"

"Why, are you offering?"

Cyrus shot him a glare, but that coy smirk told him that Lucien could see the blush coloring his cheeks. Cyrus resisted an urge to touch his neck. "No. But—Well, I suppose you don't get hungry for human food, do you?"

"Not in the same way that you do." Lucien glanced toward the trees as something took flight high in the branches. "I get cravings, but I won't starve if I don't eat. Your food doesn't give me any nutrients."

"But my blood does."

"Yes. Did you think I just drink it for fun?"

Cyrus rolled his eyes at Lucien's sarcasm, but he was still curious. "So...how long can you go without it?"

"About a month, if I must, but that's a stretch," Lucien said. "We tend to get...irritable, at best, if we don't drink often enough. Push it more than a month and things could get out of control. Personally, I try not to go more than a few days."

Cyrus wasn't great at math, but it had been at least two weeks since Lucien had drunk his blood. He glanced back at him. "Have you eaten at all since...?"

Lucien raised an eyebrow. "Now it's really beginning to sound like you're offering."

"No, I— I mean... I-If, er—"

Lucien laughed softly. "Let me know when you've made up your mind. But I'm guessing you brought up food because *you're* hungry."

"Yes," Cyrus groaned. "And I want to get off this fucking horse. Are we there yet?"

"Say that one more time, and I *will* bleed you to death."

"Don't threaten me with a good time," Cyrus mumbled.

"As it happens, we *are* nearly there," Lucien said. "Slow down. Our turn is soon."

"Wait, really?" Cyrus tugged on the reins and slowed Demeter to a lumbering walk. He peered into the trees, but there was no branching path or break in the foliage that he could see. "Where?"

"There." Lucien touched Cyrus's waist and pointed to a spot just ahead to the left. Cyrus still couldn't see a path, but he trusted Lucien's night vision better than his own. He brought Demeter to the edge of the road, where Lucien mutely climbed down from the saddle.

"We're walking?" Cyrus tried to get Demeter to move a few more steps forward, but she dug in her hooves and loudly refused. "What about Demeter?"

Lucien gathered his bags from the saddle and slung them over his shoulders, then dug into one of Cyrus's bags and tugged out a shirt. Before Cyrus could protest, Lucien went up to Demeter and gently stroked his hand down the side of her face, then tied the shirt over her eyes. She flattened her ears, but didn't protest again when Lucien led her closer to the trees.

"Huh." Cyrus hopped down and gathered his things, then fell into stride beside Lucien as they stepped onto a narrow dirt path into the trees.

"Can't say I blame Demeter for not wanting to go this way," Cyrus muttered, ducking around a low branch. He glanced up at Lucien, but the vampire appeared miles away. His eyes darted around the woods as if expecting a monster to burst out of them, and he visibly flinched when Cyrus snapped a twig under his shoe.

"Are you okay?" Cyrus asked.

"No."

The response did not invite Cyrus to press further.

The narrow road meandered through the trees and eventually brought them to a massive iron gate flanked by two stone lampposts mounted with darkened glass orbs. A towering fence bordered the foggy grounds of the mansion beyond. Proudly perched on a steep hill, the structure was a forbidding sight, all dark stone and harsh gables. Golden light shone from a window here and there, but for the most part, darkness reigned.

Cyrus glanced at Lucien and found a hard, distant expression on his face. "Have you been here before?"

A humorless smirk curled at the corner of his mouth and quickly morphed into a scowl. "A very long time ago. But standing here now shrinks those years down to minutes." He exhaled slowly and approached the gates. No sooner had he stepped up to them did a woman dressed in a crisp black suit appear on the other side.

"What do you want?" Her voice was as harsh as her dark eyes that glanced suspiciously between Lucien and Cyrus.

"I'm here on behalf of the Honorable House Vista," Lucien said. His voice came out lighter than usual, betraying his unease. "Madame Rosaura knows me, though she is likely not expecting me."

The woman didn't react. Her eyes drifted to Cyrus. "And the other?"

Cyrus opened his mouth, but Lucien spoke before he could. "My companion accompanies me on behalf of House Vista as well. If you would, we have important business to discuss with the countess."

Cyrus slowly exhaled. He didn't know why he'd worried that Lucien would reveal his family name when that would assuredly get them in all kinds of trouble, but it was still a relief.

"Very well. Enter." The woman dragged the gate open with a rusty screech, and Cyrus followed Lucien onto the mansion grounds. "I will take your horse," the woman said with an outstretched hand.

Cyrus was reluctant, but he didn't know what else he would do with Demeter, so he passed over the reins. He mumbled his thanks as the woman promptly turned and led Demeter away.

He exchanged an uneasy glance with Lucien, and then the two began their trek up the dozens of stairs leading to the mansion's doors.

Another attendant dressed in black met them at the top of the steps. He bowed deeply, then saw the two of them into the cavernous foyer. A glittering chandelier hung overhead from the peaked ceiling, casting the polished floor in dapples of gold and white. Intricate tapestries splashed muted colors on the otherwise dark walls, interrupted every few feet by low-burning candelabras tucked in niches. Directly ahead, the foyer led into a larger room with a domed ceiling; more halls, doors, and rooms branched further into the mansion from there.

"May I take your coat, sir?"

Cyrus turned his head and found the servant waiting expectantly. Lucien's coat was already draped over his arm. "Oh. Yes, thank you." He made sure there was nothing in his pockets, then shrugged off the coat and handed it over. The man bowed again and then soundlessly disappeared from the room.

Cyrus slid his hands into the pockets of his trousers and turned to Lucien. "Now what? We go speak to...What was her name?"

"Lavinia Rosaura," Lucien said quietly. He stared off down one of the halls as if facing his own death. "To us, she is Countess or Madame Rosaura."

Cyrus nodded. "So where do we find her?"

"We don't." Lucien barely voiced his words, as if this place demanded whispers. "We wait until she is informed of our presence and then we wait for an invitation."

Cyrus dearly hoped this countess wouldn't wave off their visit as unimportant. The last thing they needed was more wasted time.

"So in the meantime..." Cyrus felt uncomfortably exposed in this empty foyer. He didn't dare move any further, but he also felt like a sitting duck just standing here.

The servant who had taken their coats returned then and lifted his arm toward one of the branching corridors. "This way, if you please. I will show you to your quarters."

"Are you sure she wasn't expecting us?" Cyrus whispered to Lucien as they followed the servant down a long hallway.

"Quite." Lucien fixed his gaze straight ahead.

Meanwhile, Cyrus's eyes bounced from one side of the hall to the other as he took in the paintings on the walls, the statues on pedestals, and the gilded molding where the walls met the arched ceiling. The servant led them up a flight of steep stairs carpeted in black, and then finally brought them to a stop at a towering black door emblazoned with gold brocade.

"Here we are. If you wish to have an audience with the Countess, she invites you to her court this evening to dine and imbibe. You will find appropriate attire in your wardrobe, but if any alterations are needed, please ring for me and I will introduce you to our tailor. Should you need anything else, you need only ask."

He bowed again, and Cyrus swore he flicked a fond smile in Lucien's direction before he took his leave.

Lucien strode into the room as if in his own house. Cyrus lingered outside.

One room. This entire mansion, and they were being crammed into the same room. It was one thing when a tiny inn in a tiny town had only one space to spare, but here? Really? Cyrus was almost tempted to try another door and claim it for himself, but the last thing he wanted was to cross some sort of etiquette line in a place where Lucien seemed afraid to even speak normally. Still, he was sick of sharing spaces with Lucien.

Well...that wasn't true. He wanted to be close to Lucien, but he didn't *want* to want it. It wasn't the proximity itself that vexed him, it was the ambiguity of it. Once again, he was haunted by all of those things unspoken that wedged a barrier between them.

So speak them, said his logic, which he promptly silenced. He'd rather eat glass than tell Lucien how he made him feel.

"Are you going to stay out there all night?" Lucien called from within the room. He looked up with a faint smile when Cyrus finally joined him and shut the door. The expression vanished almost immediately. "I won't tell you we're safe here, because Lavinia is harsh and unpredictable, but you will not be harmed under this roof. You have my word."

"I don't need your protection," Cyrus muttered, dropping his bag next to a velvet chair.

"Oh, yes you do." Lucien wasn't teasing; his face was stone cold. He retrieved a cloth pouch from within his bag and crossed the room toward an opaque screen door. "We're not in Chestervale anymore, Cyrus. You need to follow my lead here. Lavinia will expect us to look our best; you ought to see what that wardrobe has to offer."

He disappeared into the next room, and Cyrus was left alone in the elegant space. Its luxury reminded him of Lucien's room in

House Vista, but this place was far darker and noticeably colder. Cyrus wished for his coat as he wandered to the wardrobe that stood beside the singular window.

Within, he found a modest array of clothes: jackets of varying lengths, fine shirts and vests, and pristine trousers without a wrinkle to be seen. Everything was either black or gray. Cyrus shifted the garments around in search of something that suited him and also looked like it would fit him, and finally settled for a black silk shirt with ruffles around the cuffs and a black vest with a broad stripe of blood-red down the back. He tried three different pairs of trousers before he found one that wasn't too long or too big around his waist, and even the one he settled on was still a bit loose. He retrieved his own belt from his bags, then turned to the giant ornate mirror behind him.

Honestly, he looked nice. The clothes suited him, and were finer than anything he owned back home. The snug vest slimmed his waist and the rich blacks brightened his eyes. Even his hair cooperated, the curls falling neatly to frame his face rather than flying randomly. The only thing missing was a cravat, but even if he could find one, the shirt's collar wasn't made to accommodate a tie; the lapels were loose and shallow, falling flat around the shirt's wide V-neck. Delicate black cords crisscrossed the opening, allowing him to tighten it, but he decided to leave it open wide. He liked the tease of skin visible beneath the silk.

Cyrus smiled to himself and turned away from the mirror just as the door across the room opened and Lucien—

Lucien?

Cyrus's thoughts scattered in ten different directions before coming to an abrupt halt. The vampire before him was undoubtedly the one he knew: same narrow face, long nose, sharp eyebrows, and vivid crimson eyes, but gone was the lithe man he'd come to know. He faced, instead, a silver-haired woman wearing Lucien's features and a shining black dress.

Cyrus couldn't get himself to stop staring. When the vampire caught him, he wordlessly raised his eyebrows.

"It's still me." Even his—her?—voice was different. Still silvery, but light and smooth. "I can shapeshift, remember?"

Right. Yes. That made sense. But Cyrus had never seen a vampire shift like *this*. Or, well, maybe he had. How would he know?

"Um." He cleared his throat. Lucien was just as disarmingly beautiful like this, and it made Cyrus's brain hazy—which was interesting, since he'd not historically felt this way toward women. "What...should I call you?"

"*Luciénne* is still of House Vista, though her exact position in the family is unknown to Madame Rosaura." She set a pair of black heeled shoes on the floor and stepped into them, adding another four inches to her height. Her hair fell in wavy cascades down her shoulders, and when she approached Cyrus he noticed that she'd lined her eyes in stark black ink. Her lips were the same vivid red as her irises.

And the dress...Sleek and gleaming, the gown clung tight to her body, accentuating every new curve. A long slit parted the skirt on her right side from her thigh to the floor. Shiny black beads decorated the rigid bodice in a sweeping pattern over the curved neckline that plunged down the center of her torso. She wore a black silk ribbon around her neck, and obsidian teardrops dangled from her earlobes.

Cyrus blinked a few times and cleared his throat again. His face was burning. "I...Sorry. It's rude to stare. I just—"

"On the contrary." Luciénne drifted closer until he could smell her sweet, floral perfume. "I quite like the way you're gazing at me. You should see your expression; it's priceless." She flashed a grin, and even a quick glimpse of her fangs had Cyrus's pulse spinning out of control again.

Get it together, Beldon.

"And if I may," Luciénne murmured, "you're looking rather fine yourself, Mr. Beldon. I like the shirt."

Cyrus swallowed, finding that his mouth had gone dry. "Thank you. I...I like the dress. Uh. This is different."

Luciénne flipped her hair over her shoulder, and the motion was so very *Lucien* that it settled Cyrus's shock a little. "I don't like to bring Luciénne out often, but she does come in handy. Though it does take a lot of energy to shift like this, not to mention it's very disorienting."

"Can I ask a really stupid question?" The words tumbled out before Cyrus could stop them.

Luciénne smiled. "I'll allow you three stupid questions."

Perfect. "Does it...feel different?"

"Yes, quite."

"Is your *whole body* different?"

"Yes. Inside and out."

Cyrus blinked a few times. "Do you like this better?"

Luciénne smirked in a way Cyrus couldn't quite translate. "No. It's like putting on a very realistic costume, while on the inside I'm still Lucien. In my mind, I see myself as I am usually, so when I see Luciénne on the outside, it's like looking at a different person."

Cyrus nodded slowly. He reckoned he'd feel similar if he put on a dress. "Do you suppose there are vampires who shift like this, one way or another, *because* it feels right?"

That one earned him a *stupid question* look. "Obviously. You're looking at one of them."

Cyrus blinked. "What?"

"Countess Rosaura doesn't know me as Lucien," Luciénne said, smoothing her hands down the front of her dress. "The last time I saw her, I looked like this. I was too young to change, even though I desperately wanted to. When I was finally old enough to manage the shift, I swore I'd never go back, but..." She shrugged. "Here, it's necessary. Useful, too, I suppose. But I'll be relieved to return to myself."

Cyrus studied her, still feeling like his brain had been flipped upside-down in his skull. "But why can't the Countess know you as Lucien now?"

"Because I don't want her to know that I'm the heir to House

Vista." Luciénne slid around Cyrus, briefly touching his waist as she did so, and stepped up to the mirror. She ran her hands through her hair and fluffed it. "She knows that Lucien Vista exists, but she doesn't know that he and I are one and the same. Let's put it this way: Madame Rosaura has, last time I checked, nine ex-spouses. No one knows what happened to her ex-husbands, but she is on cordial terms with her ex-wives."

Oh. Great.

Luciénne glanced back at Cyrus. "Including me."

His mouth fell open. "*What?*"

"I told you, it was a long time ago." Luciénne returned to fussing with her hair. "I was young and stupid and fell head-over-heels for her and oh, she knew it." She scowled at her reflection. "We were married for a year, and I have never in my life been so emotionally unstable as I was during that time. One day I was her favorite person on earth, and the next she gave me the cold shoulder. I never was sure how she actually felt about me, but the good days were *so* good that I ignored the rest. She reeled me in like a goddamned fish and I fell for it every fucking time."

She sighed and finally left her hair alone, then stood up straighter and ran her hands down the front of her bodice. She tugged at the neckline, then cupped her breasts and squished them together.

Cyrus averted his gaze.

"I was relieved when she finally decided she was bored of me," Luciénne went on, "but she didn't *hate* me, so our parting was amicable. Sort of. At any rate, she told me I would always be welcome here, should I ever need her resources or knowledge. So. Here I am, one hundred years later."

Cyrus was still processing the fact that Lucien had been married to the countess they were about to meet. Somehow that was more shocking than learning he'd started his life as a woman.

Yet, the marriage thing did make some sense. Most humans fell in love multiple times throughout their comparatively short lifetimes, and it wasn't unusual to marry more than once. Why wouldn't a vampire have the same experience? Eternity was a long time to spend with one person when neither of you would age and die. Cyrus couldn't fathom it.

And despite Luciénne's claim that that breakup was *amicable*, one didn't typically look scared shitless the way Lucien had when they'd arrived when one had an *amicable* parting with a lover. Cyrus didn't expect to hear the whole story, but it was clear that Luciénne had been hurt by this woman, and that immediately put Cyrus on the defensive.

He wasn't going to reflect on that.

"It must be hard to be back here," he ventured.

"It's been a hundred years," Luciénne said softly. "I've had plenty of time to get over it."

Nothing about the way she'd said it suggested that was the case, but Cyrus didn't push the issue. He watched Luciénne fuss with her appearance for another few minutes, then stepped closer to her so she could see him in the mirror.

"Luciénne." The name, though not wholly different, was a new shape on his tongue.

Her eyes flicked in his direction. "What?"

"You look perfect." Cyrus tried a smile, hoped it looked genuine. "Should we go?"

Luciénne pursed her lips and stood up a little straighter, throwing her shoulders back. "We should." She finally turned her back on the mirror. "But I want to give you one more thing."

"What's that?"

She stepped closer to him and unwrapped a thick black ribbon from her wrist. "May I?"

He offered his hand, confused, but she shook her head and wrapped the ribbon around his neck. Cyrus suppressed a shiver at her cool touch, fleeting as it was. When she crossed the ends over each other, pulling the ribbon snug against his skin, it lightly pressed the lingering tender spot from her bite; he sucked in a gasp. A knowing smile tugged at Luciénne's lips.

She secured the ribbon with a neat bow and then stepped back. "There. Perfect."

"What is this for?" Cyrus fought the urge to fiddle with it.

"Aside from the servants, you will be the only human in Lavinia's court," Luciénne said. "A ribbon around your neck tells other vampires to keep their hands—and *teeth*—off."

Cyrus laid his hand over the ribbon. "So it means I belong to you."

Luciénne arched an eyebrow. "If you wish to interpret it that way, then sure, it can mean that."

Cyrus might as well put his foot in his mouth at this point. "No, I—I didn't—I'm not saying I *want* it to mean that. But it sounds like you do."

"No, Cyrus, this doesn't mean I *possess* you." Luciénne rolled her eyes. "I gave you the ribbon so that you walk out of here with your life, ideally free of vampire bites."

"Maybe I want them to bite me," he mumbled, mostly to himself.

But Luciénne heard, and her expression darkened. "No, you do not. These people aren't like me, Cyrus. Honorable Ones have rules. We have a code of etiquette and conduct, and we pride ourselves on our commitment to doing the least amount of harm to our human neighbors. When I bit you, I restrained myself because I didn't want to hurt you. The vampires in Lavinia's court do not follow the Honorable Families' code, and they do not show such courtesy to humans. You are food first and a plaything second, and if there's one thing your family gets right about vampires, it is that the vicious ones love to play with their food."

Cyrus folded his arms across his chest. A few short weeks ago, he'd flung himself into a panic at a mere glimpse of Lucien's bedroom, and now he'd apparently forgotten every reason to fear vampires. He'd broken the first golden Beldon rule, and gotten comfortable.

"Hence the ribbon," Luciénne said. "You're not *mine*, but

you're not to be bothered. And if anyone lays a hand on you, I will make them regret it."

The fire in Luciénne's eyes silenced any protest Cyrus might have made. She wanted to protect him, and he realized that he wanted to let her. This was her realm, and Cyrus was more than willing to let her lead him through this house of wolves.

"Very well." Cyrus offered his arm. "In that case, Honored Vista, I am yours."

Her expression gradually softened into a smile. She linked her arm through Cyrus's and together they strode across the room. At the door, she paused briefly and took a steadying breath before leading Cyrus out into the hall.

"All right. Let's get this over with."

Chapter TWENTY

CYRUS AND LUCIÉNNE CROSSED THE LABYRINTHINE castle and approached a massive pair of dark oak doors, where four servants waited in pairs to welcome them in. Cyrus glanced at the servants as they passed and noted that *they* didn't have any sort of ribbon or tie around their necks. Their shirts and jackets were low-collared, bare skin on full display. One of them already sported an obvious bite just above their collar. Cyrus tried to catch their gaze, but though they all held their heads straight, their eyes were downcast.

Luciénne gently squeezed his arm, and he returned his attention to the room ahead. But it was not a dining hall that he and Luciénne entered; it was a ballroom.

"Don't panic," Luciénne murmured, which confused Cyrus until he remembered that she could sense his pulse. "Stay with me, and you'll be fine."

"I know how to handle balls," Cyrus hissed back, and realized a second too late how that had come out. "Er—"

Luciénne snickered and turned her lips to his ear. "You can prove that later. Pay attention."

Cyrus was more than happy to fix his eyes somewhere other than on her. The ballroom was huge; its vaulted ceiling echoed back the din of voices and sinewy music that floated over the gathered guests. Only a few scarce lanterns were aglow, their flames hushed within red-tinted glass that cloaked the room in intimate shadows. Nearly everyone was dressed in black, save for a few choice guests in red.

Cyrus's gaze drifted back to Luciénne and he found that icy, closed-off expression on her face again. His heart tugged; she'd deny it if he asked, but he could see that this place got to her. Even if a century had passed, that was likely a blink to an immortal, and even time didn't heal some things as well as one would like. Luciénne had suffered here, and no amount of denial could hide that from Cyrus.

He tightened his arm around hers. "We don't have to speak to anyone here other than Madame Rosaura."

Luciénne blinked, as if she hadn't considered that. After a moment she slowly nodded. "I want wine. Come on."

They strolled their way along the edge of the ballroom, passing beneath the balcony that curved overhead. Cyrus had to consciously keep his head up and his shoulders back, mirroring Luciénne's confident stride; he would've sooner slunk into the deep shadows of this place and disappeared. That was what he was used to at home: he was an ornament, not a guest.

Although, he supposed he was still something like an ornament here, on Luciénne's arm, but he didn't mind that quite as much.

They meandered, avoiding the throes of guests and their circles of conversation, until Luciénne spotted a servant carrying a tray of crystal goblets. She lifted her hand in the boy's direction and he abruptly changed course to meet her, bowing his head as he offered the tray. Luciénne plucked one of the glasses, but when Cyrus went to reach for one, she swatted his hand.

He hissed at the dull pain of her rings on his knuckles and glared at her. She ignored him, continuing to smile sweetly at the servant until he was gone. Then she turned to Cyrus and leaned close. "Do not drink the wine."

Cyrus's eyes drifted to the glass. The opaque crystal was decorated with intricate fractals that warped the contents, but the rich red refused to be obscured. It was not wine.

"Whose blood is that?" Cyrus whispered.

"Why, do you want it to be yours?" Luciénne reached up and lightly tugged at the ribbon around Cyrus's neck. He jerked back, scowling, and she smiled. "I should have thought to warn you that *dinner* means something a bit different here. If you're hungry, though—"

"I'm fine," Cyrus interrupted, even though he'd been famished earlier. He smoothed his hand down the front of his vest, and realized he was still wearing his family's ring. Hastily he took it off and dropped it into his pocket; that was the last thing he should be boasting here. Not for the first time, he thanked the gods he didn't look anything like Marcus Beldon.

He flicked another glance around the ballroom, searching for a sign of the woman they were here to see, but no one stood out as the center of attention. The other guests huddled in flocks of black silk, keeping their drinks close and their secrets closer. Cyrus watched as a tall woman wearing a voluminous ballgown reached out to one of the servants, but instead of taking a glass she grabbed the girl's arm, wrenched her forward, and sank her teeth into her neck.

Cyrus quickly turned away.

"Cyrus." Luciénne's voice dropped low, nearly reminiscent of Lucien. It shocked Cyrus how comforting it was to hear that familiar murmur.

She smiled when he met her eyes—a genuine softness, just for him. "Don't worry about all of them." She flicked a glance toward the other guests. "Do you want to dance?"

The question stunned him. His immediate answer was a hard *No*. He knew a few dances, of course, but while he *could* navigate his way through gatherings like this, he preferred to do so from the sidelines. He hated the feeling of everyone's eyes on him, tracking his every step and waiting for him to slip up. He swore they could all see straight through his discomfort, as if the words *I don't belong here* were written across his back.

Would it be different here? No one knew him. No one expected anything of him. Those who had seen and recognized

Luciénne probably assumed Cyrus, clearly marked as a human, was either warming her bed or about to be her dinner. Here, he wasn't Cyrus Beldon; he was a nameless human clinging prettily to the arm of an Honorable One.

"You can say no," Luciénne murmured. "It was a question, not a demand."

And given the option of refusing, Cyrus realized he didn't want to. He looked up and met her gaze. "It would be my honor to accept a dance, Honored Vista."

A smile crept across her lips. "Please, sir, call me Luciénne." She dipped into a curtsey, and Cyrus offered his hand when she straightened. She took it, eyeing him curiously. "Do you wish to lead?"

He blinked. "No." The word fell out in a breath. No, actually, if she was offering, Cyrus was more than happy to let her take the lead.

Luciénne's grin sharpened. "I didn't think so." She lifted his hand to her lips and held his gaze as she pressed a lingering kiss there; when she drew back, a smudge of red remained on his skin.

Cyrus felt as if he was moving through fog as she led him toward the center of the room, where other pairs shared intimate dances and hushed conversation. Gowns swished, shoes clicked, and shadows waxed and waned across the polished floor. The music, louder here than it had been in the far reaches of the room, wrapped and lulled and enchanted. Cyrus began to feel as if he *had* drank that wine.

Luciénne drew him to her, one arm tight around his waist while her other hand cradled the crystal goblet. Cyrus's face warmed as he gazed up at her; he hesitantly placed his left hand on her shoulder as he would if he was dancing with a man, but his other hand hovered in the air near hers, unsure where to rest.

"Typically this dance, shared by two vampires, would have us share a meal," Luciénne said. "You would hold the cup as well, and we would take turns sipping until it's empty, at which point the dance ends and we are satisfied. Though you won't be drinking the wine, hold the cup with me anyway."

Cyrus lightly touched her hand, and she entwined their fingers. He bit his lip as his pulse jumped. Maybe this wasn't a good idea. Her proximity was just as bad for him as that blood wine was likely to be.

But...what was the definition of indulgence, if not this?

"Other than the unique hand placement," Luciénne continued, "it's a waltz. Shall we?" She spread her hand across his back and held him a little tighter, a little closer.

And Cyrus was supposed to concentrate on dancing? Thank the gods he was well-practiced.

The music that swelled up was intoxicating in its own right; the moment the dance began, the rest of the room faded away. The waltz was an easy series of slow steps that kept them close as they drifted across the floor. Cyrus caught himself tipping his head forward more than once, unconsciously drawn toward Luciénne and her fragrant perfume. What did she make of this, of their closeness, of Cyrus's weakening control over his affections? He wished he could feel her heartbeat the same way she could feel his.

Did she want him as much as he wanted her?

He could find out, he supposed. He need only tip his face up slightly to kiss her, and then whatever happened from there would answer everything unspoken. It was far from the first time Cyrus had considered it.

Yet something still held him back. It was easy to flirt, to yearn, to fantasize. But to act on any of it was to acknowledge that what he felt was real, that it was potentially reciprocated, and that both of them were willing to face whatever consequences exploded as a result.

Maybe that was his hesitation: not his feelings, but the aftermath. Despite everything, Cyrus realized that he still cared what his family thought of him.

He glanced up at Luciénne's face again and his heart pulsed. Knowing that she sensed it made the next beat stronger. Did his family's approval—which he'd never had for anything—really matter more than the bond he'd unexpectedly forged with this vampire? Lucien Vista was the only person Cyrus had ever met who seemed to truly *see* him. Lucien saw Cyrus's weaknesses and shortcomings and didn't berate him for them; he bought him a sword and offered a lesson and told him he was strong. He could've turned Cyrus away that very first day with a dismissive scoff, but instead he'd given him a chance and heard him out and agreed to meet him on equal ground.

Did Lucien know how significant that simple *yes* was to him?

Oh, shit, Cyrus thought. He gazed at Luciénne and those familiar crimson eyes and it hit him all at once that he wasn't just attracted to this vampire.

He was in love.

Well. Fuck.

"Penny for your thoughts?" Luciénne's gentle voice jolted Cyrus out of said thoughts. His face flooded with warmth and he flicked his eyes away. He could handle Luciénne knowing that he was attracted to her—or rather, to Lucien—but his deeper feelings were absolutely off limits.

He could not be in love. Did he think he lived in a fairy tale? Love wasn't for people like him, with lives like his. Cyrus had never let himself fall in love before; it was useless. His life had never allowed for more than casual affairs of short-lived passion. Never commitment, and certainly never love. Beldons weren't supposed to fall in love.

Especially not with fucking vampires.

Cyrus turned his head so he wasn't tempted to look at Luciénne again, lest she see everything in his eyes. The music continued and so did their dance; Cyrus could've done these steps in his sleep and thankfully didn't have to think about it. He suddenly wished to push Luciénne and her closeness out of his mind entirely.

What was there to be done about being in love, anyway? Cyrus couldn't act on it, so the best he could do was ignore it. Distance himself. Shit, he shouldn't have even gotten this close in the first place, and he shouldn't still be this close now. If he was wise at all he would push her away and end this dance and get the hell out of her arms.

It would ruin the mood—and the rest of the night—if he suddenly broke away now, and that itself was telling of a possibility Cyrus refused to consider. But Luciénne had enough to worry about tonight, and Cyrus didn't need her worrying about him, too.

And damn it, he didn't want to distance himself. He wanted this—all of it: the flirting, the lingering touches, the twist in his guts whenever the two of them locked eyes for too long. He loved the heady rush that hit him whenever Lucien got close, and he longed to close the gap and shatter the barrier. He wanted to *scream* everything yet unspoken.

"Perhaps I *should* let you try the wine," Luciénne mused. Cyrus glanced up and found a smile in her eyes, even if her lips didn't quite match it. "You look morose."

"And you look..." Cyrus studied her. There was a new brightness to her, a glow in her cheeks that hadn't been there before. "Radiant," he concluded.

"Quite the difference a little sustenance makes." Luciénne darted her tongue over her lips.

"What does it taste like?" Cyrus hadn't really meant to say that out loud, but he *did* wonder.

"You've never tasted your own blood?" She looked doubtful. "Never bitten your lip by accident, or sucked a cut to make it stop bleeding?"

"Well, sure, but...that's hardly a taste. What is it like to... drink it?"

A sly smile tugged the corner of Luciénne's mouth. "Cyrus Beldon, you're starting to sound like a curious vampire." She tipped her face closer to his ear, touching her nose to the side of his head. "It's exquisite, to be honest. Like liquid velvet: rich, smooth, and so warm. Simply delicious."

Cyrus suppressed a shiver. Idly, he circled his fingers across her bare shoulder. "Does it intoxicate you?"

"Hmm, not really. Not unless I have a lot, and even then it's more like...a subtle pleasure. Straight from the source, though? *Oh*, it's a rush. Not unlike sex, actually, and it makes you crave more and more and *more*."

Cyrus's thumb followed a gentle line along her collarbone. "How did it feel when you drank my blood?"

"Ohh, Cyrus." Luciénne inhaled slowly and her breasts swelled against her corset. "Yours is *divine*."

He tilted his head against hers. "And do you crave more of me, Luciénne?"

"*Yes*." Her arm tightened around him.

Cyrus swallowed a whine. Gods, if that bite had felt anything to Lucien like it had to him, he genuinely admired the vampire's restraint. As it was, he had to chase off his own arousal whenever he so much as glimpsed Lucien's fangs; Cyrus could not fathom how much more distracting Lucien would be if he could smell his blood and sense his pulse.

You drive me mad, Beldon. Perhaps in more ways than one.

A smile crawled across his face and chased away his earlier angst. For this moment, Luciénne wanted him, and damned if he didn't intend to savor it.

"If you want my blood, Luciénne, you need only ask."

She nuzzled the side of his neck. "I'd rather you did."

"What, bite you?"

"No. Beg me." Her voice dropped low, a feather against his ear. "Will you beg me, Cyrus, for my bite? For my kiss?"

His knees went weak and he missed a step. Her arm tightened around him, and it was only her strength that kept him on his feet.

"Tell me," she murmured. "Would you?"

He'd already forgotten what the question was. "What?" he croaked.

"Beg."

"*Please*." The word spilled out before Cyrus could remember what he was begging for. But what else would he want other than this, other than her? Or *him*, when they were gone from this place. Cyrus wanted him— No, he *needed* him.

"*Bite me, Lucien.*"

He felt Luciénne's soft laugh like a purr in his own chest. "Here?"

"Yes. *Yes.* I don't care." His thoughts were already on their way out of his head.

She nuzzled the ribbon around his neck. "You'll care when you become a feast. No, not here. These vampires don't get to share. I want you all to myself."

Then she drew away, and Cyrus opened his eyes and came back down to earth, and somehow they were still dancing.

He let out a long, slow breath, all too conscious of the heat spinning through his body. Gods, he had to stop letting this vampire do this to him.

It took all of his willpower, but he pulled away from her embrace and brought their dance to an end. He ran his hands first through his hair and then down the front of his vest, and then looked up at Luciénne. "You drive me mad, Vista."

She grinned, fangs on full display. "And what are you going to do about it, Beldon?" She whispered his surname.

Say 'fuck it' and throw caution to the wind, he thought, but before he could manage more than a step forward, all of the lights in the ballroom abruptly went out. Darkness swallowed the space and everyone in it, but its reign lasted only a few heartbeats before a single vivid crimson spotlight flickered to life at the head of the room.

Everyone turned toward the dais at the far end of the room. Cyrus heard Luciénne swear under her breath and he went to her, taking her arm again as if the past few minutes hadn't happened. Together, they watched the Countess stride into court.

Her sharp footsteps were the only sound in the ballroom as she approached the velvet throne at the center of the dais, directly beneath the light. Shadows cloaked her, obscuring her features, but there was no doubting the strength and pride behind her movements. Various guests bowed and curtseyed as she surveyed the room; Cyrus nearly followed suit, but Luciénne stood unflinchingly tall and straight, even when the Countess seemed to stare straight at her. Cyrus held his ground.

But then the Countess's imposing gaze fell upon him, and all that blood rushing about his body ran ice cold when she said, "Do you smell that, my friends? There's fresh blood in our midst tonight."

Chapter TWENTY ONE

When Cyrus was twelve, he'd attended his family's annual ball for Darkest Night. He'd begged his father for weeks to let him go; as the youngest, he had never been to any of their formal events, especially not the solstice ball, which was not only a celebration of the holiday but Marcus's big chance to make an impression on those in high society who somehow didn't know who he was. Cyrus had heard the same excuses every year: *You're too young. You'll embarrass us.*

But that year, he'd been determined to prove himself, and he'd finally won over Marcus—or at least, pestered him to the point that he'd said yes just to get Cyrus off his back. Dressed in his finest, Cyrus had proudly stood beside his siblings while his father gave a welcoming speech to fellow hunter families and Honorable Families alike. He'd been sure he would charm everyone in the ballroom. He'd daydreamed of being the center of attention, as if this was his social debut rather than a glorified business meeting.

Instead, in his excitement, Cyrus had retched up his dinner on the shoes of a boy from the Sheridan family, moments after accepting a dance from him.

Nine years later, Cyrus still remembered the appalling feeling of every single pair of eyes burning into him with disgust and scorn. And he felt it again now, vivid as before, as a ballroom full of vampires gazed at him with hungry eyes.

He tightened his hand around Luciénne's arm and, subtly as he could manage, shifted closer to her side.

"You're okay," she whispered, but Cyrus could tell she was uneasy, too.

Madame Rosaura spread her arms to the gathered crowd. "I bid you all my fondest welcome. Most of you are not strangers to these gatherings, nor are you strangers to me or to each other. But there is someone very special indeed with us tonight, and it is my distinct honor"—she winked—"to have her and her intriguing companion among us."

Scattered murmurs drifted throughout the room; Cyrus hastily dropped his gaze to the floor so as to avoid eye contact with any curious vampires. He didn't care if they all thought him cowardly; he wasn't here to make a point, he was here to survive.

Luciénne tipped her chin up and rolled her shoulders back, outwardly unbothered by the Countess singling her out. But Cyrus knew his vampire, and he recognized an uncommon yet unmistakable edge of fear in her eyes. It made his blood boil that the Countess's mere presence in the same room frightened Luciénne; whatever that vampire had done to her, Cyrus resolved to make sure the Countess didn't lay a finger on her now.

"Well." Luciénne sighed. "That was an invitation if I've ever heard one. Come on." She started forward, and Cyrus had no choice but to follow even as his instincts balked at the idea of approaching the Countess with dozens of eyes on him.

He kept his head up but his eyes down as the two of them crossed the room together. Luciénne stopped at the base of the dais and curtseyed while Cyrus bowed. He noticed, though she bent low, that she did not take her eyes off of Madame Rosaura.

"Honored Vista," greeted the Countess in a deep, velvet voice. She sat casually in her ornate chair, chin perched on the back of her hand. Gold rings inlaid with precious jewels sparkled on her fingers, the tips of which bore blood-red nails long enough to call them claws. She was broad-shouldered and muscular, which her high-collared yet fitted dress showed off generously. Black pearls circled her throat and spilled down her chest, stark against the crimson gown. The silk skirt cascaded over her legs like liquid, spilling eagerly to the side when she crossed one leg over her knee. Her shoes' heels looked sharp enough to stake a man through the heart, and Cyrus did wonder at the fate of aforementioned ex-husbands.

"Countess," Luciénne replied. "You look well, my lady. I am honored to be back in your court, though I apologize that my presence is unexpected. I do hope it is not to your chagrin."

Cyrus doubted that sweet-talking would work on the Countess, but hell, Luciénne could turn those honeyed words on him anytime she pleased.

Focus, Beldon.

"Not at all, my dear," the Countess cooed. "It pleases me greatly to see you again after all this time. You look like a dream, as always. And please, settle my curiosity: who might be this pretty thing on your arm?"

Cyrus caught himself mid-flinch and gave another small bow in an attempt to mask it. Still he refused to cast so much as a glance at the Countess's face. "Cyrus, my lady. Cyrus Vista."

The moment the name left his mouth, he wished he could snatch it back. What had he just done?

"Vista?" Doubt dripped from the Countess's voice. "Forgive my surprise; I did not realize the Vistas were in the habit of cozying up with their cousins."

Cyrus wanted to die.

Luciénne came to his rescue with a soft laugh. "Surely not, my lady. Cyrus is my husband, of course."

There was very suddenly not enough air in this room.

Cyrus hazarded a glance at the Countess; despite her languid demeanor, she looked genuinely shocked. "Husband? My mistake, Honored Vista. I suppose I should have inferred it. And how do you find House Vista, sir?"

Cyrus felt Luciénne tense at his side. Now he made himself meet the Countess's eyes; in this dim, tinted light, they looked dark as the pearls around her neck. "They're a pleasant bunch," he said, choosing his words carefully. "Truly honorable, from what I've seen. I'm...delighted to be part of such a dignified family."

What the hell am I saying? But Luciénne had started it, hadn't she? What the hell else was he supposed to say after she'd ripped the rug out from under him with the word *husband*?

He swore this countess could see right through his bullshit, but to his relief she nodded thoughtfully. "Indeed, though my knowledge of the other Vistas is little, in my experience, the blood that runs through their House is ripe with admirable qualities." She gazed at Luciénne as she spoke, and though her lips bore a slight smile, there was something ravenous in her eyes that made Cyrus want to step between her and Luciénne.

Before he could decide if that was necessary, the Countess sat up straighter and steepled her hands. "Pray tell, what brings you both to my court? You are a long way from Chestervale."

"Indeed we are," Luciénne said, bowing her head. "I am ever so grateful for your hospitality, my lady. It's a rather serious matter that has brought us here, but if memory suits me well, you'll find it intriguing. I wonder if we might speak in private?"

"*All* of us," Cyrus added when the Countess's eyes lit up. But perhaps that wasn't the warning he thought it was, because she looked no less sly when she flicked a glance at Cyrus.

"You have my attention. Come. I can spare a few moments." Madame Rosaura rose gracefully from her throne and stepped down from the dais. Even on equal ground with Luciénne, she rose several inches taller than her. Something silent passed between them as they locked eyes, and then the Countess strode out of the light's reach. Only the sharp clack of her heels on the marble told which direction she'd gone.

Luciénne started to follow immediately, but Cyrus held her back. He met her eyes pointedly, hoping his face translated a wordless *Are you okay?* But apparently the meaning got lost in whatever shock remained in his eyes from the whole *husband* thing, because Luciénne winked at him and then tugged him along after the Countess.

They passed through a small set of double doors that brought them into a modest, quiet parlor. It was absolutely dark, more so when Luciénne let the doors shut behind them. The ballroom hadn't exactly been bright, but now Cyrus couldn't tell the difference between having his eyes open or closed.

"Lucy." The Countess softened her voice to a friendlier tone. Cyrus did not like it.

"Luciénne," she corrected, not unkindly but with a subtle edge of warning. Her gown swished as she shifted on her feet, briefly leaning into Cyrus. Not once did she loosen her grip on his arm.

"Hm." Heels clicked on the floor, and then Cyrus sensed the Countess's presence, closer than before. "How have you been, really?"

"I'm fine, Lavinia." Cyrus was quite familiar with that impatient tone. "We're not here to exchange pleasantries or play catch-up. I know you have eyes and ears everywhere, especially in the city, so I trust you've heard about the recent incidents."

The Countess sniffed. "Cutting right to the chase, are we? You disappear for a *century* and won't even tell me how you've been?"

"I owe you no such thing," Luciénne said. Her tone was sharp but still carefully controlled; Cyrus knew that if she'd been talking to anyone other than the one person who could help them, she'd have snarled those words.

Cyrus hated that she had to be here.

More, he hated that he didn't know how to help.

The Countess simmered in palpable annoyance for another several seconds, then finally backed off. Her heels clicked rhythmically as she paced a lazy loop around the room. "The *incidents*. Yes. Vampires turning Wild. Honorable Families at each other's throats, if you'll pardon the pun. And what of the Beldons? I haven't heard a peep about them, yet they suffered a loss, did they not?"

Cyrus narrowed his eyes. Was she referring to Arthur...or

Marcus? And if it was the latter, did she also know about the Vista family? Was their lie about to crumble?

"The Beldon family remains tight-fisted with their secrets," Luciénne replied casually. "Yes, one of them was an unfortunate victim of this series of Wild turns, but what Marcus Beldon and his ilk intend to do about it remains to be seen. I've been researching Wild turns for some time now, but Arthur Beldon's death was somewhat of a turning point."

"Why is that?"

"Because who in their right mind would turn a fucking Beldon *Wild*, Lavinia?"

Cyrus thought for sure the Countess would rip both their throats out for Luciénne's profanity, but Rosaura just laughed. "Indeed, who in their right mind would turn a Beldon at all? A calculated hit, but by whom?"

Cyrus shifted on his feet, and he knew the Countess probably sensed his tell, but he kept his mouth shut. How could he possibly explain how he knew exactly who had turned Arthur without also blowing his cover?

"I don't care so much about the culprit as I do about the reason for it," Luciénne said. "I'm not here to solve a murder. I want to know why this happened and how to stop it from happening again. The Beldons took care of the Wild vampire that became of Arthur, but there have been more. Namely, Leigh Harrows."

At that, the Countess's pacing abruptly halted. "The Harrows *heir*?"

Cyrus glanced at Luciénne, momentarily forgetting that he couldn't see her face. But he sensed her movement and knew she had turned to him, too, with the same thought: *Why doesn't she know that?*

"You didn't hear?" Luciénne asked.

"My contacts in the city only hear what is spoken," Rosaura said. A hush of surprise edged her voice. "House Harrows must be keeping this under very tight wraps."

"Can you blame them?" Luciénne said. "It should be impossible. Born vampires can't be turned Wild."

"But dhampirs can be."

Luciénne snorted. "If Leigh Harrows was a dhampir, we'd all know. If *any* of the Honorable Families had a dhampir in their midst, we'd know. And you especially would."

"Maybe, maybe not." Rosaura's dress rustled as she shrugged. "Tight-fisted secrets. Okay, so assume Leigh Harrows wasn't a dhampir. Draw your next conclusion. Why would she be a target?"

"That remains unclear," Luciénne said. "But if it's true that Leigh Harrows was full-blooded...it means that any human or vampire can be turned Wild."

"And doesn't that, though frightening, sound more plausible than the Harrows family keeping a secret dhampir heir all these years?"

It was the same logic that Lucien had pointed out to his father all those weeks ago in the Vista library, yet here Luciénne was, just as reluctant to believe it as Master Vista had been. Cyrus couldn't blame her, but shying away from the unpleasant and terrifying truth would not make it any less true. The sooner they all accepted that as a strong possibility, the sooner they could figure out who had inflicted the Wild turns and why.

"Yes," Cyrus answered when Luciénne still said nothing. He felt her eyes on him. "It is more plausible. And I understand why you don't want it to be true, but we have to know the threat before we can hope to eliminate it."

"Your paramour makes a good point," the Countess said, though she didn't sound happy about it. "But Luciénne, I don't think you should give up so quickly on the question of who is doing this. It's one thing for a regular, nobody vampire to turn a human Wild. It's entirely another matter to turn an Honorable One Wild, especially when that is something broadly thought to be impossible. How can you hope to put a stop to this when you don't know who you're stopping?"

"I didn't say I gave up," Luciénne snapped. "I said I don't care who's doing it, as long as I can find a way to end it. And that's why we're here: I need you to tell me if there's a way to reverse a Wild turn."

Her demand was met with chilling silence. Cyrus shifted nervously on his feet, wishing he could at least see the Countess's face. As if he'd willed it into being, a single candle flickered to life across the room, revealing that Rosaura had moved without a sound. The light caught only half of her pale, stony face, but it was enough to betray her fury.

"I don't have to tell you how dangerous even the *idea* of that possibility is."

"No," Luciénne agreed, "but if anyone could unravel the science, it's you. I believe that wholeheartedly, Lavinia."

"The time for flattery has long passed, Vista." The Countess approached Luciénne in just a few broad strides and towered over her. "I want you to think very hard about what you're asking of me, and I want you to consider the danger of that knowledge in our enemies' hands. Consider just for a *moment*, Luciénne, what Marcus Beldon would do with the knowledge that turn reversal is possible."

Luciénne's expression remained impassive, but a twitch beneath her eye betrayed to Cyrus that she was thinking of her book of research left for Emerson Beldon to find. "Do you think me so careless that I would let this information fall into the wrong hands?"

Cyrus stopped himself from wincing.

"No." The Countess narrowed her eyes. "You're not careless, but I have always known you to be too *trusting*, my dear. It is not you I distrust, but your judgment. Always giving people the benefit of the doubt. I distrust those you would call allies simply because they showed you kindness or shared a common goal." Cyrus couldn't be sure, but he swore she flicked a nearly imperceptible glance at him.

"Though...you were much younger in our golden days,"

Rosaura went on. "I wonder if the past century has knocked any sense into you."

"I don't know why you continue to pretend that you know me," Luciénne said, with obviously forced calm. Her tone iced over the room. "And I do not appreciate your condescension. You offend me, and my *paramour* as well."

Oh gods, no, don't bring me into this, Cyrus silently pleaded.

Luciénne wasn't done. "I resent your suspicion of my judgment of character. Cyrus has shown time and again that he is nothing less than trustworthy, even at times when it would have done him better to betray me. He would not be here with me now if I did not believe, wholeheartedly, that he would not turn his back on me or our cause. If you cannot accept that, Lavinia, then we are done here."

Cyrus could've kissed her. He hoped his surprise didn't show too plainly on his face, for the sake of their ruse, but he couldn't help gawking at Luciénne's words. He knew, on some level, that she trusted him, but to hear it aloud rattled him to the core.

Yet right on cue, the doubts crept in. Of course Luciénne would say all of that to build a convincing lie that they were married. Not that Cyrus thought she *didn't* trust him, but the heartfelt earnestness behind her words was very likely an act. He'd just seen how well she could sweeten her words to get what she wanted; what made this any different?

Cyrus turned his attention back to the Countess just as she replied. Her expression had softened, though she didn't look any less annoyed. Just less suspicious. "Fine. At your insistence, I'll share what I know, one scholar to another. I have not forgotten your aptitude for the sciences. However, it's on *both* of you if those damned Beldons get their bloody hands on any of this."

Cyrus had to appreciate the irony.

Luciénne smirked. "As if I would ever fraternize with a Beldon."

She flicked a teasing glance at Cyrus, but the humor instantly bled out of him. It was a joke—he *knew* it was a joke—but it still stung. His doubts and insecurities flocked him with a vengeance. Really, why *was* Luciénne still bothering with him at all?

The Countess chuckled at Luciénne's comment, which seemed to lighten the mood. Her mood, anyway. She regarded Luciénne thoughtfully, hands on her plump hips. "It's good to see you, Lucy."

"It's still Luciénne," she said, but with less venom. "You as well, Liv."

Another sour emotion joined the others roiling in Cyrus's stomach. It took him a minute to peg it as jealousy.

"You're still the only one I've ever allowed to call me that," the Countess said, shaking her head with a smile. "I recall it fondly, especially the way you'd cry it when—"

"Ah, let's leave the past in the past, shall we?" Luciénne sent her a hard look, to which she flashed a sharp grin.

If Cyrus clenched his jaw any harder he'd shatter his teeth. With effort, he eased the tension and pointedly cleared his throat. "If you're quite done reminiscing, I wonder when you might show us what we came here to see."

Rosaura sighed. "Yes, I suppose that's rather important, isn't it? But have pity, Mr. Vista, it has been so very long since I've seen my dear Luciénne."

"Your *dear Luciénne*, on the other hand, has gotten on quite well without you," Cyrus snarled.

Luciénne dropped his arm and stepped away. "And dear Luciénne does not appreciate being spoken about as if she's not *right here*." She flicked a glare at Cyrus, but turned the brunt of her anger on the Countess. "Enough, both of you. Lavinia, I expected better manners from a countess in the presence of a gentleman, namely one who happens to be my husband." She snapped the last word with a flash of fangs. "Our history is just that, and I expect you to respect that. In that regard, Cyrus is correct: I am quite content with my life, and I did not come here to rekindle any smoldering embers that might have remained on your part."

Cyrus once again found himself dumbstruck by her words.

He'd expected her to chastise his jealousy, not jump to his defense. *Part of the ruse*, he reminded himself.

The Countess, oddly, looked impressed. "Indeed you are different from the Luciénne I remember. You've gotten feisty." She glanced at Cyrus with a quirk of her eyebrow. "I bet she's fun."

Cyrus scowled.

"To return to the matter at hand," Luciénne said, "what have you got to show us, Countess?"

At last, Rosaura's expression grew serious. "A fair amount, actually. Far too much to dig into tonight. I wish to enjoy the ball, dear, not disappear from my own court. I invite you to do the same, and then we shall reconvene tomorrow afternoon. Are we agreed?"

"What?" Cyrus blurted before he could stop himself. "No! We—"

Luciénne touched his arm. "Yes, Countess, that is agreeable. Thank you."

"*What?*" he hissed, at Luciénne this time. "Luc—"

She pinched his arm, hard, and he shut his mouth. Luciénne ushered him out of the parlor in the Countess's wake, and then dipped into a shallow curtsey when Rosaura turned to take her leave into the ballroom. Only when she had disappeared into the crowd did Luciénne turn to Cyrus.

He said the first thing that came to mind. "What the *fuck* was literally all of that?"

She sighed. "You played along impressively well with my improvisation. Thank you."

"Oh, no, no, you don't just get to say 'Aww, good job, Cyrus' and leave it at that." Cyrus didn't realize how much anger had been churning under his skin through that whole interaction, but now he burned with it. "And you also don't get to tell me to fucking beg for you and then turn around and say you wouldn't fraternize with a Beldon."

Luciénne flinched and glanced over her shoulder, then grabbed his arm and dragged him down a short hallway, away from the ballroom. "*Keep it down.* Don't do this here. Are we staying?"

"I would rather leap off the roof, to be quite honest."

"Fine." She turned on her heel. "Then let's go."

Cyrus strode after her, and it wasn't until he caught her arm that he knew what he intended to do. She turned back, and he grabbed her face and crushed their mouths together.

And before he had time to even start to ask himself why he'd done that, Luciénne gripped him by his shirt collar and pushed him against the wall. She kissed him hard, fingers clawing through his hair, and Cyrus melted when he felt her fangs graze his lips. He breathed a moan against her mouth and deepened their kiss with a bite of his own, but to his dismay Luciénne then broke away.

Really? he thought breathlessly, *the vampire doesn't like being bitten?*

Luciénne released him and stepped back, breathing hard. Her gaze remained fixed on him, dark red and ravenous. Her cheeks were flushed with a pinch of color, and the paint had smeared at the corner of her parted lips. It made Cyrus want to kiss her again and again until the only red that remained was from his teeth.

Shit. He could not believe he'd just done that.

And judging by the numb shock on Luciénne's face, she apparently couldn't believe it either.

Cyrus stepped forward and started to reach for her again, because if this was happening then he wanted it to *happen*, but Luciénne stopped him with a hand on his chest. Cyrus huffed.

"Not here," she murmured. Her eyes were rather obviously on his mouth. "Not like this."

No, please. Cyrus didn't know if he'd spoken the words or only thought them, but she couldn't fucking do this to him. He held her gaze and slid his hands around her waist; when she didn't protest, he drew her closer and touched his lips to her ear. Her hair tickled his nose, and oh, he wished he could drink her scent. Now that he'd tasted this closeness, he was desperate for it.

If not here, then where? How? When? He needed to know.

"Let's go, then," he murmured. Her dress was liquid silk under his palms. "And you can be your usual self, and I..."

"Cyrus," she sighed.

Gods, he loved his name in that low voice. "Please, Luciénne."

She gripped the front of his shirt. "Cyrus." Her voice caught huskily in her throat. "I..."

"Come with me, Lucien." Cyrus whispered the name.

Luciénne sighed and turned her head as if to kiss him again, but then pulled back, yanking his hands off of her. "No. I— Cyrus, I can't. Not here." She ducked her head and turned her back on him, hugging her arms around her body.

And if Cyrus wasn't quite so frustrated or quite so riled up, he might have recognized that she needed comfort more than she needed him to kiss her, but her rejection punched hard, and all he could do was stare numbly at the back of her head. He hated how small his voice sounded when he said, "What?"

She shook her head, sending waves through her long hair. She glanced back at him once, and then fled down the hall.

Cyrus watched her go until she'd disappeared around a corner. His heart pounded, forcing heavy breaths out of him. He wanted to scream—at her, at the Countess, at this place and its dark corners. It was only because they were here that Luciénne had run from him. He was sure of it. Before, everything had been easier.

Hadn't it?

It had been clearer, then.

...Hadn't it?

They'd been on the right track, hurtling toward something more.

Hadn't they?

Had Cyrus been wrong about Lucien's feelings this whole time? Was it all truly just a game to him?

He suddenly couldn't be here anymore. He fled down the hall and chose a corridor at random, uncaring that he didn't know where he was going. All that mattered was that he didn't return to the room he shared with Luciénne. That was the last place he wanted to be, and she was the last person he wanted to see.

Well, second to the Countess.

Anger burned bright and hot under his skin as he stormed his way through the mansion's dark halls. He took turns at random, without a thought to where he ended up or who he might encounter. As long as it wasn't the Countess or Luciénne, he did not care who saw him. If any of these snobby vampires tried anything, he'd fight them. He still knew how to be ruthless, and gods knew he was furious enough.

When at last the hall he'd chosen dead-ended at a set of glass doors, he shoved through them and found himself on a wide half-circle balcony overlooking sprawling gardens below. The crisp air was a welcome balm after the sultry ballroom; Cyrus went to the iron railing at the balcony's edge, gripped it until his knuckles turned white, and inhaled until his lungs hurt. When his head started to spin, he let out the breath in a heave and released the tension in his shoulders with it.

Overhead, the midnight sky was clear of clouds. Stars painted a mural across the inky black, and the full moon cast a ghostly glow over the gardens. Cyrus stared up at the moon and felt that it was peering back at him. It was a gentle gaze, though, not a harsh, judgmental glare. The moon waited, but did not expect, for Cyrus to speak.

"I hate this," he said to the moon. His voice came out strained and thick, but out here in the Moon God's solitary company, he didn't try to clear it. He didn't have to be strong here. "I hate how we both have to act here. I hate that he has to be someone he's not just so that horrid woman will listen to us. I hate that she's the only one who can help us, and I hate that I— That I can't do anything."

He hung his head and closed his eyes. "Maybe that's it. I'm powerless. I can't do anything for him. I'm not strong, I'm not clever, I have no influence. I'm no one. And he...he deserves better than that."

His eyes swam, and he blinked the tears away. Shame washed

over him. What right did he have to be so upset over something so stupid, so inconsequential? He had no claim to Lucien or his heart. Lucien had no obligation to indulge or even acknowledge Cyrus's feelings. And Cyrus had absolutely no right to assume that those feelings were reciprocated.

Why the *fuck* had he kissed Luciénne?

"I think this is it," he muttered. "I think this is the stupidest thing I've ever done." He passed the back of his hand across his cheek to catch the tears. "And now I've ruined everything, and he's probably pitying my poor heart when I should've known that all he wanted from me was my blood." He sniffled and coughed out a noise that caught somewhere between a humorless laugh and a sob.

How had he missed it? Lucien's affections toward him had only started *after* he'd bitten him. He'd said himself that drinking a human's blood was a sensual rush—and Cyrus would bet it made the human all the more alluring to the vampire. Lucien had admitted plainly that he longed to taste Cyrus's blood again, and Cyrus was so caught up in his desire for the same that he hadn't even considered that their feelings were different.

Stupid.

And what could he do about it? They were miles from the city, and even once they went back, their work together wasn't done. Cyrus couldn't go home if he valued his life—which, though less so at the moment, he did—so he was stuck with Lucien unless he found somewhere else to go.

He didn't want to do that. Despite the emotional strife, Cyrus did not want to write Lucien out of his life. He couldn't envision his future without Lucien in it in some capacity. In just a couple short months, Lucien had found a permanent place in Cyrus's life and in his heart, and he didn't see a way to change that—nor did he want to.

Gods damn him, he really was down bad for that fucking vampire.

Cyrus dragged his hands down his face, then tipped his head up to the moon again. "Mother was right. You are a good listener. I just wish you could fix my life for me." He sighed. "But I guess that's up to me."

He didn't know how much time slipped by while he stood in silence with the moon, but when the chill started to nip his nose and numb his fingers, he finally peeled away from the balcony and retreated back inside.

The mansion's dark dreariness didn't do much to warm him or his mood, but he wandered his way through the halls with a calmer sense of acceptance that he'd made a mess and the consequences would unfurl as they would. If Lucien cared about him at all—and he was fairly confident that he did, even if it wasn't exactly in the way Cyrus wanted—he would forgive him for overstepping. And he would forgive Lucien for leading him on and then running away.

Probably.

With each turn he took that did not bring him to anything familiar, Cyrus lost confidence in his knowledge of where he was going. He didn't think he'd wandered *that* far, but he also hadn't been paying attention. It did not help that all of these hallways looked the same: dark stone walls, dark floors, faded tapestries, cobwebbed candelabras that were more for show than for light. Cyrus found no landmarks to direct him back to his room.

He shouldered through another door and descended a short set of steps—which he *really* didn't remember seeing before—that brought him into a wider hallway that was completely dark but for a slice of light spilling through a cracked door. Cyrus softened his steps and hugged the opposite wall, hoping to evade the light, and when he drew closer he realized he *did* recognize this corridor; he remembered the murals along the top edge of the walls, and he was positive that his and Luciénne's room was just after the next bend.

It was a small victory, but a victory nonetheless.

Cyrus crept by the open door, but momentarily froze when he heard a soft voice within. Quickly he stepped out of the light's reach and pressed against the adjacent wall, out of sight but within earshot.

"You know I wouldn't ask if I didn't think it absolutely necessary."

Cyrus's heart thumped. That was Luciénne's voice.

"You're not without strength," replied a deeper voice. The Countess. "This is a serious measure. Have you ever done it before?"

A heavy pause. "No. But I know the risks, and I also know the benefits. I believe the strengths outweigh whatever side effects I might suffer."

Cyrus frowned. What the hell was Luciénne asking for?

It was several moments before Rosaura replied. "If you're sure...then, here. But take care. You don't need more than a sip."

Cyrus's stomach flipped. No. She couldn't mean...?

He inched closer to the door and pressed his face flat against the wall. In the room, a tall mirror within Cyrus's sight reflected the opposite scene: Countess Rosaura lounged in a wingback chair, Luciénne kneeling at her feet.

That alone was enough to get Cyrus's blood running hot, but worse, Luciénne cradled the Countess's forearm in her hands, and Cyrus watched, stunned, as she brought Rosaura's wrist to her lips and sank in her teeth.

Cyrus pressed his hand to his mouth to muffle his involuntary gasp. Nausea twisted deep in his stomach, spreading through him with every thundering heartbeat. Only his numb shock kept him from running in there or running away; he was rooted to the spot, sick with horror...and fascination.

He fixed his eyes on Luciénne's pale face and the ecstasy that melted across her features; was that how she'd looked when she'd drunk Cyrus's blood? Or was it like ambrosia from another vampire?

Luciénne's eyes fluttered shut and she released a soft moan, but Rosaura allowed it only a second longer before she gently pushed Luciénne away and took back her arm.

Cyrus fled. He'd seen enough. And he did not need to know what might come next.

He stormed into their shared room and slammed the door, then tore off his borrowed clothes and grabbed his own familiar garments from the chair where he and Lucien had dropped their things. It wasn't until he had the shirt on that he realized it wasn't his; the fine embroidery gave it away as Lucien's, and no sooner did he notice that did he realize it smelled like him.

A sob broke out of him. He collapsed onto the couch and pulled the front of the shirt over his face, breathing in Lucien's familiar scent by the lungful. A faint rosy fragrance clung to the fabric, but beneath it was an earthier musk, like cypress. Cyrus wanted to bury himself in it.

But he also didn't want to soak Lucien's shirt with his tears, so he pulled it off his face and dried his eyes with the back of his hand. He gazed blankly across the room at the open bedchamber door, but couldn't bring himself to go sleep in there. Even if Luciénne didn't come back right away—even if she didn't come back at all— he did not want even a slim chance of being near her tonight.

It was petty, but didn't he deserve to be a little petty?

Besides, the couch was comfortable enough. He settled down and tucked himself against the back cushions, but even though closing his eyes brought some relief to his exhaustion, he knew it would be a long time before he finally fell asleep.

SOME TIME LATER, Cyrus heard the door softly click open and then shut. A light rustle of fabric was the only tell of Luciénne's movement across the room; Cyrus made sure to keep his breathing even and his body still when he sensed her approach.

For a bit, there wasn't another sound. Then more rustling, and Luciénne sighed deeply. The couch jolted and Cyrus felt a presence at his back; she'd sat down on the floor beside him.

"I know you're upset." It was Lucien's voice now. Cyrus's heart twisted. "I also know you're not asleep, but I'll forgive you this time. Gods know you have far less to be sorry for than I do."

Cyrus clenched his jaw.

"I hate this place." Lucien spoke so softly that the room nearly swallowed his voice. "I hate *her*. I had to do something drastic, and I don't know what it'll do to me, but I think—I *hope* it was the right choice." Clothes rustled. Lucien sighed again. "I drank her blood, Cyrus."

Cyrus tried not to feel any gratification that Lucien sounded disgusted with himself.

His voice was unsteady when he continued. "Lavinia is a very old and very powerful vampire. Few of us make it as many centuries as she has, and as vampires age, they grow more powerful. They gain new abilities. What Lavinia can do is godlike compared to my strengths.

"I fear we'll be facing a battle neither of us is prepared for when we return to the city." There was another soft rustle: Lucien running his hands through his hair. "I need to feel like I can fight. I need to feel like both of us have a chance. Drinking Lavinia's blood was the only way I knew to gain real, useful power. It won't give me everything she has, but it will strengthen me, and perhaps lend me an ability or two that I was not previously capable of."

Cyrus debated turning over to face Lucien, to have this conversation like a mature adult and offer some comfort after what was clearly a hard decision.

But no, he wasn't ready to see Lucien's face and the pained expression he knew he'd find there. He was afraid of what might happen if he offered any consolation.

Lucien let his head fall back against the couch. "I should be saying this to your face instead of speaking to the room and hoping you're listening. That makes me a coward for yet another reason." A heavy pause. "I'm sorry I ran away."

Cyrus squeezed his eyes shut tighter.

"I didn't want that to happen like that," Lucien whispered.

Cyrus's pulse kicked up a notch. *So you did want it?*

"Each time I imagined it, it was...joyous." Lucien sniffed. Was he crying? "Not wrought with tension or anger or...fear."

You imagined it? Us?

Lucien let out a shaky breath. "I'm so scared, Cyrus. I'm so afraid for us." He lightly laid a hand on Cyrus's leg. "I know I hurt you. I know you're confused, and you have every right to be. I've been unfair to you, and we're both at fault for that, but I..."

Heart pounding, Cyrus waited for him to say more even as he begged him, *Not like this.*

As if he heard the thought, Lucien dropped the rest of that sentence. The cushion dipped as he laid his head on it. "Will you... come to bed? I—I don't know what Lavinia's blood will do to me, and I want you close. Please." His voice was hardly a whisper by the end of his words, but the silence following them was deafening.

Cyrus's eyes burned behind their lids. His throat tightened until he could barely breathe. Every last scrap of rationality within him screamed at him to get up and take Lucien in his arms and hold him until neither of them was afraid. If Lucien needed comfort, Cyrus wanted to be that comfort. If he needed love, Cyrus wanted to be that love.

But he couldn't bring himself to do it. And he hated himself for it, but one small yet bleeding fracture in his heart wanted Lucien to feel the same sharp slice of rejection that Lucien had inflicted on him earlier.

It was cruel, and it was unfair. But there were worse things than having to sleep alone.

When a few minutes slipped by and Cyrus's response became unflinchingly clear, Lucien dragged himself up from the floor with a sigh. Cyrus didn't hear him move away, but then something soft fell over him. Lucien gently tucked the blanket around Cyrus's shoulders, letting his hands linger a moment before he finally left. A second later, the bedchamber door softly shut.

A SHRILL SCREAM jolted Cyrus awake. He bolted upright in an unfamiliar space, disoriented but on his feet in an instant. The cry came again from the next room, and without a second thought, he ran. Bursting through the door, he found Lucien on the floor, doubled over and groaning in agony.

"Lucien!" Cyrus tried to shout, but his voice escaped him. Panic spiraled through him as he dropped to his knees beside Lucien and gripped his shoulders. Lucien roughly shoved him away.

"*Don't touch me!*" His voice was strained and broken. He curled into himself, hiding his face behind his hands. His body trembled, and Cyrus heard a series of grotesque cracks and pops. Lucien groaned, and Cyrus watched in horror as his fingers blackened and lengthened to claws. When he lifted his head and opened his eyes, they were solid black.

No. No, this couldn't be happening. Not to him. Gods damn it, why had he agreed to drink that fucking Countess's blood?

Lucien's body shuddered and twitched erratically, each movement drawing a pained groan out of him. His veins darkened before Cyrus's eyes, glaring like ink on his pale skin. When he bared his teeth they were vicious, monstrously huge and sharp, and when he turned his head toward Cyrus, there was only fury in his eyes.

Lucien Vista was gone. The monster in his place lunged.

Cyrus screamed, and this time it was loud enough to wake him up.

He couldn't stop shaking, couldn't get enough air. His heart pounded sickeningly fast. He stared, unseeing, at the dark room around him and heard the echoes of Lucien's screams in the back of his mind. *I'm safe*, he tried to assure himself. *It was a dream. Lucien is in the next room. We're safe.*

No, he wouldn't believe it until he knew.

He bolted off the couch and shoved the bedchamber door open. A sting of lingering fear from the nightmare made him hesitate for exactly a second, but his concern for Lucien won out and he approached the bed.

He could hardly see in the solid darkness, but the faint light from the room behind him was enough to assure him that Lucien was there, safe and asleep.

But alone. And afraid, by his own admission.

Suddenly all of Cyrus's petty reasons from earlier crumbled to sand. He shut the door and relied on the faint moonlight to find his way to the bed, but when he pulled back the covers Lucien abruptly bolted up with a gasp and Cyrus found himself at the end of a dagger.

His mouth fell open but no words came out.

Lucien's eyes widened when he recognized Cyrus's face, and he quickly flung the knife to the floor. Cyrus reached out to him, but Lucien crumpled back onto the bed and buried himself in the covers with his back to Cyrus before Cyrus could find even a single word.

Cyrus swallowed the thick knot in his throat and then settled down, inching over until he could feel the strange coolness of Lucien's body. For several minutes he just watched him, unwilling to close his eyes on Lucien's silhouette. He could still hear him screaming. He would never forget the terror he'd just seen on his face.

Tears stung Cyrus's eyes. This vampire was far too forgiving with him. Cyrus had treated him terribly, carelessly, stringing him along only to snap the tether at the last second. For all the mixed signals Cyrus thought he saw from Lucien, he knew he was guilty of a hundred more.

Falling in love with Lucien undoubtedly created problems for him, internally as he battled everything he'd ever been taught about vampires, and externally as their entire world stood against them. This was the most conflicted he'd ever been, and never had someone so dangerous caught his interest. Nothing about the two of them was easy, and it was not about to get any easier.

Cyrus was scared, too.

But maybe, for just right now, and for all the small moments between them and them alone, none of that had to matter.

Cyrus shoved away his fear and insecurity and doubt, and then erased the final inches between himself and Lucien. He fit himself against Lucien's body and wrapped an arm tightly around him, tucking his face against the back of his neck. He inhaled slowly, and a smile touched his lips at the scent of rose and cypress.

And he couldn't be sure, in those last hazy moments before sleep fully took over, but he thought Lucien might have murmured his name.

Chapter TWENTY TWO

CYRUS WAS ALONE IN THE GIANT BED WHEN HE AWOKE in the morning, and when he shuffled out to the sitting room he found that Luciénne had returned. She was dressed more similarly to Lucien now, in a high-collared white shirt tucked into tight black pants. She sat beside the faintly crackling fireplace and drew a comb through her long hair, lost in thought.

Cyrus ruffled his hand through his own hair and purposely failed to stifle a yawn as he approached her. He plopped on the chair across from her and offered a faint smile when she looked his way.

She flickered a smile of her own, eyes softening. But she didn't say anything, merely returned to her idle task.

Cyrus searched for something to say. *Did you sleep well?* seemed like a stupid question. *I'm sorry for acting like an ass* might've been appropriate and a long time coming, but it would also open the door to a deeper conversation that Cyrus still, somehow, wasn't ready for. And everything else he wanted to say orbited that same topic.

Something had changed between them last night. He could feel it in the air now, like the space between them was holding its breath, waiting for one of them to acknowledge what had and had not been said. Last night, it had been easy to ignore his fears. Now, in the foggy gray of morning, the idea of opening that door terrified him.

He opted to keep the comfortable silence. This cozy corner near the fireplace was a welcome change in temperature after waking up in the chilly bedchamber; the warmth threatened to lull him back to sleep. He listened to the gentle hush of Luciénne's fingers following the comb through her hair and closed his eyes, allowing himself to imagine those thick strands falling through his own hands. He remembered how Lucien had felt in his arms last night, how he'd fit against Cyrus as if the two of them were made for each other.

It made his heart ache. And he knew it was his own fault; he could say something right this second and then he wouldn't have to dream and yearn anymore. He could have Lucien, and then all of these ridiculous games could end.

Not here. Not like this.

Right. Not while there was a jealous Countess in their way.

"Lavinia is going to show us her research today." Luciénne's airy voice was still startling, even though Cyrus had heard it for most of last night. "She specializes in the impossible. Experimental, risky sciences. She started out as an alchemist, but when you live for multiple centuries you tend to stop caring what the mortal world thinks is taboo. If there's anyone on this side of the world who can complete what I started all those years ago, it's her." She sighed. "And I do hate that it's her."

Cyrus certainly did too. He opened his eyes and found that Luciénne had twisted and pinned her hair back in an intricate bun. "What should I expect today, then? More balls?"

"No, I'm Luciénne today. Try again."

Cyrus snorted. "But I didn't even get to show you how well I handle them."

Luciénne burst out laughing, and Cyrus couldn't suppress a grin. That real, genuine laugh struck him straight through the heart, and it was only because of that reaction that Cyrus didn't feel a shred of horror that he'd just said that.

"As it happens, there will be no more *dances* today." Luciénne chuckled. "Lavinia got away with evading us last night, but now that she knows why we're here, I won't let her brush us off again. I hope she knows, after what I asked of her last night, how serious this is."

Cyrus didn't want to think about what he'd seen in that room. He drew one knee up to his chest and wrapped his arms around his leg. "Does she...still think we're married?"

Luciénne gave a sheepish shrug. "I'm afraid it's too late to rewrite that story. Sorry."

"It's okay."

"Are you sure?"

"Please, Vista, there are worse things for me to be than your pretend husband."

A smile smoothed the worry off her face. "I suppose so. And *you* started it, by telling her your family name was Vista. Good thinking, by the way."

"I do have a *small* sense of self-preservation, you know," Cyrus teased. "I wasn't about to declare that I'm a Beldon in a room full of vampires that already wanted to tear me apart."

"Yes, I do wish for you to keep your head on your shoulders and your blood in your body." Luciénne rose gracefully from her chair.

Cyrus looked up at her and tilted his head to the side. "*All* of my blood?"

She smirked. "Well...give or take." She left him with a wink and went across the room toward the screen door. "I'm almost ready. Are you hungry? We can ring for breakfast."

"I don't particularly want to see Lavinia's risky experiments on a full stomach," Cyrus said.

"They're not *that* gruesome," Luciénne called from the washroom. "Usually."

Yeah, no, Cyrus was not about to risk that. He went back into the bedchamber and picked out another shirt that hadn't spent the night crumpled on the floor, then grabbed the same trousers and vest from yesterday and made himself presentable. His hair was a lost cause, though; each run of his fingers through the curls seemed to make them messier.

He frowned at his reflection in the mirror. His hair was a mess, and he hated that his only clothing options were black or white. He missed his colors; monochrome wasn't him.

Pursing his lips, he went back to the wardrobe and shifted through everything again, just in case he'd missed anything different. He moved a hanger holding a crisp black suit jacket and wouldn't have given it a second glance if he hadn't glimpsed a splash of color. He parted the jacket and found a dark red shirt beneath.

Well, it wasn't his usual green or blue, but it was something. He moved the jacket and then slid the shirt off the hanger, praying for luck that it would fit him.

It was...snug. If Cyrus had slightly narrower shoulders, it would have fit perfectly. But he did manage to get all the buttons to close, even if the ones over his chest strained a bit. He left the top one open, then went back to the mirror to deal with his hair.

Luciénne had beat him there; she leaned close to the glass, carefully drawing a black pencil across her eyelid. Her eyes flicked up and met Cyrus's gaze in the glass, then she blinked a few times, straightened, and turned around.

"Well." She didn't try to make her once-over subtle. "Hello."

Cyrus looked down at his shirt. "Is it too tight? Does it look like it doesn't fit? I just wanted some color..."

"No, it's..." Luciénne cleared her throat. "It suits you. It's just different. Though..." She stepped closer to him until scarcely a hand's breadth separated them; she smelled like roses again. Cyrus tensed up as she gently undid the second button on his shirt. "There. Put that one out of its misery."

Cyrus had to remind himself to breathe. The shirt split halfway down his chest now, lower than he'd ever worn in his life, but if it made Luciénne look at him like this, he welcomed it. Though it was still odd to have nothing around his neck, the looser clothes were freeing in a way Cyrus had never expected to enjoy.

He realized Luciénne was still gazing at him and he cleared his throat. "Are we ready, then?"

"Ah—Not quite. One moment." With noticeable effort she tore away from him and went back to the mirror, shaking out her hands briefly before resuming her eye-lining endeavor. Cyrus watched in mild fascination while she finished her left eye, then offered a smile when she turned around.

"That should do it." She tucked a stray strand of hair behind her ear, then slid a curious glance toward Cyrus. "Unless you want me to do your eyes?"

She was stalling. Cyrus knew that both of them knew that. He internally laughed at himself for the envy he'd felt toward Madame Rosaura yesterday when it was obvious now that Luciénne wanted to spend as little time as possible with her. And while Cyrus was anxious to get going, he wasn't about to hurry them toward that Countess.

"Sure." He shrugged. "Why not?"

Luciénne beamed, and it was worth every minute they lost with the Countess.

She beckoned him closer to her, into the window's light. Cyrus stood obediently where she instructed him and moved his head accordingly when she gently tilted his chin down. Warmth crept up the back of his neck and spread across his cheeks, surely betraying him with a rosy blush under her intense gaze. He finally broke the eye contact and looked away.

"Close your eyes," Luciénne instructed. He obeyed, trying to relax his eyelids rather than scrunching them, but he couldn't help an involuntary flinch when she brought the tip of the pencil to the corner of his eye. "It's weird, I know. Try to hold still. It's going to tickle."

It did worse than tickle. Cyrus found that holding his breath was the easiest way to endure the strange feeling of smooth yet thick pigment dragging across his eyelid. Luciénne stroked the tip of the pencil through his eyelashes, and despite every effort Cyrus couldn't stop his eye from fluttering. When she finally lifted the pencil, he blinked rapidly to keep in the tears that wanted to escape, lest they ruin her work.

"You okay?" Luciénne smirked.

"You do this for *fun*?" Cyrus had never wanted to rub his eyes so much as he did now.

"Beauty is pain, Beldon." Luciénne chuckled. "Unfortunately, I'm not done. Look up now."

Reluctantly, Cyrus did. Luciénne resumed her work, this time dragging the pencil along the lower edge of his eye, which was somehow worse than the top half. This time Cyrus could not stop his eye from watering; he was absolutely positive the ink was smudged all over his face.

It was only a small relief when Luciénne lifted the pencil off and declared she was finished. Cyrus had two eyes.

He winced and blinked his way through the ordeal a second time, and when it was finally over, Luciénne stepped back to inspect her work. Cyrus's eyes felt raw, as if she'd shaved off his eyelashes. He was still convinced his face was a disaster, but Luciénne gradually smiled, then stepped aside so he could get to the mirror.

"Have a look."

Cyrus hesitated. "I don't like that you didn't immediately say it looks good." He went to the mirror anyway, expecting the worst, and then found himself speechless.

It was a subtle difference, but astounding to him after a lifetime of seeing the same face, unaltered, every day. His eyes were *stunning*. Bright and intense in a way he'd never seen before. He had no idea that some thick lines along the edges could make his irises gleam like that.

"Whoa." He glanced back at Luciénne, who grinned.

"Yes." She raised her eyebrows. "Whoa. Do you like it?"

Cyrus nodded once, mutely.

"Good. You look stunning." She offered her hand. "Are you ready?"

He glanced over his reflection once more and gave a final effort to smooth down his hair. No luck. Though now he found he didn't care quite as much. He went to Luciénne and accepted her hand. "As I'll ever be."

She gave his hand a squeeze and then quickly kissed it. "Then let us see what we can learn."

COUNTESS ROSAURA'S laboratory occupied a massive cellar beneath the mansion that likely took up most of the building's footprint—twisty hallways included. Cyrus and Luciénne had met a comparatively mellow Countess in the mansion's foyer, and she had led them through a nondescript door that she unlocked with a key around her neck. They'd descended several flights of musty stairs before another set of doors revealed their destination. The air had grown steadily cooler as they'd descended, and now, in the cavernous laboratory, Cyrus could almost see his breath each time he exhaled. He wished he'd brought a jacket.

For a cellar, the space was no less elegant than the rest of the mansion. Lanterns and braziers kept the room brighter than the rest of the house, and heavy curtains on the walls kept out some of the dampness. Large rectangular tables occupied most of the open floor space, each endcapped by low wooden bookcases packed with bottles, papers, and other instruments Cyrus couldn't name. Tools and vials and strange metal apparatuses cluttered the tables, some suspended over open flames, others actively smoking or bubbling. A few people in black robes pored over the tables and milled about the room, anonymous behind tinted glasses and snug coverings over their noses and mouths. They did not acknowledge the Countess's presence, and she did not acknowledge theirs.

Rosaura led them to the largest table at the center of the room and hefted a giant book from a shelf beneath the tabletop. She cracked it open and flipped to a section near the end, then beckoned Luciénne and Cyrus to take a look. Cyrus let Luciénne go ahead of him, anticipating that he would understand far less of this than she would.

"You asked me yesterday if I had ever studied a way to reverse a turn," Rosaura began. "The truth is yes, I have, but not in enough depth and unfortunately lacking the success to offer anything concrete. I do not trust the world with the knowledge of turn reversal, Luciénne. Even if I did have a solid method, I'd sooner destroy it than share it."

Cyrus frowned. "So you have nothing for us?"

"I did not say that." She shot Cyrus a glare and he glared back. "You're here about Wild turns, and that's a different story. To reverse a Wild turn would not be to force a vampire back to humanity—a feat that I sincerely believe is impossible—rather, it would ensure the turn finishes successfully and results not in a Wild vampire, but a healthy one."

Luciénne nodded once.

"However, as you probably know from your own research, Luciénne, it is often easier to prevent something than to cure it, especially a transformation such as this." Rosaura tilted the book toward Luciénne. "Everything I know about the process of Wild turns is here. And this," she presented a smaller cloth-bound journal, "documents my experiments with various solutions that *could* block or at least delay the process. Mind you, all of this is purely theoretical, as I have not had an opportunity to test it on a living subject. Even if I had one, I would need repeated, consistent results before I would even entertain the idea of success. This is by no means a definitive answer for you, but it's something."

Luciénne nodded eagerly with an excited gleam in her eyes. "It's a start, for sure. Liv, *thank you*." She smiled up at the Countess, genuinely, for the first time since they'd been here.

Rosaura flickered a smile of her own. "I'll leave you to it, then. I've got other projects that need my attention, but I'll be around if you have any questions or wish to discuss ideas."

She left and headed to another corner of the room, where she took up a pair of tinted glasses like the ones her assistants wore and then turned her attention to the contents of the table before her. Cyrus pulled out a stool from beneath his and Luciénne's table and plopped down, leaning his elbows on the table's surface.

"Don't get too comfortable," Luciénne said. "Do you expect to just sit there and look pretty? Here." She slid the giant book toward him and then opened the Countess's journal. "Read up on Wild turns. I'll handle the science."

Cyrus eyed the yellowed pages doubtfully. "I can tell you already that all of this is going to fly straight over my head."

"You've got to give yourself more credit, Cyrus." She nodded at the book. "You're intelligent. Just because it's new and unfamiliar doesn't mean you can't learn it."

He frowned, doubtful.

"Besides," Luciénne went on, "Lavinia has always had a talent for effectively explaining complex topics in a very approachable way for those who don't have her level of understanding. I owe a lot of my own interest in the sciences to her, and it's only because of her knack for sharing knowledge in plain language that I understood enough to be interested at all."

Cyrus grumbled and brought the book closer. "Are you only saying that because she's right over there?"

"Huh?" Luciénne had already dove into the journal. "No? It's true."

"I'm just saying, your attitude toward her is quite different now than it was last night."

"She's not harassing me now," Luciénne said flatly. "I'm far more willing to acknowledge the good she's done for me when she's not undressing me with her eyes or trying to drag me back to her bed." She drummed her fingernails on the table. "But even still, I am very much looking forward to leaving."

"Yeah," Cyrus said softly, again thinking of what she'd pleaded to him yesterday. *Not here. Not like this.* "Me too." He hazarded a glance at her and found her eyes already on him. He smiled.

She returned it. "Then let's get reading. The sooner we have a conclusion, the sooner we can go home."

IT TURNED out that *soon* was a relative term for immortals. Cyrus and Luciénne pored over Rosaura's notes for the rest of the day and far into the night, and while Cyrus felt like his brain had shriveled to a husk inside his skull, Luciénne and the Countess had been spinning theories left and right for the past hour. He'd done his part, poking holes in their logic whenever something they proposed contradicted something he'd read about Wild vampires, but now he was too exhausted to contribute. He'd lost track of their discussion a while ago, and had no chance of catching up.

He slouched over the table with his chin in his hands and tried not to doze off while the two vampires went on about cells and blood and neurons and infections and what might stop the first stages of a Wild turn. Cyrus was only half listening, but something about the focus of their discussion didn't seem right to him. Sure, it was a biological process, but there was something *more* to it as well, wasn't there? Something...almost supernatural? Or perhaps alchemical—one thing transforming into another, human to vampire.

But what caused that transformation? What was different about a malicious bite versus a consensual one? How did the body *know*, so to speak, when to spark a Wild transformation rather than a normal one? It couldn't just be about intention; there had to be something about the vampire inflicting the turn that changed the process.

Cyrus rubbed his temples, wracking his brain for everything he knew about turns. He knew that vampires had to be a certain age before they could successfully create another vampire, so could that have something to do with how Wild turns happened? Were they the result of a young, unstable vampire attempting a turn? But no, Leigh Harrows had turned Arthur and she was neither young nor a turned vampire herself. So it was deeper than mere age.

An idea clicked into place. Cyrus slowly straightened. "It's their blood."

Luciénne and Rosaura's conversation tapered off. "What did you say?" Luciénne asked.

"It's not the intention," Cyrus said, thinking out loud. "It's in their blood. The spark, the—the seed that causes a Wild turn—it's in the vampire's blood." He tapped his fingers on the table, mind spinning. "You told me that a vampire has to be either full-blooded or at least, what, a century old before they can turn someone, right?"

Luciénne nodded.

"So what if a similar rule applies to *who* can inflict a Wild turn?" Cyrus was buzzing. This was an epiphany to him—why weren't they reacting? He stared at them and waved his hands. "The blood! The blood has to be *old*, and it has to be *pure*."

Luciénne frowned. "I'm not sure that I follow."

Was it not obvious? "I'm saying that it's not just any old vampire who can turn someone Wild. It's *exclusively* Honorable Ones. Something about your blood contains the—the *thing* that sparks a Wild turn, and the control you have over the person you've turned—maybe that plays into it also."

"Control?" the Countess snorted. "That's a hunter's myth if I've ever heard one."

"And Honorable vampires do not *only* sire Wild vampires," Luciénne said. "We have turned plenty of willing humans safely."

Cyrus chose not to dwell on that. "Right, I'm not saying that you can't turn someone the normal way. I'm saying that you're the only ones who *can* create a Wild vampire."

"I don't see how you drew this conclusion," Rosaura said.

"Arthur Beldon was turned by Leigh Harrows," Cyrus said. Luciénne shot him a warning glance, but he ignored her. "I know," he said when Rosaura raised her eyebrows, "it seems absurd, but word got out in certain circles in the city and I promise it's true. And then Leigh—"

"Hold on, hold on," Rosaura interrupted. "Are you about to tell me that Leigh Harrows was turned by another Honorable One? Do we have *any* evidence of that?"

"No, but who else could it be?" Cyrus argued. "It would've had to be someone close to her. Maybe even another Harrows."

"This is all speculation, Cyrus." Luciénne rubbed her forehead. "Why would House Harrows turn their own heir?" Something dawned across her face, then, though Cyrus couldn't translate it. "Oh, no."

Cyrus couldn't find the conclusion she'd drawn. "What?"

Luciénne fiddled with the corner of the journal in front of her. "Damn it. I can't believe..." She sighed and glanced up at Cyrus. "There's something I haven't told you."

A cold tendril of dread licked down his spine. "What is it?"

"Before...all this," she waved a hand, "I was working with Leigh and Philip Harrows on a series of experiments very similar to our research here. With lower stakes, of course, as this was long before Arthur Beldon was turned. He was not the first recent Wild turn, but he *was* the first high-profile victim that threw this entire thing into the spotlight.

"About a year ago, a friend from House Attcourt informed me of Wild vampire attacks in some villages in their eastern territory. I looked into it, and Leigh Harrows, who had recently visited the Attcourts, offered to help. She brought her brother into it, claiming that he had a mind for science as well, and together we dug up everything we could find about Wild vampires and their biology. No one in any of the Families had seen a Wild vampire in two centuries, and Leigh, Philip, and I took it upon ourselves to find out where these recent ones had come from, who had turned them, and if there was a way to cure one. But eventually we got stuck, because there was one thing we lacked."

Cyrus's dread turned to horror. "A living subject."

Luciénne nodded gravely. "And I'll give you one guess as to

what happened almost immediately after we all realized we could not go any farther without a live specimen to study."

Cyrus stared blankly at the table as the implication of her words sank in. Leigh Harrows might have delivered the killing strike, but if not for Lucien, Arthur would still be alive.

"Cyrus." Luciénne drew his attention back up to her. She held his gaze intently. "I had *no idea* they would go to such a measure, especially not someone as high profile as the Beldon heir. I need you to believe that."

Cyrus didn't know what to think, and certainly not what to feel. He wasn't angry, but he still felt as though the earth had tipped beneath his feet. He had no love for Arthur and did not miss him, but to know that Lucien, whom he'd grown to fully trust and love, had been indirectly involved in his death, was a strange dissonance.

He met Luciénne's eyes again and read the plea there. *Please forgive me. I did not kill your brother.*

Cyrus nodded once, acknowledging Luciénne's wordless apology, and then changed the subject before the Countess could glean anything she didn't need to know. "Okay, but this still doesn't explain why House Harrows would turn their own heir."

"We don't know that they did," Rosaura said. "As Luciénne said, this is all speculation. Yes, we now have a motive for the Beldon kid's murder, but not for Leigh's. Your theory about Honorable blood is weak. We don't have nearly enough evidence to make that assertion, and even if we did, it does not get us any closer to a way to prevent Wild turns."

"It could," Cyrus argued. "If we knew what components set Honorable blood apart from an average vampire, that could help us isolate what exactly causes a Wild turn."

Rosaura pinched the bridge of her nose. "Do you have any idea how much experimentation that would take? We'd need *dozens* of willing subjects, including some who would need to consent to the risk of being turned Wild *without* a way to save them. It's unethical."

Luciénne snorted. "As if that has ever stopped you."

"Would you like to volunteer?" she snapped.

Luciénne scowled. "Cyrus, your idea is solid in theory, but I do agree that it would take ages to prove it, and we don't have that much time. We have no idea if this issue has spiraled further back home, and I would like to return with some idea of how to help."

Rosaura scoffed. "Science takes time, darling. If you came here expecting a quick answer, I've got unfortunate news for you."

No, Cyrus refused to walk out of here empty-handed. He took a different angle. "What do you normally do when you turn a human into a vampire?"

He received two matching *stupid question* looks in response. The Countess was the first to reply, "Uh, bite them."

Cyrus rolled his eyes. "Obviously. But after that. After you drain their blood and they drink yours, what happens *next*? What is the crucial next step that, presumably, is missing when someone turns Wild?"

Luciénne blinked a few times. "Care," she said simply. "Turns are not meant to be acts of violence. A turn is a mutual, intimate agreement—a trade. The expectation is that when you turn someone, you will remain with them and care for them through the entire process until they are no longer vulnerable and can survive as a vampire on their own."

Cyrus had never in his life heard it described that way. Which wasn't surprising, given who had raised him, but it made him pause and think, yet again, of all the things his family and so many other humans got wrong about vampires. How many centuries of violence could have been avoided if they'd just listened to each other?

And then Rosaura rolled her eyes. "Yes, when you are of an *Honorable* Family, that's the expectation. Some of us don't feel the need to fawn over our sires before moving on to the next sip of blood."

Cyrus grimaced. Luciénne scowled, then glanced at him and

shook her head. "I assure you, Lavinia is in the minority with that attitude."

"Am I?"

Luciénne shot her a glare, then turned her attention again to Cyrus. "What's on your mind? Why did you ask about turning?"

"Interested?" Rosaura quipped.

Cyrus ignored her even as his heart gave a completely unwarranted flutter. A very slight tick of Luciénne's eyebrow betrayed that she'd noticed.

He pretended it hadn't happened. "Because if we don't have time to find the biological component, maybe it's worth considering that it has to do with how the victim is—or isn't—cared for after the turn."

Rosaura and Luciénne exchanged a look that said neither of them had thought of that. Luciénne pressed a finger to her lips and began to pace alongside the length of the table. "That's an excellent point, Cyrus. I won't write the potential for a biological element off the table, but the transformation is also not so brief that all of the critical changes happen instantaneously. It's a lengthy, painful process, and it takes time for the body to heal and adjust. There may very well be something that occurs after the turn, during the care period, that solidifies either a successful turn or a Wild one."

"Maybe the violence is part of it," Cyrus said. "Not so much the intention, but the act itself. I mean, you're not exactly being careful if you're basically tearing out someone's throat."

Luciénne nodded, continuing her pacing. "No, and—" She stopped abruptly. "It *is* the blood."

"Huh?"

She looked at him and beamed. "Cyrus, you're brilliant! It's the blood! Not— Not who it belongs to or what their genetic makeup is—although, that could still be an aspect—but it's the *volume*. A vampire committing a hasty, violent turn isn't going to stick around long enough to fully replenish that human's blood with their own. And without enough vampire blood to supplement what was lost, the transformation corrupts."

"That—" Cyrus let out a short laugh. "Wait, but that makes perfect sense. If the human doesn't get the vampire's blood in place of their own, then what would they even become?"

"A monster," Luciénne said, grinning. "Not quite vampire, and certainly not human."

"But is it plausible? Scientifically?" Cyrus looked to Rosaura.

She considered it, then shrugged. "It's the most solid theory we have. But how do we test it? Experimental turns?"

"If we had time, yes, that is what I would do, but Liv, I don't think we even need to." Luciénne had scarcely looked so excited since Cyrus had known her. It was charming. "If the proper amount of vampire blood is the missing component, then we just need to get a few vials to a Wild vampire, get the blood into its system, and see what happens. It may actually *reverse the turn.*"

She laughed, pressing her hands to her face. "Oh, spirits... *Finally.*" When she turned to Cyrus, there were tears in her eyes.

He couldn't name the emotion that swept over him then, but it took rather a lot of his restraint not to fling himself at her and kiss her again. He settled for a smile instead, but it faltered when Luciénne approached him with her hands outstretched. Hesitantly, unsure what to expect, he took them.

Luciénne squeezed his hands. "You're brilliant. I mean that. Leave it to you, you beautiful, *wonderful* human soul, to find the answer in care, in *love.*" She grinned, and the air seemed to thin. "Oh, Cyrus Beldon, I could kiss you."

A nervous laugh bubbled out of him, because, well, she *could,* and—

And then his thoughts screeched to a halt. He watched the same horror dawn on her face as both of them realized what she'd said.

Luciénne's lips mouthed, *Oh fuck,* just as Countess Rosaura barked a cold laugh.

"I *know* I did not just hear what I think I heard."

Cyrus kept his gaze fixed on Luciénne as his brain spun into panic. What could they do? Take it back? Run?

Rosaura approached them, each step like a nail in Cyrus's coffin. Her dark eyes narrowed to slits and her features locked into a hard mask of fury. Cyrus searched desperately for an excuse, but his mind drew up blank.

Luciénne stepped in front of him. "It's not what you think."

"It's cute that you think I'll believe that," Rosaura snarled. "I should gut both of you where you stand. What *the fuck* is a Beldon doing in my house, Luciénne Vista?"

"He's not a Beldon." To her credit, her voice didn't betray a hint of the horror Cyrus knew she felt. "For all intents and purposes, he is a Vista as much as I am."

Rosaura's glare could have melted an iceberg.

"I am not lying to you," Luciénne added. "He is not a threat to you."

"This puppy?" Rosaura barked a laugh. "Of course he's not a threat. But he *is* a problem. Get out of my house."

Shit.

Luciénne shook her head. "Lavinia—"

"*Don't* make me say it again." She bared her teeth. "You bring a Beldon into my house—into this *haven* that was once your home —you *lie* to me about who he is, and then you think I'm still going to let you get away with all of my hard work?"

"Liv, please, you can't—"

"*Get out!*" Rosaura made a lunge toward Luciénne, claw-like nails swiping, and Luciénne dodged without a breath to spare. She grabbed Cyrus's wrist and ran.

But not before Cyrus had grabbed the Countess's journal from the table.

Chapter TWENTY THREE

CYRUS AND LUCIÉNNE HAD HARDLY MADE IT TO THE TOP of the cellar stairs when heavy footsteps began to follow. Panic choked Cyrus; the Countess surely had every right to be angry that Luciénne had brought a Beldon into her house, but was *chasing them* necessary?

And what the hell did she plan to do if she caught them?

At the top of the stairs, Luciénne spun around and gripped Cyrus's arms. "Do you trust me?"

He blinked. "Yes?"

"Good. Hold on, this is going to be jarring." She wrapped her arm around his waist and pulled him a step forward, and then Cyrus felt a violent tug as if his spine had been wrenched forward through his body. When he next opened his eyes they were in a different part of the mansion.

Cyrus tried to say *What just happened?* but all that came out was an uneasy groan. The room spun around him as his body caught up with the sensation of moving impossibly quickly. He was pretty sure his head was on backwards.

"Please don't vomit." Luciénne briefly touched his cheek. "I'm sorry, I know. I have to do it again. We can't leave without our things, but we need to get out of here quickly."

Cyrus blinked hard and managed a nod.

"Ready?"

He wasn't, but Luciénne grabbed him around the waist again and with a single stride forward, yanked them across space.

This time Cyrus did throw up. His knees hit the floor and he retched until he was choking on air. He doubled over and pressed his forehead to the floor and waited to stop feeling like he was hanging upside-down.

A gentle hand rested on his back. "I'm sorry. It'll wear off in a minute. I'll pack our things. I was going to blink-shift us outside, but—"

"Do not," Cyrus groaned, "do that again."

Fabric rustled as Luciénne rose to her feet. "Then be ready to fight, because Lavinia will not make it easy for us to get out of here."

Cyrus groaned and slowly lifted his head off the floor, slouching back on his heels. At least the room had stopped spinning, even if his brain still felt scrambled. "Isn't that what she wants—for us to leave?"

Luciénne was staring at him. "What is that?"

"Huh?" He looked down and realized the journal had slipped out of its hiding spot beneath his shirt. He quickly snatched it and slid it down the back of his pants, tucking his shirt over it. "Um. Just something I thought would be good to have."

Luciénne's shock brightened to a wicked grin. "You sneaky little thing! But all the more reason for Lavinia to be angry." She offered a hand and pulled him to his feet. "I hope you didn't leave your sword with Demeter."

A bad feeling settled over Cyrus. "Am I going to need it?"

Luciénne grimaced.

Are we going to die here? he wondered. Or, more accurately, *Am I going to die here?*

"We'll be fine," Luciénne said. "We just—"

"*FIND THEM!*" The Countess's voice boomed through the halls. "I care not for Luciénne Vista, but the Beldon is *mine!* Do not let him leave alive!"

Cyrus stared at Luciénne in horror. "She's going to kill me."

Distantly, doors slammed and voices clamored. Cyrus and Luciénne both flinched, and Luciénne hurried her efforts to gather their things. When she found Cyrus's sword she tossed it to him in its scabbard, but paused before reaching for her own weapon.

"I can't fight like this," she muttered, mostly to herself. "My weight is different, my balance is altered...So I guess it's time for Lavinia to meet the heir to House Vista." She glanced up briefly at Cyrus, then pressed her hands to her temples and closed her eyes. Cyrus watched, fascinated, as her features gradually changed back to the masculine form he knew. Lucien's eye twitched and a shudder ran through him, but in seconds the shift was complete and he threw his head back with a sigh.

"That's better." He rolled his shoulders and then grabbed his bag and his sheathed sword. He met Cyrus at the door and passed him his bag, eyeing him oddly. "What?"

Cyrus hadn't realized he'd been staring, but he couldn't help it. He'd missed his vampire.

Gods damn me, he chastised himself, *when did I start thinking of him as* my *vampire?*

"Nothing," he muttered. More doors slammed, closer now. Cyrus gripped the hilt of his sword. "Do we really stand a chance?"

"You and me?" Gods, Cyrus had missed that voice. "Of course we do." Lucien smiled, and Cyrus wondered for an indulgent second if he was referring to *this* incoming fight, or the other one.

Lucien started to reach for the doorknob, but Cyrus impulsively reached out and touched his arm. He met Lucien's eyes when he turned back, and all at once the confidence fled out of him. He swallowed hard and blurted, "I missed you."

Lucien flickered a smile, but it didn't quite stick. "I never left."

But you did, Cyrus wanted to argue, though he didn't know how to articulate it. Luciénne was Lucien and Lucien was Luciénne, but they were also not the same. The way Luciénne spoke, the way she acted, and her entire personality were wholly different from the Lucien that Cyrus knew. There had been a shadow of him there, visible around the edges, but Lucien had said himself that his feminine counterpart was a role—a buried, former version of himself that he'd now altered and sculpted until hardly a trace of his true self remained.

This wasn't the time to say any of that, though, so Cyrus let it go. "Right," he murmured. "I suppose that's true."

"I'm glad to be back to myself, though," Lucien said softly. He gave Cyrus's hand a squeeze. "Are you ready?"

"No."

"Yeah. Me neither." Lucien unsheathed his sword with a shrill ring of metal. "But if she wants a fight, we'll bring her a fight." He flashed a smirk. "Let's show these feather-stuffed vampires what a Beldon and a Vista can do."

Cyrus did not share Lucien's confidence, but he did his best to pack his fear into a little box in his chest and, drawing his own weapon, followed Lucien into the hall.

At nearly the same moment, three vampires in fine evening wear came tearing around the corner at the end of the corridor. Cyrus adjusted his grip on his sword and braced himself as they drew closer. Adrenaline chased off his lingering anxiety, and all at once this became familiar. This was what he'd trained for. This was what he was born to do.

Lucien leapt into action first, before the others had so much as poised a strike. He flew at them, blade swinging, and Cyrus dashed in to back him up. He spun around the vampires, dodging swipes from deadly claws until he saw his opening and swung hard. With a shriek and a wet squelch, one vampire's head dropped from its body. Cyrus whipped around and plunged the sword through its chest for good measure.

Turning to the next opponent, Cyrus caught a glimpse of Lucien just as he decapitated the other remaining vampire. Shimmering silver blood splattered his furious features, but Cyrus didn't have time to see his next move; the last vampire attacked with a howl, fighting wildly now that its companions were dead. Cyrus pivoted to avoid a slash of claws, then took the thing's head off with a wide swing. He stabbed the body through the heart before it had fully hit the ground.

When the vampire had fallen still, Cyrus heaved a breath and looked up at Lucien. A hint of regret shadowed his eyes. He passed the back of his hand across his cheek, smearing the blood there, then pushed the loose strands of his hair behind his ears and looked ahead. Wordlessly, he nodded in that direction, and together they left the corridor behind.

They made it only two more turns before more vampires caught up. Five of them now, some armed with weapons, others with only bare claws.

Cyrus didn't give any of them a chance to attack first. He rushed in and stabbed one through the heart before it knew what'd hit it, and then yanked the blade free and whirled on the next one. It met his strike with a sword of its own, eerily fast to parry Cyrus's swings. He gritted his teeth and pushed back with all his strength, but the burly vampire hardly flinched. Bigger and supernaturally stronger than Cyrus, it had the upper hand and it knew it.

But being the runt of his family had its advantages, especially when people bigger than him made the mistake of underestimating him.

Cyrus dropped to a squat, sending the vampire keeling forward with its own momentum. Before it had a chance to catch its balance, Cyrus kicked out and swept its leg out from under it, then jumped to his feet and brought his sword down hard on the back of the vampire's neck. Cold blood soaked his face as its arteries split and spurted; the vampire's shriek cut off with a gurgle as its head and then its body hit the floor.

Three more to go. Cyrus turned to seek his next opponent, only to find Lucien cornered by all three remaining vampires. Lucien held them off with his sword at the ready, but he could only look at one at a time. The one to his left lunged forward, but it was a feint; when Lucien turned, the vampire on his other side lashed out with a swipe of claws.

Cyrus heard Lucien cry out, and did not hesitate. He ran at the vampire that had feinted, aiming for its throat before it could even turn its head. His blade met flesh, but then the vampire vanished. Cyrus stumbled under his momentum, and before he could locate the vampire again, another one pounced at him. Pain burned across his side as its claws snagged him, but he ignored it and slammed his elbow into the vampire's skull. It stumbled, and Cyrus swung, but at the last second he glimpsed crimson eyes and silver hair and he swerved his strike.

"Fuck," he gasped, "don't—"

But though the vampire that faced him wore Lucien's face, it was certainly not Lucien. Its eyes were cruel, its grin manic. It was a flimsy disguise, but it had done its job and made Cyrus hesitate.

The back of his neck tingled. He realized what was about to happen a breath before it did, and without a heartbeat to spare he spun and swung. Sharp, bloody claws missed him by an inch; the vampire dropped, headless, at Cyrus's feet. Its black eyes gaped up at him, and Cyrus found a horrid sort of satisfaction in its dead shock.

He whirled on the other vampire and stabbed it through the heart before it could make another move.

Cyrus's heart thundered, but for once not with fear. His body felt aflame, *alive*, and his mind buzzed not with panic, but with exhilaration. He might never get all this blood out of his clothes or the metallic taste out of his mouth, but for the first time in his life he felt strong and capable. Like the fighter he was raised to be.

Was this it, then? Was this the rush his siblings had always described, that he had never understood?

Why did he *like* it?

A choked cry jarred him out of his daze and he snapped back into the fight. Still one vampire left, and—

Lucien.

The remaining vampire had Lucien pinned to the floor, clawed hands wrapped around his throat. Lucien struggled but weakly, while the vampire on top of him snarled a grotesque grin. Cyrus bared his teeth and strode forward, but the vampire flicked a hand toward him and Cyrus flew backwards with a blast of cold air. He crashed into a table and collapsed in a heap, stars popping behind his eyes.

What the fuck?

"Aw, how sweet," the vampire sneered. "Your little Beldon stray thinks he can save you. And you believe that, don't you? I've always known you were an odd one, Vista." It scoffed and jerked Lucien's head to the side. "Look around you. See what he can do? See how he kills with glee? These were our kin, Vista. His kind have always been and will always be *this*. The stench of blood—our blood— painting the walls of our homes."

Lucien growled and thrashed his legs, but the vampire held fast, keeping him in place with its knee pressed hard into his torso. It tightened its hands around his throat and he choked.

Help him. Cyrus struggled to see straight. His head was throbbing. The cuts on his side burned. He couldn't find the strength to move, let alone get up.

But he couldn't quit. Lucien needed him. They had to get out of here.

He shook his head to clear some of the dizziness, and, a bit unsteadily, dragged himself off the floor. While the vampire continued its taunts, Cyrus retrieved his weapon and took up Lucien's fallen sword as well, then approached the vampire on silent steps and caught its neck between his crossed blades. It went still.

Cyrus angled the blades just enough to hurt. "Let. Him. Go."

The vampire chuckled. "Got yourself a loyal bitch, Vista, I'll give you that."

Lucien finally pried the vampire's hands off his throat and coughed. "Oh, but that's not even the best part," he rasped. A wicked smirk crawled across his face and he met Cyrus's eyes over the vampire's shoulder. Cyrus knew an incoming cue when he saw one. "You want to know why I really keep him?"

The vampire growled.

Lucien grinned. "He bites."

With a single fluid move, Cyrus swiped both swords across the vampire's throat and easily cut its head from its body. It dropped like a stone, head rolling a few feet away. Cyrus looked up to find that Lucien had blinked across the room.

Cyrus went to him. "Are you okay?" He reached up toward his neck, which was already starting to bruise.

"I'll be fine. I heal quickly." He started to smile, but then his eyes widened. "Cyrus, you're bleeding!"

"Huh?" He looked down and hissed through his teeth; his shirt was soaked with blood. It stuck wetly to his ribs where the vampire's claws had torn across his skin. "Ah...that's worse than I thought."

"We need to get out of here. You won't make it through another fight like this." Lucien drew him to his side, careful to avoid Cyrus's injury. "Are you okay if I blink us outside?"

Cyrus nodded reluctantly. "Just get it over with."

"Oh, I don't think so."

Cyrus spun around; Rosaura strode into the room, an elegant sword at the ready. Hatred burned behind her eyes, and Cyrus suddenly couldn't see how he was going to make it out of this alive.

Lucien stepped in front of him and leveled the Countess with a glare, adjusting his grip on his own sword. "Let us go, Lavinia, and I promise you'll never see us again."

"Let you *go*?" Rosaura scoffed. "After you've made a fool of me not once, but twice? *No*. No, Vista, I think you've taken enough from me."

She went for Cyrus first, blade singing through the air. He parried, but the pain that radiated down his side quickly buckled his strength. He ducked and twisted out of her way, and Lucien was there in an instant to catch the next strike.

"Damn it, Liv," Lucien growled. Metal clanged as their swords clashed. "One more chance: Let us *go*. You know who I am now, so you know that this little scuffle could have serious consequences. You wouldn't want to be found guilty of attempted murder of the heir to House Vista, would you?"

Rosaura cackled. "Oh, I'd love to see *that*!" She shoved Lucien away from her and rounded on Cyrus again, but he darted out of the way. "Yes, I'm sure the Honorable Families would be *enraged* that I rightfully chased a Beldon rat out of my house. I'm sure they'd be *so* understanding of your care for him."

With a growl, she lunged at Lucien again; Cyrus managed one hard slice across her back while she was distracted. She grunted and whirled around, eyes wild and hair flying. Lucien swung; she parried, then rushed at Cyrus.

He leapt, but not fast enough. A hot burst of pain seared across his already-injured side, and he hit the floor with a cry. Blood began to seep from the new wound.

Shit. Cyrus pressed a hand over his side, then gritted his teeth and pushed himself up to his knees. The room tilted, and for a second he couldn't tell Lucien from Rosaura as they moved in a blur of blades around each other. Cyrus blinked rapidly until the haze cleared, then held his breath and used his sword to help himself to his feet.

"Cyrus, go!" Lucien briefly glanced his way as he spun around Rosaura. "I'll catch up, just—" He grunted as Rosaura elbowed him and then raised her sword.

"*No!*" Cyrus shoved his pain to the recesses of his mind and flew at the Countess with renewed fury. *You will not hurt him again.*

Rosaura blocked his first strike, but Cyrus pivoted and swung again before she had a chance to raise her blade. He saw a flash of surprise in her eyes and felt a rush of satisfaction. Her next parry was sloppy, and Cyrus struck hard. His blade sliced across her torso, and she stumbled.

"Cyrus!" Lucien grabbed him, and with a lurch, they were outside.

Cyrus dropped his sword and gasped. All of the adrenaline rushed out of him and his knees gave out. Lucien caught him, but not without straining his wounds. The pain returned with a vengeance, and Cyrus's vision went white.

"You're okay. I've got you." Lucien stroked his hand through Cyrus's hair. "Just stay on your feet a moment longer, Cyrus, you're going to be okay."

He slowly detached himself from Lucien, wobbling on his feet. The air smelled like hay and shit, and for a hazy second Cyrus thought they were all the way back home in the Vista manor's stables. But no such luck; the overly elegant space proved they were still on the Countess's grounds.

"I need to get our horse," Lucien said. His hand remained steadily on Cyrus's hip. "Can I let go?"

Cyrus nodded. He tensed all of his muscles, positive that if he shifted his weight at all he would keel over. Lucien carefully drew away, then disappeared into the shadows. Cyrus heard rustling hay, clinking clasps, and the creak of rusty hinges. Lucien murmured softly to Demeter as he led her out of the stall, then secured her saddle and bridle and then returned to Cyrus.

"Are you going to be able to climb up there?" Lucien nodded at Demeter.

Cyrus very much doubted it. "I can try."

"I'll help." Lucien went to his side and guided him up, and though he nearly blacked out from the rip of pain down his side, he managed to get into the saddle. Lucien climbed up and settled in front of him, and Cyrus didn't waste a second before collapsing against his back.

"Hold onto me," Lucien said, taking up the reins. "You need medical attention. We're going fast."

Cyrus was too woozy to hesitate. He wrapped his arms around Lucien, and the moment he closed his eyes, everything else snapped out.

"CYRUS, WAKE UP. STAY WITH ME."

He opened his eyes with a jolt that sent a sting of pain through his body. Even taking a breath felt like a fresh stab into his ribs. He groaned and turned his face against the soft, cool surface beneath his cheek. A pleasant, rosy scent—tinged with something metallic —filled his nose.

"Lucien?" he mumbled.

"Yes, I'm here. Stay awake, Cyrus. We're almost...Oh, fuck."

"Huh?"

Abruptly they came to a stop; Cyrus winced as he was jostled against Lucien's back. Demeter snorted, prancing an anxious circle.

"Damn it," Lucien hissed. "We're farther than I thought. I... Okay. Okay." Lucien twisted around, forcing Cyrus to sit up straight. But engaging his abdominal muscles made everything hurt worse.

"Shit." Lucien jumped down from the saddle and reached up toward Cyrus. "I'm so sorry. This is going to hurt, but you have to get down. Put your hands on my arms and try not to strain yourself. I've got you." He grabbed Cyrus around his waist, then gave him a quick count of three before dragging him off the horse.

Pain tore across his side and burned into his chest and back. He cried out and crumpled in Lucien's arms, and Lucien carefully lowered both of them to the ground at the mossy side of the road. He laid Cyrus across his lap and combed his hair back with his fingers. "You're okay. I'm sorry. I know you're in pain. I'm going to try to fix that."

It was dark, and Cyrus's vision was hazy, but he could see the panic in Lucien's eyes. That didn't bode well.

"Bear with me." Lucien pressed the back of his hand to Cyrus's forehead. "Okay, good, you're not feverish, but I fear you've lost too much blood, and we're too far from any towns to bring you to a physician. I need to stop the bleeding." He met Cyrus's eyes. "I'm going to take off your shirt, okay?"

Cyrus tried to grin, but he was sure it looked more like a grimace. "Buy me dinner first."

"Not the time, Beldon." Lucien carefully undid the buttons

down the front of Cyrus's shirt and peeled off the bloodstained garment. Cyrus winced as it tore away from the dried blood around the ragged edges of his wounds; he felt fresh blood leak down his side.

Lucien hissed through his teeth. "That vampire gouged you deep, and Lavinia wasn't exactly forgiving. Nor does it help that you kept going."

"H-Had to," Cyrus muttered. "You needed help."

"I could've managed." Lucien stroked his hand through his hair again; Cyrus wished he'd never stop. "You fought brilliantly back there. But let's celebrate our victories once we're out of the woods, yeah?" He looked up toward Demeter and clicked his tongue. "C'mere, girl. Can you come just a little closer? That's it. Thank you."

Cyrus watched, in and out of awareness, as Lucien dug into one of their bags and drew out a canteen of water. He opened it with his teeth and then poured the cool liquid over Cyrus's ribs. Cyrus gasped.

"Sorry, sorry," Lucien murmured. When the canteen was empty, he tossed it aside and studied Cyrus.

"What?" Cyrus prompted.

"You can say no," he led with, which made Cyrus more nervous, "but there's two steps I can take to heal you right here. Otherwise, I can bind it just well enough to rush to the next town."

Cyrus frowned. "If you can heal me, do it. Why is that even a question?"

Lucien bit his lip. "Because it involves something that might make you uncomfortable."

"I'm uncomfortable now!" Cyrus snapped. "What do you have to do?"

"Do you know why the punctures from vampire bites heal so quickly?" Lucien tapped his fingertip against his lips.

Cyrus groaned. "I'm *dying*, and you're fucking quizzing me?"

"You're *not* dying." Lucien's eyes flashed. "Answer the question. Do you know?"

"*No,*" Cyrus said. He was in too much pain to think of anything, least of all his uncle's vampire physiology lessons.

"Our bites aren't supposed to permanently mark you," Lucien said. "There's a biological component of our saliva that can heal minor flesh wounds."

Cyrus stared at him for a second, then snorted. "You could've just said you have to spit on me."

"Yes, and you would've taken that *so* well." Lucien rolled his eyes, and to Cyrus's amusement he looked embarrassed. "That's step one. Step two is because this is more than a minor flesh wound. I don't know how deep that vampire's claws went, and I don't know if Lavinia hit anything vital. Without a physician's attention, the wounds might split open again."

Cyrus was already shaking his head. "You're not about to sew my skin closed in the middle of the woods, Vista."

"No, I am certainly not." Lucien glanced away. "You'll need to drink a bit of my blood."

He said it with the same solemnity that he would've used to inform Cyrus that he *was* dying, as if such a measure would change him forever. No, it wasn't a choice to make lightly, but it wasn't as though Lucien was turning him. Just a sip wouldn't change anything, right?

Besides...He was curious.

"Okay," he said. "I'll do it."

Lucien cringed, as if he hadn't wanted Cyrus to say that. "Are you sure?"

"What, do you want me to beg?" Cyrus flickered a smirk as Lucien's lips twitched. "I said yes, Lucien."

He still looked hesitant, but finally nodded. "Okay. Try to hold still."

Cyrus clenched his teeth as Lucien adjusted his position a little, turning him slightly toward his own body. He tucked his hair behind his ear, then exhaled slowly and lowered his face to Cyrus's side. At the last second, his eyes flicked up, seeking Cyrus's gaze.

He nodded once, and then closed his eyes when Lucien's

tongue touched his skin. His cool breath hitched and he held Cyrus a little tighter; Cyrus let his head fall against him and thought, longingly, of the last time Lucien had held him like this. Lucien's mouth moved across his skin just as reverently now, but with less hunger and more care. Cyrus felt his breath stutter each time he tasted his blood, and he could only assume it was driving Lucien mad to be allowed only a mere tease.

If only they weren't in the middle of the woods. Cyrus would indeed beg him to take everything he wanted.

Lucien moved to the next gouge in Cyrus's skin, slowly and carefully dragging his tongue across the wound. The pain numbed quickly, leaving only a faint tickle where moments ago there had been sharp agony. As his pain fled, Cyrus relaxed, and by the time Lucien was done, his head was spinning for an entirely different reason.

"Are you okay?" Lucien rose and stroked his fingers across Cyrus's cheek. His eyes were heavy, his pupils blown wide. Cyrus yearned to know every desire masked behind that gaze.

He managed a nod. "M-Much better." And it was true; the deep, burning pain that had clawed across most of his torso had eased, and only a slight twinge of discomfort remained when he tried to take a deep breath.

"Good." Lucien licked his lips. "Are you still okay with...a sip?"

Cyrus nodded again. "More than okay."

"You may feel a bit feverish, after," Lucien said softly. "It will likely give you a headache that only food and then sleep can ease. After that, you shouldn't feel anything else. I won't give you anywhere near enough to affect anything deeply biological. Okay?"

Yet again, Cyrus nodded.

But Lucien shook his head. "Yes or no. I want you to say it."

A sharp, hot flutter unfurled deep in Cyrus's gut. It took him a second to find his voice. "Y-Yes. Okay."

Lucien held his gaze a moment longer, then finally conceded. "All right. When I tell you to stop, Cyrus, you must stop. I'll restrain you if I have to—"

"Promise?"

"I'm serious." Lucien glared at him. "You *cannot* have more than a sip." When Cyrus assured his understanding, Lucien raised his own wrist to his mouth and pierced his fangs into the vein, then offered the blood that surfaced to Cyrus. "Go on, then. Have a taste."

Cyrus gently took Lucien's arm, meeting his eyes briefly before touching his lips to his cool skin. His blood was quicksilver on Cyrus's tongue, sharp and bright and intoxicating. Cyrus closed his eyes and pressed his mouth fully to Lucien's arm, lapping every drop that spilled and then sucking when it wasn't enough. His body tingled with heat unlike anything he'd ever felt; it was sharper than intoxication, brighter than arousal, more addicting than the ecstasy stirred by any vice. If this was ambrosia, Cyrus couldn't *fathom* what his own blood was to Lucien.

Far too soon, Lucien started to pull his arm back. Cyrus moaned in protest and gripped his arm tighter, digging his teeth into Lucien's skin. Lucien gripped his shoulder with his free hand and, with force Cyrus didn't expect, wrenched him back. Cyrus let go, and Lucien licked the remaining blood off his wrist, closing the punctures. Then he looked down at Cyrus and sighed.

Cyrus felt simultaneously dead and alive. That ethereal energy still buzzed through him, though slightly calmer now, and he found it difficult to look at Lucien without imagining the various ways he wanted to devour him—and all the ways he wanted to be devoured *by* him. And, what, they were just supposed to get back on that horse and carry on? After all that?

"Are you okay?" Lucien murmured. "I know it can be...a lot."

Cyrus searched for the right words and came up empty. He gazed blankly at Lucien and his gentle eyes and his parted lips and that beautiful face and he *wanted*.

Not here. Not like this. The castle and the Countess were behind them. Why not here? Why not now? There was no one but the moon to judge them.

Cyrus's heart beat stronger as he made up his mind and raised a trembling hand to Lucien's cheek. Lucien blinked a few times, then traced his eyes down Cyrus's face until his gaze rested undeniably on his lips. Slowly, lest he break the spell, Cyrus began to close the space between them. His eyes slid shut just as their noses touched, but then Lucien abruptly jerked his head up.

Cyrus could've fucking screamed. "*What*—"

"*Shh.*" Lucien clapped a hand over his mouth. He went absolutely still, eyes darting around the trees. "We're not alone," he breathed.

A prickling sensation crawled up the back of Cyrus's neck. As silently as he could manage, he untangled himself from Lucien and rolled into a crouch. He couldn't see for shit, and his hearing wasn't nearly as keen as a vampire's, but his instincts were sharp enough to sense another presence. What was curious, though, was that Demeter didn't seem perturbed.

"Cyrus." Lucien's voice was barely audible. He slowly rose to his feet. "Get back to the horse."

Cyrus moved a few steps toward the road, but paused when Lucien didn't follow. "What do you see?"

Lucien didn't reply. He backed toward Cyrus and Demeter, but instead of climbing onto the saddle, he unsheathed his sword.

The scrape of metal on metal was a shriek in the otherwise silent night. Cued by the noise, the stillness shattered and five cloaked figures stepped into view.

"What do you want?" Cyrus barked. He inched closer to Demeter, seeking his sword by touch alone. When he at last felt the familiar shape, he snatched it and drew it on the strangers, whom he now saw carried weapons of their own. The moon, though behind a haze of clouds, cast just enough light to make the steel shine.

"Cyrus," Lucien whispered, "that's—"

"Well, isn't this just the most curious thing you've ever seen?"

Cyrus's heart seized along with the rest of him at the sound of the terribly familiar voice, and then one of the figures threw back the hood of their cloak and confirmed Cyrus's fear.

"Poppy?" he breathed. "What..."

One by one, the others revealed their faces. Cyrus recognized two men from the Sheridan family, and flanking Poppy were Joel and Emerson.

Cyrus exhaled a soundless, drawn-out, "*Fuck.*"

"Surprised to see us?" Poppy paced a step forward. "It was one hell of an ordeal to track you down, I'll give you that. But luckily for us, your *companion* isn't exactly low-profile." She lifted one of her shortswords in Lucien's direction. "Let him go, Vista, and we'll consider keeping you alive. Unless you'd rather join the rest of your family tree?"

Lucien bared his teeth, but Cyrus grabbed his arm before he could do anything he'd regret. "He won't be *letting me go*, Poppy, because I'm not his prisoner." He watched his sister carefully, begging her to understand. "I told you that I was going to find out why Arthur was killed. That has not changed."

Poppy scoffed. "You expect us to believe that when you're teamed up with his *murderer*?"

Cyrus recoiled. "What?"

"*What?*" Lucien echoed.

Emerson stepped forward, pacing a slow arc around Cyrus and Lucien. He brandished no weapon, but his gaze was just as sharp as one. "Ah, see, and if you had been paying attention, you would know this already. Why do you think your father challenged Alastair Vista?"

Lucien laughed dryly. "Challenged? You *massacred* my family, Beldon, with absolutely no justification to do so."

"Leigh and Philip Harrows killed Arthur," Cyrus said. "House Vista had nothing to do with it."

"Didn't they?" Emerson raised his eyebrows. "Then am I to believe that the pages upon pages of research and experiments taken from the Vista family's dwelling were the work of someone else? Leigh Harrows may have spilled Arthur's blood, but if not for the theories spun by *this* monster, the Harrows girl would have left us alone. It was because of *his* idea, under *his* leadership, that she attacked your brother." Emerson came to a stop directly in front of Lucien and leveled him with a glare. "And you still didn't get what you needed, did you, Vista?"

Cyrus's heart pounded sickeningly hard. "No," he croaked. "It's not true! He didn't—"

"I saw *all of it*, boy!" Emerson growled, whirling on Cyrus. Torchlight reflected in his furious eyes. "You would dare defend him, after everything he started?"

"He's lying," Lucien said calmly. He spoke to Cyrus while continuing to glare at Emerson. "Neither my family nor I had anything to do with Arthur Beldon's death. Yes, I researched Wild turns. Yes, I needed a live subject before I could move forward. But I never told *anyone* to go after your brother." He flicked a glance at Cyrus. "You know that."

"He's manipulating you, Cyrus, can't you see that?" Poppy shouted. She closed in on Lucien's left, while one of the Sheridan hunters circled around to his other side. Cyrus took a step toward him, only to find himself staring down the barrel of Emerson's pistol.

Cyrus froze.

"Joel," Emerson said.

Cyrus turned, but not fast enough. Joel effortlessly disarmed him, twisted his arm behind his back, and had a blade across his throat in a matter of seconds. Lucien moved to help, but halted when Emerson turned the pistol on him.

"Stop!" Cyrus cried. "Just *listen* to me. Let him go, and let us explain. We're trying to—"

"That's enough." Joel angled the blade against Cyrus's throat, just enough to pinch. They weren't sparring now, but would Joel actually hurt him if Emerson commanded it?

"What do you want?" Cyrus pleaded to his uncle. "Why are you here?"

"To bring you back where you belong." Emerson did not lower the pistol from its aim at Lucien's chest. Undoubtedly it was loaded with a silver bullet, instantly fatal if it shot Lucien through the heart. And if Emerson pulled that trigger, it would. He never missed.

"If your abandonment of your family has rewarded you *any* information regarding this conspiracy, it belongs to us and us alone," Emerson said. His gaze flicked over Cyrus's shoulder. "Joel. Do it."

The blood drained from Cyrus's face. "No!"

"*Don't—*" Lucien lunged toward him, but Poppy flung something at him and he flinched back with a cry.

Then something cold pierced Cyrus's neck, and then there was nothing.

PART THREE

Some have seen sorrow, but there are fair days yet in store.

— BRAM STOKER, *DRACULA*

Chapter TWENTY FOUR

"LUCIEN..." CYRUS SURFACED FROM FOGGY BLACKNESS with the vampire's name on his lips. "Lucien...?" It took his eyes a moment to focus when he opened them; the ground beneath him was hard and cold, the air damp, and for a hazy second he thought he was in the tower. But he saw neither the spiral stairs nor the cobwebbed room, only an empty expanse of dark.

He blinked repeatedly, but it was no use. The darkness was absolute. He couldn't hear anything, either; the stale air clued him that he wasn't outside, but where, then, was he?

And where was Lucien?

Cyrus pushed himself off the cold floor and sat up, every muscle in his body protesting. He found a rough stone wall to his right and used it to steady himself while he attempted to get to his feet, only to realize that his ankles were bound together with about six inches of slack between them. Enough to move, to shuffle around, but certainly not to run.

A prickling sense of unease crept up his spine.

Cyrus searched his memory. He remembered escaping the castle. He remembered Lucien tending to his injury. And he remembered...Poppy? Joel? Emerson? But no, why would they have been there? That must have been a nightmare. Cyrus and Lucien were miles outside the city, and had told no one where they were going. Emerson couldn't have found them.

"Lucien?" Cyrus called again. His voice scraped in his throat, as if he'd been screaming. He tried again, louder, but there was still no response. The dark, silent space swallowed his voice. He leaned on the wall and tried to push himself to his feet, but his legs refused to stay steady; he felt drained, hollowed out, and he wondered with horror if he had ended up back at Lavinia's castle.

Flashes of memory struck him: Joel disarming him, Poppy crowding Lucien with her swords drawn, Emerson aiming his pistol.

Cyrus heard an echo of Lucien's scream at the back of his mind, and swore it was accompanied by the shot.

"No..." Cyrus slumped against the wall and put his head in his hands. Suddenly he couldn't stop shaking. No, *no*, Emerson wouldn't have—Not without a reason, not an Honorable One.

But the Beldons had already proven that honor meant nothing to them—not when that honor was held by vampires. And Emerson *did* have a reason, didn't he? He blamed Lucien for Arthur's death. And why else would he have traveled all that way and spent all that time looking for Cyrus if he didn't intend to finish what he'd started?

And now Cyrus was here, alone, trapped in the dark, and Lucien...

What if it was worse? Emerson had boasted that he had all of Lucien's research notes—he'd raided the Vista manor just like Cyrus and Lucien had feared he would—which meant he could easily conduct his own experiments with Wild vampires, to whatever end he sought.

And this time he had what Lucien had not: a live subject.

Cyrus became more and more certain of it with every pounding heartbeat. Lucien would become a lab rat, caged and starved and weakened, tortured at the hand of a power-hungry alchemist chasing delusions of immortality. Emerson was going to turn Lucien into a monster and then kill him, and—

And Cyrus was powerless.

He didn't notice the tears in his eyes until they fell, didn't realize how hard his heart was pounding until the only breaths he could take were gasps. A sob forced itself out of him. Cyrus gulped in a breath, then another and another and then screamed until his voice gave out.

Somewhere across an echoing distance, a door clattered shut. Light footsteps rapidly descended twelve steps, then crunched dully across the floor until a tall figure appeared in the shadows. With a *tink* of metal, an oil lamp sputtered to life.

Emerson Beldon regarded Cyrus with exasperated boredom. "So you're awake. Took you long enough."

Cyrus didn't move from his spot against the wall. With effort, he swallowed the knot of sobs in his throat and kept his voice as steady as possible. "Where is Lucien Vista?"

Emerson tipped his head to the side. "I am so very interested to know why you care."

"Emerson." Cyrus dragged himself to his feet, relying heavily on the wall to keep himself up. "*Uncle.* Please. Tell me—"

Emerson slapped him, hard.

Cyrus stumbled back against the wall, blinking the sting out of his eyes. He took a deep breath and glared up at his uncle. "It's going to be like that, huh?"

"I've had enough of your disrespect," Emerson growled. "I am the master of this house and this family, and you will address me as such. I did not come here to listen to you snivel and beg. I am here for answers, and trust me, it is in your best interest to give them to me. *If* I am satisfied with what you tell me, I will tell you what became of Vista."

Cyrus took a shaky breath. "Fine."

"Where did you go?"

"North." When Emerson narrowed his eyes, Cyrus hastily added, "I don't know the name of the town. We were in the middle of nowhere, north of the lakes. Not far from where you found us."

To Cyrus's relief, Emerson seemed satisfied enough with that. "Why there?"

"To meet someone Luc—Er, someone Vista knew."

Emerson did not like that answer. Another slap across the face made stars pop behind Cyrus's eyes. "Do you think you're going to win with vague answers? It serves no one, least of all yourself, and lesser still your *precious vampire*, to lie to me. Tell me who you met."

Cyrus matched his uncle's furious glare and counted his breaths until he was confident he could speak without his voice cracking. "A vampire named Lavinia Rosaura."

Emerson scowled, dashing Cyrus's hope that he wouldn't recognize the name. "Countess Rosaura. Of course. An eternal thorn in my side. What could she have possibly offered that you needed?"

"Knowledge of Wild vampires." Cyrus inched along the wall in an effort to put a little more space between himself and Emerson. "I was not lying when I said that I was looking into Arthur's death. My goal—and Vista's goal—was to learn how Wild vampires are created so that we could prevent it from happening to anyone else. This all started *because* of what happened to Arthur. Tell me how that is disgraceful to this family! I was about to do something *good* for us and our legacy, rather than—"

Emerson swung again and Cyrus managed to duck, but then Emerson backhanded him and threw him off balance. He seized him by his collar and hauled him clear off the ground, slamming him back against the wall.

Every muscle in Cyrus's body froze.

"If you truly had this family's best interests in mind, you wouldn't have kept secrets." Emerson shook him; rough stone scraped up his back, clawing through his shirt. "You wouldn't have run off alone, you wouldn't have allied with an enemy family, and *you most certainly would not have let a vampire drink your blood* like a common fucking whore!"

He shoved Cyrus against the wall again as he released him, and Cyrus collapsed. He scrambled away from Emerson, hand involuntarily flying to his neck. "W-What are you talking about?"

Emerson advanced on him and delivered a hard kick to Cyrus's ribs. Cyrus recoiled, groaning, and dragged himself away until he hit another wall and couldn't go any farther. His eyes watered as he lifted his head. "I did...no such thing."

"Do you think me a fool? We all saw the mark on your neck," Emerson growled. "It's too clean to have been done against your will. You haven't been turned, either, so there is but one thing left to assume. And really, Cyrus, I never thought even *you* would sink that low."

Pain throbbed through Cyrus's body, worsening with each breath. He didn't know what else to say to placate Emerson; he had nothing more that Emerson didn't already know, and now it seemed that Emerson was less interested in information than he was in punishing Cyrus for breaking every law this family had ever laid down.

Cyrus couldn't bring himself to be remorseful. He didn't even feel guilty anymore. Why had he ever craved this man's approval?

"I didn't have a choice," he offered in his own defense.

"There is *always* a choice," Emerson snapped. "If it is *you* or *them*, we choose *us*. If the consequence is letting them die, so be it. One less monster makes us all safer."

Cyrus shook his head. "They're not what we think they are, Emerson. They—"

Emerson struck him again, this time with a closed fist. His signet ring caught Cyrus across the cheek and scraped off a strip of skin. Cyrus's head snapped to the side, and before he had a chance to recover, Emerson grabbed him by the shirt again and then flung him against the wall. Another hard kick to his side sent a fresh burst of pain across his torso.

"Have you learned nothing?" Emerson shouted. Even his voice hurt Cyrus's throbbing head. "They *lie*. They manipulate you and twist you and mislead you. Please, do you really think that monster cares about you? You're *nothing* to him, boy! You're *prey*. I'm surprised he kept you alive as long as he did."

Cyrus's ribs felt like they were cracking with every heaved breath. He felt cold dirt under his palms where they pressed flat to the ground, but he otherwise had no bearings.

"Get up," Emerson spat. "You're pathetic. Get up and face me, boy. A lifetime of training, and *this* is all you have to show for it? No wonder you let the vampires take what they want without a fight. You wouldn't last a minute against them."

Cyrus squeezed his eyes shut and struggled to scrape together the last of his strength. *I can,* he insisted. *I did.* He'd taken out three vampires in a row at the Countess's mansion. He'd killed a Wild vampire while barely able to see it. More than once, he'd bested Lucien in a spar that even Lucien was surprised to lose.

I am a Beldon. I can fight.

But against Emerson, with his feet tied, and barely able to stand? There was no point. This was not a battle he could ever hope to win. And if he'd learned anything from sparring with his ruthless brothers, it was that the best way to survive was to know when to run.

"Get *up.*" Emerson kicked him again, this time jolting his shoulder hard enough to dislocate it. Cyrus curled into himself, covering his head as another strike, and then another, pummeled his back and ribs. He tasted blood. He felt something crack. Emerson seemed to be everywhere at once. Every survival instinct within him screamed at him to get out of here, to put an end to the bright shocks of pain wracking his body, but Cyrus couldn't move. Emerson's shouts and taunts faded to the periphery of his mind, and, eventually, so did everything else.

CYRUS DID NOT DREAM of the tower, or the room at its summit. He did not dream of Lucien, or House Vista, or Wild vampires chasing him in the dark. Just when he thought he knew what to expect from his subconscious, it gave him something new.

He dreamed of a piano.

The shining black instrument sat alone on a white floor in a bright, golden room, but it was not the familiar space in Lucien's home. There were no detailed murals or marble pillars. Instead of walls there were windows on all sides, but the glass was fogged, obscuring whatever lay beyond. The sunlight was not deterred, however, and set the room aglow with such brilliance that it almost hurt Cyrus's eyes.

The room was empty but for the piano. Cyrus approached it and sat down on the velvet-cushioned bench, but hesitated to touch the keys. The ivory was pristine, unlike the worn and weathered keys on Lucien's piano. This one had been used rarely, if at all. Cyrus didn't wish to disturb its peace.

"Do you remember when you used to play?"

Cyrus turned his head. Leif sat beside him on the bench, cross-legged and dressed in all white. A gentle smile warmed their freckled face.

"What are you doing here?" Cyrus's voice remained soft; the room's tranquility remained undisturbed.

"What are *you* doing here?" Leif echoed. "I don't usually have visitors. How did we manage this?"

Now Cyrus was doubly confused. "What?"

"This is *my* dream space," Leif said, gesturing at the bright room. "How are you here? Where *are* you?"

"Am I dead?" Cyrus couldn't feel his own pulse, but he still felt a phantom of the rising panic he surely would've felt if he was awake. "Are you here to, er, guide me to the other side?"

"That would imply a number of things that I am not," Leif said. "Primarily, dead. Which neither of us is...I *think*. I come to this space when I need true rest. Perhaps that is also why you are here?"

"I don't remember where I was before," Cyrus said.

"That's normal. It'll all come back when you wake up." Leif lifted a shoulder, then inclined their head toward the piano. "You never answered my question. Do you remember when you used to play?"

Cyrus closed his eyes for a moment. He saw the brunette woman at the piano, but this time instead of a bleak room in a tower, she was in an elegant parlor with a giant fireplace. The smell of leather permeated the room; hundreds of books tucked into mahogany shelves occupied every available inch of wall. An ornate oak desk was angled by the windows in such a way that someone sitting there could see the gardens and trees that sprawled behind the estate.

The piano was small, nothing like the one in the bright room Cyrus occupied, and it was neither polished nor pristine but it was loved. The hands that expertly passed over the keys were soft and gentle, more so than any other hands in this house. They trembled from so many years of strain while dancing over these keys, but they were always there to guide and to comfort.

Tears dripped down Cyrus's cheeks. He opened his eyes and Leif came back into focus. "My mother taught me."

"You were pretty good, for being as young as you were." Leif smiled and turned their face toward the windows, basking like a cat in the stream of sunlight. "I remember when music used to fill this house. I was young, too, and I was terrified of just about everyone under this roof. I felt invisible, and it was a long time before anyone took me seriously. Not to mention that Master Beldon never hesitated to remind me that I was only there because he owed my mother a favor."

Their smile faded and they looked down at the keys. "Your mother's music was the only thing that could lull me to sleep for the first several months of my stay here. And your mother's kindness was the reason I didn't run away and find another way to take care of myself."

Cyrus's tears dripped off his chin and fell onto his lap. His memories of his mother were few and fading, but he didn't think he'd ever forget the sense of calm and comfort that she brought to this frigid house. He *had* to believe that it was not just the soft innocence of youth that gave him that feeling. It was *her*. She was the odd one out, too.

"I wish I remembered more of her," Cyrus murmured. "I guess I forget that others remember her too. No one ever talked about her after my father...Well, you know."

Everyone knew the story. It was the root of Marcus Beldon's indiscriminate vengeance against the vampires in Chestervale.

But Leif frowned. "What do you mean?"

"You're like ten years older than me, Leif, and you were there. How do you not know?"

"I know that your mother tragically and suddenly passed away when you were a child." Leif studied him carefully. "What do *you* know?"

"Marcus took her life," Cyrus said. It wasn't even a secret outside of the Beldon household. *Everyone* in high society, and probably some people beyond those circles, knew that Marcus had mercy-killed his own wife. "A vampire attacked her and turned her, and my father took it upon himself to relieve her of her suffering."

A new thought surfaced in Cyrus's mind. If his mother had been turned violently, why hadn't she turned Wild? Surely that would be part of the story if that had been the case. Unless Marcus had, for some reason, left that part out? Or...unless Natasha wasn't turned against her will.

Or, Cyrus hardly dared to think, *the story is a lie and she wasn't turned at all.*

Now he could feel his heartbeat. It pounded through his body, thundering in his head. His hands trembled in his lap. "Leif." He forced himself to meet their eyes. "What happened to my mother?"

Leif stared back at him with blank horror. "Cyrus, I think it's time for you to wake up."

And he did.

And holy *fuck*, everything hurt.

"—to fucking kill him," snarled a muffled voice somewhere

nearby. "Don't give me that look! You saw what he did to him! This is unacceptable, Leif! This is the last straw. We can't stay here."

That was Adriyen's voice.

Cyrus cracked open his eyes—or at least tried to. One of his eyes refused to open, and the skin around it felt tender. Moving his eyes sent a fresh ache through his head, but he managed to turn his head to the side, just enough that he could see where he was. He recognized the room in Leif's loft where he'd woken up after they'd forcibly put him to sleep all those weeks ago. Beyond the tapestry that sectioned off the room, soft light illuminated the lower level of the apartment; for the sake of his throbbing head, Cyrus was grateful for the shadows that remained around him.

"Look, I don't disagree with you." Leif's soft voice drifted up from below. "But where else would we go?"

"Literally anywhere else."

"And then who is going to care for them?" Leif retorted. When Adriyen didn't reply, they continued. "You and I have always cared for these children as people first and Beldons second. The new master of this house does not offer them the same courtesy. They are pawns to him, pieces on a board to be moved and sacrificed and abandoned when they do not serve him. Marcus at least acknowledged that they were his offspring, but they mean *nothing* to Emerson. Do you really think he'll bring in a new physician who will care for this family the same way you have?"

If Adriyen replied, it was too quiet for Cyrus to hear. Instead, footsteps crossed the wood floor and then creaked up the steps into the loft. The tapestry slid aside, and Adriyen appeared in the threshold.

She gasped. "Oh, gods, you're awake." She rushed to Cyrus and ever so gently set the back of her hand on his forehead, then nodded once and turned to a basin on the table next to the bed, from which she drew a sopping cloth. She wrung the water out of it, then set it on Cyrus's forehead, over his eyes. It was blessedly cold, at once soothing the aches beneath his skin.

He let out a soft groan.

"Shit, Cyrus."

He'd heard a lot of different tones from Adriyen, ranging from snappy business to sarcasm to fond softness. But he had never before heard her sound scared.

"I'm okay." His voice was a hoarse whisper.

"You are not."

"'M sure you've dealt with worse."

"That's not the point," Adriyen snapped, and then sighed. "Try not to talk so much. How is your pain?"

Cyrus didn't reply.

"Give me a number, Cyrus, one to ten. Ten? Twenty?"

"You just said not to—"

"Damn it, Cyrus!"

He winced. He'd never seen Adriyen this upset. Even when Poppy had been at death's door, Adriyen had kept her cool. But it was one thing to be injured on a job, by a monster. It was entirely another matter that the man responsible for Cyrus's current state had control over everyone in this house.

"Eight," he replied to Adriyen.

She swiftly left the room and went back downstairs. A few moments later she returned, then lifted the cloth off of Cyrus's eyes and dropped it back into the basin. She slid her hand behind his head and gently tipped it up, raising a cup to his lips. "Here. This will help. It's one of Leif's, but I promise it's not anything weird."

He carefully sipped the liquid, finding it horribly bitter. He scrunched his face, which irritated the swelling, but the reaction was involuntary. "Ugh." He struggled to swallow it.

"Yeah, it's not good, but it'll make you feel better." Adriyen waited for him to finish it, and then drew away. Her eyes darted across his face, studious and calculating, but Cyrus saw the exhaustion in her gaze too. "I'm sorry, Cyrus."

"For the gross medicine?" he rasped.

She shook her head. "How you continue to be sarcastic, given the circumstances, is beyond me."

"It's his defense mechanism when he feels too vulnerable," called Leif from downstairs.

"That hurt more than my face does," Cyrus muttered.

Adriyen cracked the slightest smile.

"Are you going to tell me how badly I'm hurt?" Cyrus tried to figure it out from her expression, but between his worsened vision and her uncanny talent for masking her emotions, he came up with nothing.

"Do you really want to know?" she asked.

He nodded. He wanted to know what Emerson had done to him, and then he wanted to know how long it would be before he was back on his feet. He didn't have time to be bedridden. Lucien could be in danger, or already dead. Cyrus couldn't just lie here and sleep his days away when he didn't know if Lucien was okay.

Stiffly, he crept his hand up his chest until he felt the key on its cord around his neck. He closed his hand around it and exhaled softly in relief.

"Your left shoulder was dislocated," Adriyen began, ticking off the list on her fingers. "Your ribs are severely bruised and possibly fractured, but I can't tell for sure. I am, however, positive that nothing is broken—for which you are extremely lucky. You had one slightly misaligned vertebra in your lower back—needed Leif's help to get that back in place, and I won't be surprised if it continues to bother you for the rest of your life—and then, of course, a litany of scrapes, bruises, and minor cuts. By the way, whoever tended to those otherwise nasty wounds on your side did an exceptional job. If I didn't know better, I'd think that was a years-old scar."

Cyrus's face warmed as he recalled just how Lucien had *tended* those wounds. He evaded the subject and considered his injuries. It was good that nothing was broken, but with fractured ribs and everything feeling as fragile as it did, he wasn't going anywhere anytime soon.

"There's another thing," Adriyen said quietly. She fiddled with her black apron. "Emerson drugged you, probably in order to bring you back here without a fight, and knowing how far you were from the city, he had to have kept you under for at least five days. You're likely to be in and out of consciousness for at least another day, and you might experience short but excruciating fevers."

She crossed her arms. "Leif and I narrowed down what he most likely gave you, but we're not *certain*, and therefore we're prepared for a variety of side effects you might experience. Be prepared to see a lot of us, because we will *not* be leaving you alone for the next few days."

So that explained the gap in Cyrus's memory. But it also sharpened his concern about Lucien. Yes, he was strong and he was clever and he'd survived well over a century of eluding hunters. But Emerson was here and presumably Joel and Poppy were too, and Cyrus knew his family. They would not have left any loose ends. If they were all alive, Lucien was likely not.

Cyrus hadn't forgotten—and was pretty sure he had not imagined—Lucien's scream right before Cyrus had lost consciousness.

He shoved the thought away and squeezed his eyes shut again. He couldn't think like that, but he also couldn't *help* but think like that. Maybe if he dreaded the worst, he'd get a miracle.

Adriyen gently touched his arm. "Leif and I are going to take care of you, and you're going to be okay. I will not let a single other person anywhere near you. You're safe."

Cyrus wanted to believe her, but while he might not be in the cellar, he was still a prisoner in this house. "Don't underestimate Emerson."

"I haven't." Adriyen's gaze didn't waver. "He won't touch you again. I made sure of it."

"How?" Cyrus narrowed his eyes.

"We made a deal." Adriyen shifted her weight to her left hip. "He approached me and ordered me to fix you so you could return to your duties. You might not be his favorite person right now, but even he has to admit that he needs you. I suspect that's why he didn't do more damage than he did; he needs you alive, for the sake of appearances, anyway."

Cyrus scowled. *Beldon first, person second.*

"I wasn't going to refuse to help you," Adriyen went on. "So I made him swear that he would leave you to recover in peace, and that he would not lay a hand on you again."

Cyrus didn't know how keen Emerson would be to uphold a promise like that, but the information brought him some relief. "Thank you, Adriyen."

"That's *Doctor* to you, kid." She smiled and started to turn away.

"Wait." He tried to sit up, but a single glare from Adriyen changed his mind. He adjusted the pillows behind him instead, and when Adriyen came over to help, he whispered, "Have you heard anything at all about Lucien Vista?"

Adriyen stilled for a heartbeat, then went back to fluffing the pillows as if he'd merely asked her if it was raining. "I have not. But Emerson did not return with an air of victory. He was angry. Interpret that as you will."

Cyrus could've cried with relief. "Thank you," he breathed.

Adriyen stepped back from the bed, but Cyrus swore her gaze found the mark on his neck before she met his eyes. "Be careful," she said, and then left him to his rest.

CYRUS WOKE some time later to the sound of aggravated voices. It took him a minute to place the sounds, but then he recognized Adriyen's snappy tone arguing with Poppy's demands.

"I just want to see him," Poppy was saying. "Last I knew, Emerson had knocked him out cold with something he cooked up in his alchemy lab. Is he okay? Is he *alive*?"

"He's alive," Adriyen allowed. "But he is in no state to have visitors."

Cyrus couldn't argue with that. Besides, his sister was second only to Emerson on his list of people he least wished to see.

Poppy had been quiet for a minute, and Cyrus wondered if she'd left. But then she spoke again, much softer. "Did Emerson hurt him?"

"With all due respect, Ms. Beldon, you'd be a fool to think otherwise."

Cyrus felt a swell of gratitude for Adriyen.

"I just..." Poppy sighed. "I thought he was different than Marcus. Less cruel, at least to us. But he's been strange lately, Doctor."

That piqued Cyrus's interest. He wished he could get up to move closer to the conversation, lest he miss something.

"How so?" Adriyen's tone softened, but by the sound of it, she had not let Poppy any further into the room.

"The best I can describe it is *unstable*. He's more irritable than normal, and he spends nearly every hour in his laboratory. I don't know what he's so obsessed with, but it's like he's slowly losing his sanity."

Cyrus had no idea what to make of that. What would have him so raptly occupied? Did it have to do with the Wild vampire situation and the notes he'd stolen from Lucien? Was he trying to replicate Viktor Stokes's experiment?

Anxiety chewed at Cyrus. He had no way of finding these answers without either speaking to Emerson directly or sneaking into his laboratory, and at the moment, both of those actions were death sentences.

"Odd," Adriyen murmured. "Indeed, he seems to be obsessed with something or other. Well, if he truly needs help, he knows where to go. Perhaps you could encourage him to see me."

Poppy snorted. "I think he'd rather perish from exhaustion at his workbench."

"Maybe so. What can you do?"

"I don't know. I'm just worried."

"Now you're entering Leif's territory." The door creaked as Adriyen, presumably, started to close it. "I'm sorry, Poppy. Next time Cyrus is awake, I'll ask him if he wants to see you. If not, well...I'm sure you understand."

If Poppy replied, her voice did not reach Cyrus's ears. Instead he heard her shuffled footsteps as they slowly withdrew, and then Adriyen shut the door with a punctuated *click*.

Chapter
TWENTY
FIVE

THE NEXT TIME CYRUS WOKE UP, HE WAS RELIEVED TO find that he felt slightly less like his bones might shatter at the slightest touch. The marrow-deep aches persisted, especially in his lower back as Adriyen had predicted, but the throbbing in his head had eased. And at least he could see out of both eyes now.

He found Leif watching over him from the opposite corner of the room, with a book balanced on their knee and a cup of tea in their hand. "Leif," he whispered.

They startled, spilling a bit of tea onto their book. They hissed and used the corner of their shirt to blot it, but judging by their scowl, the damage had been done. They grumbled and turned their attention to Cyrus. "Morning. How are you feeling?"

"Better," he rasped. "Can I ask a favor?"

"Probably."

"I need to write a letter."

Leif rolled their lips between their teeth. "Is that a good idea?"

"I need to know if he's okay." Cyrus swallowed. "Please."

Still, Leif hesitated. Cyrus almost thought they would refuse, but finally they nodded, unfolded themself from the chair, and headed for the doorway. "Just a moment."

Ten minutes later, Cyrus had pen and paper in hand, but struggled to find words. He balanced the pen on his fingers and studied the myriad of colors in the peacock feather while he overthought the greeting.

Dear Lucien was proper—well, *Honored Vista* was technically the *most* proper, but far too formal. But even a simple *Dear Lucien* seemed too *normal* for the circumstances. And just *Lucien* seemed lacking.

Cyrus deliberated over it for several more minutes, then decided it was a stupid thing to get stuck on and went ahead and wrote *Lucien* at the top of the page. He got as far as the comma after the name before he got stuck again.

This letter was a shot in the dark. Cyrus was slightly more confident now that Lucien *was* alive, but was he back home? Would he even find this letter if Cyrus managed to write it? Would he be able to write back without it getting intercepted?

Well, there was only one way to find out.

Lucien,

I don't know if you'll get this letter, but I don't know what else to do. I need to know if you're safe. And I suppose this is my way to tell you that I'm safe—as much as I can be, anyway, in a house where all but two people want me dead. Yet somehow I'm alive, and I'm okay. Our physician is caring for me, so please don't worry about me and please, Lucien, don't do anything stupid.

If you're there, if you're reading this, please write back. Address the letter to Leif Trysz and it will find its way to me.

Please be okay.
Cyrus

He read the letter five times before he was convinced it didn't sound too desperate, and then he decided he didn't care if he sounded desperate; he was. And if Lucien had any intuition at all, he already knew how much Cyrus cared about him.

Maybe someday they would have a conversation about that.

For now, Cyrus could stand to let a glimpse of his feelings bleed into this letter. Maybe it would even start that conversation.

Leif came back some time later with medicine, tea, and a few slices of bread for Cyrus. After they set down the tray on the end of his bed, Cyrus wordlessly held out the letter, safely sealed in a crisp envelope. Leif took one glance at the name and address on it, briefly met Cyrus's eyes, and then nodded once and slipped the envelope into their back pocket.

"Medicine first," they instructed. "Then food. I'm sorry the bread is plain; Adriyen insisted. Be mad at her for it."

They started to leave, but Cyrus called them back. They paused without turning around.

"Thank you," he said, with weight on both words.

Leif nodded, and then disappeared through the curtain.

Two days later, Cyrus woke from a dreamless sleep and found a cup of tea waiting for him on the bedside table. Beneath it was a small white envelope.

Cyrus nearly pulled a muscle in his haste to sit up. His still-healing body protested the swift movement, but he ignored the twinge in his back and snatched the envelope so quickly that the teacup dove off the table. He'd hear it from Leif over that, but he didn't care. He gripped the envelope with both hands and stared intently at the wax seal with its elegant letter *V* surrounded by a circle of thorns, and when he was sure he wasn't just imagining what he wanted to see, he broke the seal and unfolded the page.

His hands were trembling so hard that he could barely focus on the words. One glimpse of Lucien's sweeping handwriting sent his pulse racing, reeling with relief.

Lucien was alive. He was home.

Cyrus had to blink several times to clear his eyes enough to read the letter.

. . .

Cyrus,

My relief at receiving your letter is indescribable. I have scarcely slept since that night they took you, and all I could think about were the ways I could have acted differently in that moment. All the ways I could've helped, despite the threat. I have never felt so powerless, Cyrus, or so scared.

You warned me not to do anything you'd consider stupid, but it was only for your sake that I did not track Emerson Beldon's every move back to the city. I feared what he might do to you if I tried to intervene—especially if I failed. I know that makes me a coward. I hope you'll forgive me.

I'm home, and I'm fine. Your sister threw me a wicked surprise with a handful of powdered silver to the eyes, but thankfully much of it missed its mark. I consider myself lucky that Emerson was all bark and no bite with that pistol—now there's an injury we vampires rarely recover from. Don't tell the other hunter families.

I'm faring far better now that I know you're alive, but even as I sit here struggling to pull the right words from my mind, I wonder why I'm merely writing and not rushing to you at once. You said the family physician is caring for you—are you hurt? Are you truly safe there, Cyrus? I fear for you.

It kills me to wait, but if you truly wish for me to stir in my worries and pace these halls until you are able to come back to me, I will. Though...another letter would be a welcome remedy to this gutting solitude.

Forgive me if I sound desperate. I am. I don't think I'll rest until you're safe, and I won't be sure you're safe until you're with me.

Talk soon.

Fondly,
Lucien

Cyrus's heart was pounding. He couldn't believe he'd agonized over his letter sounding too emotional when Lucien had written *this*. If not for the lack of the word itself, this might as well have been a love letter.

The thought made Cyrus rather lightheaded.

He read the letter twice more. Just because.

He was so consumed by Lucien's words that he didn't notice Leif enter the room until they pointedly cleared their throat. Cyrus jumped and hastily folded the letter, but he knew the hot blush on his face had already given him away.

Leif offered a gentle smile. "Is he okay?"

"He's alive and unharmed," Cyrus said. Lucien hadn't sounded particularly *okay*.

"Good. I'm sure that's relieving for you."

Cyrus waited for the *but* to drop. He could tell there was a lecture incoming, or at least a word of caution, or a reminder that he was fucking insane for crossing this line with an Honorable One. Cyrus already knew all that, but if Leif was going to judge him, he'd rather they come out and say it.

"Go on," he prompted. "Tell me how stupid I am."

Leif frowned. "Huh?"

"I've wrapped you up in my nonsense. You're allowed to express your opinion about my poor taste in men."

Leif snorted. "Poor taste? Certainly not. Unfortunate circumstances, though? That's more like it." They leaned against the wall and studied him. "It's true, then? You're lovers?"

Cyrus looked away. The warmth in his cheeks sharpened. "It's...complicated."

He practically heard Leif roll their eyes. "For *that*, I'll tell you that you're stupid. But not for the mere unavoidable ordeal of falling in love. Even if it's inconvenient."

Cyrus rubbed his hands over his face, momentarily forgetting about the bruises until a throb of pain vividly reminded him. "What am I doing, Leif?"

"Is that a rhetorical question?"

"No. I want you to tell me if I'm digging my own grave."

"Can't say." Leif plopped cross-legged on the end of the bed.

"But do you remember what I told you, when all of this started, about approaching a precipice?"

Cyrus nodded.

"I saw two paths," Leif said. "At first, they were so closely intertwined that they almost looked like a single path. Then one began to pull away, farther and farther until they ran parallel, and then they reached a precipice. A cliff's edge. One veered away. The other took the plunge. It's a choice, Cyrus, and I think you've made it."

Cyrus swallowed and looked down at Lucien's letter. "I'm making a huge mistake, aren't I?"

"Do you trust your instincts so little?"

"No, but...What if I screw everything up?"

"Things that are broken can be fixed." Leif shrugged. "And if they can't be fixed, maybe they were meant to break."

Cyrus ran his thumb along the edge of Lucien's letter. Leif was right; this was not the time to second-guess anything, least of all his feelings. He and Lucien had reached a real breakthrough when everything had gone wrong, and there was still time to pick up where they'd left off—with their project, and with each other.

Cyrus was tired of being afraid of his feelings. When he saw Lucien again, he would tell him.

He looked up at Leif. "Can you bring me some more paper?"

Leif smiled. "Of course."

Chapter TWENTY SIX

RECOVERY WAS EASIER ONCE CYRUS HAD SOMETHING TO do other than sleep off the pain. When he wasn't reading or chatting with Leif and Adriyen, he wrote to Lucien, and Lucien promptly wrote back. Cyrus found himself eager to start each new day if only for the possibility of receiving a new letter.

Getting out of bed got easier every day, and after a week he could finally eat without it making him nauseous. When he had healed enough that he could venture down from the loft, Adriyen decided he needed fresh air and accompanied him outside to the gardens. She ushered him down one of the back stairwells and out a back door, never veering far from Leif's corner of the house. To Cyrus's relief, no one saw them.

Outside, Adriyen spread a blanket beside the leaf-strewn pond and invited Cyrus to sit. He did, a little stiffly, and she joined him.

The day was unseasonably warm for late autumn, the sky a bright cerulean framed by orange and gold trees that still hung onto stubborn bunches of leaves. Those that had fallen coated the rolling grounds of the Beldon estate and fluttered gently down at the slightest tickle of a breeze. Cyrus inhaled deeply and took in the crisp air and earthy scent, basking in the feeling of the sun on his face and knowing it was probably the last time he'd feel such warmth until next spring.

"Nice out here, isn't it?" Adriyen commented. She reached

down and plucked a red leaf from the pond. The carp that lived in its muddy depths popped up to the surface to investigate the disturbance, but quickly disappeared when they found nothing but ripples. Adriyen twirled the leaf by its stem between her fingers. "I've always loved this time of year."

Cyrus nodded, gazing around at the colorful leaves. "It's too short. It seems like the leaves turn all at once, and then fall, and then it snows immediately. And then it keeps snowing forever."

"Until it stops," Adriyen said. "And then spring comes back."

"Hm." Cyrus watched the leaves drift across the pond. "Some years it sure feels like winter will never end."

"It's easy to get stuck in the dark," Adriyen mused, still twirling her leaf. "We get so caught up in the dreariness and gloom of winter that we forget that the sun shines at all. It's all too tempting to embrace the negatives when the positives seem so fleeting."

Cyrus turned his head toward her. "You sound like Leif."

She scoffed. "I do not."

"You did just now. That was a very Leif thing to say." Cyrus grinned as Adriyen rolled her eyes. "They're rubbing off on you."

"Ugh. Don't tell them that. I'll never hear the end of it."

Cyrus chuckled and looked up at the sky. This respite with Adriyen and Leif had been nice, and he was extremely lucky to have their care, but anxiety needled him. "What do you think will happen, once you can't use my injuries as an excuse to keep me away from Emerson?"

"I hope you know I never intended to throw you back to him." Adriyen tossed the leaf back into the pond and dusted off her hands. "There'll be hell to pay when he learns that I lied to him, but I'll deal with the consequences. *You* need to get the hell out of here."

"And go where?" Cyrus folded his arms on top of his knees and rested his chin there. "If I leave, he'll find me again. Especially since there's only one place I'd go, and it's exactly where he'll know to look."

Adriyen set her hand on his shoulder. "I do have a plan. Sort of. A temporary solution, at least."

Cyrus met her eyes, but couldn't quite read her. She almost looked...mischievous? It was such an odd thing to see on her face when she was always all serious business. "What is it?"

"Don't sound so apprehensive." She smirked. "I think you'll like it."

Cyrus's hopes lifted. Did she mean what he thought she meant? But...how? He waited for her to go on, but she just continued smiling at him as if he was missing a joke. "Adriyen, come on. Are you going to tell me, or what?"

She turned to look over her shoulder, apparently searching for something—Cyrus couldn't tell what—and then put her fingers to her lips and whistled sharply. Plants rustled and gravel crunched; Cyrus tensed in anticipation.

And to his absolute shock, Lucien stepped into the garden.

Cyrus's jaw dropped. What was—*How* was he here?

A brilliant grin melted across Lucien's face. He held out his hands, and Cyrus snapped out of his shock.

He scrambled to his feet and flung himself at Lucien, clutching him madly as if he'd disappear otherwise. Lucien held him even tighter, and Cyrus cared not for his lingering aches.

"*Cyrus*," Lucien breathed. He buried his face against Cyrus's neck.

"*You're here*," Cyrus mumbled into his shoulder. "You're really here. How are you here? You stupid vampire, what the hell are you doing here?" He didn't know when he'd started crying, but now he couldn't stop. He finally tore himself away, just far enough to see Lucien's face—those soft eyes, that gentle smile. Cyrus had never loved the smell of roses as much as he did now.

Those letters had kept him going these past weeks, but they were a weak remedy compared to Lucien himself.

"It was Leif and Adriyen's idea." Lucien touched his cheek and Cyrus leaned into it. "They—and I—think you'll be safer with me than you are here."

"How?" Cyrus shook his head. "Emerson will—"

"No. He won't." Lucien drew Cyrus into another hug. "He won't touch you again. Even if he comes knocking, he won't get in. Not this time."

Cyrus wanted to believe him, but his fear refused to hear the logic. Still, he couldn't argue that it was better to not be under the same roof as his uncle. Anywhere was better than here, and he would rather be with Lucien than anywhere else.

He eased out of Lucien's embrace and sought Adriyen, who abruptly turned her head as if trying to appear like she hadn't been watching. She flicked her eyes his way and put on an exaggerated smile. Cyrus couldn't help smiling back. "This was your idea?"

"It was a team effort. Leif's idea, at first, but I penned the invitation." Adriyen got up and shook out the blanket, then folded it over her arm. "I thought they were crazy for suggesting it, but the more I thought about it, the more I realized that this"—she gestured at the two of them—"was exactly what you needed."

Cyrus swallowed thickly, then went to Adriyen and hugged her. She made a surprised noise, but then relented and gently hugged him back.

"*Thank you*," Cyrus murmured.

She patted his back. "Never shall you doubt my medical expertise again. Now let go." When he did, she grabbed his chin and looked into his eyes. "Listen to me. You're still healing. Do *not* do anything strenuous."

His face turned hot at the implication. He glanced toward Lucien, then back to Adriyen, who arched an eyebrow.

Cyrus couldn't make any promises.

Thankfully, he was saved from it by the hasty appearance of Leif. Adriyen released him and he started to approach them, but froze when he saw their troubled expression.

"You need to go," they said, breathlessly, shoving a stuffed bag into his hands. "*Now*. I grabbed some of your clothes and packed the necessities, as well as a couple of your books. I'm sorry it's all I had time to take."

Cyrus's stomach sank. "What's going on?"

Leif exchanged a glance with Adriyen, notably avoiding meeting eyes with Cyrus. "Emerson knows about the letters."

The blood drained from Cyrus's face. "What?"

"I'm sorry! I didn't expect one to arrive today." Leif dragged their nails across their shaved head. "He found it before I did. Here." They presented a stack of folded papers. "Take the others. The less evidence there is to find here, the better." When Cyrus took the letters, Leif pulled their sleeves over their hands and crossed their arms. "He still has the one from today. I don't know if he'll open it, but...he would've seen the seal."

"Fuck," Cyrus hissed. He looked back at Lucien, who came to his side and laid his hand on his back. "We should go, before anyone else sees you here. How are we getting there?"

"The quick way," Lucien said. "Are you ready?"

Cyrus groaned. "I guess." He looked again at Adriyen and Leif. Despite his urgency to get out of here, he wondered when, if at all, he would see them again. "Are you going to be okay?"

Adriyen went to Leif's side and wrapped an arm around them. "We'll be fine. Go."

Lucien drew Cyrus to his side. "Thank you both. My home is always open should you ever need refuge."

Adriyen and Leif both bowed their heads. "Thank you, Honored Vista," said Leif.

Lucien's arm tightened around Cyrus's waist, and with a now-familiar lurch, they were off.

It took three stops to reach the Vista manor, and by the time they arrived in Lucien's foyer, Cyrus felt like all of his organs had been rearranged and flipped upside-down. He slouched against Lucien, partially to keep himself upright, but mostly out of sheer relief that he was here, and Lucien was here, and for just this moment, they were safe.

"You're okay," Lucien murmured into Cyrus's hair. He pulled him closer. "I've got you, and you're safe here. I swear that to you. This house has intricate and strong defenses against attacks, human or otherwise. I was too lax with them before, too comfortable. But no one will get in this time."

Cyrus wished he believed it as much as he wanted to. Lucien's words were comforting, but Emerson was a wild card now. He would be furious enough to find that Cyrus had snuck away again, but the letter he'd found would only add fuel to the fire. Regardless of what exactly that letter said, Emerson would now know the true nature of Cyrus's connection to Lucien, and that put both of them in yet more danger.

Stupid. He'd gotten too careless with the letters. He should've written back just once and left it at that, but his heart had won over his brain yet again.

He closed his eyes and held Lucien tighter. The dizziness from their quick travel had worn off, but Cyrus didn't want to let go. Lucien didn't seem keen to, either. Cyrus didn't know how long they stood there, but when Lucien finally started to loosen his embrace, it was still too soon.

He tried to catch Lucien's gaze as he drew back, but the vampire's attention was elsewhere. Lost in thought, he took in the room as if seeing it for the first time.

"When we were traveling," he whispered, "I...perhaps presumptively...expected nothing other than returning here with you when our visit was done. I thought we'd pick up where we left off, and go from there." He looked down at Cyrus. "Returning here alone, unsure if you were alive, was almost worse than cleaning up my family's remains."

Cyrus took his hand and intertwined their fingers, only for Lucien to flinch back. Cyrus recoiled, remembering his ring too late.

That fucking ring. No matter how many times he took it off, it always found its way back onto his hand.

He twisted it off yet again and started to reach for his pocket, but then got a better idea. He strode to the doors, stepped outside, and threw the ring as hard as he could. He did not hear it land.

"It's such a silly thing," Lucien mused as he joined Cyrus in the entryway. Once Cyrus had stepped back inside, he heaved an iron lever to the right of the entrance. With a bone-grating groan, a heavy iron slab settled in place behind the outside doors. Lucien fiddled with his own family ring as he and Cyrus crossed the foyer. "To heap so much significance, so much symbolism, on a trinket made of metal and stone. When you live long enough, you stop seeing the point of such things. But live *too* long, and you find yourself clinging hopelessly to anything and everything that could possibly survive longer than you will." He looked up at the room again. "Immortality is a curse. Anyone who seeks it is a fool."

He headed toward the stairs, and Cyrus took his hand. "It seems lonely."

"It is. And I'm still very young, by vampire standards. I can't fathom how others make it three, four, five, or more centuries."

Cyrus couldn't fathom it, either. "Is it even possible for vampires to die of old age?"

"I don't know." Lucien glanced at him. "It's rare to find a vampire who has died of natural causes. We either starve to death without a steady supply of nourishment, or, more likely—"

"Yeah," Cyrus muttered. "Hunters."

"But," Lucien went on as they reached the top of the stairs and turned down a long corridor, "the stubborn part of me still hopes to see a time when there is no need for vampire hunters. The foolish part of me almost believes that we may have found the first step toward that possibility."

Three weeks ago, Cyrus might have shared that optimism. Now, not so much. "Yeah, until Lavinia chased us out and we lost everything."

"Not everything." Lucien smiled. "You took that journal, remember? I still have it, along with everything else from our travels. Including your horse, by the way."

Amid everything else that had happened, Cyrus had forgotten all about Demeter, but he was relieved to know that she was safe. And it warmed him that Lucien had taken care of her.

"We're not back to square one," Lucien continued as they turned down a familiar hallway toward his chambers. "Although... Emerson wasn't bluffing about finding my notes." He grimaced. "He wrecked part of my library on his way through, the bastard."

"*What?*" Cyrus was almost more offended at that than at his own injuries.

Lucien scowled. "I tidied and fixed what I could, but he thoroughly ransacked the place. There were definitely some books missing—including my notes. That's still a problem, but I think we can move forward regardless. Not yet, though." He opened the door to his rooms and let Cyrus go ahead. "Adriyen *ordered* me to make sure you continue to rest, and though I've mostly interacted with her on paper, I can tell she's not one to cross. Our work can wait. Do you want tea? Are you hungry? Oh, and it's cold in here, isn't it? I'll light a fire. Sorry, I forget..."

He darted to the fireplace without waiting for a reply, and while he busied himself with that, Cyrus lingered by the doors and relished the small miracle that he was here. This, more than anything else, felt like coming home. He hadn't realized how comfortable this house had become to him; it was a frightening thought, but he was fairly sure he'd be perfectly content as long as he never had to leave this place.

But slow that thought, because if that was to ever be a possibility, there was something Cyrus had to say first.

"Lucien." His heart was in his throat, but he'd never been more sure of anything.

Lucien turned, brushing off his hands, and came back across the room. "Yes?"

Cyrus took a deep breath. "Before you do all of that and insist on taking care of me, I— There's something I need to do."

"Hopefully not something that involves going back to the Beldon estate?"

"Gods, no," Cyrus said. He clenched and unclenched his hands. This tension was going to kill him. Less than five feet separated him and Lucien, yet the distance felt cavernous. Suddenly the simple act of closing that space felt impossible.

Lucien saved him the trouble and moved closer on his own, reaching out for Cyrus's hands. "Okay, good. Then what is it?"

Cyrus knew he wouldn't have a better chance than this. He'd waited long enough.

He ignored Lucien's offered hands as he stepped closer, slowly erasing the space between them. He held Lucien's gaze all the while, searching for a hint to tell him whether to continue or to back off. Lucien's eyes fluttered, then came to rest unmistakably on Cyrus's mouth.

Emboldened by the invitation, Cyrus slipped his hands to the back of Lucien's neck, and buried the last of his doubts when their lips met.

And the dizzying rush of relief he felt when Lucien kissed him back snapped his weakening restraint.

Oh, gods, finally, was his last coherent thought before he gave himself over. He clung desperately to Lucien and clutched him closer, *closer,* gripping his hair by the handful. Lucien locked him in a crushing embrace and kissed Cyrus with the same fervor with which he'd drunk his blood, as if he could drink the same bliss now from his lips.

Cyrus couldn't stifle a gasp when his tongue skimmed one of Lucien's fangs; shivers scattered through him, deepening his gasp to an audible moan. He kissed Lucien harder, craving more.

Too soon, Lucien broke away with a heavy breath, but only long enough to push Cyrus back against the doors. Cyrus winced at the jolt, but the pain didn't linger. Lucien pinned him there and took his face in his hands, and if Cyrus had any capacity to speak, he might've told Lucien he was beautiful.

His heart throbbed. He brought one hand to Lucien's cheek and kissed him again, softer this time. *I love him*, he thought faintly. Damned if he said it aloud, but it rang true with every beat of desire that pulsed through him.

"*Cyrus.*" Lucien tipped their foreheads together and nuzzled him. Cyrus stole another kiss while Lucien's hands carded through his hair. "*Cyrus, Cyrus, Cyrus...*"

Oh, he was certain he'd never tire of his name in that desperate murmur. Lucien repeated it like a wish, like a prayer, like a plea for it to be real. Cyrus snaked his arms around Lucien's neck and assured him that it was with every breathless press of his lips.

When he reluctantly paused to take a breath, Lucien wasted no time moving his kisses along Cyrus's jaw, and then he bowed his head to his neck, and Cyrus's breath hitched.

"*Please.*" His pulse sang; his blood ran fast and hot—couldn't Lucien sense it? Didn't it drive him mad?

Lucien hesitated. His breath stuttered, betraying his desire, and he let out a soft moan as he pushed Cyrus flush against the door.

Cyrus's eyes slid closed on their own. He rolled his head to the side, happily giving Lucien full access. Though he hoped Lucien was prepared to catch him when he inevitably lost the strength in his legs.

But it wasn't Lucien's teeth that met the sensitive skin beneath his ear; his mouth, gentle as ever, skimmed reverently down the very artery he had drunk from. Lucien gently pulled the collar of Cyrus's shirt away as he went, plucking each button open with deft fingers. Cyrus's pulse pounded beneath his skin, no doubt enticing, *begging* Lucien to break that fragile barrier. He could so swiftly, so easily, tear the very life out of Cyrus; with one snap of those fangs he could halt the pulse that teased him. Cyrus knew that Lucien would never hurt him, but still, each touch of his fangs with each bruising kiss spun a reminder through Cyrus that he was merely prey, and it only made the rush of pleasure sing louder.

Cyrus struggled to stay on his feet as Lucien continued his careful exploration of his neck. Each touch of his lips—each scrape of his teeth—was electric, yet as much as Cyrus loved it, he gently tipped Lucien's head up to stop him before he entirely lost his wits.

"Hm?" Lucien's eyes were dark with hunger. "Sorry, it...seemed like you enjoyed that."

"Oh, I do." Cyrus stroked his fingers through Lucien's hair. "But if you're going to unravel me, Vista, I want to be more comfortable."

Lucien hummed a soft chuckle. "As you wish, Beldon." He backed away from the doors, pulling Cyrus with him across the room. The bedchamber door had barely clicked shut before Lucien shrugged off his shirt and tossed it to the floor. He brought Cyrus into his arms again at once, but Cyrus paused, distracted by the necklace that Lucien wore.

Eight House Vista rings hung from a delicate gold chain around his neck. Cyrus reached up and touched them; Lucien laid his own hand over Cyrus's and then kissed him deeply.

Every press of his lips grew more insistent. "*Cyrus,*" he mumbled again and again. "I can't tell you how *long* I—"

"I've *wanted* you," Cyrus cut in, "so fucking badly..." He pulled Lucien toward the bed, and when his legs bumped the mattress he collapsed onto the edge of it, but Lucien stepped back.

"Hang on." He kissed Cyrus once more, then darted across the room. "Just a minute, I promise." He winked on his way out the door.

Cyrus groaned and flopped back on the bed, running his hands through his hair. A quiet laugh bubbled out of him; adrenaline, anticipation, and arousal rushed through him in a dizzying mix of giddiness. He needed Lucien in his arms again *now*. How was whatever he was doing more important than kissing Cyrus?

He pushed himself back up just as Lucien returned. In the room's dimness, he couldn't quite tell what Lucien had in his hand —until he raised it to his lips and took a long drink. He hummed softly as he swallowed, then approached the bed and placed the empty glass and another small bottle on the bedside table. Cyrus watched his every move until finally, he was awarded the attention he desired.

Lucien sank down beside him and pressed a kiss to his shoulder. He traced a knuckle up the center of Cyrus's chest and then plucked at a button on his shirt. "May I?"

"Please," Cyrus murmured.

Lucien scooted closer to him and gently took the edges of his shirt between his fingertips. Slowly, deliberately, he drew the garment apart and down, sliding his palms down Cyrus's arms. Cyrus shivered, never taking his eyes off Lucien's face. It might've been a trick of the light, but he swore there was something more vivid about his eyes, something redder around his lips.

Oh, Cyrus realized. *He drank blood.*

And it hadn't been *his* blood? Rude.

Lucien tossed Cyrus's shirt to the floor, then leaned in to kiss him again—but froze. Cyrus followed his gaze to the key that rested against his chest, which had not left his person since Lucien had given it to him all those weeks ago. It had become a comforting talisman, a tether to this place that had made him feel safe.

Lucien lightly touched the key, but then Cyrus realized what he was really looking at: the still-healing, hideously purple bruises that Emerson had left on his body.

Self-consciously, Cyrus leaned away and crossed his arms over his ribs. But Lucien took his hands, kissed them, and then kissed his neck, his collarbones, his chest. He made his way gently—so gently—down his center until Cyrus unwound. Lucien eased him down on the bed, cradling him with a soft reverence that made Cyrus melt. Cyrus closed his eyes and sank into the comfort, but then Lucien drew back a little. When Cyrus sought his gaze, he found hesitation there.

"What is it?" he murmured.

Lucien searched his eyes. "Are you sure?"

"Are you kidding?"

Lucien winced. "No. Sorry. It's just…" He exhaled shakily and tipped his face against Cyrus's neck. "I am...*unspeakably* desperate for you, Cyrus Beldon, and I...I need to know that you feel the same."

The words melted Cyrus to the core. "*Lucien,*" he sighed.

"Please." Lucien kissed his neck. "Please tell me you want me as badly as I want you."

"*Lucien.*" His name came out as a whine that time. Cyrus took his face in his hands and kissed him roughly. He didn't know how to say how much he wanted him; no words would come close enough, and he could barely articulate the vampire's name, let alone the depth of his desire.

"It's not just lust," Lucien mumbled between kisses. "It's so much more than that. I care deeply for you, Cyrus. I—"

Cyrus cut him off with another kiss. He wasn't ready to hear the words he feared Lucien would say next, because then he'd have to say them himself. So he poured everything into this kiss— everything implied, everything unspoken. Even if he couldn't say it —not yet—he wanted it to be known. He wanted Lucien to know every inch of his heart.

"You stupid vampire," Cyrus mumbled against his mouth. "Of course I want you." He kissed him again, tugging at his lip with his teeth. "*Please*, Lucien..."

"Oh, I do love the way you beg." Hesitation gone, Lucien kissed him ravenously as fumbling hands made quick work of their remaining clothes. Cyrus didn't have a single second to feel self-conscious before Lucien gathered him in his arms again and let both of them fall into the blankets' soft embrace.

Cyrus failed to stifle a gasp at the cool touch of Lucien's bare skin, and he must have noticeably shivered—Lucien mumbled an apology and shifted some of his weight off of him. "I'll get warmer soon. The blood helps."

Cyrus touched his fingertips to Lucien's lips. "You could've had *my* blood."

"But you're so much more to me than that." Lucien kissed his fingers, then turned his head and kissed his neck again. Cyrus shivered for a different reason this time. "I want *all* of you."

"Then have me." Cyrus swallowed another plea. From his perspective, whatever help that sip of blood offered had done its job. Cyrus was scarcely aware of anything beyond each point of contact between his body and Lucien's; even beneath his weight, wrapped in his arms, Cyrus wanted him closer. He wanted to drown.

If he was impatient before, he was desperate now. He kissed Lucien harder and bucked his hips, drawing a moan out of Lucien. Then Lucien pushed back, and Cyrus gasped, forgetting that he had his hands tangled in Lucien's hair until he pulled it, hard, and Lucien's voice cracked on a startled little noise.

Cyrus felt, quite obviously, how much he'd enjoyed that. He grinned against Lucien's mouth. "You like that, huh?"

"Guess I do." Lucien's reply came out as a breathy whine. He drew back, chuckling a little, and ran his hand through his hair when Cyrus let go. "Are you comfortable like this?" he asked softly.

Cyrus nodded.

"And you're sure you're not in any pain?" His eyes flicked to the bruises on Cyrus's ribs.

"Yes." He'd be sore tomorrow, without a doubt, but he did not care.

"Okay." Lucien smiled and leaned down to kiss him, then grabbed the bottle he'd placed on the table. As he poured the oil onto his hand, Cyrus settled back against the pillows and gazed at him. He let his eyes follow the contours of muscle down Lucien's torso, shamelessly lingering on every detail that enticed him: he wanted to tease those piercings under his thumbs; he longed to follow that coarse trail of hair with his lips. He craved Lucien's voice, his gasps, his soft noises as they mapped every inch of each other.

It struck Cyrus all over again that he loved this man. And what was everything Lucien had shown him, if not love?

Lucien climbed over him again, nudging his legs apart with his knee. He rolled his hips against him, and Cyrus gasped at the hard press of Lucien's cock against his own. Cyrus held him close and pushed back, desperate for friction. "Lucien," he breathed, "*touch me.*"

Lucien nibbled the side of his neck. "Say please."

Cyrus swallowed thickly, and even still his voice came out as a rasp. "*Please* touch me. And—"

"And?"

"Please—" he started, but his voice escaped him when Lucien fulfilled his wish for touch. With that, his thoughts silenced. In their place, warm pleasure bloomed.

Soon their duet of gasps and moans drowned Cyrus's racing mind, quieting everything but Lucien's name on his tongue. He lost every worry about his family and what they might do, every concern about the other Honorable Families, every fear of Wild vampires. The only vampire that mattered was *this* one, and as Lucien pushed Cyrus closer and closer to the edge, *worry* lost all traction.

"*Cyrus.*" Lucien's voice was a murmur at the back of his mind. Soft, melodic; it wrapped him in shivers and wound him tighter.

Cyrus gripped the sheets in his hands and threw his head back, arching his spine as Lucien thrust harder, faster. "*More*, Lucien, *more...*" He was so close; he just needed—

"*Lucien, bite me.*"

Lucien leaned down and roughly kissed his neck. "*Come for me, Cyrus,*" he breathed, and sank in his fangs.

Cyrus crashed, crying Lucien's name as Lucien rode out his own release. He quickly passed his tongue over the bite he'd left on Cyrus's neck, then collapsed on top of him, breathing hard. Cyrus held him close, grounding himself with lazy strokes of his fingers through Lucien's hair as they both came back down to earth.

Oh, how long had he yearned for this? How many daydreams, fantasies, and thinly-veiled desires had Cyrus tried to smother and hide? He didn't know when he'd stopped scolding himself for being drawn to Lucien and started hopelessly longing for him.

What had started as a superficial attraction had sunk deeper, rooting in Cyrus's heart and blossoming. Lucien was right; it was more than lust. They would've found themselves intertwined far sooner if all they were to each other was a quick release of endorphins.

Where they went from this, after tonight, didn't matter yet. Cyrus didn't care about the future when all he wanted—all he needed, for this soft moment—was here in his arms.

He had no intention of letting go anytime soon.

Chapter  TWENTY SEVEN

CYRUS DIDN'T DREAM OF THE TOWER THAT NIGHT. HE woke slowly from a deep, comfortable rest, and when he found Lucien beside him, a smile came involuntarily to his face. Last night, just before he'd fallen asleep, a very small part of him had feared that he'd wake up and regret everything, but now, all he felt was calm. Like something had finally settled into place. Cyrus's heart didn't hurt anymore.

Lucien slept on, peaceful in his slumber with his lips slightly parted. His silver hair was a hurricane around his head; Cyrus reached over and gently moved a stray strand off his cheek, smoothing it back with the rest of his thick tresses.

Cyrus found himself quite obsessed with Lucien's hair. He couldn't get enough of it, especially not after discovering that Lucien reacted beautifully when he pulled it a little. He longed to run his hands through it now, but he didn't wish to wake Lucien too soon.

Cyrus turned onto his back and smiled up at the canopy over the bed. He felt a little foolish, but he also hadn't felt so *light* in a long time. It wasn't even the glee of having his feelings reciprocated or the bliss of exceptionally good sex; rather, for the first time in longer than Cyrus could remember, he had something that he deeply wanted. He had been granted this victory—being here, alive, and happy with Lucien—and with the rest of his life exploding in his face, this slice of contentment was everything to him. It made the rest seem tolerable, if not solvable. It made him feel like he was good for something, even if he couldn't fix the mess he'd made with his family.

It reminded him that he *could* be happy. He could, every now and then, have what he wanted. He didn't have to hopelessly wish and yearn forever.

Lucien stirred and turned over onto his other side, pulling the blankets with him. Cyrus shifted closer to him—wincing as a twinge of pain shot up his back—and slipped his arm around him. He gently moved Lucien's heap of hair out of the way, then pressed a kiss to the back of his neck. Lucien's body was cool against his own, but Cyrus welcomed the slight chill beneath the blankets' warmth. He pressed more light kisses to Lucien's skin, drinking in the rosy scent of him.

Lucien inhaled deeply as he woke, murmuring a soft noise. His hand found Cyrus's and he intertwined their fingers. Cyrus pressed another kiss to the back of his neck. "Morning," he whispered.

Lucien made another low noise that sort of sounded like the word *morning*. He didn't stir for another minute, and Cyrus thought he'd fallen back to sleep, but then he mumbled again and turned over to face Cyrus, nestling close.

Cyrus ran his fingers through Lucien's hair, marveling that he was lucky enough to know this side of Lucien. Seeing him like this, sleepy and affectionate and completely at ease, was a treat that Cyrus had barely dared to dream of. His fantasies had all ended with them tangled in the sheets; even his subconscious hadn't ventured farther. This softness had seemed like too much to wish for, too much to hope for.

Yet here they were.

Lucien heaved a long sigh. "Don't want to move."

"Good," Cyrus murmured. "Neither do I."

"Are you hungry?" Lucien mumbled into the pillow.

Cyrus smiled to himself. Awake for a minute, and Lucien was already trying to take care of him. "Nah. Er...are *you*?"

Lucien opened one eye and shot him a sly look. "I know where you're going with this."

"Guilty." Cyrus grinned. "But really—"

"I know." Lucien propped his head up on his hand and studied Cyrus closely. "But I have stores. I don't need—"

"I know you don't," Cyrus said. "But you could."

He didn't want to push *too* hard, lest he rouse the grumpy side of Lucien and spoil their soft morning, but he also didn't understand Lucien's reluctance. What vampire repeatedly turned down multiple blatant offers for fresh blood from a willing donor?

"That doesn't mean I *should*," Lucien said softly. He reached up and gently touched Cyrus's neck, caressing one of many tender love bites. "I shouldn't have bitten you like that last night. Not while..." He glanced away as his face reddened. "I'm sorry."

"You most certainly do not have to apologize for that." Cyrus smirked, and Lucien's worry gradually smoothed from his face. Still, he wouldn't quite meet Cyrus's eyes. "What's your hesitation?"

Lucien shook his head. "It's...silly."

"Clearly it's not," Cyrus said gently.

"It's just..." Lucien sighed. "After that first time, each time you begged me to bite you, it made me feel like...that was all you wanted from me." He glanced up at Cyrus. "That's why I tried to bury my true feelings for you. I didn't think it went any deeper on your end."

"Lucien." Cyrus touched his cheek and leaned forward to kiss him. "No. No, it's so much more than that. I promise."

"I know that now," Lucien murmured. "So..."

Cyrus drew back, pulse jumping. "So?"

Lucien smirked knowingly. "If you're *sure*, then...breakfast in bed sounds lovely."

Cyrus grinned. "Absolutely. Um..."

"Turn over, with your back to me." Lucien scooted back a little to give him space. "Get comfortable."

Cyrus shot a smirk over his shoulder. "Yes, *sir*."

"That's *Honored Vista* to you, Mr. Beldon." Lucien settled behind Cyrus, drawing him close. Cyrus shivered at the cool press of Lucien's body as he nestled into the pillows. Anticipation tensed his muscles and quickened his pulse; he couldn't stifle a gasp when Lucien softly kissed his neck.

"Keep still. Try to relax," Lucien murmured. He placed one hand on Cyrus's hip. "And let me know if you want me to stop. Okay?"

Cyrus nodded and released a slow breath, loosening the tension in his shoulders. He closed his eyes and bit his lip, but still moaned when Lucien's fangs sank into his flesh. They pierced deep, a sharp ache far beneath his skin that pulsed with each racing heartbeat. His head swam with pleasure, and soon it wasn't pain that throbbed from the punctures, but a dizzying, dazzling sparkle of activated nerves. Lucien's steady, insistent sucking on the wounds only intensified the feeling, and Cyrus couldn't hold back another groan.

Too soon, Lucien slowly drew back, leaving a wet kiss on the mark he'd left as he withdrew his fangs. He sighed deeply and nuzzled the back of Cyrus's neck. "You're delicious. Thank you. Are you okay?"

"Mhm." Cyrus slouched against Lucien and closed his eyes. His pulse was a drumbeat in his ears, and though Lucien had closed the wound on his neck, its heat still tingled beneath his skin.

"Cyrus," Lucien murmured against the nape of his neck.

"Hm?"

"You know that I care for you for more than your blood, right?"

Cyrus turned his head over his shoulder, but he couldn't see Lucien's face. "Of course."

"Good," Lucien whispered. "But your blood is fucking sublime, too."

Cyrus chuckled and turned over to face him, rolling neatly into his arms. He brought their faces together and kissed him. "You are welcome to it anytime."

"*Any*time?" Lucien nuzzled his neck and gently skimmed his hands down his sides. "Be careful what you wish for."

Cyrus knew *exactly* what he was wishing for.

He nestled closer to Lucien and lazily stroked his fingers through his hair. He again found himself smiling, content in this feeling that nothing outside of this room mattered. The rest of the world had paused, it seemed, at their whim.

"Can I tell you something?" Cyrus twirled a strand of Lucien's hair around his fingers.

"Hm?"

He coiled Lucien's hair tighter around his hand and tugged it lightly, pulling a soft gasp out of Lucien. "I'm surprised you didn't know you liked this."

Lucien traced his fingers along Cyrus's collarbone. "No one ever did it before. Would it discredit me to admit that I don't do this often?"

"Not after last night."

Lucien smirked. "I don't seek out casual affairs. I've never been able to wrap my head around the idea of taking someone to bed after a mere conversation or a few drinks. I need a deeper connection—I want to know the *person* first." He touched Cyrus's cheek. "You caught my interest because of all those ideas and hopes in your heart. You came to me with a puzzle, and what other choice did I have but to solve it?"

Cyrus kissed him. "When did you know, then, that you wanted me?"

"Is someone feeling a little insecure?"

"No, I just like it when you praise me."

"Oh, Cyrus, if it's praise you want..." Lucien kissed him again and then pushed him onto his back and leaned over him. "I may never stop."

"Yeah?" Cyrus pushed him off and then climbed on top of him, straddling his hips. He bent forward and kissed Lucien's neck, nibbling just below his ear. He grinned when he felt Lucien's breath hitch. "Let's hear it, then. We've got all day."

LATER, Cyrus sat contentedly curled up in a plush armchair by the fireplace in the library, with a cup of hot tea in his hands and one of Lucien's cardigans draped over his shoulders. He watched the flames flicker and absently stirred his tea while Lucien, similarly nestled in his own chair on the other side of the low table between them, paged through one of the few books they had deemed useful all those weeks ago.

When Lucien had said that Emerson Beldon had raged his way through this library, Cyrus had expected the worst. Even though Lucien had said he'd cleaned up, Cyrus had still held his breath when he'd come through the doors, and then was shocked to find only a few scarce traces of Emerson's meddling—a broken shelf here, a scuffed chair there. The books that Cyrus and Lucien had left on this table the night the Beldons had raided House Vista were all still here—if they'd been moved, Lucien must have found them —and all that was missing, as far as Cyrus could tell, was Lucien's notebook.

Cyrus had not stopped kicking himself for leaving that book behind. He shuddered to think what Emerson might have already accomplished with Lucien's work.

Lucien muttered something to himself and set the book he'd been reading on the table with the others, tucking a scrap of paper into the crease to keep his place. He grabbed the Countess's journal next, but only glanced at a page or two before dropping it back on the table. He slumped back and looked up at Cyrus. "Don't get me wrong, you're quite good at sitting there like a very handsome statue, but might you be interested in helping?"

"Sure, if I knew what you were looking for." Cyrus sipped his tea.

Lucien responded with a vague wave of his hand and then got up and started pacing. "Your theory that Wild vampires are the result of a corrupted, incomplete turn is very sound. It also implies that the remedy— No, the *key*, the *catalyst* is in the vampire's blood. Without that genetic material telling the body what to do next after its human essence is drained, it goes berserk. It turns monstrous. It takes the base instincts of a vampire—fear, hunger, and anger—and remakes the body with that framework." Lucien pivoted by the fireplace and paced back the other way, gesturing pointedly as he talked. "However, this assumes the victim is human to start; I still have no idea what could cause such a transformation in a vampire. But, to continue our hypothesis, in order to correct a Wild turn, the victim would need an injection of vampire blood."

Cyrus held his hope at bay. "Could it really be that easy?"

"It's hardly easy." Lucien came back toward Cyrus. "You'd need a *lot* of blood. More than the equivalent of what you lost. The timing would need to be absolutely precise, and that would mean we'd need to know exactly when a turn occurred so we could get there in time to administer the antidote before the victim is too far gone. I suspect that once the Wild transformation has begun, there is a very small margin for reversing it. We can't be sure without intricate experiments—then again, we can't be sure of *any* of this without experiments." He mussed his hair. "It's not perfect, but it's something. And if we can find a way to *reverse* a Wild turn, it will likely lead us toward a way to *prevent* Wild turns altogether."

Cyrus found himself smiling. "I love it when you talk like this."

Lucien glanced at him and blinked a few times, then tucked his hair behind his ear. "Just...thinking out loud. Rambling, really."

"It's endearing." Cyrus sipped his tea. "So...where do we start? Aren't we going to run into the same problem you did with Leigh Harrows? We need a Wild vampire."

Lucien plopped back down in his chair. "Afraid so. I think it may be time to pay a visit to House Harrows."

Cyrus stared at him and waited for him to understand how stupid an idea that was, but Lucien's expression didn't waver.

"What?" he prompted.

Cyrus raised his eyebrows. "I shouldn't have to tell you that that's a terrible idea."

"What would you suggest instead?" Lucien flicked his hand at the table. "Books will only tell us so much. I need to speak to a firsthand witness, someone who was there when Leigh was turned. Master Harrows is a brutal and obsessive scientist; if he led this experiment, he'll have extensive notes. I need to see them. If the answer we're looking for is anywhere, it'll be there."

Cyrus couldn't disagree with that, but he didn't like it.

"I need to know what House Harrows is up to," Lucien continued. "Why Arthur? And why Leigh? What was the goal, and if Leigh was truly my ally, why was I kept in the dark?" He rubbed his forehead.

"Let's hope they're willing to talk to us, then," Cyrus said.

"No." Lucien met his eyes. "Not us. Me."

Cyrus recoiled. "What?"

"You're going to stay here—"

"*Lucien.*"

"—where you're *safe*, and I'm—"

"Seriously?" Cyrus set his teacup down with a *clack*. "I'm not a child! You really think—"

"They'll hurt you? Yes." Lucien clenched his jaw. "They killed your brother, Cyrus. The *heir* to the Beldon family. What do you think that makes *you* to them?"

"*Excuse* me?"

"You're nothing to them, Cyrus," Lucien snapped. "You're disposable, even more so than your brother was."

Cyrus scoffed and bolted to his feet. "Yeah, just like I am to my own fucking family, thank you."

He started to turn away, but Lucien stood and caught his arm. "Listen to me. That's obviously not what *I* think of you, nor do I wish to reinforce the lies your family told you. But I need you to understand that House Harrows does not give a shit if you're the heir or the last born—in their eyes, you're nothing, because you're human. House Harrows is one of the oldest Honorable Families, and they fully believe that vampires are a superior species. Remember how I said the vampires at Lavinia's court saw you only as food? That's *indifference* compared to how Harrows vampires would see you."

Cyrus looked away. He knew Lucien was right, but admitting it and folding to his request felt like succumbing to his own weakness. He was a Beldon; he wasn't supposed to *need* to stay home where he was safe.

Lucien's hand tightened on his arm, but gentler this time. "I lost you once," he said softly. "I can't lose you again. Please, Cyrus, *please* stay here."

He grumbled a vague agreement. He wasn't happy about it, but fine. He'd play along.

Lucien pulled him into a hug. "Thank you."

"I wish it didn't have to be like this," he mumbled. "I wish I could be literally anyone else."

He longed for the anonymity he'd enjoyed in those little towns by the lake. It was refreshing to not be recognized, to be just another face in the crowd. Most people he met around here already knew his name, and already had an opinion about that name. It had been nice to have the chance to be *anyone*. Even someone as foolishly bold as Cyrus Vista.

"Trust me, I know how you feel." Lucien let go of him. "Vista is no small mantle to carry, either."

"At least people respect you." Cyrus smirked. "Want to trade? I'd like to see you stroll up to my family's house and announce that you're a Beldon now. I think my uncle would keel over on the spot."

Lucien laughed. "Ten generations of Beldons would turn in their graves."

"Especially my father." Cyrus shook his head and slid his hands into his pockets. "I find it hard to believe that we've only ever been enemies. I know that vampires feed on humans and that naturally creates some tension, but clearly it doesn't *have* to be like that. Do you really think, in all those years and all those lifetimes, *no one* from either a hunter family or an Honorable Family ever found themselves in love with the other?"

"I'm certain they did." Lucien stroked his fingers across Cyrus's cheek. "And I'm sure that if we looked hard enough, we could find the stories about them."

Cyrus gazed at the thousands of books surrounding him without really seeing them. "What if there are none? What if no one ever bothered to write them down? Or what if they were erased?"

"Then we'll have to be sure that our story is not forgotten." Lucien drew him close and pressed his face to his hair. "There's one such story that has survived, quite famously, though most people only know part of it. Do you remember the song we played together, just before we went north?"

"The one about how humans aren't worth loving?"

"The very same one that claims vampires will trick you and break your heart." Lucien smiled in reply to Cyrus's confused look. "It's the same song. Different verses, each from a different perspective. But there's a third verse that everyone forgets, and it goes like this:

But that woman and her creature of the night
Stayed together
As promised, all their lives
And they loved each other
For all time,
Ne'er to be apart again.

Lucien murmured the last words against Cyrus's ear, then kissed his temple and started to draw away, but Cyrus pulled him into his arms—partially to hide the tears that had welled in his eyes, and partially to prolong Lucien's departure. He closed his eyes and breathed in the smell of roses and cypress.

"We're not destined for tragedy," Lucien whispered. "But even if we were, it would not stop me from caring about you."

"Likewise," Cyrus murmured. He finally let Lucien go and stepped back. "All right. See what you can learn from House Harrows. I'm sure I can keep myself entertained in the meantime."

Lucien smiled with obvious relief. "Thank you." He kissed Cyrus once, then turned and left with a wave.

"Please be safe," Cyrus whispered to his back. Then, when Lucien was gone from sight, he turned to the nearest bookcase and lightly touched the leather spines. "All right, beauties. What will you show me today?"

CYRUS WAS SO ENGROSSED in the book he'd settled with that when the shudder of doors announced Lucien's return, he couldn't be sure if Lucien had been gone for twenty minutes or two hours. Even as he heard Lucien call his name, he couldn't quite tear his attention away from the page.

"Cyrus?" Lucien called again, moving closer but still two floors down.

"Up here!" Cyrus said, unhelpfully. He was curled up in a chair in a secluded corner of the third floor, in which he'd found an exquisite collection of literature and poetry spanning centuries. The library had practically thrown this book at him as he'd been browsing, and Cyrus had been pulled in from the very first page.

He could still hear Lucien searching for him. Sighing, he reluctantly marked his page as he came to the end of a chapter, then brought the book with him to the nearest balcony overlooking the center of the library. He leaned over the railing and spotted Lucien on the main stairs. "Lucien, I'm here. How did it go?"

Lucien looked up, then took a step forward and vanished in a blur of silver and black. A moment later, he stood beside Cyrus.

Though he'd expected it, Cyrus still jumped. "That is never going to stop being weird. How do you do that, anyway?"

"It's called blink-shifting," Lucien said. "I can only do it in short bursts, and admittedly it's only thanks to Lavinia that I can do it at all, but it comes in handy. It's like—" He cut off abruptly, and Cyrus realized his eyes had fallen on the book Cyrus carried. "What is that?"

Cyrus blinked. "It's this brilliant invention called a *book*."

Lucien shook his head. "No, I mean—May I see?"

Skeptical, Cyrus passed over the volume. "It's...a romantic adventure novel. Nothing related to our work."

Lucien smirked and flipped through the book, lingering notably at the place where Cyrus had left off. Cyrus's cheeks warmed—the chapter he'd just finished had been particularly... passionate—but Lucien didn't comment. A small, fond smile eased across his face as he acquainted himself with the book, and then he handed it back to Cyrus with an expression Cyrus couldn't translate.

"Favorite of yours?" Cyrus asked. The author was somewhat famous among the right readers, but Cyrus hadn't expected Lucien to know them.

"You could say that." Lucien leaned his arms on the railing and maintained that weird look on his face. "You didn't notice, did you?"

Cyrus flipped the book around, searching for something he might've missed on the otherwise plain leather cover. He opened the front and scanned the endpages for something interesting, but they were plain, too. "Notice what?"

"The author's name."

Cyrus frowned and turned to the title page. "L. A. Atsiv? What about it?"

Yet Lucien was giving him that *stupid question* look again. Cyrus studied the name on the page for another minute, and just when he was about to demand an explanation, it suddenly clicked.

Atsiv was *Vista* spelled backwards.

Cyrus's mouth fell open. Lucien grinned when he looked up at him. "Y-You wrote this?"

"Technically speaking, L. A. Atsiv wrote it." Lucien smirked. "But sometimes, very secretly, L. A. Atsiv is also known as Lucien Alastair Vista."

"You *write books*?"

Lucien shrugged, as if writing books wasn't one of the most extraordinary things a person could do. Cyrus was at a loss for words. This book was *brilliant*. The prose was like poetry, the plot had utterly captivated him, and the romance—gods, the *romance*... It had just the right amount of heat to make him swoon. Suddenly it made perfect sense that Lucien had written this, given the affection he had shown Cyrus last night and this morning.

Cyrus fanned the pages and felt a pang of regret at how close he was to the end. He'd burned through this book so quickly that he hadn't even savored it; clearly, he'd have to read it again. "Do you have more?" he asked.

Lucien nodded. "A few. Nothing terribly recent, though. That was one of the last ones I finished before I got...disenchanted with the hobby."

"Lucien, this book is exceptional," Cyrus said. "I wish I was reading it right now. I haven't put it down since you left. How long were you gone, anyway?"

He shrugged. "Perhaps an hour."

"Could have been five minutes, for all I was paying attention." Cyrus tucked the book under his arm and leaned on the railing. "I'll restrain myself from interrogating you further, but this won't be our last meeting, Mr. *Atsiv*." He grinned, but now when Lucien smiled back, it didn't stick. Cyrus cocked his head. "What's wrong?"

Lucien sighed. "A lot. House Harrows are bastards, the lot of them. If I ever had an ally in that family, it was Leigh. No wonder they fucking killed her."

Cyrus's eyes widened. "They told you that?"

"Chester Harrows stated, *very* solemnly, that Leigh *sacrificed herself* for her family and for *the greater good*." Each emphasized word dripped with contempt. "He can act as innocent as he pleases, but I don't buy it. He murdered his own daughter and turned her into a monster, probably to turn the Beldons' suspicion away from the family. And then he had the audacity to tell me I should understand *perfectly* that sacrifices are often necessary for the good of the Families."

Cyrus recoiled. "What the *fuck*."

"So that's when I left."

"Good."

"But." Lucien drew a folded square of paper out of the pocket on his vest. "Not before taking a page from your book. If you'll pardon the pun." A faint smile softened his eyes as he passed the paper to Cyrus.

He unfolded it, and his blood ran cold when he recognized his uncle's handwriting. "Oh, fuck." He glanced up at Lucien. "This is bad."

"Read it," Lucien prompted. "It gets worse."

Reluctantly, Cyrus read.

HONORED HARROWS,

This is splendid news. I know my brother's demise was an unforeseen inconvenience for all of us, but as I said in my first letter, he and I have similar interests in this regard—as it seems you and I do. I'm more than happy to continue the negotiations that Marcus started, and I expect this arrangement will bring both of us closer to our goals. You, my friend, are far more accommodating and understanding than stubborn old Alastair Vista. Years of cordialities and favors, and still he refused to award me a fraction of the trust that you have already lent me. I do appreciate your courtesy.

Ah, I digress. Admittedly my days have been occupied with family matters, but I wonder if we could agree upon a time to meet in this coming week. I would like to hear more of your history with House Attcourt, as well as anything else you might know of them. Of all the Honorable Families, they have remained the most distant and

the most mysterious, haven't they? I think it's time for them to share the wealth, don't you?
   We'll talk soon.

Sincerely,
Master Emerson Beldon

Cyrus stared at the last paragraph until his eyes slid out of focus and blurred the words. "What the hell is he planning?"

"I don't know, and that's what scares me." Lucien raked his fingers through his hair. "Tension between Harrows and Attcourt is nothing new, but I don't understand why Emerson Beldon thinks he has anything to do with it."

"I'm afraid I need a history lesson," Cyrus said. "Why are Harrows and Attcourt at each other's throats?"

"Oh, there's hardly anything mutual about it," Lucien said. He coiled a strand of hair around his fingers as he talked. "Harrows has been waiting to pounce on Attcourt for decades. Centuries ago, when each of the Families had its own little empire, Harrows and Attcourt's northern lands neighbored each other. I don't know who started it, but a Harrows had a problem with an Attcourt and it sparked a conflict that ended with House Attcourt gaining part of House Harrows's territory. This all happened right before the Families convened to agree upon the alliance that eventually became the Century Truce, so Harrows never got back the land that Attcourt took. To this day, Attcourt still technically controls the western region outside the city."

Cyrus rolled his eyes. "Really? All of that over a scrap of land that became the shittiest part of Chestervale? How long ago was this?"

"Probably close to three centuries at this point." Lucien pursed his lips. "It seems petty, yes, but remember that to a vampire, three hundred years might as well be thirty. And Chester Harrows is not exactly famous for his compassion."

"Ah, so I'm sure he and my uncle get along splendidly." Cyrus passed the letter back to Lucien. "But this doesn't explain...well, any of it, really. Why would Leigh Harrows murder Arthur if my father and her father were working together? What does my uncle want from House Attcourt? And what does he think he'll get from House Harrows if he helps them? What did my *father* want from them?"

"I don't *know*." Lucien put his head in his hands. "The pieces are all here, Cyrus. Why can't we see the picture? What are we missing?" He rubbed his hands down his face. "Damn it, I shouldn't have left so quickly. Maybe I could've gotten more out of Master Harrows. I was just..."

"Offended?" Cyrus offered gently.

"A fucking coward."

Cyrus laid his hand on Lucien's arm. "No. You had every right to walk away when he said that to you. It was cruel and uncalled for. If that's how Chester Harrows treats other Honorable Ones, then he's not deserving of anyone's respect."

"Still, it was a childish move on my part." Lucien pushed away from the railing and slunk toward the stacks, looking more defeated than Cyrus had ever seen him. "I should be stronger. *Honored* Vista, *Master* Vista...What do those titles mean if I can't live up to them? I'm the only one who speaks for my family and its legacy now, and what do I do at the first sign of conflict? I run away."

Cyrus started to follow him, reaching out. "Lucien."

But then Cyrus blinked, and Lucien had disappeared.

Chapter  TWENTY EIGHT

CYRUS WAS BACK IN THE GODDAMNED TOWER.

He faced the door at the top of the stairs, which was open and beckoning to him. He looked into a dim, cluttered room with a generous dusting of cobwebs in the corners. A piano stood against the wall beneath a tiny window, and a woman sat at the piano.

Cyrus didn't know how he hadn't recognized her the first time. After all, his brown curls looked just like hers. And if she turned around, he was certain he'd see his own green eyes gazing back at him.

"Mom?" His voice caught in his throat; he cleared it and tried again. "*Mom*, can you hear me?"

She didn't move. Didn't seem to hear. She sat perfectly still, perfectly straight, with her hands on the keys. Her clothes were dusty and threadbare, as gray and bleak as the rest of this room.

Cyrus stepped into the room, and was faintly surprised to find that the dream let him move. Candles flickered on the windowsill and threw shadows across the room. It was cold; there was no hearth to warm the space, and the tower's stone walls hoarded the chill.

"What are you doing here?" Cyrus moved another step forward, only for an unseen barrier to halt him. He tried to push ahead, but the empty air might as well have been brick.

His mother still did not acknowledge him. "Mom," he tried

again. "Mom, please, it's me! You told me to come here, and I'm here. Why can't you—"

She whipped around, and a gust of wind flung Cyrus backwards. The door slammed. The mirror shattered.

Cyrus woke up in Lucien's bed.

His heart was thundering so hard it was difficult to take a full breath. It was several seconds before he fully came back to himself, at which point he found Lucien hovering over him with his hands on his shoulders as if he'd shaken Cyrus awake.

Cyrus exhaled slowly. "Sorry."

"Don't be." Lucien stroked Cyrus's hair back off his forehead. "You seemed like you were having a nightmare. Are you okay?"

Cyrus rubbed sleep out of his eyes. "I guess. I keep dreaming of that tower. Leif told me what it means, but I'm certain there's more to it that I *don't* know, and I've no idea how to figure it out. I need to, though. I don't think the dream will go away until I do."

He had tried not to dwell on what Leif had told him, in that strange dream plane, about his mother's death. Leif hadn't offered any explanation after Cyrus had woken up, and Cyrus had been too afraid to ask. But now there was no one to ask, and he had nothing.

He itched to know, but at the same time, what good would it do him to learn that what he knew about his mother's death was a lie—and that the truth was possibly worse than what he'd been told?

"You've been dreaming of a tower?" Lucien's soft voice surfaced him from his thoughts. "Is it a place you recognize?"

"Yeah." Cyrus rolled over to face him and propped up his head on his hand. "It's the old stone tower behind my family's house. It used to be part of a castle that was there before the estate was. My father was the only one allowed up there, so I've never been inside. But it's been showing up in my dreams, and once, it...called to me."

He cringed as Lucien raised an eyebrow. "That sounds crazy, I know. But it feels like something is trying to get me to go there."

"Indeed, it would seem that way." Lucien touched his fingertip to his lips as his brows knit in thought. "What do you see up there in the dream?"

"My mother," Cyrus whispered.

At that, both of Lucien's eyebrows shot up. "Oh. Well, that's interesting. She passed away quite a while ago, didn't she?"

"Yeah, when I was a child. I don't remember much of her, but I think...I think she's the one calling me to the tower. The dream won't let me talk to her, though. I can see her, but she can't hear me and I can't get close to her." Cyrus sighed and flopped onto his back, dragging his fingers through his tangled curls.

"Seems like she has unfinished business with you," Lucien said.

"But what? I was six when she died. I know her death was horrible, but what could I have done about it?" He rubbed his eyes. "The dream changes every time I have it. Sometimes I'm stuck climbing the tower's spiral stairs, other times I'm at the top but I can't open the door. Always that tower, though."

"Well," Lucien scooted closer to him, "what's stopping you from investigating?"

"The guarantee of a bullet through my skull if I went anywhere near the Beldon estate," Cyrus said.

"Fair, but you said the tower is *behind* it, yes? On the grounds, but not close to the house?" Lucien raised his eyebrows. "We could go right now. No one will see us under the cover of night, and I can blink-shift us there and back easily. No one will know we were ever there."

Cyrus waited for him to crack a grin and wave all of that away as a joke, but if anything his expression grew more eager the longer Cyrus stared at him blankly. "You're insane," Cyrus told him. "Didn't you tell me you hope I never have to see my family's house again?"

"Yes, but we're not going to your family's house," Lucien said. "Only the tower. It must be a bit of a distance, right? Because I didn't notice a tower when I met you in the garden."

"You were too busy looking at *me* to pay attention to anything else," Cyrus teased, playfully tapping the end of his nose. Lucien scrunched his face.

He was right, though: there was a small stretch of woods that separated the tower from the rest of the estate. They *could* go there without being seen, but despite Cyrus's itch to know what secrets the tower kept, he was reluctant.

"Or, we can stay here," Lucien said softly. He touched his knuckles to Cyrus's cheek and traced his thumb along the scatter of freckles. "We don't have to go. I won't drag you if you don't want to. But if you do want to, it's no trouble to blink us there."

The obvious answer was to stay, at least for now, in the warm comfort of Lucien's bed and the steady security of his embrace. Yet something made Cyrus hesitate to turn down the offer to investigate. Would he get another chance to find out what was in that tower? Would the dream ever go away if he didn't follow its call? What if it revealed something about his mother that added a connecting piece to the puzzle that he and Lucien couldn't seem to complete?

There were too many what-ifs. Cyrus would never be able to sleep with all of that on his mind, anyway. He sat up. "Let's go."

"Really?" Lucien rose, beaming. "Right now?"

"It's going to weigh on my mind forever if we don't," Cyrus said. "So, yes, let's go, and let's hope it's worth it."

"You are so wonderfully full of surprises." Lucien kissed him, then threw back the covers and climbed out of bed. Cyrus followed suit and found yesterday's clothes on the floor, and once they were both dressed, Lucien pulled Cyrus to his side.

"We're going straight from here?"

"Why not?" Lucien tightened his arm around Cyrus's waist. "Ready?"

"I guess." He screwed his eyes shut and braced himself. The jarring wrench was quicker this time, and when they stopped, Lucien let go. Cyrus waited for him to blink-shift them again, but when he didn't, he opened his eyes.

The Beldon estate loomed before him, aglow in all its proud glory.

The sight of it unsettled Cyrus's stomach. He turned his back on the house and stepped into the shadows beneath the trees on the edge of the grounds. Lucien remained close at his side as Cyrus led the way into the woods. There was allegedly a footpath that went straight to the tower, but in the dark, Cyrus couldn't tell where his own feet were, let alone a dirt path. He trudged through the foliage by feeling alone until he tripped on a root and nearly smashed his face into a tree.

Lucien caught his arm. "You can ask for help at any time, you know."

Cyrus grumbled. "Fine, okay, can you find the path?"

"It's right there." Lucien pointed at the ground to his left, about a foot away from where the two of them currently stood. Cyrus couldn't make out his features, but he could sense the smug grin on the vampire's face. "Shall I lead?"

"Be my guest, Honored Vista." Cyrus flourished a hand in the vague direction of the path.

Lucien chuckled and linked arms with Cyrus. "Your dramatic flair never fails to amuse me. I expect it'll be obvious when we reach the tower?"

"I'm not dramatic," Cyrus muttered, fully knowing that was an astronomical lie. "And yes, it's not far. Can't miss it."

Indeed, it was only a few minutes before the trees tapered off and revealed the crumbling cobblestone structure. Abandoned and left to rot, it shrouded itself in the darkness cast by the trees; if not for the sliver of light from the half moon overhead, Cyrus might've mistaken the tower for a shadowy mirage.

He gazed up at the structure and crossed his arms as a chill ran down his back. This thing had a *presence* about it that he couldn't fully name.

Cyrus glanced at Lucien at the same time Lucien glanced at him. "I'm not sure what I expected," Lucien said softly, "but this place feels like a tomb."

Cyrus shivered and tried not to dwell on that. He took a deep breath and strode forward.

Overgrown, dying brambles surrounded the structure, forming nearly a perfect ring around its cylindrical perimeter. With Lucien's guidance, Cyrus found a narrow break in the thicket and followed a path of buried, broken cobbles up to the tower.

"What are our chances of finding an unlocked door?" Lucien glanced up and down the tower as he slowly made his way around it.

Cyrus went the other way, but with more thorny bushes in the way, he couldn't tell if there was a door at all. "That'd be too easy," he muttered.

"Was there a clue in your dream as to how to enter?" Lucien asked.

"No." Cyrus met Lucien at the back of the tower. "Can you blink us in there?"

Lucien shook his head. "I can't blink-shift to places I've never been. That's why we ended up in front of your family's house and not precisely here."

Of course, because the incredibly convenient method of rapid travel couldn't be *too* convenient.

Lucien hummed and traced Cyrus's steps back around to the front of the tower, examining the brambles as he went. Cyrus watched curiously, then winced as Lucien shouldered his way into the thicket of thorns. He rummaged and shoved aside the bushes as if the thorns didn't bother him at all.

"Did you know," he said over the crackle of snapping twigs, "that vampire hunters used to think that rose bushes could keep vampires out?"

Cyrus scoffed. "Remember who you're talking to. Of course I know that, and even I know it's just a myth. Clearly." He inched closer to the hole Lucien had carved through the thorns. "Doesn't that hurt?"

"Not really." Lucien continued thrashing his way through the bushes. "And while it *is* a myth that prickly branches have a supernatural barring effect on me, it's thanks to that superstition that hunters and common folks alike got in the habit of hiding important things among rosebushes. Like, for instance..." He grunted and broke another branch with a loud *crunch*, and then Cyrus heard a distinct knock of knuckles on wood. "A door!"

Cyrus let out a disbelieving laugh and peered through the thorns. "Are you serious?"

Lucien rapped his knuckles on the door again. "I certainly am! Come on, then. Keep your head down so you don't tangle those beautiful curls, and you'll be fine."

Cyrus eyed the thorns doubtfully, despite the somewhat clear path Lucien had forged through the bushes. He tucked his hands to his chest and hunched his shoulders, ducking as he moved into the thicket. Branches tugged at his sleeves and thwacked his ankles, but he managed to avoid getting torn to shreds and met Lucien at the ancient-looking wooden door. Cyrus felt around for a knob or handle, but if there had been one once, it had not survived.

Lucien gave the door a hard shove; it groaned, but didn't budge. He frowned and threw his shoulder into it, and the door ceased its protests. The rotting lock gave way with a splitting *crack*, and Lucien flashed a grin before darting inside.

Almost reluctantly, Cyrus followed.

Absolute darkness swallowed him. Cyrus couldn't see an inch in front of his nose, yet somehow he knew this place at once. The damp smell of moss and rot were chillingly familiar, and he knew that if he moved forward, he'd find the stairs.

He didn't realize he'd actually moved until he tripped on the first step. Instinctively, he caught himself on the wall to his right. He looked up, and for a moment was confused that there wasn't an enticing light ahead.

"Lucien?" His voice cracked on the name, but to his relief he could speak.

"I'm here." Lucien came up behind him and gently touched the small of his back. "Do you want me to go first?"

"No. I know the way." Cyrus reached out with his left hand

and found Lucien's arm, then felt his way down to his hand and gripped it tight. "But stay close to me. Please."

He hated how scared he was, but he couldn't forget about the times that this dream had become a nightmare.

"Of course," Lucien murmured.

Cyrus took a deep breath and started up the stairs. He didn't need light to find his way forward; the stairwell unfolded before him like it always did, curving up and up and up. The dampness sank into Cyrus's bones and the darkness pulled him deeper and deeper until all he knew was the sound of his own pounding heart. If not for Lucien's hand clutched in his own, he would swear he was still asleep.

Or maybe he was. Maybe Lucien was part of the dream now. Or maybe the cool palm pressed in his hand wasn't real at all.

When Cyrus went to take another step up and found that there were no more to climb, he froze. Here he was, at the top, and he couldn't see a single thing.

"Lucien," he breathed.

"I'm here." Lucien squeezed his hand and moved to his side. "There's another door in front of us. It's closed. Do you want me to try to open it?"

"There's nothing else?" Cyrus cursed his feeble human sight.

"No. We're on a small square landing, and all there is is the door."

"What does it look like?"

Cyrus sensed the confusion in Lucien's pause. "It's...plain. Normal. Wood, with iron hinges."

"It's not a mirror?" Cyrus could hardly hear his own voice beneath his pulse.

"No." Lucien squeezed his hand.

"Is this real?"

"Yes." Lucien lifted Cyrus's hand and kissed it. "I'm going to see if I can open the door. Can I let go?"

"No." Cyrus clung tighter to him. He knew he was being foolish—childish, even—but the dark was consuming, and Cyrus didn't want to be alone in it for even a second. He was usually good at swallowing his fear, but not here.

"Okay. Then come with me." Lucien gently tugged him forward a few steps, then stopped. Cyrus heard a dull clatter as Lucien jiggled the doorknob, and then with a sudden *snap* that made Cyrus jump, the door creaked open.

A stale smell of dust and earth wafted out of the room. Lucien moved forward, but Cyrus stayed rooted to the spot until his only options were to follow or let go of Lucien's hand. Lucien waited patiently until Cyrus finally decided that he'd rather face whatever was in this room than let go. He stepped inside.

Faint moonlight slanted through a small window high on the wall. Cyrus blinked as his eyes adjusted, and then he could make out familiar shapes. Bookshelves, tables, a chair, the piano.

"Ah, here." Lucien struck a match and lit three half-melted candles arranged crookedly on a brass candelabra. As the flames grew, Cyrus could finally see.

Dusty, cobwebbed, and cluttered with the unfinished remnants of someone's life, the space was frozen in a messy stasis that suggested its inhabitant had left unexpectedly and had not returned. Cyrus finally released his grip on Lucien's hand and slowly poked around the room, careful not to upset anything as he explored. He didn't know what he was looking for, exactly, but if something had been calling him up here, he hoped that same insistent spirit would show him whatever it wanted him to see.

He glanced back at the piano again, and swore he glimpsed a shadow of someone sitting there. But then he blinked, and it was gone.

Just a trick of the light.

"This doesn't make any sense," he muttered, mostly to himself. What was he supposed to find here? The room was essentially an attic, full of things that hadn't been thought about in years. Old furniture made a maze out of the square space, coated with dust and inhabited by spiders. Moth-eaten sheets slouched over a couple of chairs with moldy upholstery, and a dirt-smeared mirror with pieces missing from its shattered face leaned against the wall behind them. Cyrus glanced at his splintered reflection as he crept by, but startled with a gasp when he saw a figure behind him.

He whirled around, already assuring himself that it was just Lucien, but there was no one there. Lucien was on the other side of the room. All that stood behind Cyrus was an old bookcase that looked ready to collapse.

Cyrus stared at it, heart pounding. The back of his neck prickled, but he squashed the urge to look in the mirror again. *Just a play of the light,* he told himself. The shadows danced and shifted in here; of course his eyes were tricking him.

"Are you okay?" Lucien asked.

Right, he could probably hear Cyrus's frantic pulse loud and clear. "Yeah. Just...startled myself." He laughed it off, but the sound was weak even in his own ears.

Pull it together, Beldon, he scolded himself. He shook his hands and resolved to search the bookshelf when something fell off of it, sending him jumping a foot backwards.

He caught himself on one of the chairs. Before him, an old and tattered journal lay open on the floor. Some of its pages had come loose on impact, and it had coughed up a small picture in a square frame.

Cyrus bent down on his knee and carefully picked up the frame. It held a graphite drawing of a young child, but he couldn't make out any further details in the dim light. He collected the journal and its fallen pages, then moved closer to the candelabra and tilted the picture toward it.

His heart stuttered.

"Oh...gods." The drawing showed a child of maybe two, with a pudgy face, round eyes, a smatter of freckles, and a thick mop of curls on his head. Nearly two decades later, Cyrus more or less had the same features, minus *some* of that youthful roundness in his cheeks.

"What did you find?" Lucien joined him at the candles and

leaned over his shoulder. "Is that you?" He failed to mask the delight in his voice.

"Yes," Cyrus whispered. He flipped the picture over and found his name, his age, and the year in his mother's handwriting. In the bottom corner, she'd written, *My only joy.*

Cyrus swallowed and turned the picture face-up, then considered the journal. He tucked the drawing inside the back cover, then flipped the book to the front and fanned the pages. Endless lines of his mother's looping handwriting filled the space from margin to margin, interrupted frequently by sketches of birds, insects, mice, and a few vague faces. He glimpsed several pages of music notes toward the middle, but then everything abruptly ended three-quarters of the way through the book. A section of at least a hundred sheets remained blank and untouched.

"She must have been in the middle of this one when she died," Cyrus murmured. He flipped all the way to the back and glanced over the last few pages in case she'd scattered random notes there, but there was nothing. *Come on, Mom, tell me something*, he thought with a frustrated grumble. *Why did you bring me here? Why were* you *here?*

What was up here that Marcus didn't want anyone to find?

Cyrus split the journal open as far as it would go without completely breaking the binding, and with a crack of glue, a pocket opened on the inside of the back cover. The edge of a loose page poked out, and Cyrus triumphantly tugged it free.

But before he'd unfolded it even once, Lucien laid his hand on his arm. Cyrus eyed him. "What?"

Lucien studied him closely for a minute, and then Cyrus saw him bury whatever it was he was going to say. "Nothing. Sorry. I just...I imagine this is a lot for you, and I want you to know...I'm here."

He flickered an appreciative smile. "Thank you."

Lucien kept his hand on Cyrus's arm as Cyrus unfolded the page and read.

If you are reading this, you are too late. You failed, I won, and I'm gone. You remain to wallow in your misery and hate, and I am free.

I am finally free.

And as you read this, I hope it hits you—I hope it pierces you like one of your precious silver blades—that it is because of you that I'm gone. It is because of you that I could not stand to live another day. It is because of you and your <u>cruelty</u> and your <u>rage</u> and your utterly <u>rotten</u> heart that my only choice was to leave everything—even my children, who will now all grow up without a mother's love—because you were too selfish and proud and cruel.

Well, Master Beldon, I hope you're proud now. And I hope you're miserable. Because despite your best efforts, I no longer am.

I'm free.

Cyrus didn't realize how hard he'd started breathing until Lucien pulled him into his arms and he found he couldn't take a full breath. The note and the journal fell from his shaking hands. He didn't know how his lungs were still working, his heart still beating; he felt like everything—the earth itself—had stopped.

That was...That was a suicide note.

His mother had killed herself.

But— But no, no, this didn't make any *sense*. *Everyone* knew the story. Cyrus had heard that story for nearly his entire life. It was what had kept Marcus devoted to his bloody hunting career, and it was what motivated Arthur and Joel and Poppy to follow in Marcus's footsteps. It was the root of Cyrus's own hatred of vampires; he had believed for fifteen years that it was a vampire's fault that his mother was dead.

But it was all a giant lie?

"Cyrus." Lucien held him tightly and murmured comforts incoherent to Cyrus's ears. "I'm so sorry. I didn't realize you didn't know."

At that, Cyrus tore away from him. "What?"

Lucien broke his gaze. "The story about your mother being turned and Marcus having to kill her...I knew it was a lie. Most of the Families do. But we also understood that if Marcus knew we'd seen through his lie, there would be hell to pay. So we stuck to the story even though it was glaringly obvious that it didn't make any sense. No Honorable One in their right mind would attack the wife of Marcus fucking Beldon. Such a breach of the Century Truce would have been unthinkable at the time."

Cyrus couldn't breathe. A red haze clouded the edges of his vision, pulsing with his pounding heart. He wanted to scream. If he didn't think someone in the house would hear it, he would. He wanted to tear this room apart and—And what? Find more evidence of his mother's misery? Find something worse?

He wished he could rip that note from his mind, but at the same time he felt a terrible compulsion to dig through everything else until he knew the entire picture. What had Marcus done to her? How cruel had he been to her? Was this tower her sanctuary... or her prison?

No wonder Cyrus had been forbidden from this place all his life. But had the others been? Had Arthur been up here? Did Marcus treat it as some kind of sick coming-of-age rite that Cyrus was never going to deserve? Or did Arthur, Joel, and Poppy know the truth because they were older when it happened? Hell, even Leif, who wasn't related to the Beldons at all, seemed to know what had really happened to Natasha.

It was just him, then, who was kept in the dark?

Cyrus sniffed and rubbed his nose. "You know...I get why they didn't tell me as a kid." His voice wobbled around the words but he didn't care. "How do you explain to a lonely child that his mother took her own life because his father was cruel to her?

"But Poppy and Joel were children at the time, too. They were probably told, eventually, what had happened. Why wasn't I? Why do I continue to be treated like I'm not part of this fucking family?"

Cyrus took a shaky breath and tried to keep his voice low, but his anger won. He spun away from Lucien and slammed his hands down on the piano keys; they cried a discordant chord. "*I'm sick of it!*" he shouted. "I *hate* this place, I hate this family, and I hate that I'm part of it. And you know what, I get this too." He turned back to Lucien and swept his arm across the room, ending with a gesture toward the note on the dusty floor. "She got as far away from that house as she possibly could while on Marcus's leash, and when this wasn't enough, she went where he couldn't follow her. I get it. I do."

Cyrus braced his hands on the piano bench and hung his head. "This fucking family is *poison*. They've been trying to bury me for my entire life, and all I've ever wanted is to survive to see a day when I can leave them behind. They want me gone? Fine. But if they want to bury me like they did my mother, then I'm dragging them down with me."

Hot tears spilled from his eyes and he hastily wiped them away with the back of his hand. He sniffed again and looked up at the window over the piano. "My mother chose freedom in the only way she knew how. I will too, but I won't let them break me like they broke her. If I owe one thing to my mother, it's to bring this family to ruins."

It started with you, he'd said to Julius Beldon all those weeks ago. *It'll end with me.*

"How?" Lucien asked softly.

Cyrus turned back to him; he still lingered by the candelabra, but he'd picked up the journal and Natasha's note. When Cyrus approached him, he could see wet streaks on his cheeks.

Cyrus gently took the note from Lucien and tucked it into its place at the back of the journal. "This city sees the Beldons as an idyllic, infallible family. This"—he waved at the surrounding room—"shatters that image. If people knew the truth, it would taint their rose-colored view of the family."

"Potentially," Lucien allowed, "but is it enough?"

"Not nearly," Cyrus said. "But why does everyone *really* look up to the Beldons?"

"Because you're wealthy," Lucien muttered.

Cyrus scoffed. "Pot, kettle. Your house is bigger than mine."

"Oh, I don't think we need to go there."

Cyrus rolled his eyes. "The Beldons' real influence comes from our reputation. People look up to us as courageous protectors. We know everything there is to possibly know about vampires and killing them. We keep the city safe and we keep the monsters under control." He held up a finger to acknowledge Lucien's scowl. "Or so everyone *believes*. I'll be the first one to admit, after everything I've learned from you, that what the Beldons know is little more than superstitious fairy tales. But my father spent his entire life maintaining my ancestors' image of heroism and expertise, and he solidified it so strongly that every human in this city believes that without the Beldons, no one would be safe. The city would be rife with violence. Vampires would run amok. The Honorable Families would take over the world. My family, in the eyes of the average citizen of Chestervale, is the line between peace and mayhem."

"And we can conveniently ignore the mayhem and bloodshed your family *causes*," Lucien muttered.

"Exactly. The people who look up to the Beldons will ignore *anything* as long as they still have reason to believe the family will keep them safe. The truth about my mother, horrible as it is, isn't enough to shake that belief. We need, instead, something to prove that Emerson does not have the city's safety as his top priority."

Lucien tilted his head and touched his fingertip to his lips. "If we can dig up more information on this arrangement your father had with House Harrows, and find out what your uncle is planning with them now...would that be enough?"

"We'd need a lot of details," Cyrus said. A collaboration between the Beldons and House Harrows—or any of the Families—might cause a stir, but it wouldn't necessarily spell ruin. Not unless that collaboration revealed a truly nefarious plan. "But it could lead us to something. It's a place to start."

Lucien sighed and took Cyrus's hands. "We keep finding places to start. I would love it if we could find a conclusion."

"Can't have that without a beginning, can we?" Cyrus squeezed his hands. "These pieces are all connected, Lucien. I can sense it. We just need to fill in the gaps."

"Easier said than done," Lucien murmured, "when neither of us can show his face at House Beldon."

"No," Cyrus agreed, "but we may not need to. There's still House Harrows."

Lucien cringed. "I think I blew my chances there."

"Maybe not all of them." Cyrus shrugged. But even if Lucien had, *he* hadn't. House Harrows wouldn't know a thing about Cyrus's recent exile from the Beldons. In their eyes, he was still one of them, which meant that if he played his cards right, he might be able to get something out of them.

Lucien wouldn't like it, but Cyrus didn't see another way forward. So, until he successfully got some answers out of House Harrows, Lucien didn't need to know.

Better to ask forgiveness than permission, right?

Chapter

TWENTY
NINE

It was nearly dawn by the time Cyrus and Lucien returned to the Vista manor, and Cyrus was so exhausted—emotionally and physically—that he pushed his brewing plans out of mind and crashed into bed for six hours. The tower no longer haunted him, and blissfully, he slept.

He woke sometime in the late morning and then happily succumbed to Lucien's attention for a while, but by the time he'd bathed and dressed and eaten, he was itching to get going. Rest had eased some of his shock and anger from last night, but he was no less motivated to collapse the empire his family had built.

Logically, he knew he couldn't entirely destroy his family's legacy. It was too deeply rooted in this city—and probably beyond it, too. But he could shake it. He could poke and prod until it started to crumble, and then hopefully it would collapse under its own weight.

Cyrus followed Lucien to the library after they enjoyed the lunch Lucien had made, and while Lucien went straight to the directory and began noting various sections to search for whatever it was he wanted to find, Cyrus tried to figure out how to slip away. He didn't want to just disappear and cause Lucien unnecessary distress, but he also couldn't tell Lucien where he was going. Cyrus knew his reasoning for going to House Harrows was sound, but Lucien *would* talk him out of it with his worries and his big pleading eyes that Cyrus was not immune to.

Cyrus knew that Lucien was afraid that he wouldn't walk out of House Harrows if he went, and Cyrus understood that fear. But he also wished Lucien trusted him a little more. Cyrus had been raised with the necessary survival skills for interacting with Honorable Families, and despite what Lucien had said about the Harrows family, Cyrus didn't really think any of them would lay a finger on him. Arthur's case was different; clearly, Leigh and her brother had gone rogue. If Master Harrows cared about the Century Truce at all, Cyrus was in no danger.

He wished Lucien would see that. Cyrus didn't want to lie to him, but...well, Lucien would have to forgive him.

Yet another hour slipped by before Cyrus finally made up his mind. He had wandered away from Lucien while Lucien searched for books and Cyrus pretended to, and as he found his way back to the table they'd claimed, he consciously calmed his nerves and made sure his pulse was even. He leaned over the back of Lucien's chair and poked his shoulder.

"Hm?" Lucien kept reading for a moment before he looked up. "Did you find something?"

"Not yet. I can't focus. There's a lot on my mind." That, at least, was completely true. "I think a walk would help."

"Do you want company?"

Cyrus figured he'd ask that. "I'd rather be alone this time. I won't go far."

Lucien eyed him warily, as if the mere thought of Cyrus being out of his sight was already wearing on him. Cyrus could tell there were a thousand protests on the tip of his tongue, but he didn't voice any of them.

Cyrus leaned down and kissed him, meaning it to be a quick reassurance, but Lucien didn't let him go for a minute. When he finally did, Cyrus drew back with a smirk. "You're very persuasive, but I'm still going. I won't be long, I promise."

Lucien nodded, but still looked reluctant. "Be careful."

"I'll do my best," Cyrus promised, and tried not to walk *too* quickly as he made his way out of the library.

HOUSE HARROWS WAS NOT SO MUCH a house as it was a castle. Perched on a hill to the north of Chestervale, it loomed over the valley below with a sharp, watchful eye. Pines trimmed like coiling spires were planted like sentinels along the sloped path leading from the road to the front doors, and larger trees with bare, tangled branches surrounded the castle and its dark towers.

Cyrus left Demeter secured to the iron fence along the side of the road that had brought him to the outer gates, then trekked up the hill while fruitlessly assuring himself that the trees were not watching him.

Places like this were designed to intimidate, to leech the confidence from your bones until you second-guessed your decision to come here and turned around. Cyrus had felt similar trepidation when he'd approached the Vista manor for the first time, but visiting an Honorable Family for academic reasons was one thing. Walking up to the doorstep of his brother's murderers was a very different story.

But if Emerson and Marcus really did have a negotiation on the table with Master Harrows that would betray the other hunter families and break their vows to protect the city, Cyrus could not back down until he had documented proof in his hands. Fear be damned, he needed to walk out of here with something solid.

He was as prepared as he possibly could be without knowing how he'd be received at the door. He had a script, a goal, and a plan to flee if things got hairy. He'd even resumed his old habit of covering his neck, partially to avoid suspicion that he was anything other than a loyal Beldon, but also partially to adhere to the vampires' own meaning of a tie around the neck: *off limits.*

Though, given what he knew about the Harrows vampires, he doubted a social cue would stop one of them from ripping his throat out if they really wanted to.

He tried not to think about that.

When he finally reached the top of the hill, winded and sweating, he took a minute to collect himself. He straightened his cravat and smoothed his hands down his vest, then tugged on the lapels of his coat and took a deep breath. Steeling himself, he grabbed the knocker and struck the door.

It felt like a hundred years before he finally heard footsteps on the other side of the massive black doors. When they groaned open to reveal a man dressed in a gray suit, Cyrus drew himself up as tall as possible. "Good afternoon. I'd like to speak with Master Harrows. Is he in?"

The man raised a thin eyebrow. He was younger than Cyrus would expect of an Honorable Family's butler, but there was a coldness in his near-colorless eyes that hinted he'd seen more than his wrinkle-free face would suggest. "I will see if he's available. Whom shall I say is here to visit, and on what business?"

"My business is my own," Cyrus said carefully, "and I'm here on behalf of the Beldon family."

The man's eyes widened slightly, but he hid his surprise quickly by bowing his head. He stepped aside to allow Cyrus to enter the foyer, then shut the doors. "Very well, please follow me, sir."

Cyrus let out a slow breath as he followed the butler through a series of dim, spacious rooms and finally into a parlor. First victory achieved: he was in, and he hadn't been immediately turned away when he'd offered his family name.

The butler left him with a promise to return shortly—with or without Chester Harrows. Cyrus stepped toward one of the leather chairs by the parlor's narrow windows, but didn't sit. He was far too anxious to sit still; he felt like he was on thin ice occupying *any* space in this house, let alone making himself comfortable. He lingered by the chair and absently looked around the small space. A massive framed painting took up the majority of the wall opposite him, while tall, narrow windows brought in pale light behind him. Sheer white curtains filtered the afternoon daylight, and Cyrus noted there were no oil lamps nor a fireplace. On the far wall where one might have been, there were instead two towering bookcases with an oak desk between them.

Cyrus resisted his curiosity of the bookshelves; he *was* here to gather information and snoop around, but the Harrows family's books weren't part of that. Besides, he doubted there was anything useful on those shelves, unless the Harrowses were *really* confident about hiding things in plain sight.

Well, on that note, what if they were? The Vistas—or, mostly Lucien—kept their secrets safe by organizing their library with such intricacy that no one else would know how to find anything. Maybe hiding things in plain sight was the Harrows family's method.

Or maybe Cyrus just really wanted to look at the books.

It was something to do other than stand here and be nervous, at any rate. He went across the room.

Even if the books weren't directly useful, they would still reveal something about the Harrows family that Cyrus would not otherwise have known. What sorts of literature did they keep? Who had collected these, and who had read them? You could tell a lot about a place and its people by the books they kept, but most people overlooked such details and assumed them to be inconsequential. Cyrus knew better.

He folded his hands behind his back and skimmed the titles emblazoned on the leather spines. Novels, mostly, with some plays and collections of poems scattered throughout. He could tell by the titles that they were fictitious: *Last Bite. Wretched Twilight. Mircalla: A Tragedy. The Lost Poems of A. Tepes.* It amused him to see that vampire writers leaned toward the dramatic just as much as humans did.

Cyrus didn't recognize any of the books, which thrilled him; before him now was an entirely new sphere of literature—of *vampire* literature. He made a mental note to ask Lucien about some of these titles, and if he'd read them. And more importantly, if he had them in his own library.

Unable to resist, he reached for one of the volumes and started to slide it off the shelf when he heard a loud *click*, followed by a hollow thunk and then the creak of hinges. Cyrus shoved the book back in its place and scrambled away from the bookcase just as a section in its center swung open inwardly.

He had hardly registered the appearance of the hidden door when someone stepped through it, shocking him anew.

Cyrus stared at the gray-haired man. The man stared back at him. And just as Cyrus realized he knew him, the man started laughing.

"Well, well, *well*, isn't fate a funny thing?" Viktor Stokes clapped Cyrus on the shoulder as he shuffled around him. He reached for a book near the corner where the shelves met the wall and pushed it in; the passage closed with a deep grinding noise. Viktor then turned to Cyrus and chuckled again. "Now, what on *earth* are you doing here, Mr. Beldon?"

Cyrus forgot every ounce of etiquette he'd ever been taught. He stared like a gaping fish at the man and tried in vain to connect literally any of the dots. Viktor Stokes, the man who had allegedly reversed a vampire's turn, who had given Cyrus the book of Lucien's research—which he'd, for some reason, had in his possession—and set Cyrus upon this entire mad Wild vampire endeavor...was also connected to House Harrows?

What?

Cyrus finally managed to shut his mouth after a minute of staring. He remembered his manners and hurriedly offered his hand. "I—I beg your pardon, Mr. Stokes, I am...very shocked to see you here."

"Likewise, sir!" Viktor shook his hand with a bright smile. "Well, let's have a chat, shall we? Tell me how your research is going! Ah, I was very sorry to hear about your brother. And your father! Such tragedy befalls these hunter families..." His eyes clouded. "Such tragedy."

Cyrus followed him to the chairs by the windows. Viktor invited Cyrus to take a seat, and Cyrus spent a minute studying him and trying to piece all of this together. Viktor didn't *look* like a prisoner; surely if he was, he wouldn't be wandering freely through secret passageways. He looked healthy—content, even—and was dressed in clean, fine clothes. The only odd detail was his notable lack of cravat.

Cyrus filed the observation away and brought his attention back to their conversation. "I appreciate your condolences. Those losses weigh heavily on my family. Much has changed since we last spoke, that's for sure."

That was putting it lightly.

"Indeed." Viktor nodded thoughtfully. "House Vista also suffered a tragedy, did they not? Is it true—were they all lost?"

Cyrus couldn't help but feel like this was a test. He slowly shook his head. "All but one, so I hear."

Viktor grimaced. "Devastating. And the late Master Beldon was lost in that battle, yes?"

Okay, so whatever Viktor's position within House Harrows, he was tightly in the loop. Interesting.

"Yes," Cyrus said. "My father was killed in the...altercation with House Vista. I'm afraid I don't know more than that."

Which wasn't *entirely* false.

Thankfully, Viktor didn't press the issue. He nodded, rubbing his scruffy chin. "I see. Well, forgive me for dredging up difficult memories. But tell me, Mr. Beldon—"

Cyrus couldn't take it anymore. "Cyrus is fine, sir."

"Ah, then call me Viktor, my friend. No need for formalities. I won't bite your head off—I'm no Harrows!" He laughed.

Cyrus forced a smile and a soft chuckle, then jumped on the topic while he had it. "Speaking of which...Er, forgive my candor, but what *are* you doing here?"

"Oh, I work for the family." Viktor pressed his palms together. "Master Harrows has quite an interest in alchemy, though he hasn't the brain for it. Can't wrap his head around the theories—too abstract. Master Harrows is a man of practicality and hard science. He wants numbers and formulas, but alas, alchemy can only offer so much of that. It is a science with a *spirit*, my friend, and that spirit only speaks if one is willing to listen."

Alchemy, huh. So that gave Master Harrows and Emerson Beldon something in common beyond whatever agreement the letter suggested. No wonder Emerson had jumped on the chance to take over Marcus's alliance with House Harrows.

"So you're the resident alchemist," Cyrus confirmed.

"The one and only." Viktor looked rather proud of himself, and Cyrus wondered what Master Harrows offered him in return for his scientific services. "And say, the new Master Beldon is quite the accomplished alchemist himself, is he not? I've read some of his research, and it's gold standard. I'd *love* to discuss theories with him. Now *there's* a man with a mind for the spiritual science!"

Cyrus cringed, earning himself a curious look from Viktor. Cyrus tried to shrug it off. "He's...very serious about his work. He has a strong agenda, and, to be honest...I don't know if that agenda and his goals are..." He trailed off, hesitant to imply too much.

Viktor leaned closer to him. "Are...for the greater good?"

Cyrus nodded once. "I think *he* thinks he's working for the greater good, but to me, he seems to be advancing only his own fame and fortune. Not even the family's—just his."

"I see." Viktor frowned. "What's his goal, then? What does he want?"

Cyrus prayed that he could actually trust this man. It was a stupid risk to be talking about this at all, but he'd much rather get the information he needed from Viktor than from Master Harrows. He could deal with the consequences later. "What every alchemist wants," he said quietly. "Immortality."

Viktor murmured the word as it left Cyrus's mouth. "Of course." He sighed, suddenly looking exhausted. With a slight grunt, he pushed to his feet. "If you can spare a moment, I'd like to show you something. Come with me."

Cyrus stood, but glanced nervously at the door. "Er...I asked for an audience with Master Harrows. If he comes looking for me..."

"He'll assume you changed your mind, as many do, and he'll return to whatever he was doing." Viktor waved a hand and went back to the bookshelves. "Come now, before he decides to take up the business he has with me."

Cyrus sent a silent apology to Lucien for taking yet another risk, and then followed Viktor through the passageway behind the bookcase.

Unlike the hidden passage in the Vista library, this one *wasn't* pitch dark; small candles enclosed in little niches behind iron lattices followed the stairs' descent, throwing shadows but creating just enough light that Cyrus didn't fear he'd miss a step and break his neck. Viktor moved swiftly down the steps and nimbly turned each tight corner through the narrow passage; Cyrus suspected he hardly needed the light to find his way through what was clearly a very familiar space.

Cyrus wondered about that. Why not just walk freely through the halls, if he worked for the family and was obviously respected by them? Was he encouraged to stay out of sight like a servant? But wouldn't an alchemist, especially given Master Harrows's interest in the science, enjoy a place of honor in the family?

Additionally, if Viktor lived here, why did he also have that big dark house out in the country?

This was all very curious.

Yet Cyrus kept his questions to himself and silently followed Viktor's lead. At last they came to a plain door at the end of a narrow corridor, and Viktor grabbed a key from his belt to unlock it. He hummed to himself as he pushed through. Cyrus hesitantly stepped into the room.

Before him sprawled a massive laboratory illuminated to near-daylight with a multitude of oil lamps, candelabras, and a giant chandelier overhead. A stone hearth shaped like a fish's mouth housed a roaring blaze that chased off the cellar's chill. Several pots of bubbling and steaming liquids hung on iron hooks over the fire, and the long wooden tables placed throughout the room displayed colorful substances in oddly-shaped glass containers. A sharp metallic smell permeated the air.

"Welcome to my corner of House Harrows," Viktor said with a proud smile. He made his way around smaller tables and stacks of crates, beckoning Cyrus to follow. Pausing at one of the long worktables, he waved Cyrus to his side. Cyrus went, confused; Viktor had brought him to the only empty table in this entire room.

Before he could ask, Viktor lifted the tabletop up, revealing a deep compartment packed with books and papers. "A contraption of my own invention, this is." He grinned at Cyrus's amazed expression. "Fireproof, waterproof, and accessible only with a key forged specifically for this lock. A key which never leaves my person, mind you, and even if it did, there's a lot of things in this room that have locks. Would take someone all day to figure out where this one fits, and by then I'd likely have noticed it was gone."

Unless you're dead, Cyrus thought glumly.

"And in here..." Viktor tapped the cover of one of the books. "All my notes from all my years as an alchemist. Some, even, from my years as a hunter."

That raised Cyrus's eyebrows. "You were a hunter? From which family?"

"Well." Viktor shrugged. "It depends on who you ask. I like to say I was from the Barlow family, as they were the closest thing to *family* I ever got, but they do not like being reminded of that."

Cyrus could sympathize with that, at least. But this, of course, also raised more questions. Namely, if Viktor had been raised by the Barlow family, why didn't he adopt the surname? Did they force him to drop it, or did he choose to? And why had Cyrus never heard of this? The families were secretive, yes, but the gossip was ruthless. Even if it had happened several decades ago, he was surprised the situation hadn't been turned into a cautionary tale.

He was relieved, for Viktor's sake, that it hadn't. No need to rub salt in the wound.

"Water under the bridge," Viktor assured him. "Anyhow, this is my trove. Anything and everything I work on—including the work Master Harrows asks of me—is here."

Cyrus eyed him skeptically. "Why are you showing me this?"

And what the hell was the catch?

Viktor slowly turned to face Cyrus, and though he kept his head ducked, his eyes lifted to meet Cyrus's gaze. There was a fire there that Cyrus hadn't seen before, something well-hidden, buried beneath decades of reluctant yet necessary obedience.

Cyrus recognized that quiet rage as his own.

"Because, Cyrus Beldon," Viktor said, "I believe there are those whose power has gone to their heads. And I believe those who try to fly too high deserve a reminder of why we were not built with wings."

"Viktor." Cyrus lowered his voice. "What did Master Harrows ask of you?"

Viktor opened the book on the top of the pile, swiped up a page, and handed it to Cyrus. A single sentence in thick black ink stretched diagonally across the paper.

Find us our eternal life.

Of course. It was what all alchemists sought. But why would a vampire—namely an Honorable One—need immortality if they already had it?

"I know what you're thinking," Viktor said, "and it was precisely my question. But what Master Harrows refers to here is not immortality, but *invincibility*."

Cyrus looked up at him. "Invincibility to *what*? He's already immortal, and has more strengths than the average human can even imagine. How is that not enough?"

"Indeed, how?" Viktor nodded. "See, vampires may have the *ability* to live forever, but very often they do not. They cannot catch illness or grow old like we do, nor are they harmed by wounds that would be fatal to humans. But they *can* die by a trained hand, and in this city, they very often do. Master Harrows wishes to change that."

Cyrus blinked. "By alchemically making vampires resistant to silver?"

"Silver, yes, and everything else as well." Viktor eyed the page in Cyrus's hand. "He wants his kin to be impossible to kill, even by a hunter's expertise."

Cyrus spun this information in his mind, trying to find a way to thread it with the rest of the puzzle. He let the paper fall back into the table's compartment. "So Master Harrows wants vampires to be invincible. And Emerson Beldon wants to achieve vampire-like longevity. Of course they're working together."

"Oh, their alchemical interests are similar, certainly," Viktor said. "In an ironic way, too: one can't have immortal hunters and invincible vampires. The fight would go on forever, neither ever winning. I don't know if Master Beldon knows about Master Harrows's alchemical goal. Their negotiations are much less... metaphysical."

Cyrus frowned. "What do you mean?"

Viktor's eyes darted away and he busied himself with the contents of the table, idly shifting things around. "I admit I can't give you many details, as what I've heard has been mere snippets of a much larger circumstance. But what I know is condemning enough. Are you sure you wish to know?"

"Yes." Cyrus tried to catch his gaze. "Viktor, please. What do you know? What is my uncle planning?"

Viktor still wouldn't meet his eyes. "It could spell ruin for the Beldons," he whispered.

Cyrus stepped closer to him until he finally looked up. "*Good.*"

Viktor's eyes widened, and Cyrus saw the understanding dawn on him. "Ah. I see. I see..." He took off his glasses and rubbed his eyes, then pulled a handkerchief from his pocket and set to work cleaning each lens. "Do you know of the feud from the years before the Century Truce?"

"The one between Harrows and Attcourt?" Really, this again? "Yes, and I know that House Harrows still holds a grudge."

"Very much so." Viktor continued cleaning his glasses. "Each master of House Harrows since that bloody year has made sure the next generation will not forget. That rage is alive and well in Chester Harrows's heart, and with a power-hungry, like-minded alchemist at the helm of the Beldon family, he has finally found the tool he's been lacking."

Cyrus didn't like where this was going. "So he's using Emerson to further his own revenge on House Attcourt? How?"

"Well...it would rather break the Century Truce if Master Harrows personally attacked House Attcourt and made a grab for that lost chunk of territory. But no one bats an eye if the Beldon family kills a vampire now and then, even an Honorable One, especially if that vampire is out of control and harming civilians. Certain circumstances call for the extreme, and...if one has the means to alchemically fabricate such circumstances..." He grimaced.

Oh.

Oh, no.

Everything clicked together in Cyrus's head, and he staggered back a step. "Holy shit."

There it was: the answer to that last confounding question of how born vampires turned Wild. Master Harrows must have found a way to corrupt their biology through alchemical means—which Viktor had likely conjured for him. What was it, then? A poison? Would the solution that Cyrus and Lucien had theorized—a significant dosage of vampire blood—still be able to reverse it, or was every Wild vampire a lost cause?

And if Master Harrows's ultimate plan was to use Wild vampires to pick off members of the Attcourt family, then why was Arthur turned? As an experiment? And what about Leigh Harrows?

And furthermore, *why*? What did House Harrows gain from a bit of land they hadn't controlled in centuries? And what did Emerson get from helping them? If Master Harrows was so dead-set on that territory that he'd go to these lengths to get it back, it wasn't as though he'd turn around and share it with the Beldons, of all people. Emerson was a fool if he was convinced that was the case.

Oh—But it wasn't Emerson who had started these negotiations. It was Marcus. And what had Marcus Beldon wanted, for as long as Cyrus could remember? Fame. A legacy. Unshakeable power over Chestervale—*and* the rest of the province. So what if it wasn't physical territory that Master Harrows had promised Marcus, but *influence* there? Jurisdiction to hunt rogue vampires even outside of the city, giving the Beldons a one-up on the other hunter families.

And if Master Harrows was the one determining who the Beldons killed, he could keep his own hands clean while targeting his enemies one by one.

Emerson might be primarily focused on his quest for immortality, but if allying with House Harrows brought him closer to that information, he was still Beldon enough to jump at the chance to seize more power and eliminate a few Honorable Ones along the way.

A perfect circle of vengeance.

Cyrus pressed his fists to his forehead and hissed, "*Fuck.*"

Viktor chuckled, but the sound was humorless. "I don't know how any of this will come to fruition, Cyrus, but I advise you to be careful with this information. Much of it is piecemeal, and the conclusions I have drawn—though potentially logical—are, in fact, guesswork. We may both be seeing connections we merely wish to see, while the truth could be very different."

Cyrus dragged his hands through his hair. No, it wasn't piecemeal, not anymore. Here it was: the completed puzzle. Cyrus still had a million questions about each of these pieces, but they were together. And Cyrus and Lucien were tangled at the center.

Cyrus had no idea how to go about stopping any of this.

He let out a slow breath, collecting himself. He just needed to think it all out, then present it to Lucien and let him pick it apart. Then, somehow, they could weave a plan.

But...gods, this scheme was centuries in the making. Was it even worth it to try?

No, of course it was. Cyrus couldn't start thinking like that. A revelation like this *could* rattle the Beldons' legacy and ruin their image—at least in the eyes of the other hunter families. Marcus and Emerson had crossed lines that were, by society's standards, unforgivable. That had to mean something, right?

Cyrus brought his attention back to Viktor. "Thank you for telling me this. I don't know what will happen in the coming days, but for your safety and for mine, I was never here. Do you understand?"

Viktor nodded.

"I have two more questions for you." Cyrus pushed his hair back off his forehead. It was suddenly uncomfortably hot in this room. "Did you really reverse a vampiric turn?"

Viktor went to reply, then hesitated and closed his mouth. He rubbed his chin. "No. I reversed a Wild turn."

Cyrus's mouth fell open. "*How?*"

"Don't you remember?" He gave a sad smile. "I don't know. I managed to pull it off exactly once, and then never again. I dearly hoped that you would continue where I had left off, but..."

His disappointment was palpable. Cyrus wanted to sink into the floor.

"I tried," he said, a touch defensively. "I found the author of those notes and we have a reasonable hypothesis. Testing it will be tricky, but I'm not about to give up." He took a deep breath. "I will find a way to cure Wild turns, but right now, I need to try to halt whatever my family is plotting with House Harrows. My second question for you is this: Do you still have contact with anyone in the Barlow family?"

Viktor winced. "Yes...somewhat. I occasionally exchange letters with Quincy Barlow, but our communication is very much a secret. It's better if Master Barlow doesn't know of an open connection."

Cyrus considered the chest full of books and records, and his gaze found the order from Master Harrows. By itself, it was too vague to prove anything, but there had to be some written proof of what Master Harrows really wanted, *and* what he and Emerson were—

Oh! The letter! But was *that* enough, without any details?

"What are you thinking, my boy?" Viktor murmured.

"We can't keep this to ourselves," Cyrus said. "Neither of us can go personally to the hunter families, but..." He met Viktor's eyes. "If I could bring you evidence of Harrows's and Beldon's plan, could you take it to the hunter families? Nothing spreads like wildfire faster than a scandal, and this is more than that. This is betrayal."

Viktor narrowed his eyes. "And is what you wish to do not also *betrayal*, Mr. Beldon?"

Cyrus tipped his chin up. "I renounce my position in the Beldon family. They have done nothing to deserve my loyalty. I owe it to someone I lost to expose the family for what it is: a rotten pit of greed and lies."

Something changed in Viktor's eyes, though Cyrus couldn't quite name it. His brows pinched together, but he no longer looked skeptical. Only sort of...sad. "Oh, my friend, I fear we are more alike than we ought to be. You remind me of myself, and that frightens me."

Cyrus didn't see how that was his problem. "This isn't about you and me. It's bigger. We both know how powerful and influential the hunter families are. How much longer can this shaky truce really last when they're all getting bored of the power they already have? My father all but declared war when he attacked House Vista, and I have no idea how my uncle has managed to hold the other Families at bay, but something is going to give soon. If this whole damned city is going to collapse, I want to make sure the Beldons can't get back up."

Viktor started to shake his head, but Cyrus didn't think it was a rejection of his words. More like an acknowledgment of how insane this was. Cyrus agreed with that, at least.

"What would you have me do?" Viktor whispered.

"Meet me in the city," Cyrus said. "Tomorrow, at dawn. You know that little park on the corner of Magnolia and East? The one with the pond and the big fountain?"

Viktor nodded.

"I'll be there. Don't be alarmed if there's someone with me. It *won't* be another Beldon," he added hastily when Viktor looked nervous. "I'll be there with the evidence I have, as well as a written account of everything I know combined with what you've just told me. Bring anything from your notes that can be tied in—anything to do with Harrows's vengeance against House Attcourt, about his work regarding Wild vampires, and his negotiations with Marcus and Emerson. I'll put it all together, and then I need you to get it to your contact in the Barlow family. Can you do that?"

Several heartbeats ticked by. Cyrus never took his eyes off of Viktor. He knew he was taking a huge chance—his life and Lucien's life in his hands—and if this went wrong, if Viktor bailed or if he turned out to be a traitor, Cyrus might as well have just dug two graves.

But there was something about Viktor—something serendipitous that Cyrus couldn't explain. Cyrus had found him on the slightest of whims, and now here he was again by pure chance. Cyrus didn't really believe in fate, but he did believe that something—a sense or an energy that he couldn't name—had placed this chance in front of him. He'd be a fool not to take it.

Finally Viktor looked up and straightened to his full height. He offered his hand, and when Cyrus took it, he shook firmly. A small smile softened his weathered face. "I can. I will do everything in my power to make this known. They will listen."

Cyrus let out the breath he'd been holding. "*Thank you.* Let's bring the Beldons to their knees."

Chapter THIRTY

CYRUS HAD ANTICIPATED A GRUMPY VAMPIRE WHEN HE returned to the Vista manor, but he had not expected Lucien to be the first thing he saw when he stepped through the doors.

So much for having an excuse prepared. He'd spent the ride back from House Harrows reviewing everything Viktor had told him, and he'd planned to consider what he'd say to Lucien while he made his way through the house to find him. But here he was, leaning against the nearest column with his arms crossed and his shoulders tensed, watching the doors.

Judging by the anger in his eyes, he'd been standing there a while.

Cyrus shut the door behind him and sighed. "What, do I have a curfew?"

Lucien didn't say anything.

Ah. It was going to be like that, was it? Cyrus crossed his arms and leaned back against the doors. "I'm not a child. And unless I've *vastly* misunderstood the parameters of our relationship, I'm not your ward. You can be concerned for my safety, but do you really need to glower like a hawk?"

Lucien continued to glare.

Cyrus swallowed the anger that surged up inside him. He took two small steps toward Lucien and spread his hands. "If you have something to say to me, Lucien, for gods' sakes just say it."

Finally Lucien pushed off the column and approached Cyrus,

but stopped with a few feet still between them. His guard didn't fall. If Cyrus wasn't quite so good at reading the subtleties in people's expressions, he wouldn't be able to detect Lucien's anger at all, but he could *feel* it.

It seemed rather disproportionate to the situation.

Cyrus threw up his hands. "What do you want me to say? I'm sorry? For making my own decisions and taking a situation into my own hands? Do I need your fucking permission to step outside these walls? Fucking hell, it's like I never left home!"

A muscle twitched in Lucien's jaw. "Where were you?" His voice was dangerously low, forcefully calm.

But now he'd pissed Cyrus off, and if Lucien was angry, Cyrus wanted to see it. "Are you keeping tabs on me now?"

"Just answer the fucking question!" Lucien let out a frustrated growl and wrung his hands. "Why does everything have to be a fight with you? Where were you? Because I *know* you didn't just go for a little stroll through the woods. You were gone for almost two hours."

"And I didn't die, did I!" Cyrus snapped.

"Tell me," Lucien bit out, "where you were."

For once, it was Cyrus deploying the *stupid question* look. "Where do you *think* I was, Lucien?"

All at once, Lucien was in front of him. Cyrus reflexively flinched. Lucien froze and then fell back a few steps. He let out a slow breath, and as his anger calmed, Cyrus saw what was really behind that glare.

Fear.

Cyrus loosened the tension in his shoulders. "Lucien, I—"

"Tell me you didn't go to House Harrows," Lucien whispered.

His hesitation was all the answer Lucien needed.

Lucien closed his eyes and let out another sigh. "*Fuck*, Cyrus."

"What did you expect me to do?" Cyrus snapped. "Wait around here and wander aimlessly while you try to solve everything yourself? This isn't just about you and your family, and it's not even just about Wild vampires anymore. This mess surrounds both of us, and we both know that I have resources that you don't. You said it yourself that you blew your chances with House Harrows, so I took mine. And, by the way, thanks for asking, I learned enough to put the pieces together."

Lucien blinked, anger momentarily forgotten. "What?"

"Uh-huh." Cyrus lifted his chin. "I know what's going on, and I have a plan. But I need your help to make sure I'm not missing anything. So are you going to let me tell you, or would you like to finish your tantrum?"

Lucien turned his head, scowling, then sighed again and took a step back from Cyrus. "I'm sorry. Spirits, Cyrus, I'm sorry. I just..."

Cyrus inched closer to him and hesitantly extended a hand. "Hey."

Lucien looked up, but didn't quite meet his eyes.

"I forgive you, but don't ever do that again." Cyrus lightly touched Lucien's arm. "I can't make you stop worrying about me, and gods know nothing will make me stop worrying about you, but if you can't trust me, Lucien, then..." He trailed off with a shrug.

"I do." Lucien touched his cheek. "I do trust you, and I'm sorry."

"You don't," Cyrus countered, calmly this time, "when you get *that* upset that I left for a couple hours."

"It's not that you left," Lucien murmured. "It's that you lied to me."

All right, that was fair. Cyrus took his hand and squeezed it. "I'm sorry I lied. But I knew you'd try to stop me if I'd told you where I was actually going."

"Of course I would have!" Lucien gently pulled him closer and nuzzled his hair. "If that had gone badly, Cyrus... I wouldn't have known where you were. I wouldn't have been able to help you."

Oh. There was the fear. And knowing the root of it, it no longer seemed disproportionate. Cyrus slipped his arms around Lucien and held him tight. "I'm sorry."

"You could have told me," Lucien murmured. "You're right, I

wouldn't have liked it, but I know I wouldn't have been able to stop you, stubborn as you are." He drew back a little and flickered a smile. "You know that you can come and go from here as you please, Cyrus. You don't have to tell me your every move. This isn't your prison, and you're certainly not my ward." He stroked his thumb across Cyrus's cheek. "I do trust you. Just...don't lie to me again, okay?"

Cyrus turned his face to kiss Lucien's wrist. "I promise."

"Thank you." He kissed Cyrus—just once, not enough—and then drew back and intertwined their hands. "So, tell me what you found in that dreadful castle."

CYRUS WAS VIBRATING, partially from exhaustion but mostly from the truly unhealthy amount of coffee he'd drunk in the past six hours. He didn't even know what wee hour of the morning it was, but he and Lucien had been huddled over the dining room table for the entire night and their labors were not about to stop now.

"Okay," Lucien said, confidently, for the hundredth time. "Is this everything now? Because the last time we thought it was, we remembered more."

Cyrus gazed longingly at the cushioned chair beside him, but he knew if he sat down he wouldn't get back up. His back hurt and his brain hurt and his eyes felt like rocks in his skull and he didn't even really care about the hurricane of papers on the table anymore. In fact, he rather resented this heap of evidence for keeping him from Lucien's delightfully soft bed. He dragged his gaze up to Lucien, intending to suggest once again that they should call it a night, and found Lucien looking at him expectantly.

Ah shit, had he asked him something? "What?"

At least Lucien looked sympathetic. "I know, you're exhausted.

I am, too. But if we're meeting this Viktor Stokes fellow at dawn—"

Cyrus groaned. Dawn was probably in twenty minutes.

"—then we need to be sure *everything* is here." Lucien straightened and stretched his back with a groan. "Let's go over it one more time."

"And then we can go to bed?" Cyrus grumbled.

"If there's time." Lucien dragged a hand down his face. "Okay. Three hundred years ago, right before the Century Truce was enacted, House Harrows lost part of their territory to House Attcourt." He cleared off the map of the region he'd spread out on the table, then placed two cards—one labeled HARROWS and one labeled ATTCOURT—next to each other. "The Century Truce happens, snatching away any chance at vengeance that House Harrows could have taken. The Harrows family bides its time for a few centuries, then Chester Harrows decides he wants his territory back."

Lucien placed a card labeled CHESTER beside the family name. Then he grabbed three more—LEIGH, LUCIEN, VIKTOR STOKES—and arranged them around the HARROWS card. "Chester Harrows tasks his alchemist with finding a way to make vampires invincible to human attacks. Leigh Harrows and I begin researching Wild vampires. Viktor Stokes allegedly reverses a Wild turn, and allegedly creates a way to artificially turn a vampire Wild."

"Allegedly?" Cyrus cut in. "He told me he did it."

"Then I hope he brings evidence of it," Lucien said. He pushed his hair back from his face. A card labeled BELDON joined the others on the map. "Marcus Beldon begins negotiations with Chester Harrows. We still don't know what Marcus was offered—"

"Jurisdiction outside the city," Cyrus said.

"That's our *theory*, but we have no way to prove it without Viktor's evidence," Lucien said. "But whatever it was, clearly it was a good deal for him and him alone, prompting him to keep it a secret from everyone else. But then..." He slapped a card labeled

ARTHUR onto the table, and moved LEIGH closer to it. "His son is killed and turned Wild. You begin researching Wild vampires. You find Mr. Stokes, you find my notes, you find me." Lucien moved a CYRUS card onto the map and moved his own beside it, separating them from Leigh's card. "We start looking into a way to reverse a Wild turn, but then..."

"Marcus murders your family," Cyrus muttered, saving Lucien from having to say it.

He grimaced. "And Marcus dies, and Emerson becomes Master Beldon." He flicked Marcus's card to the side and replaced it with EMERSON, moving it close to CHESTER. "Emerson resumes Marcus's negotiations with— Oh."

Cyrus raised his eyebrows. "What?"

Lucien stared at the table, suddenly breathing hard. He clenched his jaw, nose flaring, then dropped into a chair.

Cyrus had never seen him look so exhausted.

"I know why Marcus went after my family," he whispered.

Oh. Cyrus was ashamed to realize that he'd forgotten they still didn't know that—not for sure, anyway. Emerson had implied that he'd framed the Vistas for Arthur's murder, but that was a weak case.

"He was never going to attack House Harrows." Lucien's eyes were fixed, unblinking, on the map of names. "They were allies. Of course Marcus wouldn't turn on them. But he'd appear weak if he did nothing after his heir was so blatantly murdered, so he had to go after *someone*, and I had just enough involvement..."

His voice broke, and his composure along with it. His face crumpled and he slumped forward, dropping his head into his hands. He clawed his fingers through his hair, gripping it by the fistful. "*Fuck*, it's all my fault."

Cyrus went around the table and placed his hand on Lucien's back. "No, it's not."

"*They're gone because of me*," Lucien hissed. "Because of *my* work and *my* stupid research." His shoulders shook under Cyrus's touch.

"They're gone because of Marcus fucking Beldon," Cyrus snapped, not unkindly. He sank to his knees and gripped Lucien's shoulders, forcing him to look at him. "Listen to me." He reached up and tucked Lucien's hair back, then cupped his tear-streaked cheek in his hand. "Lucien. Blame anyone else—Marcus, Emerson, the entire damn Harrows family, hell, even me—but do not blame yourself. You were working to *help* your family. You did not choose to put them in danger. What Marcus did was his own damning choice, and there was not a thing you could have done differently to change that."

He studied Lucien's eyes, looking past the bleary exhaustion and raw sadness to find the fiery passion that he knew was there. It was faint—he was so tired; both of them were so tired—but it still burned. Stubbornly, defiantly.

"You can't lose hope now," Cyrus murmured. He slid his hand down to Lucien's chest, pressing over his heart—over the spot where his life had nearly drained out of him. "We're so *close*, Lucien. We know what's going on, and we know who's behind all of the pain that both of us have endured. Don't pin that atrocity on yourself when there are those who actually have Vista blood on their hands."

Lucien just looked at him, tears silently running down his face. Each slow blink released a fresh wave. His lips moved in the shape of Cyrus's name, but his voice didn't follow. Cyrus tipped his head forward and kissed Lucien's forehead, then rose to his feet.

He turned to the table, keeping one hand on Lucien's shoulder. "Marcus attacks your family and dies. Emerson becomes Master Beldon and resumes negotiations with Master Harrows—who very well might owe him a favor now that Marcus has turned his vengeance away from House Harrows. We leave the city. Emerson steals your notes and—presumably—uses them to try to find the secret to immortality so he can achieve it himself.

"Meanwhile, Chester Harrows is experimenting with alchemy and turns Leigh into a Wild vampire." Cyrus grimaced. "Are we safe to guess that...it was Viktor's work that...?"

Lucien shrugged. He was facing the table, but his eyes were unfocused.

Cyrus squeezed his shoulder and continued. "So far, no one has made a move against House Attcourt—not that we know of, anyway. Viktor, Harrows, and Emerson are playing with alchemy, and Emerson and Harrows both want more power and each wants the other to not be able to kill him, but both of them are fine with killing other vampires if it gets them the power they want."

Cyrus moved the card labeled EMERSON and the card labeled CHESTER beside each other. "That's our focus: the Beldons are playing both sides, betraying the other hunter families in order to gain power alongside House Harrows, whom they are also very likely to betray once Emerson is confident that he can't be killed by the Honorable Families. One way or another, the Century Truce is shattered. And everyone in this city—possibly beyond it—could become a victim of those alchemical experiments. Is *that* everything?"

Lucien was quiet for several minutes, and Cyrus feared he'd gone catatonic. But then he nodded and stood, a little unsteadily. "The Beldons have broken the Century Truce. That's our accusation. Now let's hope Mr. Stokes has evidence of the experiments that took place within House Harrows to back up our claim. That's everything."

"Great." Cyrus leaned against Lucien. "Bed?"

Lucien turned his head, and Cyrus followed his gaze to the clock on the fireplace mantel. "It's after five already. It'll be dawn soon, and we still need to get up to the High District."

Cyrus groaned and slumped down into the chair Lucien had just vacated. His eyes slid shut almost immediately, but though his head swooped with drowsiness, the combination of caffeine and anticipation kept him clinging to consciousness. He heard Lucien gather up all the papers and notes, and then something lightly tapped his head.

He looked up, squinting. Lucien was holding an envelope toward him. "What?"

"It's all right here. Our half of the puzzle." Lucien set the envelope in front of Cyrus. "Are you ready for this?"

Yes, he thought instantly. Then, *Gods no*. He itched to shove the Beldons off their pedestal, yet despite everything, the sight of that crisp envelope containing his family's damnation made his stomach turn.

He knew this was the right choice, and he knew there was no one better suited to soil the Beldons' fame than himself and Lucien. But at the same time, part of him still wished it didn't have to be him. For his siblings' sakes, mostly. Well, for Poppy's sake.

Well. She wasn't exactly his friend or ally anymore, was she?

"I don't know," he replied to Lucien's question. "But it has to be done."

Lucien nodded. "It has to be done."

Cyrus sighed and slid the envelope toward Lucien, but the vampire frowned.

"What are you doing?"

"What? Giving it back to you. I thought you were just—"

"Cyrus, you dug all this up. You put the pieces together. This is *your* vengeance." Lucien slid the envelope back to him. "Our goal is the same, but your family's ruin should come from your hands. Not only to avenge your mother and everyone else hurt by that family, but to avenge *yourself*. Take it."

He was right, and Cyrus agreed with him, but he also felt like he didn't deserve to take this credit. It had been a joint effort, after all, and without Lucien's help, he wouldn't have gotten anywhere close to these conclusions.

"Cyrus." Lucien touched his chin. "This is your victory. Be proud of it."

That, Cyrus couldn't do. Not yet—not until he *knew* it was a victory, and even then...well, two decades of being told he was incompetent were hard to shake off. But he must have learned something in these months with Lucien, because he claimed the envelope anyway.

Lucien smiled and took Cyrus's hand, pulling him to his feet.

"Come on, then. The sooner we meet Mr. Stokes, the sooner we can get some sleep."

VIKTOR WAS PRECISELY where Cyrus had told him to be. He waited on a bench along the cobbled wall that surrounded the little park, hands folded on his knees. Pale, foggy dawn blanketed the city, just dim enough to allow the streetlamps to stay awake a little longer. Viktor sat within the golden pool of one lamp, but his face was shadowed by his top hat. He looked up at once when Cyrus drew near, and when his eyes darted to Lucien, he abruptly stood.

"Master Vista!" Viktor bowed. "Forgive my surprise! Mr. Beldon informed me that he would bring company, but I did not expect... Ah, you have my deepest condolences, sir. I was very sorry to hear about your family."

Lucien bowed his head politely. "I appreciate it, sir. But please, I come to this meeting as a friend. Cyrus has assured me that you are trustworthy, and for that I am grateful. There seems to be too little honesty going around these days." He offered his hand. "I'm pleased to meet you, Mr. Stokes."

Viktor shook Lucien's hand, then Cyrus's. "Yes, yes, likewise. And good morning to you, Mr. Beldon. Er...you have it, yes?"

Right to business, then. Cyrus presented the envelope, unable to mask the trembling of his hands. He hoped Viktor didn't notice. "This is everything we know. I trust you brought your own evidence?"

"Indeed." Viktor opened his coat and brought out a folded bundle of parchment tied snugly with twine. "Every experiment Master Harrows demanded of me, as well as a number of letters between the late Master Beldon and Master Harrows. I believe we have everything, then."

Cyrus nodded. "I hope it's enough."

"Will you call a gathering?" Lucien asked Viktor.

Viktor's eyes widened. "Oh, dear, no. I have no such authority. I imagine the families may, once all this gets out. My contacts may be few, but I trust their integrity. They will not let this be swept under the rug. I'm happy to light the spark, but my Barlow friend can fan the flames."

"Barlow, eh?" Lucien cocked his head. "They're perhaps the only humans in this city less forgiving than the Beldons. I wouldn't have chosen a better family to drag Emerson Beldon off his bloody stage."

Viktor chuckled softly. "One must tread carefully with all of them, Master Vista. Of course, you'd know that well, being an Honorable One."

"All too well," Lucien murmured. He cast a smirk at Cyrus and nudged him with his elbow. "This particular Beldon especially."

Cyrus scowled as Viktor guffawed. "Ah, he's a stubborn one, that's for sure!" But his eyes were kind when he turned to Cyrus. "You are headstrong, my boy, but don't think that's a bad thing. To hell with Emerson and Marcus and their ilk. This city needs more Beldons like *you*."

Cyrus's breath caught.

"I couldn't agree more," Lucien said softly.

Cyrus lost his words. He swallowed hard and ducked his head, sliding his hands into his pockets. "Yeah, well...I'm trying." Warmth crept up the back of his neck. He glanced at Viktor and scrambled for a change of subject. "Anyway, we've no time to waste, and it's been a long night. Viktor, thank you again. I owe you more than I could ever repay."

"No, no." Viktor grasped Cyrus's hand between weathered palms. "You owe me nothing. We will *all* benefit from the fallout of these truths, Mr. Beldon. This is not a favor to be repaid, but a victory to share."

There was that word again. *Victory*. Cyrus had to appreciate the irony of it being spoken now by someone whose name doubled as the word for the bringer of said victory. If the universe or the gods or whatever was out there had a sense of humor, Cyrus hoped they directed it in his favor. Let them all be victors.

"Spirits willing, we will," Lucien replied to Viktor.

"Indeed." Viktor shook Cyrus's hand, then Lucien's.

"Good luck," Cyrus said. "If you need to contact me again, come to the Vista manor. *Don't* send a letter. Come in person, and knock twice."

He saw a flicker of suspicion—no, more like intrigue—pass over Viktor's face, but a nod cleared it away. "I expect we'll all know when this information spreads. Take care, Mr. Beldon. Master Vista." He tipped his hat, then tucked the envelope from Cyrus into his coat along with his own papers, and then shuffled away toward East Boulevard.

Cyrus released the breath he'd been holding all night. It was out of his hands now, and all that was left to do was wait.

Chapter THIRTY ONE

A DAY PASSED. CYRUS AND LUCIEN HEARD NOTHING. Cyrus checked the newspapers obsessively, combing through every page of the morning issue in search of any mention of the Beldons. He found nothing.

Sure, it had barely been twenty-four hours since he'd passed his evidence to Viktor, but journalists couldn't get enough of this type of thing. He'd expected it to explode. He thought he'd wake up to the whole city talking about it.

But no. Not yet.

He was on his third read-through of the morning papers when Lucien finally took them away from him. "The words didn't change since the last time you read them." He neatly folded the crinkled leaves. "We'll know when something happens, Cyrus."

And Cyrus knew that, but he also needed to know the *minute* something changed. What else was he supposed to do? Sit here and be anxious? He knew he absolutely could not focus on a book or even a conversation, so instead of wearing a rut in Lucien's floor with his restless pacing, he decided to wander.

His feet brought him to the library. He hadn't been trying to go there—there were a lot of other corners of this manor that he wanted to explore—but he unconsciously drifted toward the oak doors no matter which floor he chose.

Apparently House Vista had something to show him.

"Okay, what is it?" Cyrus grabbed a candle from one of the

niches in the hallway and then entered the library on the fourth floor, glancing around to get his bearings. The space seemed emptier than the lower levels of the library; the stacks were farther apart, many of them with empty or half-full shelves. The books stored on them were falling apart; some were no more than bundles of yellowed paper wrapped in fraying twine. Cyrus was overcome with a desire to fix them all up. Why had all these books been left up here to rot? When was the last time someone went looking for one of them?

Cyrus dipped down one of the aisles and gingerly lifted the cover of one of the more intact volumes. A gritty coating of dust caked the leather; Cyrus moved it as slowly as possible so as to avoid a noseful of it. He peeked at the faded text on the title page, only to realize it was in a different language. He grumbled and carefully set the book back in its place.

He turned around, scanning the other shelves for another book that wouldn't break if he touched it, but then froze in his tracks when his gaze landed on a portrait on the wall at the end of the aisle.

It was dusty, faded, and half covered with a tattered sheet, but Cyrus would recognize those vivid eyes anywhere.

Why the fuck was there a portrait of Julius Beldon in the Vista family's library?

Cyrus approached the picture, positive that his eyes must be playing tricks on him. He brought the light as close as he dared to the dusty painting, stepping to one side and then the other as if the image would change from a different angle. Julius's eyes seemed to follow him, though his gaze wasn't quite so harsh in this depiction as in the portrait at home. He wasn't proudly boasting his prowess as a hunter in this picture; he was relaxed, leaning one shoulder against a doorframe while a book balanced in his hand. His head was tilted down but his eyes pointed straight ahead, as if he'd glanced up at an interruption to his reading.

And there was something about his eyes. They were bright and

intense in the painting back home, but here they were sort of...
glowing? Glinting? No, *reflective*, almost like—

Cyrus blinked and laughed at himself. No, there was no way. It
must be just a quirk of the artist's style, the way they toyed with
light, or something like that. It must be, because otherwise it
implied—

"Now how did you find your way up here?"

Cyrus practically jumped out of his skin at the sudden voice.
He spun around and found Lucien approaching him, shadowed by
the bookcases on either side of him. His eyes reflected the light
from the candle Cyrus carried.

Cyrus glanced at the painting of Julius, then back at Lucien.
"Why is this here? And why does—Why are his eyes...like that?"

Lucien went to Cyrus's side and considered the painting.
"Spirits, it's been a long time since I've seen this. I thought my
father would have destroyed it ages ago."

"Lucien." Cyrus couldn't keep a tremble out of his voice.
"Why is this here?"

It could be a very mundane answer, of course. Maybe a long-
ago Vista had stolen it from the Beldons as some sort of prank and
it had been rotting here ever since. But something told Cyrus that
the answer was more complicated than that.

And something told him he wouldn't like it.

"Julius Beldon..." Lucien sighed and met Cyrus's eyes. "Well,
we both know that your family loves to keep secrets. So does mine."

"What do you mean?" Cyrus's hands shook, making the
candle's flame flicker. "What does *this* mean?"

Lucien set his hand on Cyrus's shoulder and turned his
attention to the painting. "He wasn't a vampire. Let me first clarify
that, because I know that's what you're thinking. But he was a
dhampir."

An incredulous laugh bubbled out of Cyrus. "N-No. He can't
be. He—"

"No, think about it." Lucien held up a finger. "Many
dhampirs, unfortunately, choose to reject their vampire side and

become hunters. Caught between two worlds—not human enough, and not vampire enough—dhampirs often feel like they have no place at all, and this breeds resentment toward their vampire parent. With almost all of the traits that make vampires powerful, a dhampir is essentially predisposed to vampire hunting —and they're better at it than the average human hunter. Someone with those skills would easily make a name for themself in a time when crying 'vampire' was everyone's solution for getting rid of people they didn't like."

Cyrus nodded along with Lucien's explanation. Okay, so Julius Beldon being a dhampir and then becoming one of the most famous hunters in history wasn't *entirely* hypocritical. But it still didn't answer the biggest question.

"Lucien." Cyrus stared at the painting. "Was he...of House Vista?"

"Yes," Lucien said quietly. When Cyrus turned to him, alarmed, he added, "Not by birth! Sorry, I should have said that sooner. He was dropped on the doorstep of this house as an infant with no hint as to who his parents were. The Vistas raised him as their ward, and as far as any of the other Honorable Families knew, he was one of us. But...then he found out the truth." Lucien grimaced and turned his head down.

"He killed the man who was Master Vista at the time," he said softly. "Tried to kill the man's wife, too, but she managed to fight him off and escape. The family chalked it up to madness at first; Julius disappeared for almost two years after that incident, so everyone brushed it under the rug. The woman who had raised Julius, my great-great-grandmother, became the head of House Vista and made everyone swear never to mention Julius's name again. She had every image of him removed from the house and all of his belongings burned. If he were to come crawling back, the family had orders to kill him on sight."

"Shit," Cyrus muttered.

"She was furious and devastated," Lucien went on. "But she had raised him like a son, and part of her still loved him." He nodded toward the painting. "This portrait had hung in her favorite spot in the library. She took it down, and everyone thought she had destroyed it with the others, but in truth she'd hidden it, and probably continued to visit it every so often for the rest of her life. My grandfather found the painting when he was young and brought it up here, and here it has stayed with the other forgotten items that no one cares about."

Cyrus eyed the broken books, then looked up at Julius again. Now that his initial shock had eased, he realized he sort of felt bad for Julius. Not that what he did was justified, but finding out the truth about his presence in House Vista must have been staggering. To learn that he had begun life as an unwanted throwaway—perhaps even tossed to the Vistas as *food*—would undoubtedly have been traumatic. Cyrus could sympathize with that.

Never would he have expected to sympathize with the honored and deified founder of House Beldon, but Cyrus understood a thing or two about being unwanted.

"Puts everything in a different light, doesn't it?" Lucien murmured.

Cyrus shook his head. "It really was a circle of vengeance right from the beginning, huh?" He ruffled his hair. "What gets me is that it could have been different, you know? The founder of the Beldons, a child of House Vista—this story could have proven that at the beginning, we were not enemies. But no, he had to bathe his legacy in silver blood and then bury his history. And now here we are."

Lucien leaned closer to him and took his hand, threading their fingers together. "It won't be like this forever," he murmured. "I need to believe that. And I know you want to, also."

"I do," Cyrus sighed.

"That can start with us," Lucien whispered. He brought Cyrus's hand up and kissed it. "It already has, in a way. After all, you've refrained from killing me so far."

Cyrus flickered a smile. "And somehow, you don't hate me."

"No." Lucien kissed his hand again. "I certainly don't." He

held Cyrus's gaze a moment longer, then looked to the dusty stacks. "I haven't been up here in ages. The lower floors of the library have been my priority, but I've neglected this room for too long."

"I can help," Cyrus offered. "I know how to fix old books. Just say the word, and I'll happily bring all of these back to life."

"Really?" Lucien brightened. "You'd do that?"

"In a heartbeat," Cyrus said, smiling.

"Well, then." Lucien grinned. "You're hired. And I guess that means you're here to stay, because..." He gestured at the rows upon rows of broken books.

Cyrus certainly had his work cut out for him, but work with books was rarely tedious. He was tempted to start now and call it a distraction from the whole Beldon case, yet despite Lucien's permission, he hesitated.

He squeezed Lucien's hand. "You mean that? I can stay?"

Lucien blinked. "Of course you can stay. Did you think I would kick you out once our role in this whole mess is done?"

"Well—No, but..." Cyrus shrugged. "Sort of."

"Cyrus." Lucien tilted his head. "Do you still not see how much I care about you? Not for your usefulness to me, not for your role in our project, and certainly not for your blood. You've brought brightness and life to this old house, Cyrus. I don't know what I would do if you weren't here. You've saved me in so many ways, and I...I don't think I can tell you how much that means to me."

Cyrus's first instinct was to brush off Lucien's words, but the deep sincerity on his face silenced any deflections Cyrus might have thrown. He tried to shove away the doubts that screamed that he didn't deserve that care that Lucien confessed, but those efforts failed to ease his anxiety about what Lucien might confess next.

"Sorry if that seems like it came out of nowhere." Lucien tucked his hair behind his ear. "I found some old things—letters and such—that dredged up memories. I think it's finally hitting me that I'm...alone. I'll never see any of them again."

He blinked hard and visibly swallowed. Cyrus pulled him into his arms.

"I'm fine," Lucien insisted, but didn't resist the hug. "I'm fine. It's just...Did they know that I loved them?" He sighed and rested his chin on Cyrus's shoulder. "Family is a strange, complicated thing, especially for us. We acted like colleagues more than relatives most of the time. But I did love them." His voice cracked. "I did."

Cyrus held him a little tighter. He didn't know how to assure Lucien that anyone who knew him likely couldn't help loving him, and he didn't know what words could soothe his pain. He didn't know if anything could.

"Sorry." Lucien sighed and drew back, just enough to see Cyrus's face. He flickered a faint, teary smile. "We've got enough on our minds without me spilling my emotions everywhere."

Cyrus touched his cheek. "You don't have to apologize. It's okay. I don't want you to feel like you have to hide your feelings from me."

Lucien stared at him as if no one had ever told him that before. And Cyrus understood; emotions had been discouraged in his own house as well. But Lucien had had a lot longer to perfect the careful art of bottling everything up, and Cyrus knew it would be a long time before Lucien dropped the habit. Even if he never fully did, Cyrus wanted him to know that his feelings were safe with him, that *he* was safe with him.

Lucien held his gaze another moment, then softly kissed him. Cyrus's heart missed a beat; it was far from the first time he'd kissed Lucien, but something about this tenderness—this softness, this gentle, simmering intimacy—made his heart beat harder. He knew Lucien could sense it, this jittery rushing of his pulse, and he wondered what Lucien thought of it. What did he think was still unsaid, now that so much of the tension between them had eased?

He *must* know. Cyrus couldn't fathom how he wouldn't. Lucien had seen straight through Cyrus's poorly-concealed attraction to him, and now Cyrus was certain that Lucien knew his deeper feelings, too.

He wanted to say it. But he would also rather swallow nails.

"Cyrus," Lucien murmured against his lips, "I..."

Oh, gods.

Cyrus drew back to meet his eyes, caught between anticipation and terror, but then Lucien abruptly jerked his head toward the stacks.

"What is it?" Cyrus listened, but the library was silent as death.

"The evening paper just arrived," Lucien whispered.

"What!" Cyrus exchanged a wide-eyed glance with Lucien, then both of them took off at a sprint toward the library doors. They scrambled down the steps, skidding around corners on each landing until they reached the first floor and hauled across the manor. Cyrus nearly wiped out on every sharp turn, and when they made it to the foyer, Lucien blink-shifted outside, then back in, bundle of papers in hand.

"Holy shit," Lucien breathed.

"What?" Cyrus made a grab for the paper, but Lucien batted his hand away and simply turned the page around for him to see. The headline stole the remaining air from Cyrus's lungs.

BELDON FAMILY BETRAYAL?

"Holy *shit*," Cyrus echoed. He stepped to Lucien's side and hurriedly read the accompanying article. It was short, barely scratching the surface of the situation, but its mere presence in the papers just one day after Cyrus had passed on the information was astounding.

Viktor had done it—and the Barlows had wasted no time leaking the story to the press.

Cyrus read on until he reached the last paragraph, which he read aloud. "'A formal gathering has been called among the hunter families to discuss this matter and to allow the Beldon family a chance to defend themselves against these serious accusations. Honorable Families are permitted to attend, but the hunter families ask that they abstain from testimony at this time. The gathering will commence tomorrow, noon sharp, at the city meetinghouse.'"

"We have to go to that gathering," Lucien said.

Cyrus agreed, but he also feared what Emerson would do if he showed his face—especially since he'd be siding *against* the Beldons. "How?"

"I will, of course, represent House Vista," Lucien said. "And you will accompany me."

Cyrus snorted. "As what? Your traitorous lover?"

"No. As my favored one."

"Oh, come *on*." Cyrus scoffed. "You might as well call me your pet at that point."

"Would you rather have them all know the true nature of our relationship?"

"Of course not," Cyrus said. "But that would at least paint a better picture than me being a favored one."

Despite what the title suggested, it wasn't exactly a position of honor. Colloquially, Cyrus had heard favored ones referred to as *bedbugs* more than their actual name. It implied that the one in question, usually human, wasn't important enough to the vampire to be their lover or partner, but the vampire still wanted them—for sex or blood or both—and offered them protection from other vampires.

While Cyrus quite enjoyed occupying Lucien's bed and was more than happy to offer his blood to him, that didn't mean he wanted it to look like he was *only* wanted for that.

"I know it's not ideal," Lucien said. "And you are obviously more to me than a favored one typically is, so yes, it is insulting, and I'm sorry. But I don't see another option."

"We could tell them nothing." Cyrus glanced over the article again. "It says the hunter families are requesting that any Honorable Ones in attendance remain silent. If I'm there with you, for House Vista, neither of us will have to speak."

"Right, but to them, you're not of House Vista," Lucien said.

"You might have renounced your family, but everyone there will still see you as a Beldon."

True, but it would send one hell of a message if Cyrus showed up to that gathering with Lucien, sat with him, and didn't say a word while his family fought for its dignity. That action alone would betray him as the one who had sparked this fire—but that was a problem for later.

Of course, if he *really* wanted to stir some drama, he could stick a ring on his left hand and pretend to be Lucien's husband again.

But no, entertaining as that might be, it would create a disaster. This was not the time to masquerade anything that wasn't true. He looked up at Lucien again. "Look, it's not that I disagree that calling me your favored one is a safe idea—even if I don't like it. I'm more concerned that if we say *anything* about what we are to each other, *that's* going to become the talk of the city. We'll be a scandal, and that'll overshadow everything we've put up against the Beldons."

Lucien frowned and touched his fingertip to his lips. "Hmm. I didn't think of that."

"I really think our safest choice is to say nothing. Let everyone assume what they will, and we won't confirm or deny anything."

It was the best course of action Cyrus could see, and still it turned his stomach. The thought of being in that room surrounded by all those judging eyes—including his uncle and siblings—made him want to hide with Julius Beldon on the fourth floor until the whole storm blew over.

But he had started this, and he needed to see it through. This was his work and his plan at play, and this was not the time to be a coward about it.

"Your uncle is not going to react well to seeing us together," Lucien murmured.

"Trust me, I dread it as much as you do," Cyrus said. He leaned against Lucien's side and wrapped an arm around him. "But we have to go."

"I know." Lucien sighed and folded the paper, then dropped the whole bundle on the table next to the doors. "Spirits willing, this will be over soon."

Cyrus couldn't imagine it being over. Now that he'd set the Beldons' downfall in motion, part of him expected to be dealing with the aftermath for the rest of his life. His family was too powerful to just disappear overnight; one trial would not be the end of them. This fight was far from over, even if the trial itself was a significant step. He could rest assured, at least, that *someone* in the city had heard what was happening and took it seriously. For that, he was grateful.

Still, he didn't know how he was going to sleep tonight.

LUCIEN APPARENTLY WANTED tomorrow to come even less than Cyrus did; they found a welcome distraction in each other in the darkening hours after dinner, yet afterward as they lay tangled together with the sheets twisted around them, Cyrus still didn't want to fall asleep. He was exhausted—Lucien had made sure of that—but though his body begged for rest, he refused to close his eyes.

"I wish we could stay like this forever," he whispered.

Lucien nestled closer to him, tucking his face against Cyrus's neck. "Me too."

Cyrus lazily ran his fingers through Lucien's hair. "I know you said before that immortality is a curse, but it must be nice to have so much time. I feel like I've already run out of it."

"We're not going to die tomorrow, Cyrus," Lucien murmured. "We have all the time in the world."

"It's not that, it's just..." He sighed. "I feel like I've wasted all these years—almost a quarter of my life—just trying to get through one more year until I reached some unknown point where I could finally be free. I don't know what I thought would happen, or what would finally cut me free from my family, so all I could do was keep waiting." He turned his head to rest against Lucien's. "I certainly never expected this."

"Not in a thousand years," Lucien agreed.

Cyrus nuzzled his hair. "You said earlier that I had saved you, but I can't imagine how when there's about a million ways that *you* saved *me.*"

Lucien lifted his head to look at him and smiled, touching his thumb to Cyrus's chin. "Maybe it's mutual."

"Maybe it is." Cyrus's heart thudded, and he knew that if there was ever a time to say the words that had been on the tip of his tongue for weeks, it was now. No, they weren't going to die tomorrow, but this still felt like a precipice—the hanging end of a chapter. Cyrus didn't want anything left unsaid when they stepped into that courthouse tomorrow.

He opened his mouth, but Lucien spoke first.

"We should sleep, love. The sun will rise whether we want it to or not."

Cyrus had barely heard anything past that word. If his heart was racing before, it was *pounding* now. He stared at Lucien, and all that came to his lips was that singular, tiny, monumental word: "Love?"

A small smile softened Lucien's face. "Isn't it obvious?"

Cyrus was speechless. *No*, it wasn't obvious. Or—hell, maybe it was. Maybe Cyrus had known all along and had chosen to ignore it, because it was easier to suppress his own feelings if he assumed they were unrequited. It was easier to squash his hopes, even now, when part of him hesitated to believe that this relationship with Lucien was deeper than casual sex—even if the way Lucien had kissed him, touched him, held him, and worshiped him was anything but.

But, honestly, how could it be? Lucien had just dropped the word *love* like it was the most obvious thing in the universe, and Cyrus couldn't fathom it. *How* could Lucien Vista possibly love him? How could a man who had been alive for nearly two centuries, who had likely loved dozens of people, not be completely jaded to the concept of falling in love? How could he choose Cyrus, who was basically nothing in comparison?

It seemed so impossible.

Yet here they were. Here *Lucien* was, with his heart on his sleeve and overwhelming affection in his eyes.

Cyrus Beldon was a fucking idiot.

"It probably was," Cyrus said, finally letting a grin melt across his face. He touched his forehead to Lucien's. "I'm just a fool."

Lucien hummed a soft chuckle. "Yes, well, we both know how much you love denial."

Cyrus snorted. "Maybe so. But more importantly, we both know that I love *you* more."

"Do we?" Lucien stroked his fingers through his hair.

"I do," Cyrus whispered. "And I hope you do, too."

"I suspected as much." Lucien kissed him softly. "But it's still nice to hear you say it."

Cyrus was surprised to find he agreed; now that he'd said it once, it seemed easy to say it again.

Even now, his doubts scratched at the door, but they were easier to ignore. He didn't want to continue denying that Lucien cared deeply for him. He wanted to be the person Lucien had fallen for, faults and all, and he didn't want to care whether he deserved it or not.

Lucien loved him, and that was enough.

MORNING CAME and brought a day for which Cyrus was utterly unprepared. He lingered in bed, huddled beneath the covers long after Lucien had gotten up, and when he finally dragged himself out, he got stuck again at the wardrobe. His own clothes occupied a tiny fraction of the space compared to Lucien's, and while he'd so far been unbothered by borrowing Lucien's shirts, he couldn't fathom doing that today. But none of his own were formal enough. But did that even matter? Oh, who was he kidding, of course it did. Cyrus might not be going to this meeting representing House Beldon, but it was still high society. There were expectations.

Grumbling, he gave up on the wardrobe for now and wrapped himself in one of Lucien's dressing gowns that was quickly becoming his own. Lucien had a variety of them, but this one was clearly older than the rest, soft and lived-in and slightly worn out. And it smelled like him. Not like that rosy perfume that clung to nearly everything in this house, but like *him*. It was like wearing a hug.

Cyrus shuffled out of the bedchamber and found Lucien in his chair by the fireplace. He was still in his own dressing gown, and the only sign that he'd ventured downstairs was the steaming teacup in his hand. A book balanced on his knee, but Cyrus could tell he wasn't actually reading. Still, it took him a second to look up.

"Oh. Good morning."

Cyrus grunted a noncommittal noise. It certainly was a morning. Not so much a good one.

Lucien closed his book and set it aside, then reached out his hand. Cyrus went to him and Lucien took his hand and kissed it. "The world's not going to end today, you know."

Cyrus perched on the arm of Lucien's chair. "Then why does it feel like it will?"

"Because we're scared." Lucien wrapped his arm around Cyrus and leaned his head on his shoulder. "But there will still be a day after this meeting. The afternoon will pass, and evening will come, and night will fall, and then tomorrow the sun will rise again. And we will still be here, together." He tilted his head to look up at Cyrus. "I promise you that."

Cyrus wished he believed it. How could Lucien promise

anything, when neither of them had any idea what would happen today? Cyrus didn't want to expect the absolute worst, but...

But he was terrified. Simple as that. He was terrified of his uncle and the power he held—over Cyrus himself and over the city as a whole. He was terrified for Lucien, who was a loose end and a glaring target as long as he lived. Emerson Beldon was utterly unpredictable, and now that his carefully-plotted schemes were coming into the light, Cyrus wouldn't put anything past him as *too far*.

He blinked the sting of tears out of his eyes and pressed his cheek to the top of Lucien's head. "I'm so afraid of losing you."

"Darling, you won't." Lucien held him closer. "I'm not going anywhere, my love, and neither are you."

Cyrus hoped to every fathomable divine power that he was right.

Too soon, it was time to get ready. Cyrus only picked at the breakfast that Lucien made for them, and then took entirely too long to settle on an outfit while Lucien told him time and again that he looked fine. Which was easy for him to say; he was dressed sharp and sleek, in all black but for a blood-red tie around his throat. He pinned his hair loosely at the back of his neck, then pulled a long, black coat from the wardrobe and threw it over his shoulders with a flourish. He looked magnificent, truly an impressive and imposing image of House Vista, and as Cyrus drank in the sight he couldn't decide what he wanted more: to enjoy these fine clothes on Lucien, or to take them off of him.

Cyrus himself finally settled on one of Lucien's fancier shirts and paired it with his own vest and trousers he'd brought from home. Lucien provided a green silk cravat and an emerald brooch to dress it up a bit more, and then Cyrus let him line his eyes again, and then it was actually time to go. Cyrus opted to wear one of his own coats, even though it wasn't quite formal enough; he already felt like he was more Vista than Beldon, and he was nervous to add more evidence of that.

They stepped outside to a foggy, rain-soaked morning.

Covering their heads with their coats, they hurried into the carriage house, where Lucien prepared one of the smaller coaches for them. Cyrus fed Demeter an apple while Lucien got her hooked up to the carriage, then Lucien came around front and gently took Demeter's face in his hands. She went oddly still.

Cyrus stared at him. "What are—"

Lucien's eyes flashed briefly in that strange, reflective way, and then Demeter tossed her head and snorted. Lucien released her, tracing his hand along her side as he approached the carriage door. "Shall we?"

Cyrus was still caught on the previous two minutes. "What the hell did you just do to my horse?"

"Nothing harmful," Lucien assured him. "I just told her where to take us so that I don't have to sit out there in the rain to drive."

That explanation did not, in fact, explain anything. "What?"

"I can temporarily compel animals," Lucien said. "Demeter will bring us safely downtown. No need for a driver."

Cyrus had too much else on his mind to try to make sense of that. He shook his head and climbed into the carriage. "Sure, okay. Let's get this over with."

Lucien stepped in after him and knocked once on the inside of the carriage door once it was closed. The coach lurched, and they started on their way.

Cyrus sat doubled over with his elbows on his knees and his head in his hands for the entire ride into the city. If Lucien tried to talk to him, he wasn't aware of it. His head was ringing. His insides felt scrambled. He feared that if he tried to speak or even look at Lucien, he'd break down. Over and over, his thoughts screamed one phrase: *What the hell am I doing?* And swirling around that question were a million segments of other fears and doubts that didn't fully form in his mind but brought a nauseating feeling upon him regardless. There were so many things that could go wrong and so many things he feared and he couldn't articulate any of them.

The carriage seemed to bump and sway for an entire year

before it gradually slowed and then stopped. The knots in Cyrus's stomach coiled tighter. Maybe if he didn't move even an inch, the day wouldn't go on. Maybe if he didn't look up, everything would disappear.

A gentle hand settled on his back. "Cyrus, we're here."

We're here. No going back. The spark had been lit, and it was time to fan the flames until the Beldon legacy crumbled to ashes. Cyrus didn't know if he could really do this, but he'd gotten this far. He couldn't give up now.

He took a deep breath and sat up straight, exhaling slowly as he looked at Lucien. He hid his fear well, but Cyrus could see it in his eyes. Oddly, it gave him courage. If they were both terrified, then it wasn't just Cyrus's own weakness holding him back. They both had genuine reasons to be scared, and that scrap of validation was just enough to push Cyrus forward.

He leaned in and kissed Lucien once, then opened the carriage door before his fear could freeze him again. He looked ahead at the steps leading up to the limestone building and its columns and statues and he tried to tell himself that whatever happened today, even if it wasn't favorable, he would still go home with Lucien later and they would still be together. Even if everything went wrong, and even if this case wasn't enough to topple the Beldons, Cyrus did not have to be part of it. He and Lucien could leave all of this behind.

Lucien stepped to Cyrus's side and offered his arm. Cyrus hesitated, then smothered his anxiety and accepted. He held his head high as they ascended the steps together, and at the top, he met Lucien's eyes.

"Are you ready?"

"Not at all," Lucien said. "Are you?"

"Not even a little." He tightened his grip on Lucien's arm. "Let's do this."

Chapter THIRTY TWO

CYRUS AND LUCIEN WEREN'T THE LAST TO ARRIVE, BUT they were far from the first. A section of seats toward the back of the meetinghouse had been reserved for the Honorable Families, and Cyrus recognized vampires from House Attcourt, Downings, Astra, and of course, Harrows. Only Master Harrows was present from his House; the others had two attendees each.

As much as it wracked Cyrus's nerves to be accompanying Lucien, he was glad, at least, that Lucien wouldn't have to sit here alone.

He swore he felt every pair of eyes on the two of them as they strode down the center aisle separating the two sections of seats. Lucien chose a row near the front of the Families' allotted space, but on the opposite side of the room from the others. Cyrus wanted to yank him back and insist they sat as far from the front as possible, but he swallowed his panic and tried to appear confident as he took his seat beside Lucien.

No one spoke. The silence was suffocating. Cyrus had thought the Honorable Ones would at least chat idly with each other, but clearly there was no such expectation among them. Cyrus avoided looking at any of them as his eyes bounced around the room, but then he feared he appeared too nervous and dropped his gaze to his hands in his lap.

He still thought his left hand looked strangely empty without his family ring. He'd scarcely thought about it since he'd thrown it away, but now its absence glared at him. It was easy to not be a Beldon in Lucien's house. Here, he suddenly felt like he belonged nowhere.

As if his thoughts had summoned the Beldons, the meetinghouse doors clattered open and Emerson stormed in, trailed by Joel and Poppy. Cyrus clenched his jaw and glared at his uncle, who breezed by without notice, but when Poppy followed, she locked eyes with him. She scowled, but Joel pulled her along before she had a chance to say a word.

Cyrus didn't take his eyes off his siblings until they'd settled in their seats at the front of the room. At least a dozen more people filed in and filled the remaining benches; Cyrus spotted Viktor Stokes among them. He avoided the Barlow hunters in attendance and sat in the back, close to Master Harrows but not daring to occupy the same row.

When several more minutes passed and no one else arrived, the main doors clunked shut and two men in gray robes swept up the middle aisle. They each took a seat on either side of the dais at the front of the room, and then five judges dressed in black strode onto the dais from a door off to the side. One of them, a woman with gray-streaked hair, approached the podium in the center while the others took their seats in a row behind her.

The woman in front retrieved a pair of glasses from within her robes and put them on as she placed a stack of papers on the podium. Cyrus vaguely recognized her but couldn't conjure her name through his nerves; she'd been the First Judge—the one who led and guided the others, and if needed made an executive decision —for as long as Cyrus could remember. Half the city loved her, and the other half hated her.

Marcus Beldon had been in the latter half, primarily because she didn't tolerate bribes. That made Cyrus feel a little better about the potential outcome of this gathering.

The judge placed her hands on top of the podium. "Good

afternoon. First Judge Bridget Hargreeve shall commence this unconventional gathering with the intention of uncovering the whole truth of the situation and directing proper justice. I am no stranger to the ethics and codes that the hunter families have upheld for generations, and I am confident in my ability to judge the actions of the Beldon family accordingly. Likewise, I am versed in the laws and ethics of our Honorable Families, and therefore House Harrows shall be judged as well."

A few of the vampires in attendance exchanged frowns and shifted in their seats, but no one dared to break the oath of silence. Cyrus glanced at Lucien; the slight crease between his brows confirmed Cyrus's understanding that the First Judge typically did not have jurisdiction over the Honorable Families. Cyrus had never heard of the city's laws governing the Families. Not successfully, anyway.

Unconventional day indeed.

"I see your confusion, Honored Ones," Judge Hargreeve continued. "You have my gratitude for upholding your promises to listen without comment. Let me clarify: we are here today to shed light upon these rather disturbing accusations and isolate the truth. I shall not—nor do I have the authority to—convict or condemn any Honorable Family. That decision, should it be necessary, is your own. The Beldon family, however, answers to the city of Chestervale."

Her stony gaze flicked to Emerson, then she addressed the room. "I invite Mr. Quincy Barlow to the podium to present the evidence he brought to the House of Justice this week."

Cyrus exhaled slowly and spread his palms on his knees. He'd been wringing his hands so hard that his fingers already ached. He partially wished he still had his family ring just to have something to fidget with.

Quincy Barlow rose from his seat and strode to the front of the room. He was around forty, with a stocky build and a dancer's grace. He had a somewhat famous reputation among the hunter families for his skill with a bow. Old fashioned, but he'd refused every hunter's attempt to get him to use anything else. After a while it had become a running joke to suggest increasingly absurd things that Quincy should use as a weapon in place of his bow, and if it bothered him, he never showed it. He was frightening with the bow; Cyrus had heard rumors that he had so much strength behind his shots that he'd cleanly decapitated numerous vampires with a single well-aimed arrow.

As Quincy took up the podium and presented the information that Cyrus, Lucien, and Viktor had passed to him, Cyrus let his attention slide. He focused instead on keeping still; more than once, he caught himself bouncing his leg even as he consciously tried not to. Then he realized his jaw was clenched painfully tight, and then minutes later he had to stop himself from chewing the inside of his cheek to shreds. Then his leg was bouncing again. He again wished he'd thought to put a ring or two or ten on his hands.

Quincy's deep voice droned on. Cyrus tuned back in every few minutes to make sure he wasn't missing anything he didn't already know, but Quincy had only gotten as far as explaining the agreement between Marcus and House Harrows. He confirmed everything Cyrus had suspected, citing letters Viktor had swiped from House Harrows: Marcus would get jurisdiction outside the city, and Harrows would get his enemies eliminated one by one. Cyrus tuned Quincy back out and once again caught himself bouncing his leg.

Lucien, on the other hand, hadn't moved a muscle this entire time. Was he even breathing? Cyrus flicked a glance at him and found the stony mask of Master Vista fixed securely on his face. He betrayed nothing, his attention pinned to the front of the room. Cyrus might as well not exist.

A few minutes later, when Cyrus resorted to wringing his hands again, Lucien inched his hand toward him and dropped something into his palm. Cyrus looked down and saw that it was one of Lucien's rings: a gold band with tiny roses etched in the metal.

Cyrus flicked another glance at him. Lucien didn't exchange the look, but drew Cyrus's attention to his hands by flexing one of them and then turning his family's signet ring around his finger.

Oh. It was something to fidget with. Great, so Cyrus's restlessness was probably obvious to the whole room.

He worked the ring onto his middle finger, absently hoping it didn't get stuck since it only barely fit, and then became so occupied with twisting it around and around that he didn't notice that Quincy Barlow had finished his testimony until he stepped down from the dais.

Cyrus held his breath again as Judge Hargreeve resumed her spot at the podium. "Thank you, Mr. Barlow. This is some disturbing information, indeed. But before we hear from Master Beldon, I wish to call Mr. Viktor Stokes to the podium, so that he may elaborate on the alchemical work he has provided to House Harrows and the purpose for said work. Mr. Stokes, if you would?"

Cyrus risked a glance in Viktor's direction, but his eyes caught first on Master Harrows, whose face was coarse with fury; Cyrus prayed he hadn't condemned Viktor by getting him involved in this. He was a little surprised that Viktor had offered up his own identity in his evidence at all.

Master Harrows's glare would have kept Cyrus firmly in his seat had it been directed at him, but Viktor stood and made his way to the front of the room, seemingly unbothered. He did not look at Master Harrows. He did not look at Cyrus. He nodded respectfully to the judges and then stepped up to the podium.

"Good afternoon," he began. "My name is Viktor Stokes, and I have been employed by House Harrows as their alchemist for nearly forty years. I have worked closely with Master Harrows in his ambitious scientific endeavors. Judge Hargreeve, I am willing to share any relevant information you might seek."

"Thank you, Mr. Stokes." The judge stood to the side of the podium with a page of notes in hand. "You've said that Master Harrows had certain scientific ambitions. Can you tell us what he sought with this work?"

"Of course, Judge. He seeks pure, true immortality. That is, invincibility to any fatal injury a human hunter may inflict upon a vampire."

Murmurs scattered throughout the gathered hunter families. Emerson Beldon twisted around and glared straight at Master Harrows. Poppy and Joel exchanged an alarmed glance.

One hard look from Judge Hargreeve silenced the whispers. She turned again to Viktor and asked, "And has Master Harrows been successful in this endeavor?"

Viktor shook his head. "No, Judge. Given my great knowledge of the alchemical arts, I am confident when I say that it is impossible."

"What of your other experiments, then?" Hargreeve went on. "Mr. Barlow mentioned a series of studies pertaining to Wild vampires, which the late Leigh Harrows, her brother Philip, and House Vista were all known to have participated in as well. Can you elaborate on your role in such studies, Mr. Stokes?"

Cyrus started to pray in earnest.

Viktor shifted on his feet and adjusted his glasses on his nose. "Well...to put it simply, I was tasked with isolating the core switch of vampiric turns. I was ordered to identify the biological change at its root and alchemically replicate it."

"For what purpose, Mr. Stokes?"

He fiddled with his glasses again. "To force a corrupted turn upon a born vampire, thus creating a Wild vampire."

A chorus of gasps broke the silence. A glare from the judge didn't quiet them this time; even after she loudly cleared her throat, a few murmurs persisted.

Cyrus dared another glance at Master Harrows. He white-knuckle gripped the back of the bench in front of him, but to his credit he did not say a word.

"Settle," Judge Hargreeve snapped at the attendees. "Mr. Stokes, I implore you to tell us more. Were these experiments successful? Were they conducted on humans?"

"Yes, Judge." Viktor licked his lips. "Humans and vampires. An...Honorable vampire, to be precise."

"Impossible!" someone shouted.

"Are you truly implying—"

"You dishonor House Harrows!"

"*Settle!*" Judge Hargreeve snapped, and the few hunters that had bolted up dropped back into their seats. Two attendants escorted three Honorable Ones out of the room for breaking the oath of silence. Once they were gone, Judge Hargreeve tucked her hands behind her back. "Mr. Stokes, this is alarming. Who was the Honorable One who suffered this fate? And by whose orders? Or have you just confessed to a crime before us?"

Viktor closed his eyes. "It was Leigh Harrows, Judge, and the experiment was ordered by Master Harrows himself. You will find evidence of it in my notes."

Cyrus braced himself for another outburst, but seconds dragged by and the room remained deathly silent. Even the judge looked stunned. But she recovered herself quickly and nodded. "One more question, Mr. Stokes: why might Master Harrows have ordered this of you? Why use his own daughter—his own heir—in such risky experiments?"

"Because she stepped out of line," Viktor said, and genuinely sounded like he regretted it. "Master Harrows said it himself as he administered the serum I had transmuted: Leigh had crossed a line by attacking Arthur Beldon, and...if she needed a live subject for her study so badly..." He lifted his hands.

Cyrus had suspected as much, but the revelation didn't lessen his horror.

"I see," Judge Hargreeve said, and even she sounded rattled. "Well, then, Mr. Stokes, I thank you. That is all I will ask of you at this time."

Then the room exploded.

"*That's all?*" Master Harrows surged to his feet. The other Honorable Ones around him flinched; even Lucien startled.

"These accusations are preposterous, and you're all fools to believe it! My daughter was killed by the Wild vampire that became of Arthur Beldon, and—"

"Untrue!" Emerson barked, bolting to his feet. "I killed that monster myself, long before—"

"*Master Harrows*," snapped Judge Hargreeve, "that's quite enough! You have broken your oath. Attendants, please escort Master Harrows out of the room. Master Beldon, I implore you to take your seat."

"You'll rot in hell for this, Stokes," Harrows snarled even as the attendants took him by the arms and dragged him, thrashing, from his spot. "After everything I did for you! You disgrace House Harrows, just as you disgraced House Barlow!"

That set the Barlows on their feet, all shouting over each other. Master Harrows finally shut his mouth and wrenched himself out of the attendants' grip as he stormed out of the meetinghouse. The building shuddered when he slammed the doors.

Somewhere in the jumble, Viktor Stokes had disappeared.

"Settle, all of you!" ordered the judge. "That's enough. We will speak no more of House Harrows now that there is no representative in the room. I will leave it to the other Honorable Families to review the evidence I have been given and then act accordingly. For now, I will call Master Beldon to the podium, and I *beg* you all, mind yourselves. I will not tolerate any more ruckus."

If Cyrus was uneasy before, he felt ill now. He watched his uncle stand and stride up the dais and he wished he could take Lucien's hand. Instead he moved so his arm was slightly pressed against Lucien's; a subtle touch, but better than nothing.

Lucien glanced at Cyrus, then reached over and quickly squeezed his hand.

Emerson Beldon stepped up to the podium and smoothed back his hair, then straightened the lapels of his coat and fixed the room with a hard glare. He brought no notes with him that Cyrus could see, and though his frame was wrought with anger, not a hint of it showed on his disturbingly calm face.

And then he looked directly at Cyrus, and his stoic control did little to hide his disgust.

Cyrus clenched his hands and forced himself to hold his uncle's gaze until Emerson finally looked away.

Emerson took a moment to collect his thoughts. "I know you all think I am here to defend myself, my family, and our honor—and I am. But as Judge Hargreeve said, we are here to bring the truth to light, to clear the murky water into which we've all been submerged, and find the pearl in the sand. The accusations brought against myself, my late brother, and House Harrows—an *Honorable* Family—are severe, shocking, and uncharacteristic of our noble society."

Gods, he sounded like Marcus. And worse, he radiated a sort of charisma that Marcus had always lacked. Where Cyrus's father had relied on his gruff voice and commanding demeanor to get what he wanted, Emerson had mastered the art of luring everyone into his graces.

"Today we have heard Mr. Barlow share accusations that I have broken the ethics that have been honored by the hunter families for generations," Emerson continued. "I say these accusations are groundless, pieced together with weak and insubstantial evidence used to paint a picture that certain individuals in this room wish to see. My brother's sins are his own, and what is to be done about a dead man's wrongs? I have been trying to *ascend* my family. With my work in the alchemical arts, I will raise us—and, in time, the other hunter families—to the same level of divinity and honor as the Honorable Ones, so that as long as there are vampires, there will be hunters—stronger and better than ever before—to keep them in check. No longer will we humans be at a mortal disadvantage. There will be *balance*, as the gods intended."

Emerson paused and scanned the room, but notably did not look in Cyrus's direction again. "You're all looking for someone to blame, someone to hold accountable for betraying our ways. The one you're looking for *is* in this room, but it's not me."

He reached into his coat and produced a crisp envelope.

All of the blood drained from Cyrus's face.

Lucien exhaled a single, barely audible gasp.

"Something quite peculiar is going on, my friends, and it has nothing to do with Wild vampires or alchemy." Emerson stepped away from the podium, still holding up the envelope. "Allow me to present my own evidence, and then I will ask you who you would judge."

No. Cyrus couldn't breathe. He needed to run. He and Lucien needed to get the hell out of here. But he couldn't move.

Emerson opened the envelope and read: "'My dear Cyrus, my heart breaks for you... If I am on your mind every waking hour, then you are in my thoughts even in my dreams...' And on and on and on... 'Spirits willing, I will see you soon.'"

Emerson looked up, directly at Cyrus. "'Signed, with *deep fondness*,'" he finished, "'Lucien Vista.'"

Cyrus felt every pair of eyes in the room as if each glare was a dagger piercing his flesh. If he tried to move, to stand, to *run*, he was certain they would sink deeper and shred him to pieces. He was trapped.

He had failed.

And he had fucked up.

"Do you see?" Emerson tossed the letter with a flick of his hand. "My work with House Harrows may seem dubious, but I assure you, both I and Master Harrows have the city and its citizens' best interest in mind. I have not broken our codes by allying with House Harrows. But a disgraceful, disgusting boy hardly deserving of the name Beldon has shattered, stomped on, and dirtied the standards that hold our society together. He has crossed a line that none of us would dare to toe, and if I may be so bold, the Vista heir is equally guilty."

The room's wordless shock broke. Voices erupted, people leapt out of their seats—hunter and vampire alike. The judge demanded order, but even Cyrus could hardly discern her voice over the others. *Beldon, Vista, betrayal.* Cyrus's ears rang with the words, over and over and over.

And he couldn't take his eyes off his uncle.

It took Lucien hauling him to his feet to break him out of his horrified trance. All at once he remembered how to breathe and gulped down panicked lungfuls of air, but each one detached him further from the room, from his body. He grasped Lucien's coat and the thick fabric in his hands was the only thing keeping him grounded.

"*SETTLE*," Judge Hargreeve hollered, and in the second she got in return, Emerson jumped on the chance to speak again.

"Listen, I'm not done!" He paused as everyone settled. "An illicit affair is scandalous indeed, but that's not all. It has come to my attention that my nephew has been colluding with this vampire for quite some time, chasing the very same scientific secrets that Master Harrows sought from his alchemist. He, too, sought the creation of Wild vampires." Emerson's face twisted into a smirk—a devious one that said he knew he'd already won. "I do wonder how far back these investigations go, and if, perhaps, the death of Arthur Beldon was not so much a tragedy...as an experiment gone wrong."

What?

"After all, it was Lucien Vista's notes and studies that led to Arthur's death in the first place," Emerson went on. "How do any of us know for certain that the boy was not also involved?"

Cyrus wanted to scream. He opened his mouth to insist that Emerson was lying, but nothing came out. His chance to speak then vanished with more outraged shouting.

Emerson glanced at Hargreeve and nodded once, then stepped down from the podium. "That concludes my defense, Judge."

He didn't take his eyes off Cyrus until he sat down. The hunters seated around him surged to their feet and smothered him with demands and questions that overlapped into a mad, senseless cacophony. Cyrus tried to hear his uncle's voice beneath the noise, desperate to know what he was telling them, but it was useless. His own thundering pulse muffled it all.

Then Poppy stood up. She turned around and glared at Cyrus

with that familiar fire in her eyes, lips pressed tightly together. Then she mouthed a single word:

Run.

And that finally got Cyrus unstuck. The room and its noise and its stifling heat and his shaking body and racing heart and burning lungs all rushed back into sharp relief. He grabbed Lucien's arm and stumbled out of the row, then made blindly for the doors.

The judge's voice rang out over the room. "A decision of justice cannot be made today," she declared. "We will have our conclusion in three days' time."

"*Three days?*" someone shouted. "Did you hear a *word* he said?"

"They're a risk to all of us!" screamed another. "They insult the dignity of the Families!"

"Emerson Beldon, if they are the problem, *eliminate them*! Clean up your fucking mess! Are you a hunter or not?"

Silence fell.

Cyrus stared at Lucien in blank terror.

Lucien grabbed him around the waist, and in a blink, they were outside.

Cyrus couldn't catch his breath. He felt like he was going to vomit. He clung to Lucien even after the dizzy effects of the blink-shift wore off, and when Lucien tried to break away, he held tighter.

"Cyrus—We need to get out of here." Lucien stroked his hand through his hair. "I—I'm sorry. Fuck, this is all my fault. I shouldn't have risked another letter without telling Leif to expect it, and—"

"No, no, none of this is your fault," Cyrus mumbled. Finally he made himself let go and dragged his hands through his hair. "*Fuck.* I was stupid to think this would work. I was stupid to forget about the letter. I should have known Emerson would turn everyone on us. I..."

Panic clawed up his throat. Everyone in that room—some of

the most powerful people in Chestervale—wanted Cyrus and Lucien brought to justice, and knowing how those people defined justice, nothing short of bloodshed would be enough.

None of them, least of all Emerson Beldon, would rest until Cyrus and Lucien were dead.

"What do we do?" Cyrus looked to Lucien. He could still hear the muffled voices from inside the meetinghouse; were they getting louder? Closer? How much time did they have before someone came after them?

"We have to go," Lucien said. "We need to get out of the city, and we need to hide. At least until this calms down."

"Is it going to?" Cyrus argued. "They're not just going to forget about us in a couple months, Lucien. I *wish* we were that low-profile. Do you really think they're going to give up if we disappear?" He went to him and grasped his arms. "We'd have to go *far*, Lucien, and I don't think we can ever come back."

Lucien closed his eyes for a minute, then stepped back and lifted his chin. "No."

"What?" Cyrus glanced nervously at the meetinghouse doors as the voices inside surged again. They were running out of time.

"I will not let Emerson fucking Beldon chase me out of my family's home." Lucien straightened his coat and turned on his heel, striding toward their carriage where it waited on the side of the road. "If we need to run now, fine, but I refuse to hide forever."

Cyrus followed him to the carriage, confused. "What the hell are we to do, then?"

"Have a look under the seats." Lucien wrenched open one of the doors.

Cyrus climbed in on the other side, feeling around under the cushioned bench until his hand bumped something long and smooth. He dragged it toward him and revealed the scabbard of the sword Lucien had bought for him back in that lakeside town.

His stomach lurched.

"You expected this to go poorly, didn't you?"

"I hoped it wouldn't." Lucien slid another sword from beneath the other seat, this one longer but thinner. "But I wanted to be prepared in case it did. Your uncle does not rule this city; it is yours and mine too. And we're going to show him that we won't flee without a fight."

Scarcely a heartbeat later, the meetinghouse doors crashed open.

Chapter  THIRTY THREE

CYRUS CAUGHT ONE GLANCE OF EMERSON BELDON storming down the meetinghouse steps before Lucien grabbed Cyrus and blink-shifted them away. Cyrus teetered on his feet when they halted, head spinning, and when his vision cleared he found the gates to the Beldon estate looming before him.

"W-Why are we here?" He anxiously glanced around, as if Emerson would appear with a vampire's speed. "I thought—"

"I told you," Lucien said, pushing through the gate, "we're not running away without a fight. And you wanted to bring the Beldons to ruin, yes?"

Cyrus glanced over his shoulder once more, then followed Lucien through the gates. "Yes, but..."

But this was different than fighting a few anonymous vampires while running from an angry countess, or facing Wild vampires in the woods. Cyrus could fight, but could he fight his uncle? His brother and sister? Could he face, with intent to harm, the people who had surrounded him for his entire life?

And was he even strong enough?

"You know as well as I do that few things matter more to Emerson Beldon than his life's work," Lucien said. "*If* he walks away alive today, I want him to be left with nothing. Are you with me?"

Cyrus swallowed his fear and looked up at Lucien, then

grabbed the front of his coat and kissed him. "Yes," he murmured. "I'm with you, always."

Lucien held him close. "Whatever happens, Cyrus, know that I love you. And I want to love you for as long as the spirits will allow me, whether that be for a day or a year or a lifetime."

"And I, you, Lucien," Cyrus whispered, and tried not to think about how much that sounded like a goodbye.

Lucien kissed him again, then drew back and started toward the house. "Come on. We don't have much time before they—"

In a blurred streak of black, Emerson Beldon appeared at the end of the walkway.

Impossible. Cyrus backed toward Lucien to put more space between himself and his uncle. Lucien mirrored his alarmed glance; there was only one way Emerson could have gotten here so quickly.

But that was absurd.

Emerson took two unsteady steps forward, his body jerking with the movement as if he was a puppet on uneven strings. "How poetic, that your blood will spill so close to where your brother's did. And look, we'll have more Honorable blood to nourish the flowers. I wonder if they'll all sprout up silver come spring."

He grinned, baring fangs, and Cyrus's suspicion doubled over into horror.

"What the *fuck* have you done?" he said, drawing his sword. Beside him, Lucien shifted into position.

But Emerson didn't raise the daggers clutched in his hands. His grin widened into something manic. "What have I *done*? What I've always done, boy—made sacrifices for this family. Risked *everything* for this family. It's precisely as I said: I will ascend us, and as long as I was mortal, that was not possible. So I became *more*. More than a mere human, and more than a mere vampire. *This* is the harmony I have always sought—*I* am the great work."

"How did you survive it?" Lucien snapped. "Vampires don't fully mature for nearly a century. You should be ash right now, still susceptible to sunlight."

"Aha, and I would be, if I was indeed a mere vampire."

Emerson crossed his daggers behind his back. "The invincibility that Master Harrows sought might be impossible, but my alchemical work was not for naught. With my expertise combined with that fool Stokes's research, and a bit of yours, *Master* Vista"—he spat the title—"I was able to bypass the weaknesses suffered by a typical vampire. Sunlight can't hurt me, and neither can *you*." He fixed Cyrus with a disgusted glare.

Cyrus tightened his hands around the hilt of his sword in an effort to still their trembling. He would've had a hard enough time winning this fight before, but now...Was he asking for death just by trying?

Yet something about Emerson's boasts didn't seem right. Cyrus hadn't delved into the science of turning in nearly as much detail as Lucien had, but he knew enough to confidently believe that the process couldn't simply be *sped up* with alchemy. Either Emerson was bluffing, or he had yet to encounter the consequences of toying with risky experiments.

Maybe Cyrus had an advantage after all. Regardless of whether Emerson had endured the turn a week ago or a month ago, he was still a fresh and unstable vampire. Cyrus had fought far worse than that.

He adjusted his grip again, but just as he readied himself to swing, footsteps thundered up the path.

"Uncle!" Poppy's voice tore across the grounds. She ran toward them with both of her swords drawn, Joel on her heels with his own blade in hand.

Cyrus didn't give them a chance to interfere. He swung at Emerson, who blocked the strike easily, catching Cyrus's blade between his two. He deflected the blow, and Cyrus spun around to aim another one.

He was faintly aware of Lucien keeping his siblings occupied in his periphery, and he silently thanked Lucien for it; he had enough to juggle with Emerson alone.

The man fought effortlessly, hardly lifting a finger against

Cyrus's swings; meanwhile, Cyrus's arms already ached and he felt his strength waning.

More than anything, it pissed Cyrus off. He had killed Wild fucking vampires. He'd slashed his way out of a house of snapping wolves. Emerson could not possibly be stronger than the monsters Cyrus had bested, vampire or not. He was still only a man.

Emerson spun out of reach of another strike, but stumbled as his body shuddered. He stood hunched over, breathing hard, and Cyrus seized his chance. If this would be Emerson's only moment of weakness—

In the same second Cyrus started to swing, Emerson transformed and hurled himself at Cyrus, claws outstretched. Cyrus barely managed to dodge, and the black-coated beast pivoted to attack again. Cyrus braced himself, prepared to strike, but inches away from colliding with him, the wolf-like creature collapsed to the dirt. Its body heaved and contorted, and then Emerson lay before Cyrus again. Blood streaked down his chin, staining his newly sharpened teeth. He lifted his bloodshot eyes to Cyrus and snarled.

"Cyrus!" Lucien called.

He turned just in time to feel a bright swipe of pain across the back of his shoulder. Poppy darted back from him, blood dripping off one of her curved swords. Cyrus didn't have time to so much as raise his blade before she attacked again, and then he had no choice but to turn his back on Emerson. He blocked blow after ruthless blow from Poppy, and then Emerson swung at him again and he narrowly avoided a slice across his torso. He twisted away and stumbled back, holding both of them at blade's length.

They paused, exchanging a glance. Behind them, Lucien had Joel pinned against a tree with his blade across his throat, and though Joel was struggling, he wasn't bleeding. Lucien's eyes were locked on Cyrus, caught in the same dilemma that Cyrus himself faced.

He couldn't win against both Emerson and Poppy. Not without Lucien's help, and they were still outnumbered.

"Give it up, boy," Emerson snarled. "We made you what you are. We taught you everything you know. Do you really think you can use that against us? Against *me?*"

Cyrus held his gaze. "If I give up, if I leave, you'll let me go?"

Poppy scoffed. "You never learned a goddamned thing, did you?"

She sprang toward him, but Cyrus had seen it coming; he pivoted and slammed the hilt of his sword into her chest, sending her staggering backwards, and then turned and swung his blade toward Emerson. Emerson raised his weapons to block the strike, but at the last second Cyrus turned his wrists and jabbed the blade upward, aiming for the heart.

It sank into flesh, but not Emerson's.

Cyrus stumbled backwards, dropping his weapon as his sister's body collapsed to the ground. Poppy wheezed and brought a shaking hand to her chest where the sword had pierced straight through her. She looked up at Cyrus; blood spilled through her lips when she opened her mouth.

Cyrus couldn't catch his breath. "P-Poppy? *Poppy?*" He was suddenly on his knees, unaware of falling. He grabbed his sister and pressed a hand to her chest, frantically and fruitlessly trying to stop the bleeding. "Poppy," he gasped again, "Poppy, please, no, *no*, I'm so sorry, I—I didn't—Why would you—"

"*Get away from her!*" A hard shove sent Cyrus sprawling across the dirt. He scrambled up and faced Joel, who sank to his knees beside his twin's crumpled form.

Cyrus took one step toward them, but then Emerson was in front of him again.

"Let's end this." He dropped his blades and then drew a pistol from his coat.

Cyrus's mouth went dry. He glanced at his fallen weapon, then dove for it.

The shot cracked.

Cyrus flinched, expecting an explosion of pain, but it didn't come. A scream echoed across the grounds, and Cyrus scrambled to his feet, blade in hand, just in time to see Lucien stagger and then fall to his knees.

All of the air rushed from Cyrus's lungs.

"*NO!*" He whirled on Emerson without a second thought and sliced his right hand clean off; it dropped to the dirt, pistol still clutched in the twitching fingers. Emerson growled and recoiled, and Cyrus rushed at him.

He didn't give Emerson a chance to move another muscle. He drove the sword straight into his chest, breaking through bone and shredding sinew to pierce directly through his heart.

Emerson howled. His body jerked and Cyrus heard his bones cracking and popping. Twitching and twisting, his body was attempting to change itself, but Cyrus held tightly to his sword and twisted it deeper.

Silver mixed with muddy red gushed over Cyrus's hands. Emerson's breath hitched as blood bubbled up his throat and spilled through his lips; he coughed and shuddered, and when his strength finally left him, Cyrus let go of the blade.

Emerson swayed, and then crumpled. His body spasmed violently, and Cyrus watched, frozen, as the flesh rotted before his eyes. Ashy gray blight crawled up from Emerson's fingertips, spreading rapidly to his neck and over his face. In seconds, his body was a smear of bloody ash in the dirt.

Reality crashed back. Cyrus shook himself out of his shock and sprinted to Lucien. He was doubled over, one hand on his chest while the other weakly held him upright. Cold, silver blood soaked Cyrus's shaking hand where it pressed to Lucien's chest, pouring steadily from the bullet's violent entrance.

"No, no, no, no, *no, no, NO.*" Cyrus pressed harder, but Lucien's blood only flowed faster. Panic threatened to close up Cyrus's throat.

Lucien gripped him by the shoulders and tipped their foreheads together; Cyrus wasn't sure if the trembling he felt was his own or Lucien's. His lover's breaths came in rattling, raspy gasps, and more blood leaked from his chest with each heave.

SILVER BLOOD

Cyrus squeezed his eyes shut, releasing a torrent of tears. "*Listen to me*," he choked out, "*you're not going to die.*"

Lucien made a pained noise. "Cyrus...th-the b-b-bull..."

"Shhh." Cyrus shook his head. "Don't. Just—Just hold still, Lucien, I've got you. You're going to be okay and I'm going to get h-help and we're going to fix this and you're going to be *fine* and—"

"*Cyrus*," Lucien hissed, "*the bullet.*" He tried to bring his own hand to his chest again, but gave up halfway. His remaining strength bled out of him and he slumped against Cyrus; Cyrus had no choice but to lay him down.

Then he froze, unable to do more than stare blankly at the dying vampire in front of him.

Dying vampire. No, dying *man.* Dying fucking love of his life. For just a moment, Cyrus hated him. Hated his stubbornness and his pride and his honor. *Why couldn't you have been a coward? Why didn't we just run away?*

"*Cyrus*," Lucien wheezed. His voice was weakening, his breaths growing more labored. He groaned in agony with each inhale; tears spilled from his eyes and smeared blood down his cheeks. "C-Cyrus...you have to...get it *out.*"

"What?" He shook his head, panic clouding his understanding. Get what—?

Oh. The bullet! Of course—he'd heal from the wounds if the silver was out of his body. *He'd heal from the wounds if the silver was out of his body.* But would it work, even though the bullet had pierced his heart?

Cyrus tore open Lucien's coat and ripped the hole in his shirt wider, using the fabric to clean away as much blood as possible until he could clearly see the bullet's entrance wound—and the glint of metal embedded deep in his flesh.

An inch away from hitting his heart.

Relief hit Cyrus with enough intensity to make him dizzy. "Holy shit," he breathed. "He missed."

Emerson Beldon had fucking missed. Cyrus had been granted a miracle.

"Okay." He took a deep breath and tried to soak up more of Lucien's blood with his already-sodden shirt, but it was little use. Reluctantly, he glanced to Lucien's pale face. "I'm so sorry, but this is going to hurt."

Lucien weakly grasped his arm. "I trust you."

That was great, but it wouldn't lessen the pain. Cyrus hurriedly took off his belt and held it up in front of Lucien. "Bite down on this." He waited for Lucien to take it between his teeth, and then braced himself and dug his fingers into the bullet wound.

Lucien cried out as his body convulsed. Cyrus blinked the sting of tears out of his own eyes and forced himself to keep going; he could feel the metal, warm amid Lucien's cool blood. He quickly lost track of how many times he'd murmured *I'm sorry* as Lucien's ragged sobs continued. Nausea roiled in his stomach and the smell of blood was unbearable, but he swallowed it all back and focused.

I have to save him. He didn't know how he would go on otherwise.

When he finally freed the bullet, Lucien slumped back on the ground with a pained gasp. Sobs wracked his body; Cyrus pressed both of his hands to Lucien's chest in a final effort to slow the flow of blood as his body healed, but he knew it wasn't enough.

Cyrus slid his hand under Lucien's head and gently tipped it up, then held his other forearm in front of Lucien's face. Lucien glanced up at him.

"Bite," Cyrus commanded. "Drink."

Lucien didn't have to be asked twice.

Cyrus barely felt the fangs pierce his skin. As Lucien drank his fill, Cyrus curled himself around his body and held him. Tears welled in his eyes and he did nothing to stop them from spilling down his cheeks, dripping into Lucien's hair. Without meaning to, he broke down, as everything that had just happened caught up with him. Emerson, a vampire. Poppy, dead—by Cyrus's hand. Emerson, dead—*by Cyrus's hand.* The gunshot. Lucien, falling.

His blood. His pain. His agonized sobs and the terror in his eyes and the sheer horror that Cyrus had almost lost him forever.

And the relief, stark and almost unbelievable, that Cyrus had saved him.

He cried all of it out, and only drifted back to himself when Lucien finished and tucked Cyrus's hand against his chest. Cyrus held him tighter, tears still spilling from his eyes.

Then he realized they weren't alone.

Cyrus looked up at Joel—quiet, calculative, quick-thinking Joel. He was neither ruthless like Arthur nor relentless like Poppy, but he was the wild card. Cyrus did not know what to expect.

But the longer he stood there, merely staring, and the longer Cyrus studied his deep-lined, exhausted face, the more certain he became that Joel Beldon was not a threat.

"You actually love him, huh?" he said, voice ragged.

Cyrus nodded once, holding his brother's gaze.

Joel sighed and swayed on his feet, dragging a hand through his hair. He looked up at the house, then glanced back briefly at the ashen remains of Emerson Beldon. Joel's hands fell limply to his sides. When he turned to Cyrus again, there was no anger in his eyes. Just defeat. "You should go. Both of you."

Cyrus tightened his arms around Lucien. "And you?"

"I'm all that's left." Joel swallowed. "Someone has to be Master Beldon. But...I don't think Master Beldon has to be like *him*." He nodded toward Emerson's remains.

"No," Cyrus agreed. "He doesn't."

Joel took a deep, shuddering breath. "I can't protect you here, not alone. Go, and go *far*, because the other families—Honorable and otherwise—are still out for blood. If anyone asks what happened here..." He ruffled his hair again as he gazed at the fallen Beldons. "Emerson betrayed us and made an attempt on our lives. Poppy was murdered. I killed Emerson in self-defense. He was a rogue vampire, and I did my duty."

Cyrus stared at the back of his brother's head. "Joel."

"Are we understood, Cyrus?" Joel did not turn to look at him.

Lucien gently squeezed Cyrus's hand, and met his eyes pointedly when Cyrus looked at him.

Cyrus swallowed. "We are."

"And you." Joel turned his head over his shoulder, eyeing Lucien. "Take care of my little brother."

Lucien nodded. "I swear it, Master Beldon."

Joel bowed his head, then after a minute threw his shoulders back and approached Poppy's body. He heaved her into his arms, glanced back at Cyrus once, and then carried his sister toward the house.

Lucien untangled himself from Cyrus's arms and stood, a little unsteadily. When Cyrus didn't join him, he gently pulled him up, slipping an arm around his waist. Cyrus stumbled a little as he tried to walk, leaning heavily on Lucien as they made their way toward the gates.

There, Cyrus paused and took one last look at House Beldon. It seemed to shrink away, cowering, burying itself and all its shame. Gone was that snarling pride; it might as well have gone up in smoke.

Cyrus knew that he and Lucien had not won. Far from it. They would leave the city not in victory, but in fear. But the Beldons hadn't won, either, and for now—for today—that was enough.

Cyrus turned his back on the house and met Lucien's eyes. He searched for something to say, scraping for that optimism Lucien loved so much, but he came up with nothing. He was just tired. So fucking tired.

Lucien took his hand. Maybe words weren't needed. Maybe it was okay to just walk away, together, and let the fire they'd started run its course.

So they did, and Cyrus didn't look back again.

Chapter THIRTY FOUR

ONE MONTH LATER

CYRUS WATCHED DAWN BREAK OVER THE SEA OF TREES that met the horizon. From this vantage point on the fifth story of a six-story castle which perched on a hill amid endless pines, the trees seemed like all there was. It was a thriving, bustling forest, bursting with life, but nonetheless isolating.

It wasn't home. Cyrus was starting to doubt it ever would be.

The place still felt temporary. They'd been here almost five weeks, and a few ventures into the nearby riverside village had provided them with enough goods and supplies to settle in and make the place seem somewhat lived-in, but a castle built for multiple branches of multiple generations of multiple families was never going to feel homey or alive with only two people to wander its halls. Lucien had told him that the castle, which once belonged to a distant Vista ancestor, had only been empty for about twelve years, but it felt far lonelier than that. Cyrus could sense the ghosts, and they were gloomy.

He knew Lucien wasn't thrilled about being here, either. It had been in rough shape when they'd arrived after ten days of steady travel, so before they could rest they'd had to chase off the spiders and clear the dust and find temporary fixes for a dozen broken windows and rotted doors. It was another couple of weeks before they'd finished the major repairs, but the cleaning was endless.

It was something to do, sure, but Cyrus never wanted to pick up a broom again.

Today would bring more odd jobs to brighten and fix the weary old place, and Cyrus should have gotten more sleep. These days wore on him, dragging him into heavy fatigue that leeched away the energy he *wanted* to spend on Lucien. Yet even though they were together and alone and out of danger, Cyrus had never felt so distant from him. They didn't talk like they used to. There was a barrier between them, something transparent and perhaps thin, but still solid and still *there*. Cyrus wished he knew what it was so he could break it.

He wanted his Lucien back.

Across the room, nestled in bed, Lucien stirred. He turned over and stretched with a soft groan, hands poking out from beneath the heap of blankets. He spread his arms wide, then bolted up with a gasp, eyes wide and alert. Cyrus stood from the window seat, and when Lucien spotted him, he relaxed.

Sorrow tugged at Cyrus's heart. This wasn't the first time Lucien had panicked when he didn't find Cyrus beside him when he woke up, or vice versa, and he knew it wouldn't be the last.

Cyrus slid back into bed, nestling into Lucien's arms. "I'm here," he murmured. "I couldn't sleep. Was it the nightmare again?"

A minute slipped by in silence. Lucien's eyes were closed, his face pressed against Cyrus's chest. His hair shadowed his one visible eye; Cyrus gently stroked it back.

"No," Lucien murmured after another minute. "Not the nightmare."

"You okay?" Cyrus said.

"No. Not really."

"Yeah," Cyrus sighed. "Me neither."

"I hate this place. I want to go home."

"You sound like a child," Cyrus teased.

"No, I sound like you."

Cyrus scoffed, and Lucien chuckled softly. Cyrus smiled to himself and nuzzled his hair; this was the first glimpse of *real* Lucien that Cyrus had seen since they'd come here, and it warmed him.

But yes, he wanted to go home, too. He missed the Vista manor. When he thought of a comfortable space where he could rest and be himself, it was there. Its grand halls and shimmering chandeliers, its intricate statues and dozens of paintings. The piano, the ballroom, and the little family dining room where he and Lucien had shared their meals. The gardens, the *library*...Gods, Cyrus missed that library. He'd been so excited to fix all those old books on the fourth floor! And he hadn't gotten a proper chance to explore the farthest reaches and stick his nose in every bit of knowledge and literature the place had to offer. He wanted to find the oldest book in those stacks and marvel at it. And he wanted Lucien there to tell him *everything* about all of it.

"What are you thinking about?" Lucien asked, interrupting his yearnings.

"Huh?"

"Your pulse quickened." He traced his fingers along Cyrus's collarbone. "Daydreaming?"

Cyrus bit his lip. "You could say that."

"Yeah?" Lucien lightly teased his nails down Cyrus's neck. "Anything you'd like to share?"

"Well..." He twirled a strand of Lucien's hair around his fingers. "If you ask nicely, I'll tell you."

"Oh?" Lucien kissed his neck. "Please do, I'm so very curious."

Cyrus was glad Lucien couldn't see his face in their position; he was sure he wouldn't be able to stop himself from giggling. "I was thinking..." Just to be cheeky, he slid his knee between Lucien's thighs. "...how much I want you..." He paused one more time as Lucien kissed his throat again, then finished in a whisper, "...to show me everything in your library."

A beat passed. Lucien's confusion was palpable. "What?"

Cyrus laughed. "I was thinking about your library."

"Seriously?" Lucien pulled back, just enough to look at him.

Cyrus grinned. "Yes."

Lucien pouted, but the frown didn't last long. A smile eased its way across his face, and then he chuckled and tipped his forehead against Cyrus's. "You are the only person I know who would get so excited thinking about *books* that your heart rate actually increases."

"Other than you."

"...other than me."

Cyrus laughed and kissed him. "And that's why I love you."

"Just that?" The pout returned.

"Hmmm." Cyrus pretended to study him seriously. "I guess I can think of one or two more reasons."

"Only one or two?" Lucien playfully pushed him onto his back and leaned over him. "I simply must do better."

"I'd like to see you try." Cyrus smiled against Lucien's lips and savored his soft kisses, for once not looking to escalate anything. Lucien eventually settled against Cyrus's side again, tucking his head against his shoulder.

Cyrus loved this—he did—but he realized as they lay there that the core of that feeling of distance was a desire for *more*. This softness with Lucien made him feel safe, and he treasured their intimacy, but he also missed the unpredictability of their days on the road. He missed exploring new places and experiences with Lucien. He wanted something that felt like a normal partnership—or at least, as close to normal as the two of them could get.

He didn't know if that was possible, but maybe now that he had words for it, it was worth talking about.

"Can I say something crazy?" Cyrus murmured.

"Hm?" Lucien propped his head up on his hand.

"What if we left?" He turned his head to meet Lucien's eyes only after the words were out. "I know we can't go home, but why do we have to stay here? We could go anywhere."

Lucien studied him for a long minute. "We're safer if no one sees us. Too many people know who we are, and it would be too easy to be followed."

"Not if we go far enough." Cyrus sat up. "Lucien, we have nothing tying us to Chestervale anymore. We're free. Why are we imprisoning ourselves in this miserable castle when we have the world?" He searched Lucien's eyes for even a hint that he agreed. "Besides, our work isn't done. We can still help victims of Wild turns. We know how they're made now, and we have a theory of what to do to reverse it. There's still a chance for us to help people, maybe even more so now with Emerson out of the way."

He could see that he was getting through to Lucien, but whatever was making him hesitate seemed to be winning. He sighed and sat up, drawing his knees up to his chest. "I don't know, Cyrus. I...I agree with you, but I don't know."

"Do you want to stay here?"

"No."

"Right, so—"

"But we're safe here because no one knows where we are," Lucien cut in. "All it takes is one person who recognizes one of us, Cyrus, and then our anonymity is lost. The Beldon threat might be gone, but Harrows could still come knocking, and..." He shook his head.

Cyrus leaned against his side. "Nothing we do is going to be without risks. We can't let fear tie us down forever."

Lucien scoffed. "Optimism is wonderful until you're dead. Cyrus, look at me."

He already was, so he raised his eyebrows instead.

"It's too soon. I doubt the dust has settled back home. We have no idea how the Honorable Families or the other hunters have reacted to what we did. To what *you* did. They could be looking for us. Do you really want to risk...?" His voice cracked and he tried again: "I won't risk losing you again. Not for anything."

"And I don't want that any more than you do," Cyrus said. "Of course I want us to be safe. But I also want us to *live*."

Lucien held his gaze a moment longer, then pulled him into his arms. "One more month. We'll stay here one more month, just to be safe, and then..."

Cyrus's spirits lifted. "Then?"

"We can go." Lucien drew back and cupped Cyrus's cheek in his hand. "Just the two of us, anywhere we want."

"No hunters on our tail," Cyrus said. Hoped.

"No Honorable Families breathing down our necks." Lucien stroked his thumb across Cyrus's cheek. "We could go west. See what's beyond all these woods. Or north, across the lake, into the mountains. Although, we may need to find a second horse. Demeter may abandon us if we ask too much more of her."

Cyrus chuckled. "Demeter is more honorable than all the Families combined. She would never abandon us."

"Truly, we should start addressing her as Honored Demeter." Lucien smiled, and Cyrus saw a spark of happiness in his eyes that had been missing for the past month—perhaps longer. But even amid the grief and fear and misery, Cyrus had always managed to find that flicker of hope in Lucien's eyes. It had been all the more noticeable, then, when it had disappeared. His relief at seeing it again now was dizzying.

Cyrus wasn't so naïve as to think that running off to gods-knew-where would solve all of their problems or fix all of their pain. He didn't expect it to. But they didn't need a magic cure for their grief; they needed a fresh start. A balm. A purpose. A soft place to land. This was not it.

There was a place out there for them; Cyrus knew it. They would wander from one town to the next, one region to another, and then they would settle. Together, he hoped, and one way or another, they would be content, and they would be safe.

Despite the chaos they had left in their wake back home, Cyrus felt more centered than ever. No one was making decisions for him or telling him how to act or what to be. Without the weight of his family's expectations on his shoulders, he was sure, for the first time in his life, that he had a purpose other than being a Beldon. He didn't know what that purpose was or where he would find it, but he knew it was out there—and now there wasn't anyone to tell him to stop looking. His life would not begin and end under the shadow of House Beldon.

He wouldn't be like the rest of them; neither proud of his family nor defeated by it. His name was his to rewrite, and his future was his to forge.

He couldn't wait to see who he'd become.

ACKNOWLEDGMENTS

It's always surreal to get to this page, and as always, I don't know where to start. This book was a freaking beast, I'll tell you that. And without the unwavering support from so many dear friends, it wouldn't be here in your hands.

Firstly, I must sing praises of my brilliant cover artist, Jan Falk, who wrapped this book in the most stunning art I could have asked for. It's beyond everything I imagined. Thank you, thank you, *thank you*.

Many thanks, always, to my Queer Lodgings pals. My pocket friends. My hype squad of fellow indie authors. You're all so very special to me, and I'm proud to know you.

One thousand thank-yous to Rita for being an insightful and enthusiastic beta reader, and also a great friend!

Infinite thanks to Nemy, for not only listening to my stream-of-consciousness rambling about this book for the better part of like two years, but also for beta reading a monstrous early draft. No wiser words were ever spoken before you told me, "Sometimes you need to go insane to get better." Well, here you have it: the product of that very insanity. Go ahead, give it a chomp.

Thank you also to early readers who provided blurbs and reviews: Josie Jaffrey, Rita A. Rubin, Cara Nox, Juniper Lake Fitzgerald, Senna Byrd, Carolina Cruz, and Jake Vanguard. Your kind words mean the world to me.

Hi Mom. Don't speak to me about the sex scene. Lmao. But thank you for your constant support and everything you do for me. PTLN!

Many thanks to my friends and my wonderful, ever-tolerant partner, who encouraged me along the way and also endured my hyperfixation on vampire literature as I wrote this book. Thank you for putting up with my nonsense! <3

Finally, thank you, dear reader, for making it to this page. It may seem like a small thing, but it means the world to me as an indie author each time a reader gives my books a chance. Thank you for seeing this journey through to the end.

CRAVE MORE?

Cyrus and Lucien's story continues in *Sweet Sorrow*, a companion novella that takes place several years after the end of *Silver Blood*.

Time brings changes for ex-hunter Cyrus and his vampire lover, but when the two reunite after years apart, they are quick to remember what drew them to each other in the first place.
Sweet Sorrow is for adult audiences.

Learn more:
undernightfall.carrd.co

And don't miss the conclusion of Cyrus and Lucien's story in "Soft Eternity," a short story found in *Transcendence: An Anthology of Change*. Learn more at tallimorgan.com/shortfic.

BONUS CONTENT

Lucien,

Your letter has left me quite speechless. I resent my uncle and siblings all the more for causing you as much hurt and distress as they've caused me. But I'm so relieved to hear that you're home safely. I just wish you didn't have to endure what must be a painfully quiet manor all alone.

You know, it's strange. We've spent so many days in each other's company, it feels odd to be without you now. I keep looking for you, hoping to share a comment or a thought, only to find myself alone. Not that Adriyen and Leif aren't good company, but it's not as though they can spend every minute with me.

I don't ever remember being this lonely before.

Another letter from you, I think, would bring some much-needed comfort. Until we can meet again, anyway.

Fondly,
Cyrus

Honored Vista,

Forgive me for interrupting your correspondence with Cyrus, but I promise I'll be brief. My name is Adriyen Snow, and I'm the Beldon family's physician. I've been taking care of Cyrus as he recovers, and while I'm doing everything I can for his physical health, there is only so much comfort I can bring him. That brings me to the purpose of this note. I have a request.

Cyrus will only be safe in my care for so long. He needs to get out of this house, and I know there is nowhere he'd rather be than with you.

I know it's dangerous, and frankly rather stupid. But I don't know whom else to turn to. You are his hope.

Please reply back and we can arrange the details. Thank you. --Adriyen

Luci

You
sibl
as t
saf
pai

You ... , it's strange. We've spent so many days in each other's company, it feels odd to be without you now. I keep looking for you, hoping to share a comment or a thought, only to find myself alone. Not that Adriyen and Leif aren't good company, but it's not as though they can spend every minute with me.

I don't ever remember being this lonely before.

Another letter from you, I think, would bring some much-needed comfort. Until we can meet again, anyway.

Fondly,
Cyrus

Cyrus,

I'll save us the trouble of continuing to dance around the words and just say it: I miss you, too. You're right: after so many days with you constantly at my side, within arm's reach, these days between us now feel like ages. And that's quite the comparison, coming from someone to whom decades pass like singular years.

It soothes my worries, though, to know you are cared for. I'm relieved to hear you have at least two allies in that house. I'm sure you're keeping them on their toes with your refusal to lie still and rest. We both know I'm equally terrible at being motionless, but if it's any incentive, the sooner you feel better, the sooner we might see each other again.

I know that's what has been keeping me going, but it's not getting any easier to remain here while you are there.

Write soon.

Fondly,
Lucien

Cyrus,

I'll save us the trouble of c...
words and just say it: I'...
so many days with you con...
reach, these days between u...
quite the comparison, comin...
pass like singular years.

It soothes my worries, tho...
I'm relieved to hear you ha...
house. I'm sure you're keeping the... ...es with your
refusal to lie still and rest. We both know I'm equally
terrible at being motionless, but if it's any incentive, the
sooner you feel better, the sooner we might see each other
again.

I know that's what has been keeping me going, but it's not
getting any easier to remain here while you are there.

Write soon.

Fondly,
Lucien

Dr. Snow,

I'm pleased to make your
acquaintance. Any friend of Cyrus
is a friend of mine, and I must
express my gratitude for your care of
him. I'm sure it goes without saying
that he has become quite dear to me.
Tell me when to be there, and I will be.
Lucien

Lucien,

Seems we're together in our misery. I've been thinking of you often; if I wrote it all out, I'd fill a book. You've really managed to plant yourself in my thoughts, you know. I've hardly been able to sleep, and frankly, how dare you? Don't you know I'm supposed to be resting? Adriyen would have a sharp word with you if she knew you were the cause of my insomnia. I've even started to consider sneaking out, but I fear Adriyen's wrath too much. That should tell you all you need to know about her.

I am feeling better, though, slowly but surely. Every day I can move a little easier, and the aches are tolerable. At this point the bruises look worse than they feel. I consider myself lucky. Emerson could've done a lot worse. I know that doesn't excuse what he did do, but I could very easily be dead.

Much as I try not to, I've been wondering why I'm not. Why did he let me live? Why not just bury the wayward Beldon, once and for all? It scares me, Lucien. I feel my safety ticking away slowly with each minute.

I don't say this to worry you or make you fear for me. But I also can't pretend — and don't want to make you falsely believe — that everything is fine and peachy. Your letters are the only things reminding me that I can still hope for something better than this. I miss you terribly.

Fondly,
Cyrus

Lucien,

Please, as a friend, call me Adriyen. Thank you for your note. If it's not any trouble -- and I mean that: only if it's not any trouble -- I can find an excuse to get Cyrus out of the house within the next four days, if the weather permits. Let the sun be your signal to pay us a visit. We'll be in the back gardens by the pond. I trust that you'll follow your instincts to join us in the safest way possible for your sake and for ours.

I'm endlessly grateful for your agreement to this reckless plan of mine. Such wild things we do for those we love, no?

You're truly honorable, Lucien. Thank you again.

Adriyen

Cyrus,

My heart breaks for you. I know all too well how it feels to drown in hopelessness and misery, but I promise that the utter loneliness you are feeling will not last. It's so hard to hope, so allow me to hope for you. For both of us. There is more to this life than struggle and loss. I must believe that. How else do you think I've survived over a century?

Oh, and Cyrus, if I am on your mind every waking hour, then you are in my thoughts even in my dreams. I feel that you're with me always, even as I feel your absence like a wound. Spirits, it sounds so dramatic and foolish; you must think me ridiculous for waxing poetic in all of these letters. Yet I find it's easier to put such thoughts – such feelings – in pen rather than in words.

Indeed, that makes me a coward, too.

I hope you continue to heal. I wish I could soothe all of your worries and assure you of your safety, but for now, the most I can do is leave you with these words and this hope.

Spirits willing, I'll see you soon.

With deep fondness,
Lucien

ABOUT THE AUTHOR

T. L. Morgan, who also publishes as Talli L. Morgan, writes fantasy books for adults and young adults. When they're not writing, Talli enjoys drawing, playing D&D, and thinking about writing. You are also likely to catch them in the library as they go about their day as a professional question-answerer.

You can learn more about Talli's books on their website, tallimorgan.com.

Follow Talli online:

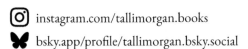

instagram.com/tallimorgan.books

bsky.app/profile/tallimorgan.bsky.social